When We Do Mee

C000064398

Historic fiction at its finest! An intriguing mystery, time travel love story you won't want to miss!

Brilliant Chicago surgeon, Dr. Stephen Templeton, needed a sabbatical to combat his overwhelming depression. A drive down River Road in Vacherie, Louisiana--outside New Orleans--promised to be just what the doctor ordered to relieve his stress, when a ruined antebellum mansion beckoned for him to purchase and restore it.

That's when he met her. The ghost of its former mistress, Isabella Durel, who was murdered December 25,1838--in this, her plantation home. It wasn't long before he found her portrait and fell in love with her. But, there was another picture lurking in the far corner of the attic. That of her husband...Emile. Stephen's exact likeness.

Can Stephen give her the second chance at life and love for which she's yearned for over a hundred years? Can he find sanity in her loving embrace? Can he find a murderer and reverse her fate before it's too late? Only if Time Travelers, Incorporated can work their magic and send him through the time tunnel so that he may return to his wife and his life as Emile Durel *circa* 1838.

Destination--Durel Plantation
    Vacherie, Louisiana
E.T.A. --**December 22, 1838!**

Only a love stronger than time can bring her back into his arms!

"I have my own plans for celebrating Mardi Gras," said Isabella.

"You have?" Stephen took a sip of wine from the crystal goblet and gazed at her.

"We never tangoed tonight. And you promised me."

"You want to tango—now? With no music?" he said.

"We need no music. Just rhythm." She let the dress drop to the floor. She stood before him in a corset and pantaloons. "Take off your clothes."

He placed the glass of wine on a small table, removed the fancy shirt and the big belt, then sat on a nearby chair to kick off his black boots.

She took off her underclothes—slowly—pulling at each little ribbon of her camisole and then undoing the corset's hooks with careful attention. She sat down on the side of the bed, slipped her pantaloons from her hips, and skillfully rolled each stocking from her long legs, being careful not to slash them with her nails. When she was done, she stood and undid her long hair from its chignon so that the dark mass of curls fell over her shoulders. The look in her eyes would have defrocked a priest.

He stood naked before her, his long legs, and muscular thighs flexing in anticipation of the dance movements they would soon perform.

"Care to tango?" He reached his hand to hers and gave a secret 'thank you' to Emile.

She took his hand, never dropping her stare from his, and smiled. "Avec plaisir."

<u>When We Do Meet Again</u> by Hollie Van Horne

An original publication of Time Travelers LLC

Time Travelers LLC
Columbiana, Ohio
44408

Original first printing copyright 1999
Second edition copyright 2004
  by Hollie Van Horne

ISBN: 0-9674552-3-5

Library of Congress Control Number: 2004090855

First printing of original: October 1999
Second revised edition: February 2004

When We Do Meet Again

Hollie Van Horne

Time Travelers   Book Four

When We Do Meet Again

When we do meet again,
When we do meet again,
When we do meet again,
T'will be no part.
Brother Billy, fare you well,
Brother Billy fare you well,
We'll sing Hal-le-lu-jah,
When we do meet again. *

* From Slave Songs of the United States which was originally published in 1867 and was compiled by William Francis Allen, Charles Pickard Ware, and Lucy McKim Garrison--Applewood Books

Author's Note

This novel is the fourth in my time travel series, but it is the first book to introduce Time Travelers, Incorporated. The brothers, Jim and Sam Cooper, meet Bruce Wainwright in <u>Reflections of Toddsville</u>--book one. Sam's vacation to 1722 in <u>Wild Roses for Miss Jane</u> coincides with Wainwright and Jim's travels to 1066 England in <u>McKnight's Revenge</u>-- books two and three. These three men are secondary characters, and have, so far, only aided the hero or the heroine on his or her adventure.

The three joined forces to create the lucrative business entitled Time Travelers, Incorporated. <u>When We Do Meet Again</u> is their first assignment. If you enjoy this novel, you will want to read the others and discover how this odd friendship and unique company originated.

The past time depicted in this novel will be shown as it truly was—not as one might fantasize it should have been. I have uncovered historic data from the personal journals, diaries, and letters of men and women—both free and enslaved—who lived and worked on Creole sugar cane plantations in Vacherie, Louisiana, during the 1830s. I let the past speak to me from the words of the people who lived it. The characters depicted in this novel are real not romanticized. Their speech, manners, and customs may surprise you at times, but it is my goal to make your reading experience as real and as entertaining as possible. Time Travelers, Incorporated will send you to the past, but they cannot create it to fit your own personal biases or fantasies. I only wish to draw aside the curtain that shields the past from our eyes so that you may see more clearly. I want *you* to time travel to the past with my characters. Wainwright's even waived the asking price of $150,000.00 to just the price of this book. So sit back, relax, fasten your seat belts, and put your feet up because *you* are about to time travel to 1838 New Orleans.

P.S. You will notice a dangling pocket watch on the spine of this book. The time on the watch's face indicates the number the book is in the time travel series. Ex. Four o'clock on this book means that it is the fourth in the series.

Enjoy!

For Bruce

Dance with me, Isabella
by Emile Durel --1838

Dance with me, Isabella,
Take my hand to start.
Beauty, grace, clouds of lace,
Sway inside my heart.

Dance with me, Isabella,
Twirl inside my arms.
Two steps--glide--by my side,
Free from fear or harm.

Dance with me, Isabella,
Eyes so bright, so bold.
Secret kiss; stolen bliss,
Charms my very soul.

Dance with me, Isabella,
Shadows part the night.
Lost and mourned; heaven born,
Spinning out of sight.

Dance with me, Isabella,
For a rest it seems.
Embrace me bride; from the other side,
And waltz inside my dreams.

Dance with me, Isabella,
Loathsome destiny.
The tune imparts a broken heart;
And love's sweet memory.

December 1, 1838

"I'm going to kill her; I swear to God I will!" screamed Emile Durel.

The old man listened and shook his head to show his disapproval. "Emile, for shame. You can't mean it. You'd never do such a thing to your wife."

Emile threw up his hands in exasperation. "And why not, I should ask? You heard what those men said. She has made me the laughingstock of New Orleans! She has been seen unescorted about town, may be having affairs with God knows how many men, robs me of every penny I manage to secure on this plantation, refuses to stay at home choosing to travel to the city every evening instead and dine there or go to the opera or the theater, yet will not allow me—her own husband—into her bed. Before we were married she couldn't bear to leave my side. Now that we are united, she wants nothing to do with me—except financially, of course. She has made it clear that she will never agree to having a child. A family might dampen her 'social calendar', I suppose. How could I have given my heart to such a woman?"

"Isabella's a modern woman, intelligent, willful at times, temperamental, I grant you, but very beautiful," replied the old man.

"A curse in itself, for what good is beauty in a wife if her husband never delights in it? Every man wants her within seconds after meeting her. Does he get her? My associates laugh at me. A constant joke, n'est ce pas? I'm powerless to prevent her lest I show anger towards the woman and have her destroy my family's good name as well as my personal image as a man before my friends. I am sworn to uphold the Durel family name while she destroys it."

"You're upset, Emile. You mean her no injury," said Dr. Gayerré, Emile's father's long-time friend.

"Don't I?" Emile poured a glass of copper-colored brandy for himself, sniffed it to see whether it was agreeable, and then poured one for the old gentleman. His hands trembled with emotion. His eyes were filled with rage. He handed the goblet to the doctor and then sat in the armchair across from him.

Gayerré swirled the brandy around the base of the glass and then sniffed at it and smiled—then frowned. "Take her lead and have a bit of fluff for yourself. The slaves are pretty here. It's your due. Show her that you can take lovers as well. It'll improve your image. You *are* a Creole gentleman, by God, living in the modern world of 1838 Louisiana. If she can have others—so can you. T'isn't right for you not to have a mistress anyway."

Emile groaned. "She has not one particle of feminine modesty. What can she be thinking? She was brought up by proper Creole parents, after all. Now she displays a bitter temper towards me and is immodest in public."

His voice softened briefly. He ran his hand back and forth across his forehead. "And I loved her so much—*once*. Still do." His eyes filled with tears. "Oh, God, how wrong could I have been about her? I vowed never to tarnish my marriage vows by lying with another woman. I know other men have mistresses, but I chose not to. It was a personal vow. I loved her too much to break the bond between us. After I lost my parents, all I could think of was to fill this plantation with Durel heirs so that our family's name would never die. I'm probably the only plantation owner in all New Orleans who doesn't have a mistress or two on the side."

He looked directly at the old man. "You see my dilemma. I will not stoop to her level of perversity by committing adultery, yet could callously commit murder by strangling the life from her body with my own two hands. No, a sexual affair will not solve my problem. I hate, despise, and *loathe* her now. I can't think of enough words to explain how her haughty manner, angry eyes, hand gestures, clothes—those damnable evening gowns—all displease me."

He turned his face from Gayerré's curious stare. "She *dares* to disobey me." Emile opened a cherry humidor on the table next to him and offered his guest a cigar.

"Then divorce her." The doctor chose one of the large Cuban-made cigars.

"Would that I could," he said, choosing a cigar for

himself and then closing the canister's lid. "We're Catholic, you know that, and even if I could divorce her, it isn't such an easy task these days. She would probably take all of my money in the settlement." He stood up and walked to the fireplace, bit off the tip of the cigar, and spat it into the flames. Then he took a small piece of kindling and lit his cigar and then the doctor's.

"You can't be too sure of that."

"I can't risk it either. My plantation and my father's fortune would go out the door with her voluminous luggage. She'd get her way *and* my money."

"Dear me."

"I have to devise a way of killing her so that I won't appear responsible."

"You don't really mean to do this, Emile." Gayerré's eyes grew wide. His fingers tightened around the brandy snifter. "Do you?"

"I do," said Emile, as golden flecks of cruelty burned in his brown eyes, "and I need you to keep quiet about it. I have everything planned. I'll wait until I'm sure she'll be home. She'll be here for the holidays. On December twenty-fourth, Christmas Eve, I will ask her for the favor of sleeping with her; she will naturally refuse me. I shall be kind, romantic, and bring her a goblet of wine to make my intentions clear. She'll make some excuse, of course. I shall offer her the wine, and when she drinks it, she'll become violently ill, need to be rushed to her bed, the doctor—you—summoned, and by morning, be stone-cold dead. December twenty-fifth. I purchased poison in town today."

Emile folded his arms across his chest in an expression of determination. "And I've done some research on the subject."

Gayerré stared at his young friend for a very long time. His face showing warranted concern. "You can't. I won't let you do it."

Emile spun his body so that he could make eye contact with the good doctor. "I can and will. I just have to make sure she drinks the wine."

"A human life? This is not like you at all, Emile. You just came home from France, overheard some gossip which may not even be true, and you haven't even asked her about the allegations."

11

He ignored the doctor's pleas. "Her body will lie in state in our library room. You see, I have it all planned. I've even fancied how she'll look as she awaits her final trip to my family's tomb in the city. That expensive gold gown she claims came all the way from Paris that she is so fond of should create a nice effect next to the red cherry wood of the coffin." He waved his hands through the air to paint the picture in his mind's eye. "Roses—white, I think, and glimmering candles in solid gold holders. Her hair assembled high upon her head—which rests on a gold satin pillow—and allows escaping ringlets to curl down her forehead and cheeks and onto her soft, delicate shoulders. I want her to look lovely—for she is. Her hands, those long, graceful, fingers—wearing *only* her gold wedding ring of course—shall be folded prayerlike across her bosom. One perfect white rose rests in her hand."

"Mercy," sighed Gayerré.

"The final moment comes when the grieving husband is allowed to look one last time on her perfect, oval face just before they close the lid of her coffin and seal it for all eternity. I'll sing mourning hymns at her funeral, shake hands with the guests—her many dubious friends like that pigheaded actor she's so fond of. He'll probably miss a few performances over her death. I'm looking forward to that moment when the priest motions to me that I should toss the white rose, which I carried with me to her grave, onto her coffin as it is placed in our tomb. The rites spoken in French, n'est ce pas? We walk outside, into the fresh air, the sunshine of a new beginning, a new life. One last quick look backwards to watch them permanently seal her eternal prison. Farewell, Isabella. Oh, God."

Emile fell into a nearby chair. He covered his eyes with both hands to mask the grief in his eyes. He appeared to be in pain. "Everything I've worked for, dreamed for, is gone."

Gayerré moved uncomfortably in his chair. "This horrifies me. You're sincere?"

Emile wiped his eyes with his handkerchief. "I reserved a coffin for her; I'm sincere."

"And you mean to do it during the holy season? What if you're caught?"

His voice held a chill. "I won't be. Especially when my own family physician," he pointed to the doctor, "Dr. Gayerré, pronounces her dead of—ah—some horrid disease. Maybe the plague. That'd be appropriate, eh? Yes, indeed, the plague should do nicely."

Gayerré shook his balding head. "You expect me to lie, as well? To be an accomplice to this hideous crime?"

"Of course. You've been like a father to me these many years since his death. I need you to do this favor for me. A minor one, as I see it."

"I am honor bound to heal the sick not kill them. I've seen enough of death for one lifetime. I'm Isabella's doctor, don't forget. No."

"*You* won't be killing anyone—just turning your face away when I do." Emile swallowed the last sip of brandy in his goblet. "We live so far from the city, who will doubt you when you say she suddenly took ill. Living on the Mississippi River, so far from New Orleans, death happens quickly and with little notice after so many plagues have terrorized our people. She goes into town so often, it's only natural she would become infected. No one will question her untimely death." He raised his eyebrow and smiled.

"I lost my own wife not so very long ago," said the old man sadly. "I think about her every moment of every day. I can't imagine you trying to live without your lovely Isabella. I won't let you do it. Perhaps she'll change her ways. Rumors are simply that—rumors. They may be fantasies bred of jealousy. A little patience, monsieur. After all, you've been away during the work season. Traveling so far from home and for so long, it would put a strain on anyone's marriage. Perhaps she's just tired from trying to run this whole plantation without you. It's difficult and lonely work. You'd be shocked to know how many planter's wives I see daily complaining that they think something is horribly wrong with them when all that is really wrong is that they are beyond exhaustion. Now that you're home, maybe she'll settle down."

"She'll settle down all right, inside a sealed coffin, in the family crypt."

"Mercy."

Emile placed his empty goblet on a tray, which rested on the table next to his chair, and rose to leave.

"I don't know you anymore, Emile. What's wrong with

you? How could you have changed into such a...a..."

"Monster? Live with Isabella for a week. Try to love a woman like her. Be rejected repeatedly by a woman you adore, and you'll see what I mean all too quickly. She has her own room now. Won't let me near her. Won't even *sleep* with me. I hope I can convince her to let me lie with her one last time on Christmas Eve."

"Mercy."

Emile stood and walked towards the door of the library. "You repeat yourself. No mercy shall be given to her. None," he said. "She has broken my heart." He stopped for a moment. Angry tears and intense emotion prevented him from speaking. "I'll be *damned* if she's going to wreck everything my poor father, mother, and entire slave population worked their whole lives to establish. Unfortunately, I am the only son who survived and, therefore, sole owner of this plantation now. It's my responsibility to see that it doesn't trickle through the dainty fingers of my wife. I haven't much money left. The depression has almost ruined us. I've almost nothing left in my bank account. She's taken it all. It appears that she's frivolously spent our entire fortune. The fortune that might have saved Durel Plantation. I've—we've—worked too hard for that, all of us. The slave huts are falling apart, and I haven't the money to fix them. They speak of running—-of freedom."

"Times are difficult. You've been away and don't understand the economy—what she's been through."

"What she's been through is the last of our money. We are virtually bankrupt."

"Well...there are many ways to tame a wife without killing her. What if she calls for help? Cries out in pain. I'll not watch the lady suffer."

Emile arched his back and stretched his muscular torso to its full height. "I'm told the poison works slowly and makes the victim violently ill. Spasms of life and death, darkness and light, breath and suffocation. When it looks as if her time is up, I'll send for you, old friend, who will just happen to be staying the night with us. Wonderfully appropriate, don't you think? We can say that you were invited to have Christmas dinner with us. It'll be too late for you to do anything for her, of course. What could you do anyway? I'll say I slept too deeply, groggy from our night of lovemaking, and did not hear her cries for help." He paused and looked down at his empty glass. "Making love to her—when we were first married—-was so wonderful for me. I enjoyed her beauty with complete and utter satisfaction. Why does she refuse me now? I'll never understand her."

"Try."

Emile leaned close to Gayerré's face. "Please help me. On the vow that you made to my father on his death bed to help me. Your sworn oath. There's not enough money to continue this huge estate. I'll have to sell it in two months if she goes on another shopping spree for new gowns. *Help me.*"

"Why not just tell her she mustn't leave the plantation anymore? Are you not master of your own house? If it's cash you need..."

"That won't help. Whatever you give me, she'll squander."

"I see."

"Since I've been gone, she's created this amazingly tight circle of new friends. She would complain to them that I was being harsh with her, demanding that she not attend the parties or the theater with them anymore, and she would continue ruining my good name by saying that I'm a total beast to her. Besides," he said slowly, "when a woman has lost her honor—that sweet, gentle femininity that she should cherish as she does her rosary, as well as her husband's good name—death is the traditional punishment."

"I've always been fond of Isabella." The old man's voice broke with sadness. "She's so full of life. Always laughing at my jokes. And she has a way of making every man in the room feel imp—." He looked at Emile,   "Oh, I'm sorry. Forgive me."

"You'll help me? On your oath to my father?"

He looked at his young friend and gave a heavy sigh before regretfully saying, "I will aid you in this hellish idea, but only because I assume you'll come to your senses before December twenty-fourth. I'll pray earnestly that you'll change your mind."

"*Never.*"

Emile clapped his hands together and then shook Gayerré's. He waltzed around the room before heading for the parlor door. "By the morning of December twenty-fifth, I shall be free from her forever. I can't think of a more wondrous gift than the final destruction of Isabella Durel."

Later, in his room at Durel Plantation, Dr. Gayerré cried and prayed, "Dear Father in heaven, change *his* mind and *her* heart. Emile needs you right now. So does Isabella." Then he took out his journal, and with a shaking hand, and an uncertain script, he wrote what his heart prompted him to say to the Almighty. At the end of the entry, he added, *"God in heaven, save her."*

Chapter One

November 1, 1998

Dr. Stephen Templeton was growing fond of the woman's spirit who nightly visited him in his room at the ruined, but soon to be restored, Durel Plantation on River Road, Vacherie, just outside New Orleans, Louisiana. But who was she? Her eyes were mesmerizing, her body tantalizing in that gorgeous, golden gown, and her lips inaudibly begging him to do something. But what? To a lonely man who'd overcome his initial fear of ghosts upon seeing her that first night, she'd become more than a messenger from the other world. Much more.

He found her portrait in the attic and wondered why it'd been placed there instead of on the wall in the dining room. Such a captivating face should be witnessed, scrutinized, adored. Her oval face was lovely, but it was her big, brown eyes that riveted him. Mesmerizing. Sad. Intelligent. Lively. They seemed to reach into his very soul and touch his heart.

Her dark, brown hair, piled high on top of her head, framed her small ears, long, graceful neck, and high cheekbones. Her head was tilted just a bit to the side as if she was asking you to explain yourself. Her eyebrows veiled her eyes seductively, beckoning him to kiss her full, red lips. The golden gown encircled her delicate shoulders, exposing a bountiful bosom. A fragile necklace caressed her skin. It was not as ostentatious a piece of jewelry as one might have expected. It was a thin, gold chain with a gold and diamond encrusted bow that subtly fell just above the crease between her breasts. Her hands were folded on her lap, and she held one perfect white rose. On the third finger of her right hand was a tiny cameo ring. He couldn't see her wedding band because one of the rose's petals covered that finger. The rose was probably a love gift from her devoted husband, and she wanted it in the portrait. Stephen wondered who might have given her the cameo ring and that simple, but perfect, necklace.

Such a rich plantation mistress could have demanded diamonds, rubies, and emeralds if she but smiled and tilted her head in the same flirtatious way she did in the portrait. She was perfection in feminine form.

Then he'd been forced, by sheer curiosity, to peruse the dusty, cloth covered journals and personal diaries he'd found in the library to determine her name. It had been Isabella Durel who died December 25, 1838, at her home. Cause of death—unknown. Nothing written there. Empty. Blank. Why? Signed by Dr. Gayerré and her husband, Emile Durel. Who was this Emile person, he wondered. Stephen was jealous of him already.

It took some hunting, but eventually he discovered Emile's portrait, hidden further back in the attic, turned back side out, and wedged behind some prints. He dusted away the dirty film until the man's handsome visage peered forth from the thick oil paint. Stephen was impressed with the man. Darkly handsome. Lean, strong face and features. High cheekbones. Dancing brown eyes. Black hair. Thin, drooping mustache. Long, slender, but strong fingers. Definitely Creole. He was dressed to kill in an aristocratic, black frock coat of classic 1830s cut and design; wearing a long-sleeved, white shirt with gold buttons; black ascot, tailor-made, white vest with white buttons; two gold chains that dangled from underneath the top button and traveled to the vest pocket that probably held his pocket watch, and a red sash that outlined his vest's wide lapel. Wearing a devilish grin on his long face, his manner was authoritative— maybe even cruel. Stephen couldn't tell for sure. Emile's brown eyes were intelligent, passionate, masculine, proud. His form appeared muscular beneath his garb, and his posture was regal, even aggressive. A man used to giving orders—and being obeyed. Stephen stared at it, off and on, for the entire day. It drew him, and he wasn't sure why until he suddenly realized that the face was his own.

Take away the mustache and Dr. Stephen Templeton, thirty-one-year-old owner of Durel Plantation and number one surgeon at Cook County Hospital in Chicago, Illinois, was a duplicate of the Creole planter. With one distinctive difference—he had no haughty veneer about him, no wicked smile, no patronizing look in his eye, but he did know how to give orders in the E. R. room with that same determined look Emile displayed. "Funny," he thought. "The last master of this mansion was a dead ringer for its new one."

It explained a great deal. Why Stephen had been drawn to this run- down plantation when he loved modern architecture. Why he'd paid their initial offer to obtain it. Why he wanted to restore it. Live in it. Why he had abandoned a successful medical career in Chicago to study the Victorian time period. Why he had suddenly grown a passion for antiques. Why he'd broken his engagement with his fiance. Why, though he'd always despised the South, he moved there. Why he'd been depressed for so long. And why he felt so happy now that he was "home." His therapist had almost given up on him. Stress had taken its toll on Stephen's emotional stability. And now, with one swipe of a cotton rag, everything had become clear.

He placed the portraits across from each other on the dining room wall. They glared at each other. So this was the man who married the beautiful lady. The man who had loved her or "owned" her. Stephen half hoped she had room left in her heart for a 1998 doctor, since she seemed so fond of visiting him every evening. Unless...she thought he was Emile.

That tenet troubled him. He wanted her, but knew she couldn't be his. Another man, in her real world, spoiled his romantic image. He couldn't erase Emile from her past.

Emile and Isabella Durel never had any heirs according to the family Bible he found on the shelf in the library, so there could be no blood connection to him in any way, but he knew that there was a spiritual one. If there wasn't, he was insane. Obsessed? Possessed?

According to the diaries, Emile never married after Isabella's death. He had been thirty-one-years old at the time of her demise; she, a mere twenty-eight.

He sat down on the floor in the library and held his head in his hands. Stephen's medical friends had told him that stress was a killer, and that he needed a break. If they had any idea what was going on in his life right now, they'd think he'd gone over the edge. And maybe he had.

It wasn't a topic you casually discuss with a neighbor or a stranger in the grocery store. "Hello. Nice to meet you. My name is Dr. Stephen Templeton. Yes, I *am* the new owner of the

Durel Plantation, and I'm in love with the ghost who lives there. Ah, yes, you have one too? Well, I'll show you mine if you'll show me yours. Ha Ha."

But in love with Isabella Durel was the only way to describe what was happening in his heart. He wanted her.

Every evening, at twelve o'clock, she came to him, with her dark hair and golden gown flowing behind her. Her face was breathtakingly beautiful, to his way of thinking, despite the sunken cheekbones. Her skin was the bluish gray of a harbor fog. Her big brown eyes, so sad and lonely, were rimmed with dark circles. Compelling and frightening. A specter to be sure. No mistaking it. She would reach her arms out to him, and her lips would move. What was she trying to say? Then, in seeming desperation, she would disappear. If he hadn't seen how beautiful she'd been in that life, he might have perceived the encounter differently. His love for her blinded him to the obvious pallor of her complexion.

Try as he might, he could not sleep after her visits. He took naps in the afternoon to ease his aching body, but his mind only dreamed about her. He had to know why she'd died so young, and why the cause of death wasn't mentioned on the death certificate. The answer to that question was the reason she haunted the mansion. He had to know what she wanted from him. Did she think he was Emile? Maybe he should just pick out a nice silver and china pattern and live eccentrically for the rest of his life with this lady ghost as his constant companion.

He grew a mustache just like Emile's.

He also found it serenely satisfying to reconstruct the mansion from the original inventory of items in the house at the time of her death.

He loved the bizarre, garish home as much as he loved its occupant. It was a large, antebellum mansion whose design was unique compared to the others he'd seen. The whole house sat on red brick pillars. Windows, shutters, and arches, which had an odd pagoda look to them, outlined the exterior. A wide porch ran the perimeter of both floors. Every room in the house had French doors that opened to the porch. He had a decent amount of cross ventilation when the windows and the French doors were left open.

Beneath the house was a cool basement that had been used

for a wine cellar. There were rows of tiny cubicles where the wine would have been stored, and the house's strong beams were visible there as well. He was even lucky enough to find some primitive tools lying on the dirt floor.

The yard around the house was reminiscent of every Southern farm he'd ever seen. Tall oak trees, which must have been standing for more than a hundred years, waved their arthritic branches in the breeze. There were green bushes and tangerine-colored flowers—he didn't know their names. Rusting kettles, once used for making sugar, were filled with rainwater, leaves, and bugs. There was a dried-up well in the backyard. Acres and acres of green grass with yellow flowers covered the plantation like a quilt. Old, run-down, slave huts dotted the yard. He noted that each hut was just one wooden structure, divided into four sections, with one room per section, and doors and windows in each of those sections. "Not very homey," he thought. He found the cookhouse and a smokehouse, lying almost on their sides, near the main house.

The grand mansion had two floors. On the bottom floor was a dining room, parlor/library, and pantry that some later occupant had turned into a kitchen. There were no hallways save one small foyer by the entrance door, but there were doors everywhere that enabled one to get from one room to another. There was a long staircase leading to a second floor that had one large master bedroom and several smaller guest bedrooms. The master's bedroom, which Stephen claimed for his own, still had, what appeared to be, original wall covering hanging on the walls.

The previous owners had left the old-fashioned pump in the sink. He could almost envision a slave woman smiling as she drank a cup of water she'd poured from it. If he closed his eyes, he could see Emile filling a bucket of water from it so that his horse could drink after their long ride. There were bookcases that still housed ancient epistles on their shelves, and the old, ruined pages seemed to beg for someone to read them. A harpsichord, covered in a white sheet, still sat, probably because it was too cumbersome to move, against the library wall. Every once in a while he could swear he heard a melody being played on it. He found white and blue floral print china in a china closet in the dining room. "Had someone asked for tea," they seemed to ask when he inspected them. Of course, there were the paintings of Emile and Isabella to add the proper historical touch to what remained of a long-forgotten time.

The old tools. The trees. The diaries. The lady ghost. Cups and books. Huts and buttercups. These emblems of bygone days, coupled with acres and acres of land a man on horseback could ride over for hours, drove Stephen's imagination to thoughts of wealth and power, of being the lord and master of his plantation. It belonged to him now. Maybe it had been his in another life.

He hired an architect to decide what to do about restoring it. Take off the ghastly exterior paint, he'd said. Yellow house, white steps, orange bric-a-brac, green shutters—hideous, he'd said. Stephen fired him after the first consultation. It just seemed that the original colors should be repainted, not covered. There had to have been a good reason for the original owner's choice.

Besides, *she* hadn't liked the idea. Hadn't liked the man. No idea why he felt her mood on the subject, he just knew. Stephen felt it as instinctively as if she were his wife staring at the man's designs over his shoulder and disapproving of all of them. The two of them seemed to be in some sort of odd, eternal union, and he loved it. He would restore the home for *her*, based on *her* tastes, and hope to find an architect worthy of the task, but, until then, he was on his own.

"Physical labor is sometimes good therapy for mental fatigue," he said to himself.

The master bedroom was the first to be stripped of its wall covering. He took the old, weather-stained piece of fragile cloth to a shop behind Jackson Square. He showed the man the material and asked if they could find a duplicate. The man had smiled obligingly at him. His stare made Stephen wish he'd gone elsewhere with his request.

Special order? Very expensive. Well, why should he care? His father managed four hospitals and had a heavy patient list. Money was no object. Whatever *she* wanted. Hang the expense.

The rolls of wall covering took weeks to arrive, so he spent the time purchasing 1830-style Victorian furniture from an antique store that was close to the paper-and-paint shop on Royal Street.

Eventually, the rosy, wall covering pattern came. He'd asked the man to give him some pointers on how to do the job himself, then bought more than enough supplies. Taking one step at a time, he cautiously started the job. He found that his nimble fingers and surgical-cutting abilities created a professional effect.

He hoped she'd like it, but all she did when she saw it was tilt her head to the side as if she thought it looked odd. One could never be sure with spirits. He could feel her coolness next to him while he worked. Was she looking over his shoulder or kissing his cheek? Could this be possible? Real? He grinned as a secret lover might after making love to his mistress.

The night he finally completed the room, she came to him, again, trying to articulate her eternal message. She came closer to his bed than she had on any of her other visits. He no longer noticed her pallid complexion and deathlike eyes. Her bony fingers reached out to him, so he moved his hand next to hers. She shook. Seemed to be crying. Then she smiled. Those incredible eyes. So sad. So lonely. So frightened. So in need of his help. But for a moment, she seemed happy that he'd made the room pretty again.

"Do you like the wallpaper...and the drapes...and the furniture?" Stephen asked, waving his hands at his work. "I bought you a little vanity table with a mirror. There. See it. Even found this silver vanity set of brushes, combs, and mirror. Do you like them? I saw some antique clothing too, but wasn't sure you'd want it. I'll go back tomorrow and get it for your closet if you want me to."

She nodded slowly, and it seemed as if this simple action took all her energy.

"I did it for *you*. All for you." He became bold with her. "I know who you are."

She looked startled.

"You're Isabella Durel, and you once lived in this house. In this room." A strange sensation of ownership came over him, and he stepped from the four-poster, Victorian bed, tossed the sheets and thin blanket aside, and stood before her. He was wearing only his underclothes, but she didn't look at his nakedness. "This is *my* house now."

Her lips moved.

23

He shook his head in despair. "Isabella? I can't understand you. What are you trying to say to me?"

Her head turned towards the door.

"*No*, don't leave me. I command you to stay." He had no idea from where this sudden burst of chauvinistic manhood emanated. It wasn't how he wanted to be with her. He'd discovered that this behavior got him nowhere in his many failed relationships with the opposite sex. It certainly hadn't worked with his ex-fiance. He wasn't like that with people he worked with, but with women, something just came over him.

Seeing that she was leaving, mourning, he changed the tone of his voice. "Wait," he said in a lover's whisper. "I'm sorry. I was harsh with you." He held out his hands to her departing light, hoping she'd reach out to him again.

The specter dissipated.

"I'm a bastard, Isabella, okay. Don't go." He searched in the darkness for her shadow. "I'm sorry I was harsh with you. Stay. Shit, I'm no frigging good with women." Then in a louder voice. "God in heaven, don't leave me, Isabella. Come back tomorrow night. Please. I'm working my ass off for you. And I don't know why."

There was that cool breeze on his lips. He smiled. She was with him. He closed his eyes and enjoyed it, and then went back to bed. Ever so faintly, her cold breath rested on his cheeks and lips. It was enough for now.

"You're here? In bed? Are you here in the bed with me?" he said aloud.

"I'm sorry, Isabella. May I call you that? I don't want you to be angry with me. Not what I intended at all."

He fell into a deep sleep.

Chapter Two

Stephen began speaking to her in the daylight even though he knew she wouldn't materialize or talk to him.

"The next room I redecorate will be of my own choosing. I want to redo the dining room. Somehow I feel that it is the most important room next to the master bedroom. A showplace for your portraits. We might have guests—from Chicago maybe. It really doesn't matter whether you want me to or not. See. I'm not controlled by you, you know."

Then privately he said, "Yeah, right. Not much you aren't."

He rested his hands on his hips. "Did you have Emile wrapped around your little finger like you have me?" he said laughing.

He picked out white lace curtains and heavy green drapes for the large windows in the room, first making sure the old frames were airtight. He replastered the walls where they needed it and painted them a light green. He ran a border, that matched the drapes, across the top of the walls. After that, he stripped the wood floors and restained them with a walnut color he'd seen in the corners of the room. Then he polished the floor until it gleamed. He ordered an Oriental rug for under the 'new' antique mahogany table, that sat twenty that he'd purchased in the city. He'd considered himself lucky to have found such a grand manor table which came with its own matching chairs. It correlated, in austerity, with the opulent decor he hoped to achieve in the room.   Lastly, he replaced her portrait on the western wall and her Emile's on the eastern wall of the room. They glared at each other again. Maybe it was just the light in the room, but they looked as if they were about ready to fight.

He finished the dining room with an old-fashioned corner cupboard, a long serving table under her portrait, and an antique bar under Emile's. He even found a few potted ferns to place in the corners.

"Isabella. I believe I've missed my calling in life," he said aloud. "I should restore old homes for a living."

During the whole of two week's travail, he spoke to her in a manner that resembled a man asking his wife for help on every domestic detail. He found himself speaking to her when he was looking at items in the antique stores, too.

"What do you think about this table for the dining room?" he'd say to her. "No, Isabella, that lamp is far too garish. Just because you like it, mon cher, doesn't mean it suits your time period." Her spirit was near him always, or at least, her personal style was.

It took him a few days to realize that he was speaking in a formal, high-Victorian manner that fit her time period, not his. His way with her was altogether perplexing and new to him, for he was, by nature, a kindhearted, sensitive man, never showing anger and was relatively calm in any given situation. This seemingly positive personality trait was driving him to an emotional instability that further complicated his present malaise.

He never lost his temper with nurses or other doctors back home. Rude patients and their families didn't ignite his ire often. He couldn't be aggressive with people who insulted him. But for some unknown reason, he was becoming more and more irritated with Isabella. It must have been her inability to communicate her message to him. He told himself that it really wasn't her fault. He didn't know much about the supernatural, after all, and a little metaphysics might have been useful at a time like this.

"Well, after all," he said to her one afternoon during his lunch break, "you're the one who understands the other side, not me."

That thought immediately translated into an idea. He could talk to the other world if he found a clever psychic. "Check that thought, pal, you don't even believe in that sort of thing."

He knew she was listening, so he told her everything. All his plans. She never responded except during her nightly visits. The night before he went to Jackson Square to speak with one of the fortune tellers who inhabited the outside booths there, she came to him. He could feel the energy bristling around her. He wasn't sure whether she was pleased with the idea of the psychic or not.

"What do you want from me? I'm getting tired of trying to understand you. It's futile. I'm a living person. I'm not a gifted psychic."

Then he heard the moan. The first audible link to her mind.

He came towards her, and his voice softened.
"Ah...Isabella, I don't mean to be harsh with you, but I can't help you if I don't understand your needs."

Her eyelids lowered in such agonized rejection that it broke his heart.

"You think there's no hope for us, don't you?" he said.

The soft, feminine moan.

"I'll help you if you tell me what's wrong."

Her hands reached for him. Her hair flowed behind her beautiful, oval face. She wanted him.

He was pleased and smiled at her. "Well, this is a twist. Can you speak to me in my mind? No? Then I'll have to bring in the psychic. Will you be a good girl when they come?" he whispered to her.

Her eyes went wide with amazement. She was responding in the only manner she could.

He repeated, "Will you be a good girl?" He focused on her eyes until she was forced to raise her chin so that she could look at him. Direct eye contact with a being from the other world. His blood ran cold, and his nerve endings tingled. His heart froze. Different voice. Different man. *"You will do as I say, Isabella. I am the lord of this house now, and it is my wish that you obey me in all things."*

That was the first time he saw her cry. Unmistakable. The large drops of vaporous wetness fell upon her cheeks and blue-gray lips. The tears sparkled silver with a luminous light. He regretted his roughness with her, but it wasn't his voice.

"Don't go," he said to her departing form. "I'm sorry. I don't know what's come over me."

She turned to regard him.

"Please stay and let me talk to you," he said.

She didn't move and glanced at him over her left shoulder.

The gold-but-graying gown, tattered and torn from the grave, billowed behind her. Her lips parted. She spoke again. Slowly this time, she formulated each word to perfection so that he might read her lips.

He crossed his arms over his chest and shifted his weight to a casual stance. One that he thought looked rugged, manly, and in control. "You don't want the psychic here? Some fear of what she might do to our relationship. I can't tell what you're saying, but the subtext is coming through loud and clear. You're jealous. You don't want a...woman." His eyebrows raised as he said the last word.

He laughed. "No competition there. No woman could hold a candle to you." He moved towards her. "I'm getting to the bottom of this, Isabella, whether you like it or not. I've got to find out if I'm a lunatic and get on with my life. I want to stay in this house, and to do that, I need to find out all about you."

A sudden, cruel streak burst inside his heart. *"Maybe get rid of you for good,"* he growled.

Her eyes opened to his gaze, and she tilted her head to the side—just like the portrait pose. What had he done now? He'd done something terribly wrong that was for sure. She vanished.

He called to her frantically. "I didn't mean that. I'd never want you to leave. Look. I'm crazy. I'm a lunatic on a sabbatical. Okay? I shouldn't have said that. I didn't mean I'd get rid of you. Something weird came over me."

He ran through the house, room to room, calling her name. Then he rushed downstairs and into the dining room to stare at her picture. In reverence he stood, before her portrait, with his hands tightly clasped in prayerlike fashion. Tears streamed down his face.

"I didn't mean that," he sobbed. "You just have to understand that I'm new to this possession thing—this haunting stuff. I'm not savvy with the other world, and I need someone who is, who can help me find you. Isabella? Are you listening to me?"

Nothing. All the work he'd done for her wasted with one stupid statement. He crumpled to the floor and sobbed. "Don't leave me. Please don't leave me. I'll find a good one, okay? One who will be sensitive to our unique bond."

He heard a moan coming from the master bedroom, and he

raced up the stairs, like a madman, two steps at a time, to find her. She stood before him.

He stayed in the door frame pretending to block her only exit. It seemed stupid to say it, but it came naturally to his lips. "I love you," he said and he meant it. "I love you, Isabella. I wouldn't think of hurting you."

She moved to him. Stared at him. Touched his lips with her index finger and smiled. She loved him, too.

Chapter Three

Stephen awakened the next morning in a tranquil state, as a lover might after being with the woman of his dreams, and slipped out of his bed. Wearing nothing but the shorts he had slept in, he swaggered down the stairway and into the dining room. He finger combed his hair and rubbed his face with his hands as he looked quickly at her portrait before waltzing into his kitchen.

This room was the only one in the house that had a semblance of modern decor. He had kept the old cupboards, sink, wooden counters, cutting block, and the basic furniture, even the pump at the sink, and he'd filled the shelves with antique china dishes, cups and saucers, and crystal goblets. Some of the original blue floral-patterned china remained, and he used it often.

The former owner had wired the house, so he had electricity. He'd purchased all the modern equipment he would use: a new stove, refrigerator, microwave, dishwasher, and coffeemaker. He had the telephone company install a new phone line into the kitchen and jacked up his computer in the wall socket over the small kitchen table. He had the coffeemaker on the table nearest the old pump-style sink and a microwave right next to that.

The sun was streaming through the lace, amber-colored curtains which draped above the big window over the sink. He had a few potted ivy plants sitting there waiting for their morning drink. He obliged them while he poured water into his coffeemaker.

There was some rattan furniture on the stone patio just outside the open archway leading to the courtyard and what used to be a fenced-in garden. As soon as he took his shower, he would make oatmeal, toast a bagel or two, and have his breakfast out there in the morning sunlight.

He had created a bathroom with a toilet, shower stall, sink, and washer and dryer, where the old pantry door and shelves used to be. He walked into the bathroom and began his morning routine. He was happy and had no idea why. He shaved, splashed cologne on his cheeks, smoothed down his mustache, and then slipped into a hot, steamy shower to wash away yesterday's sweat and grime. He ran the musk-scented soap all over his body until it was one enormous bubble. His muscles were getting stronger from his labors, and the hot water soothed them. He felt tough, strong, capable, masculine, healthy, sexy, and in love. He started singing at the top of his lungs.

The words came to his mind easily, and the melody was an old rock and roll song he'd heard on the radio the other day. "Dance with me, Isabella, sway inside my heart—ooh—ooh. Dance with me, twirl inside my arms—ooh—yeah. Dance with me, Isabella, eyes so bright, so bold—ooh, ooh—baby, baby." He swiveled his hips and bounced up and down as he sang and bathed.

When he emerged from his shower and towel dried himself, he started dancing to his own song, moving his hips, and flailing his arms like a rock star. Naked. He put the towel behind his back, rubbing it against his skin to the beat of the song. His thighs tightened as he touched each toe on the tile floor and twisted his feet as he danced. He looked at himself in the full-length mirror that was on the back of the bathroom door. "Emile Durel wishes he looked this good," he said. "Ooooh, Ohhhh."

His toothbrush became his microphone as he scrubbed his teeth and sang another garbled chorus of the only verse he knew. He was completely nude when he felt her coldness near his body. Her icy hands encircled his waist from behind him.

"Good morning, beautiful," he said, smiling. "I know you're there, you bad girl. Spying on me while I'm in my birthday suit?" He looked around to see if she might be visible. He added with a wicked sneer, "Like what you see, baby?" He swiveled his hips.

He wrapped the towel around his waist and tied it. "Later, sweetheart. Boost up your energy, and we'll have one sweet time tonight, okay? Or will your husband get jealous?"

A small bowl, which he'd put out for his hot cereal, fell from the counter near the sink. No reason; it just crashed to the floor. He stopped everything he was doing and listened. Stephen walked into the kitchen, bent over the broken pieces, and said, "What the..."

He collected the sharp pottery and threw it away in the wastebasket. Then he went back to the bathroom and finished his routine. From the dryer, he took underwear, a pair of half-wet jeans, a sleeveless sweat shirt with Chicago Cubs written on it, and a pair of white socks. He dressed quickly.

The coffee was hot and delicious with just the right amount of chicory. He added some skim milk to it. Then he poured water into his bowl of dry Quaker oats and nuked it. He watched as it 'grew' like a volcano inside the microwave. He ate the cereal while his bagels toasted. When they were done, he spread raspberry jam over the top of them, placed them on a small dish, filled his cup with more coffee, and went outside. He sat down on a cushioned rattan rocking chair and sighed. He was so happy here. As if he were meant to live here forever.

He'd decided to start reconstructing the library today. He was excited about the prospect of slowing down the work so that he could look through all the ancient volumes amassed on those dusty shelves. He hoped to find more information about the Durels.

He went inside again to pour another eye-opening cup of Cafe Du Monde coffee when he noticed his computer. He hadn't checked in with any of his cronies for days. Maybe he had e-mail.

He sat on a stool, clicked on the power, and opened the Internet connection. The horns and whistles told him that he had picked the right time to go on-line. An idea struck him. Why not check the Internet for a good psychic who might live in the area?

He did have mail though. He wasn't sure if he should read it or not. He had been told by his therapist to avoid all encounters with work-related stress, but he couldn't resist peeking. It was from the new surgeon who shared a clinic with him—Tony Cameron. Tony had been kind enough to send a pleasant message and mentioned how smoothly things were going. There was a message from his therapist asking him how he was faring in his new home. His father had sent him a message that he should call his family if he needed anything, so he e-mailed him that he was doing fine, and that he needed nothing. He never mentioned Isabella to any of them. What kind of message would it be anyway?

"Dear friends, I have fallen hopelessly in love with a dead woman. We are happily setting up house together, and I think we'll tie the knot soon provided her husband doesn't oppose the idea. But, after all, when you die the marriage is over, right? He has no rights here now. Love, Stephen."

Then he tapped into the search engines with the keyword PSYCHICS. After a few wheezes and clicks, he had more than enough "hits." He book marked the ones in his vicinity. A Gloria Bradford looked young and pretty and mentioned in her bio that she'd had several encounters with poltergeists. She was expensive, but he e-mailed her his problem. "Sorry, Isabella," he said.

On a whim, he hit the "More Like This" phrase and found an odd addition. It didn't have anything to do with psychics, but it was intriguing just the same. "Time Travelers, Incorporated, Bruce Wainwright—president. Contact the great beyond, check out your family tree, cure that longing for a trip to the past. If you want to find a way to relive history, call us today. Research done on a three-month rate." There was even a picture of the man who looked sane.

Stephen sipped his lukewarm coffee. He book marked the spot. Time Travelers? What a riot. Had to be a gimmick. People can be duped by anything. He looked at the face of the man on the first page of the web site one more time. Wainwright looked like an honest man though—but who could say.

He didn't e-mail him and shut off the computer. Time to go to work on the library and maybe later head for the store. He needed to replenish his pantry. He wondered if Isabella had looked at the computer. He envisioned her standing beside it, bewildered at the odd equipment. The many marvels he would show her if their relationship continued.

He stared at the library's old, wooden bookcases and tried to determine if he should tear them down or reconstruct them. There were volumes of dusty books that were merely classic tomes from authors long deceased, and there were a few odd fiction books that looked as if they might have been love stories. Romance novels? Nothing worth saving. There were some interesting educational epistles that must have been used to teach the Durel children. When he reached to take one from the shelf, it crumpled into a pile of papers on the floor. He would see if that antique store on Royal Street would purchase the good ones from him. They were over a hundred years old.

He spent the rest of the morning and long into the afternoon, cleaning and reading the books. And then, he saw something that sparked his heart and imagination. A safe was hidden behind a broken panel. The wood crumpled when he touched it. It must have been loose from age.

Stephen ran his anxious fingers over the lock. The safe was old, but not the lock. How could he open it? With a hammer and a chisel, he guessed. He went back into the kitchen to find his tool chest. His mind pondered all the wonderful things that might be found once he opened the family's safe. Treasure. Emile and Isabella's legacy.

There was no point in being delicate about opening the old cache, so he tore into it savagely. It yielded after a few hard knocks.

He closed his eyes and reached into the gapping hole. Papers. Maybe a book? A box. Jewels? The excitement of found treasure seized him. It was his house and therefore his booty.

He opened the black velvet box and found Isabella's bow necklace, the one she had on in the portrait. It was beautiful. Dangling from a soft, dainty chain was a gently draping gold bow with quarter-carat diamonds all around it.

"I found your necklace, beautiful." He placed it on the floor next to his feet. Then he opened the papers and perused them. Just old deeds and documents that he'd look at later. He brushed the dust from the face of the old journal. Dr. Gayerré's medical diary. Who the hell was he? Oh, yeah, the doctor who signed her death certificate.

Stephen sat on the floor and let the dying sunlight illuminate the pages. There were sheets and sheets of yellowed paper, full of details on the plague and family illnesses. He could not read much of the old man's strange, old-fashioned handwriting. And then, he found the last page.

"Dear Father in heaven, change his mind and her heart. God in heaven, save her."

What the hell was he talking about? Change whose mind? From what? Was the woman Isabella?

Stephen was suddenly weary. His eyes over tired and strained. His sinuses were about ready to burst. Time for a long dinner break, another shower maybe, and a glass of brandy. He'd curl up with the good doctor's journal and learn all he could about Emile and Isabella.

As he staggered into the kitchen, he decided to check his e-mail. The computer was his only outlet, and in the blur of redecorating the two rooms, he'd forgotten it. It might have been therapeutic, after all. He was supposed to get away from his practice and his colleagues. The house and Isabella had taken his mind off his problems at home.

There was a message from Gloria. She wanted to know more about his poltergeist. Poltergeist? What a funny thing to call Isabella. Where exactly did he live, and did he want her to come over? He wrote back that he wanted her to come as soon as possible, and that he would pay her transportation fees as well as her rate. He stared at the journal, which he had placed on the kitchen table, and at the wastebasket filled with a broken china bowl. Yes, he said to the computer screen, come quickly before I go mad.

Chapter Four

December 1, 1998

Stephen set the date with the psychic for after Thanksgiving because he had to make a quick trip to Chicago to visit his family. He was back to Durel Plantation by Sunday evening. Even three days away from Isabella was too long.

He wasn't sure what to expect from Gloria. He cleaned the house and made a small lunch of tuna salad for the two of them, with fresh grapes, melon, and strawberries on the side. "I bet psychic women love this shit," he thought.

At her request so that she would not be prejudgmental as to the severity of his case, he had told her only the barest of details. They had set up an appointment for the afternoon and this perplexed Stephen. He thought that she would want to be around for the ghostly unveiling at twelve o'clock. Apparently that wasn't necessary. The fee was set. The time of the meeting affixed. Directions given.

Gloria had told him that if he decided to have the ghost, or poltergeist, removed there would be no extra charge. She would bring her cards if he wanted a complimentary reading of his future. Well, he thought, the supernatural has gone professional. Even has a bonus gift with every service. Like a physician, she assured him that she could heal him of this "lady." He didn't want to be healed, he wanted to be helped, and he wanted some questions answered.

She arrived ten minutes early, explaining that she had done so in case she got lost, it being such a distance from New Orleans. She was uniquely beautiful, and he knew in an instant that Isabella would hate her. She had silver hair, wore her hair totally straight with bangs that framed a slender face, chiseled cheekbones, and violet eyes. At first, Stephen thought that they were that color because she was wearing contact lens, but she assured him, when he asked, that they were not, and then smiled demurely at the intimate question. She wore a multicolored gypsy skirt of the palest blue and purple hues, and her violet blouse, gathered at the bodice and cuffs, made her eyes even more beautiful. She had a three-inch black belt that made her waist seem even smaller than it was, and she was covered from head to toe with gold jewelry and gold coins. If there were a spot on the body where one could wear gold, this woman had it covered.

He offered her tea or cola, and she wanted none of them. She threw something on the floor. It looked like silver dust. He could have sworn he heard Isabella sneeze. A wicked grin crossed his lips. "You're in for it now, sweetheart," he said to himself.

The woman waved her hand at him, as if she knew what he was thinking, and bowed her head to inspect the floor. "If she's here, we'll see her footsteps."

Then she rolled her eyes up and under her eyelids and seemed to go into a trance. Stephen was impressed.

She mumbled, and then her eyelids opened wide as if she had been stuck in the back with a dagger. "Upstairs! She's upstairs hiding from me. She is angry with you for inviting me," she said turning her head to look at Stephen, "but she'll get over it."

He liked the sound of firm control, wisdom, and coolness in her voice. She laughed and said, "She has no choice."

She looked at Stephen. "You two have a special bond, don't you?"

"Yes."

Gloria eased her way up the long staircase. "She's up here. I can feel her, see her. Not a pretty sight now, but quite something in her day, I'll bet."

She grasped her stomach as if she were becoming ill. She moaned loudly. Stephen wondered if her movements were normal or if the woman really were sick. Then she spoke with Isabella. "Isabella," she said in a stern voice. "You don't have to be afraid of me. I'm here to get your side of the story. I'm not interested in your man."

"Can you really talk to her?" Stephen said.

"Only if she trusts me."

"I can't make out what she's saying to me. How do you do it?"

Gloria said, "Do you mind if I touch you?"

"What?"

"If you want to hear her, I have to touch you."

"Oh, okay, fine." He was thrilled, closed his eyes, and waited for her touch.

She waved her hands over his back as if brushing something off his shirt, then she reversed all her movements by flailing her hands in front of him. After that, she pressed her finger to his chin. Next, she massaged two spots on his forehead. He relaxed instantly. As a finishing touch, she rubbed his sides.

"That feels wonderful," he said.

She stopped for a moment and then touched the soft spot on his head with her thumb.

"Oh," he said, barely able to control his body anymore.

She repeated the process. After waving her hands over his back, and running them, in similar fashion, down both arms, she touched his throat and then his temples. She took his hands in hers and massaged each finger.

She stopped suddenly. "Have you heard her make any sound at all?" she whispered.

"Recently. I can hear her moaning. I feel these cold spots, and I think I know when she's near me. It's like she's kissing me or touching my face." He opened his eyes. "Does that make any sense to you?"

Gloria smiled, and her incredibly beautiful violet eyes twinkled with spiritual light. "Do you feel better now?"

"Wonderful. You're going to have to teach me how to do that, so I can use it on my patients."

Gloria patted his hand. "She's here all right." Then in a louder voice she called to Isabella. "I'm not here to hurt you, or take him from you. Do you understand?"

He felt the coldness next to him. "She's standing next to me."

"I know. She trusts only you." Gloria looked up at the far corner of the master bedroom. "Isabella? Why are you in such desperate need of his help?"

"She needs help? What kind of help?" He heard the concerned physician's tone in his own voice, and Gloria gave him a warm smile. "She wants you."

Then she swayed as if about to fall. "Oh, my. Oh, no,"

she said.

Stephen sensed a need to rescue Gloria, Isabella, or both. "What's wrong? Is she speaking to you?"

"Yes, she trusts me now. She will be able to speak with you soon. After I leave. She died in this house. In the master bedroom. Right here," she said pointing to the bed. He saw tears in the mystic's eyes. "She was poisoned." She opened her eyes and looked at Stephen. "She was murdered."

An icy coldness took a hold of him. He would never have suspected such a thing, and for a moment, he doubted Gloria's abilities. "How could anyone? She's so sweet. I can't believe it."

"I'm sorry. You wanted the truth. Not everyone felt as you do about her. She has no idea who killed her, and she can't rest until she finds out who did it. She cannot follow the light, or her husband...Emile...into heaven because she died before her time. Some misunderstandings that were never healed. He came after—later. Am I right about his name?"

"Yes. She can't go on?"

"That's right. And...you look just like him?"

"Yes, I do. Does she think I'm him?"

"You *look* like him, but...she heard you...in the...shower the other day...singing? And she knows *now* that you're not him. Apparently, you displayed a certain behavior," she said, smiling, "that her husband would never have done."

Stephen backed away from the woman. "How could you have known that? Incredible."

Gloria waited a minute and then said, "Born again at another time, but once Emile to her."

"How can that be?"

She opened her eyes and spoke to him as a teacher would. "Reincarnation, Dr. Templeton. You have come back to the house you owned, to the land you worked, and to the woman who was your wife, to the woman you loved."

Stephen took his time before saying, "Did Emile kill her? I must know."

She shook her head. "I don't know. I can't see it. I'm being given the barest details. Emile and Isabella were married in 1831. She died seven years later in this house. Such a short time to be married. Now, she and you are together in this lifetime and in this bizarre situation."

"She's dead; I'm alive."

She looked at him. "You still love her as you did then—maybe more. And she wants you to do something for her."

"What?"

"She...I'm not sure...what she's saying? Hold on."

She touched the wall of the bedroom to keep herself from falling. Her voice changed to a soft, feminine whisper. It had to be Isabella's voice. *"Give me a second chance."*

"A second chance?" Stephen asked.

Gloria stopped meditating. "That's all I can get right now. 'Give me a second chance,' she keeps saying over and over again."

"For what?"

"I'm not sure. Probably at life—or love. She wants to relive a certain part of her life and change it. She wants to make something right that was misunderstood. It's really bothering her. Poor dear. How hopeless. So sad."

"Hopeless?"

"She can never live again, Doctor. What has been done in the past, her death, the fact that someone took her life at such a young age, can never be changed. She may always haunt this house and never cross over. Of course, I could end her misery if you want me to."

Stephen didn't like the sounds of that. "What do you mean?"

"Let's go downstairs and have some tea and talk." Her voice was like a parent's, wanting to speak out of earshot of the children.

"But...Isabella..."

She spoke softly, "Mustn't know what we're planning on doing."

Stephen reacted defensively. "She won't leave my side. She won't stay in this room. She'll follow us anyway. So what's the point in leaving?"

She whispered. "We have to help her go on, exorcise the house of her spirit." She touched his shoulder reassuringly. "I have the candles and the holy water. It won't hurt her, and you'd be doing her a favor."

"No!"

"Tea, Dr. Templeton? You're getting much too emotional about matters beyond your control."

"You sound like I do when I tell a patient bad news. We'll go into the kitchen, but believe me, I'm not going to hurt her."

She smiled. "The bond is very strong. Perhaps the strongest I've ever seen."

Gloria sat at the small table at the center of the kitchen and watched Stephen boil water in a teapot. He offered her a assortment of blends, and she chose peppermint.

"I know you two love each other, but she has to go onto the other side where she'll be happy."

"How can she be happy if she has no clue why she died so early in life? Why she was murdered? Who murdered her? I couldn't rest if I thought that someone I loved might have killed me. And where is Emile?"

The tea kettle whistled. A cool breeze on a cloudless day came into the kitchen with such force that the kitchen's screen door whipped open and banged against the cupboards.

"Oh, he's here—with you," Gloria said.

"Well," he said, pacing around the kitchen, "tell his spirit to get lost. This is my kitchen, my house, my..."

"Wife?" she said, finishing his thought.

"Wife," he said meekly. "She isn't, is she?"

She observed the hot steam that floated above her cup. "That all depends. One, he's dead which ends the marriage bond. Two, a woman has the right to pick the man she loves and wants to live with. Three, you're alive and strong. I sense a great deal of power inside you. Spiritual power and passion, and a great desire to heal people who are hurt and heartbroken. But I don't know what you can do if he..."

"There's nothing he can do," Stephen said, defiantly.

"Well, there is *one* thing."

Stephen finished making his tea and sat down opposite her. He sipped the hot liquid, stared at her, and waited for her to speak.

"If he's the one who killed her, and I am not saying that he is," she told him, "he could prevent her from contacting you anymore. He could keep her in limbo forever by confusing her spirit. Torturing her with the mystery of her death by never telling her the truth."

"Doesn't he love her? Want her to be happy?"

She looked into the distance. "I don't like what I'm picking up here. Man, these Victorian Creole guys are a nasty lot. Not willing to take a back seat to anyone—even the living. He tells me that Isabella must do as he says, and that you should stay out of it."

His hand closed into a fist. "I'd like to see him try to make me."

Gloria looked at him and smiled at the force of Stephen's words. "He's laughing. He tells me that he's already taken matters into his own hands by entering your body and forcing words out of your mouth. He says that he'll keep doing that as long as he wants. He doesn't think that you have the power to stop him."

Stephen dropped the cup onto the saucer. "So, that's why I've been so bastardly to her."

"All the time?"

"No," he said sheepishly, "just once in awhile."

She touched his hand. "She knows you don't mean it. She understands. She loves you as you are. In your shower, with your towel, singing silly songs out of tune."

"I do *not* sing out of tune."

She laughed. "Isabella doesn't mind. I guess that really got to her. Isabella Durel meet Dr. Stephen Templeton, the man who loves you."

"So we're going to forget about the exorcism stuff, right?"

She smiled again and took a sip of her tea. "I think you should put her out of her misery. It's the kindest thing to do."

"You make her sound like some animal we're going to put to sleep."

"Dr. Templeton, Isabella has been kept away from happiness, peace, and eternal joy for a very long time. Let me say the words to send her to heaven, and she will never haunt this house again. She isn't supposed to be here."

Stephen stood. "I think it's time you left. I appreciate everything you've done for me. Thank you very much."

"Spirits aren't supposed to be on earth." She followed him down to the entrance hall. "They're *supposed* to be in heaven with the ones they love."

"How can she be happy in heaven when she knows one of her 'loved ones' might have poisoned her? Would you rest 'peacefully,' Gloria?"

"Well..."

"Exactly." He handed her the check he had written earlier.

"But there's nothing you can do about it?" she said.

"I hope you find the ride back to New Orleans a pleasant one." He opened the door for her.

"Here's my card. Call me if you change your mind."

"I won't."

"You can't go back and change the past."

He shut the door on her words, scratched his chin, and headed for the kitchen.

"The hell I can't."

He turned on his computer and opened the Internet bookmark to Time Travelers, Incorporated.

"Okay, Wainwright, show me what's the going rate on a first-class ticket to 1838."

Chapter Five

Bruce Wainwright e-mailed him this reply:
Leave your name, address, and directions to your location, and I will give you a free consultation in your own home. Time travel is for three months with no exceptions, so if this is a serious inquiry, you need to start planning now. Travel arrangements are made with the Internet's help, and you may depart through a time tunnel nearest your home soon. Next traveling date will be December 22.

December twenty-second? Just a few days away from her death date. He had to try it. He had to give her that second chance. He gave Wainwright all the information he'd asked for, and prayed that he would get back to him as quickly as possible.

He wondered if Isabella would come to him that night. He couldn't sleep for fear that she might have been offended by Gloria and her "fairy dust."

He heard a voice call to him in his mind just before twelve, but it wasn't Isabella's voice he heard. It was a man's. Emile's? He manifested himself right before Stephen's eyes. Tall, arrogant, still handsome in a bluish sort of way, and as domineering as he could be. Stephen told himself to be firm.

"Get out of my house, you trespasser," he said.

"It isn't your house anymore, it's mine," Stephen said, his courage building.

"Ridiculous to be called away from sheer pleasure in heaven to discuss Isabella."

"I don't find her an irritant in the least. I think she's wonderful, don't you?"

"You don't know her like I do. Leave her to her misery."

"Don't you care about her? What happens to her?"

The ghost tried to hide his eyes from Stephen by turning away. *"I loved her once. Who are you to judge me?"*

He moved closer to Emile's ghost. "Hey, big shot, don't you notice the similarity? Hello. I'm you; you're me. And I'm not interested in your attitude, pal, so drop it. I'm going to do everything in my power to free Isabella from her date with death, from her destiny, from whoever murdered her, from bad karma, or whatever you call it. By the way, was it you who poisoned her?"

The ghost turned away from Stephen. "*Leave me to my grief. I lost my wife, man. Have you no sentiment at all? No compassion?*"

Stephen folded his arms across his chest. "Just answer the question."

"*She was poisoned!*"

"If not you? Who?"

"*You think you understand her, but you don't. She took all my money, never made love to me, ran around with every wealthy or artistic man in New Orleans, and refused to show me the least bit of respect for my family's name. She drove me mad with jealousy. She's dead. Leave her that way. Tis God's own judgment on her—a curse.*"

"No, *you* leave *us* alone. You don't want her; I do. And I'll risk my sanity to save her soul because someone has to pity her. Obviously her husband couldn't satisfy her needs." It was a cruel statement, and Stephen meant it to be.

"*Sir, you are a silly romantic in love with a woman who will betray you and break your heart. Don't waste any more of your time or your money on her.*"

"Try to stop me."

"*I will.*" And he was gone.

Stephen was torn between hatred, jealousy, and awe. He'd just spoken to the dead. The bastard had tried to stop him from giving her a second chance. How could a woman like Isabella live with such a man? Then the demons started to stir in his mind. Was she an adulteress? Did she frivolously throw away Emile's hard-earned cash? Was she cold? Was he wasting his time with a dream? Maybe she wasn't what he thought she was just as Emile had said. Maybe his emotional instability had caused him to fall in love with the vision of a woman who never existed. If he traveled in time, would he be wasting his time, as Emile had suggested?

A horrid thought crept into his thoughts. He doubted his heart. She didn't visit him that night.

The next morning, he awakened clear headed and well rested. After his initial fears drifted away, he fell asleep. There was no vision to disturb him, no lady to kiss him good night, and no specter to drive the sleepy coils from his brain.

He ate his breakfast and sipped his coffee while checking his e-mail. True to his word, Wainwright answered him within hours of his first message. "Does this guy have a life?" he wondered.

Wainwright was in New York but promised to be in New Orleans as soon as he could get a flight. He would e-mail Stephen the estimated time of arrival. When he arrived, he'd take a taxi to the plantation if Stephen gave him directions. A New Orleans taxi drive all the way out to Durel Plantation? Stephen laughed. "Good luck, pal."

He e-mailed him specific instructions and asked him to call when he arrived at the airport so that he'd have a good idea when to expect him. Stephen's plantation was an hour's drive from the airport.

Wainwright also told him that all his air fares and taxi rides would be a part of the whole cost if Stephen decided to time travel. The consultation was free. Stephen added, in his own letter, that he would pay for his air fare and welcome him to his house with accommodations and food.

He wanted to make Wainwright feel as if he'd fallen into the past—the hospitality of the Templeton Plantation. Emile could go to hell. It was his estate now. He made a shopping list.

He didn't feel her presence all day, and he tried to pretend it didn't matter to him. She was a jealous little girl if she thought Gloria was a threat to her. Maybe she was worried that he believed Emile's words. Why should he? The man had only been her husband, after all, and hadn't Stephen kept her safe from Gloria's incantations and candles? Of course, maybe she wanted to go to heaven. Nah! She wanted to be with him. She could just go haunt the attic if she thought that he would change his plans for her whims.

This was all for her—about her. The second chance she wanted. She should appreciate his generosity. It was costing him a hell of a lot of money, for perhaps, nothing.

He busied himself redoing the library, which wasn't as tough a job as he had first thought. He dumped the old and dusty books into a box, threw them into the back of his Lexus, and drove to New Orleans. He found a parking place near the Cafe du Monde and walked to Royal Street.

The man at the antique store was excited about the sale and would give him a handsome fee, when Stephen noticed the coin collection resting under a long, glass case.

"You wouldn't happen to have any currency from 1838 or before, would you?"

"A true collector? In the back. Follow me. We don't keep that sort of thing in the front of the store."

Stephen followed him to the small office and watched as the man opened the safe and took out old bank notes and coins from a special tin box.

"You've got quite a collection," said Stephen.

The pinched-faced man in the business suit said, "Yes, indeed, it is, sir. Are you interested in a particular piece?"

"Are all these from 1838 or before?"

"Yes," he said.

"The entire collection?"

The man was getting perturbed. "Yes, sir. Some are in better condition than others, of course, and that effects the price. What would you like to see?"

"How much would this entire collection go for?"

The man looked away as if he were slightly amused. "A collector would know."

"Look. I asked a question, be civil enough to answer me." Stephen was shocked at himself. He was forceful, domineering, controlling. He sounded like Emile. Well, he thought, there might be something to be said for possession, after all.

"I could add it all up for you, but it would take a few minutes."

Stephen said, "I have all the time in the world."

The man went back to his desk, took out a calculator, weighed each coin on a scale, and then added the sum. He opened a book and checked something and then returned.

"The set is worth $350,000 by today's market. In 1838, it would amount to $100,000." He waited patiently, expecting that Stephen would need a long time to decide what he wanted. The twisted grin on his face, which he tried to hide, gave the impression that he expected Stephen to cough politely and say that he would think it over—and then leave.

"Can I use the money from the books as part of this sale?"

"Why, yes, of course," he said.

"How much would you take off on this purchase?"

"Which item?"

Stephen scowled. "On all of it, man. Why would I waste my time on one piece?" There it was again. The powerful, type A personality coming through again.

Stephen whispered softly into the air. "You do know something about business, don't you, Durel?"

"What did you say, sir?" the man said, jerking his head up from his mathematics.

"I was just talking to myself. The price?"

"For all of them?"

"Put them in a velvet bag as if they were diamonds. I'll write you a check today." He smiled sweetly. "If that's all right with you."

The man beamed. "Oh, yes, of course, Dr. Templeton. I had no idea you were so fond of old coins. You hardly glanced at them when you came into the shop the last time. Forgive me. I thought you just wanted a souvenir of the past. Let me go ring this up and subtract the discount. Stay right here."

Stephen said aloud. "Alright, my girl, I now have something you can't resist, *cash*. Enough to keep you in gold gowns, fine dinners, and opera tickets, to be sure. But unlike your husband, I intend to see you pay me back. *With interest*."

In his mind, he heard Emile say, "*You're a fool, Templeton. A complete and utter ass*."

"But I mean a hell of a lot more to her than you ever did. And I intend to show her the love you neglected to give her. And even more than that, you bastard, I'm going to give her back her life. Something you, or whoever it was, took from her. So bug off, Bozo."

The man returned to the office just as Stephen said, "Bug

48

off, Bozo."

"What did you say, sir?" the man said, timorously.

"Ah...I said...isn't this King Borco from Spain? The profile—on the coin?"

"Oh, no, I think that's the Queen of Spain, sir."

"Yeah, I guess you're right. The light's playing tricks with my eyes. Still," he said like a true connoisseur, "if you ever do find a dated coin with King Borco of Spain on it, I'd sure like to buy it."

The man twisted his head in bewilderment, puzzled by Stephen's statements. "Yes, sir," was all he said.

Stephen made the sale, and while he was writing out the check, noticed a small cameo ring in the jewelry case near the cash register.

"That ring? May I see it?" he said.

"Which one, sir?" he said, getting his key.

"The small cameo ring."

"Oh, this one, here? You have good taste and a keen sense of your 1838 date. From the same time period. It has a legend, too."

He handed the ring to Stephen who smiled in recognition of the familiar piece of jewelry he'd seen in the portrait. "So many women must have had rings like this."

"As a matter of fact, they didn't. This cameo, as many others, was designed specifically for the woman who would wear it. It's her profile. Very expensive, and not easy to get a hold of in Louisiana. It might be French."

"I don't suppose you know who owned this one?"

"Oh, yes, the legend's quite clear." He read a card that had been hidden under the ring. "This is the beautiful face of the notorious Victorian beauty, Isabella Durel." He let Stephen hold the ring.

Stephen almost dropped it when he heard him say her name as if he'd known her all his life. His hand shook.

"Notorious?" he said.

"A renowned lady known for her beauty as well as her grace and gentleness...and for her lovers."

Stephen blanched. "Lovers?" he said.

"Rumors only. Gossip. But never the less, a possibility. It's said," he moved closer to Stephen so that he could be more

49

confidential, as if someone from 1998 knew the lady he was about to make infamous by his speech. "It's said that her husband poisoned her when he grew weary of her many sordid affairs and spending habits."

Stephen's face grew pale, and he almost fainted. He forced himself to breathe.

"Are you all right?" said the man, concerned that he might lose the customer before he'd signed the check.

"Water."

The man raced to the water fountain, took a paper cup, and poured Stephen a drink.

Stephen stared at her face on the ring. "No," he said to it. "I don't believe it."

Then with more force and much louder, he said, "You lousy bastard."

"Excuse me, sir," said the man, "I came as fast as I could."

"No, I didn't mean you...oh, never mind. I'll take the ring."

The man was overjoyed for the second time that day. Even if Stephen were a raving lunatic, his credit was good all over the world, so he hastily rang up the second sale. He placed the ring in its broken, but original, velvet box—a plus as far as Stephen was concerned. He had her money, her diamond bow necklace, and now her ring.

"Any time you need any more coins, just let me know," said the man, as he shook Stephen's hand enthusiastically and slipped him his card.

"Thank you."

"And I'll keep a sharp look out for that rare King Borco of Spain coin."

Stephen was feeling far too ill to explain and wanted to get out of the store. "You do that. And thank you very much for your kindness," he said, handing him the empty paper cup.

He walked down Royal Street and back to his car. He placed the package of coins in the trunk and locked it. Then he decided to have some beignets and coffee, a rare treat for him, at Cafe du Monde, while he watched the psychics read people's fortunes, the carriage horses wilt in the heat, and the artists render portraits of tourists. Jackson Square.

He let the sugary pastry melt in his mouth and then swallowed it with a swig of chicory coffee. It was a sunny day in New Orleans, but his mind was going mad with the man's words "many lovers." Was that all Stephen was to her? Is that why she was so good at pulling him into her web of helplessness and seduction? Past master—mistress—of the art? And Emile? Had he poisoned his wife? He'd never really received a straight answer from the man—spirit.

"God, help me," Stephen said. "Don't let me play the fool. I've already spent so much money on her, on this mad dream, this metaphysical love affair, that I may have to go back to my practice sooner than I'm able just to pay her bills. Is this how Emile felt? Did he kill her rather than lose his mind as well as his heart?"

The ring was still in his pocket—in its bag and box. He took it out of the worn, velvet box, and let it rest on his little finger. Her unique profile was even more distinct in the sunlight. Her sweet angelic face. "How could you?" he said.

Then tears came to his eyes. "This is crazy, Isabella. You aren't worth this grief. Adulteress. Not mine."

The waiter came by and broke his mood. "More coffee, sir? More beignets?"

"What?"

"Say," said the young man, eying the ring, "who's the ring for? It sure is a beaut."

"It's for...it's for..." He paused before he could say the words. "It's for the woman I love."

"Well, she's one lucky lady. That's a real treasure. The profile is lovely."

"Yes, it is. And so is she."

He paid the boy, leaving a sizable tip, placed the ring back into the box, back into his pocket, and drove back to his plantation. He wanted to have a long talk with a certain female ghost.

Chapter Six

Stephen didn't go straight home; he stopped at a local grocery store and purchased enough food for his house guest. In a whimsical moment, he purchased champagne, caviar, and a box of small wheat crackers. His plan was to invite Isabella to a "spiritual date" where they could discuss his concerns about her past. He needed more information about her life, especially since he was about to embark on an incredible adventure to save her from a dismal fate. He knew, in his heart, that it didn't really matter what she'd done. That thought pleased him. He loved her unconditionally. He now understood what the term meant. It didn't matter what anyone said about her; he trusted her. That didn't mean he didn't want the story from her own lips.

She obviously needed someone to love her. He'd studied enough patient psychology to know that if someone is behaving to a degree of reckless abandon, they might just be seeking affection. Emile, and perhaps other family members, had been a little shy on this aspect of her life.

How could he tell? It was in her eyes. In the portrait. Hauntingly sad eyes. Big brown orbs of depression and loneliness. Her eyes had attracted him first. Both in the portrait and as a ghost. The eyes were the mirror of the soul—and the heart—and they never lied. She was begging for someone to love her.

When he'd put away all his groceries, he went into the library and started working. He thought the room would make an excellent place for them to discuss his time-traveling expedition, and he wanted it to be ready for Wainwright's visit. The furniture had arrived yesterday afternoon, and he had the men place it in the foyer until he'd finished polishing the floor.

He made it shine, and then threw a new tapestry rug

across the width of it. He moved a round oak table into the center of the room, and tossed a Victorian piano shawl of burgundy and green over its top. He brought in two leather chairs—one red and one green—and put one at the north corner and one at the south corner of the open space. There was one window that he now draped with the same curtains and border as the dining room windows. "At least we have three rooms to live in now, Isabella," he said.

There was an old harpsichord in the room. It was long overdue for a tuning, and he resurrected it as best he could. He had a gut feeling Isabella knew how to play it. It might have been something she treasured. As a finishing touch, he found two brass candelabras in the attic, and placed one on the table and one on the harpsichord. He needed to create a romantic mood.

Since it was near dusk, he made himself a ham sandwich, poured a glass of wine, and lit the candles of the candelabras.

"Isabella?" he sang to her. "I have *champagne* and *caviar* and *candlelight*. I haven't heard from you lately. Are you angry with me? Why don't you visit me at twelve like you used to?" And, as an afterthought he added, "I don't believe him, you know."

He heard Emile whisper, "*Fool.*"

"Yeah, yeah, why don't you go walk around your plantation, or haunt the stables or something, and leave us alone. You scare her, and I can see why."

It occurred to him that he wasn't dressed properly for their date, so he bolted upstairs and dressed in his formal togs. He regarded his reflection in the mirror. "She won't be able to resist me. I may look like her husband, but I'll see to it that she catches the difference between us as soon as she materializes. It's all or nothing tonight, baby. You want me to give you a second chance, and I want you. Why should I lie about it? I love you, and I know you want me too. There, I've said it."

He felt a rush of cold air up his neck. It tickled the hair on the lower part of his head. "The thought gets to you, doesn't it? I'm not going to use you like everyone else did. I'm going to change that expression you're wearing in that picture to a big smile and sparkling eyes." He held up his index finger to where he felt the chill. "Hold that thought."

He went back downstairs and placed the champagne in a

silver ice bucket filled with crushed ice. Then he opened the caviar, placed it at the center of a china plate, put crackers around it, and a small knife on the plate's side. "Only the best for you, sweetheart."

He took the appetizer into the library, put it on the table, and then waited. He sauntered towards the harpsichord. "Do you know how to play this, Isabella?"

"*Yes*," came a whispered reply. It was the first word he'd heard her speak. Soft, angelic, breathy, seductive, sweet, and alive.

He twirled to find her standing by the red, leather chair. She looked different in the candlelight. Almost real. Almost alive.

"Would you like some champagne?" he asked, popping the cork expertly.

She laughed. Throaty, spooky, but nice laughter. He'd made her laugh. She touched the stem of the glass, and it stayed in her hand. She was using a great deal of energy tonight. Maybe she realized how important this date was to Stephen who was wrestling with Emile's accusations. She pressed the glass to her lips and drank.

He became bolder. "Cheap grocery store caviar, mon cher."

"*Yes*," she said, and smiled at him. She opened her eyes wide so that he could drink in the golden brown hue of them.

He placed a teaspoonful of the glossy black fish eggs on a cracker and handed it to her. "You know something, Isabella, *you* are a woman of few words." He raised his right eyebrow. "I like that."

She let her eyelashes flutter, not daring to look him in the eye. "*Yes*." Beguiling, coquettish, feminine, sexy, soft.

He poured a glass of champagne for himself. Then he positioned himself as close as he dared to her beauty. He touched the tip of her goblet with his. The pure, crystal glass rang—a bell to raise a spirit—to bring it nearer to earth. "Here's to us. To eternity. To second chances."

The vision glowed. The blue of her transparent spirit form turned into a flesh and blood beauty.

"Are you taking all of my energy?" he asked, with the underlying meaning of the remark being sexual. He moved closer to her so that his face was just above hers.

Her eyelids fluttered open again. Her head tilted as if begging for a kiss. "*Yes,*" she said, with a voice as willowy and refreshing as a cooling breeze on a hot, summer night.

He gave her a masculine, wry smile. "You *are* good. How I want you. Do you want me?"

"*Yes,*" she said, and moved closer to his lips.

"Then tonight I may have to write a new chapter in Gloria's textbook. How to make love to a ghost."

She didn't answer his comment. Instead, she went over to the harpsichord, opened the lid, and sat down to play.

"It doesn't work." He regretted the statement immediately. If she could be physical for even a moment, then the harpsichord would play. He had to remind himself that he was not dealing with reality anymore. Her fingers first caressed the keys, and then she rested them on the familiar notes of a long-forgotten song.

The most ethereal music came from the instrument. She had amazing talent. "You love music, don't you?" he said, standing behind her.

She answered and then giggled, "*Yes.*"

"You know I'm not Emile, don't you?"

"*Yes,*" she said, and arched her shoulders high to reach the musical crescendo correctly.

He took the risk. "I hope that doesn't bother you."

She stopped playing, stood up, turned around quickly, and with fear in her eyes, touched his lips with her fingers begging him to say no more.

"All right. All right. No more talk of 'him.' May I...kiss you now? Is it...permitted?"

She closed her eyes, moved her chin up to meet his lips, and said, "*Yes.*"

"Thank you, Lord," Stephen said.

Just then the doorbell rang.

He turned his head away from her. "Ah, shi...ta...hey, I'll be right back. Probably some Girl Scout selling cookies for voodoo camp or something. Don't be afraid. Don't move a muscle. Here, drink more champagne, I want you very happy tonight, if you know what I mean. Spirit-filled spirit."

She laughed at his joke.

Stephen ran to the door. He hadn't realized it was storming like mad outside. No little girl would be out selling cookies on a night like this. He opened the huge door to find two men dripping warm rain on his porch.

"Can I help you?" said Stephen, protecting his tuxedo from the swirling wind and dampness.

"Rather the other way around. Bruce Wainwright of Time Travelers, Incorporated, at your service," he said, offering his hand to Stephen. Stephen shook his hand absently. "Got a special Internet discount on a flight to come down this morning and couldn't resist saving you money. And this is one of my business associates, Samuel Cooper."

Sam shook Stephen's hand and said,"Ah...it's a little wet out here. The taxi driver refused to bring us any closer to the door. Something about haunted plantation houses. He crossed himself three times before he got our luggage from the back of the cab and hurled it onto the roadside." He cleared his throat. "Ah...may we come in?"

Stephen had been stunned into impolite behavior. "Oh, yes, of course, come in. May I help you with your luggage? I was just having a small snack before going to bed."

Wainwright's right eyebrow rose in disbelief. "Really?"

"Yeah," said Sam, "I always wear a tuxedo when I want to lay back and act casual." Sam slapped Stephen on the shoulder as he walked past him.

Stephen thought how slow and dumb witted he'd sounded to these men, how observant and professional they seemed, and how Isabella would be beside herself with joy when she saw the two attractive men in her home. "Timing, Stephen," he said to himself, "is everything." He knew she would have dematerialized as soon as she heard the men's voices.

A bevy of emotions coursed through his veins: irritation, impotence, embarrassment, agitation, and relief. It was a comfort to have someone else in the house. Other males who would understand his situation and help him go back to her. He was inwardly glad that Wainwright had found that other flight, yet his lips were still burning from the nearness of hers.

"Forgive us for the late hour," said Wainwright. "We had a problem in Atlanta."

Sam coughed.

Stephen asked, "Understandable. Here let me take your coats."

Sam said, "Where's your computer?"

"Oh, right through here, in the kitchen."

"I need to e-mail my brother and tell him we made it here in one piece." Then Sam winked and whispered close to Stephen and out of Wainwright's earshot. "Something to do with Wainwright's whacky super saver Internet plane routes. Puddle jumpers. Always looking for the best deal, he sometimes books us on the strangest planes out of the weirdest terminals."

He showed Sam the computer while Wainwright ran back outside to get more luggage.

"Here let me help you with that," Stephen said, while dragging the heavy suitcase up the stairs to one of the unfinished but furnished guest rooms. Had they brought everything they owned? Stephen hadn't expected Sam, but he liked and trusted him immediately. He and Wainwright went through his master bedroom to get to the smaller room.

"I'm just redoing the old place. By myself, you see. I haven't managed all the rooms yet."

"And doing a formidable job of perfecting the time period, I must add. That 1838 date all the way through the plantation?"

"Yes."

"Good. Listen, I know it's late, and you may not want to give me all the details tonight, but I need to know one thing before I unpack."

"Yes, of course, what is it?"

Sam came rushing into the room. "Oh, there you are. It was a little *spooky* down there. Cold chills in New Orleans and in December yet. A cool breeze right up my neck."

Stephen smiled. "Isabella."

"Huh?" said Sam.

"You'll get used to it. I'll tell you more later. You were saying, Mr. Wainwright?"

"I need to know whether you're really going to time travel to 1838, Dr. Templeton."

"Oh, yes, indeed, Mr. Wainwright."

"Despite personal loss or gain, and even if it costs a

fortune to get there and back."

"May I ask *you* a question first?"

"By all means."

"Can you produce a three-month stay in the year 1838 on *this* plantation for me?"

Wainwright smirked, and Sam grinned. "Yes, Dr. Templeton. We can."

Stephen opened the collar of the tuxedo's shirt and grinned. "Good night, gentleman, we'll talk more at breakfast. Only bathroom in the house is in the back of the kitchen near the pantry. You are my guests, and if there is anything you desire you need only ask. Welcome to Durel Plantation."

He turned to leave and then had a second thought. "And yes, Mr. Cooper, this house *is* haunted just as the taxicab driver informed you. They won't bother you much so don't be alarmed. They are very distinguished ghosts, too. The last true Creole master and mistress of this mansion. You can see their portraits in the dining room if you wish. Have a pleasant night."

Wainwright and Cooper gave each other a curious look, just as Stephen closed the door on them.

"Isabella, you naughty girl. Stay out of their room," he said to her.

"*Yes*," she whispered into his ear.

"*Now what?*" said Emile. "*Good Lord! Yankees in my home.*"

Chapter Seven

Stephen was becoming as skillful in the kitchen as he was in surgery. He made bacon, eggs, toasted bagels, and pancakes for his guests. The conversation began after breakfast.

"Okay, Wainwright, how does this time travel work, and why do you know so much about it?" said Stephen, pouring himself another cup of coffee and offering them another cup as well. He wondered if Isabella was listening.

"Time travel has been available for centuries. We have documented records going back as far as 650 b.c."

Stephen laughed. "What did they have to go back to?"

Wainwright didn't find the joke funny.

"It's a natural phenomenon that works with the changing of the earth's sphere. You depart at the solstice—when the sun crosses the equator and shifts the earth's atmosphere thus opening black holes and various spots on the earth's surface. When they open, and you are near a portal, and you are emotionally linked by your thoughts to a specific time, you may enter the time tunnel and travel to the past. You'll stay in that spot until the equinox—when all holes are closed again—and the time traveler returns. You may travel five different ways. The easiest way to travel is a general transfer which means you want to visit and come home—rather like a vacation for three months. The second way to travel is a slot transfer which means you go back in time and become time. In other words, you were born in this time period to go back and live in the past. This happens very rarely, but we have conclusive evidence that it does happen. The next mode of travel is a death transfer, and this happens when someone replaces someone they resemble who's died on the eve of the solstice. Another rare one but, again, we have evidence to substantiate it. Now the ones most frequently asked for are the next two: genealogical transfer and reincarnation

59

transfer."

Stephen sat down completely fascinated with Wainwright's speech. Sam Cooper was smiling at him and nodding his head in agreement. "You say you think that you might be the reincarnation of this Emile Durel? I saw the portrait in the dining room. It does seem to corroborate your psychic's perception. Later, with your permission, I'll hypnotize you and scan your unconscious to see whether that's true."

"Is that really necessary what with general transfers being an option?" said Stephen.

"It is if you plan to help your spirited friend. It would take you too long to make your presence known to the Durel's to be of any help to her. The Gemini Effect would be a lot faster."

"Gemini Effect?"

"In genealogical and reincarnation transfers there is a blood and soul sameness, as well as an anatomical exactness. This makes blending with the other person's physical body a possibility. In a death transfer, there is no need since you are taking someone's place because they have left this world. In general transfers you are making a whole new persona so no one cares whom you are provided you don't try to pretend you're someone important like, say, Napoleon. Two in one harmony is the rule. The stronger personality usually takes control of the intimate bond. Of course, since we're more advanced now, the ancestor usually stays totally dormant, allowing the stronger ego from the future to take over for them. Naturally, certain likes and dislikes, hobbies and talents from the other soul may rise to the surface. Sam did it accidentally once, and he swears he had no idea he was his own ancestor."

"Much to my surprise, I found out that my loving wife was my great-great-great grandmother. So, Dr. Templeton, we've been testing the waters of this River of Time—or time tunnel—before we would ever make it available to anyone."

"And we have to make sure that you are Emile Durel so that your trip will be all that you want it to be. Satisfied customers are future endorsements."

"You say the stronger personality may control?" said Stephen.

"Yes, that's right."

"Emile is a controller, master of the plantation, passionate, aggressive, and a type A if I've ever met one. I'm a classic type B and have been going to analysis for a year about it. I almost had a nervous breakdown from not being able to deal with the stress. I can't release my emotions, but ever since I met Isabella—well, it's been sneaking out. For some reason, I've become a real son of a bitch with her."

Wainwright looked into his coffee cup for some time before saying, "Then this may be exactly what you need."

"How so?"

"You said that you wanted to save his wife from a murderer?"

"Yes. The psychic said that she was poisoned. Isabella's ghost wants me to give her a second chance."

Sam touched Stephen's shoulder and softly said, "To be able to do that, you may have to force Durel into a passive role. Not an easy undertaking. If you mean to save her, you will have to use *his* aggressiveness and *his* strength to do what, apparently, he wasn't able to do in his own time—save her life."

"Something else bothers me," said Wainwright. "How do we know he wasn't the one who killed her?" His voice was soothing but businesslike.

"I don't know for sure. Can't I save her? Can't history be changed?"

"History can be changed on a small scale. The Civil War will not be erased, but a death certificate, and whether a little boy is saved from drowning, can be. Was there trouble between them?"

"I think. Hold on, let me show you something." Stephen went to the library, and the two men followed. "This is Dr. Gayerré's journal. I found it in a hidden safe. It says, 'Change his mind and her heart.' Her death was Christmas Day 1838. If you can send me back to December twenty-second, I could stay with her and try to stop it."

Sam said, "You'd have to follow her everywhere and check everything she ate or drank—who she was with."

"Well, I wouldn't mind doing that." A boyish smile graced his lips.

"And continue doing it for three months. You'd have to keep fate away from her until the equinox," said Wainwright.

"You mean watch her continually for three months?"

"A difficult task considering you would have to work the plantation during that time as well."

"He could take one of us with him," said Sam.

Wainwright explained, "Sam and Jim Cooper are from a time traveling family whose journals and adventures have helped us put together this business."

"My brother owns an antique business in Milford, New York, and I run the family business, a string of summer cabins near Richfield Springs, New York. Two years ago, my brother used the Internet to locate other time-traveling families, and, with Wainwright's European connections, we were able to locate almost all the time tunnels on the globe. With this information, the five ways to travel, and our extensive research, we can take you to and from 1838, watch over your 1998 holdings, as well as keep your family and friends clueless as to where you are. Most people cringe at the idea that their families might think they're nuts for trying such a thing."

"That's for sure," said Stephen, "especially in my case."

Sam continued, "So my brother is watching the Internet as well as the cabins, Wainwright and I are here to help you do the legwork, but only one of us has to stay behind to watch your home and talk to your friends if they decide to visit."

"You lie for me," Stephen said.

"Exactly," said Wainwright.

"I *will* come back though?"

"Like a canceled check," said Sam.

"Can I die or be hurt while I'm there?"

Wainwright sat down in the green leather chair. "Excellent question. If it's your time to die in 1998, then you will die in 1838 on that day and in that month. But on genealogical and reincarnation transfers, it's unlikely that you would die since someone else's body and yours are linked biologically speaking. You would have double the energy, and most people find that they're stronger during this time."

Stephen pondered all that they'd said. "Then time is nothing but a continual..."

"Flowing river. You are on the banks and may enter anywhere, but those in the water must remain there. Hence, we do not arrange future trips. Modern books and movies would have you think that you can go into the future, but it isn't so. Recorded time only. Too much can alter the future, so there is no way you can have a clear perception of it, and thus not be able to fantasize about it enough to go to it."

"We should also mention that you'll be affected by any storms that shake up the atmosphere. If you're near your entrance portal, you can flash back until the storm has passed. If you aren't, then you experience flu-like symptoms," said Sam.

"You said that I didn't have to go alone. Why would I want to take another person with me?"

"Part of our service. We're used to traveling and can transfer easily to any destination. It's sometimes nice to have someone with you to guide you through the experience. It's up to you. Under such mysterious circumstances, Dr. Templeton, you may need more than one pair of eyes to keep Isabella from harm. Fate, history, death will want her life, and will try, in those three months, to claim her just to keep the record straight. Two heads are better than one, as they say. It sounds as if Isabella had many enemies, and one of them is trying to take her life. When they are thwarted on December twenty-fifth, they may try again."

"Well...who would go with me?" Stephen said.

"I'd like to volunteer," Sam said bowing. "My specialty is the 1700s, and I might fit the manners and custom of your 1838 time period better. Wainwright is more inclined towards the ancient Euro-Asian world. Of course, we'd have to do a great deal of research on her family, Emile's, and their habits, if we're to keep her alive. I would need a persona, a name, that I could role play." Sam smiled for a long moment and then added, "I think this is very caring of you, Templeton, to spend all this time and money to save a woman you've never met."

"Oh, I've met her all right. She haunts this place as well as her husband. I hired a psychic to get some answers from her, but Emile is keeping his mouth shut on the subject of her murder and refuses to help me. I'm keeping her close to the house until I can find a safe way to send her to her eternal home."

"Hmm," said Wainwright, "maybe Emile knows who

killed her. Do you love the woman in the portrait?"

The question spoken for all three to hear sounded so odd to Stephen, "Yes," he finally said, "is that odd?"

"Nothing is odd to us, Doc," said Sam. "Besides, we have a happy ending slot transfer 1890s story that started with the photo of a Victorian man."

"Must you go there?" said Wainwright stiffly.

Sam looked at Wainwright. "Sorry."

"Can I save her then?" said Stephen.

"We'll do the best security job anyone can hope for. We need to find out why anyone would want to kill her in the first place."

"And try to solve the mystery of a bruised marriage," said Stephen.

"Ah," said Sam finally catching on. "Playing her former husband and her present lover, you think you can give her a second chance at happiness? Namely—you."

"If you saw the way, she looks at me with those big sad eyes."

"Like in the portrait?" said Sam.

"Yes. You just *have* to want to see her life change—made happy."

Sam smiled. "You're more than a physician; you're a saint."

"Physician heal thyself?" said Wainwright.

Stephen looked at him and said nothing. "I don't know what you mean by that remark."

Wainwright didn't comment; he just grinned. "My price includes the historical research, location of the nearest portal, proper clothing for you, manners rehearsed, and house sitting. I will also be at the arrival portal to make your transition to your own time period easier for you."

"How much?"

"$100,000 plus $50.00 a day, after you leave, to mind your affairs for you. All this is assured in a legal contract. Half is paid up front, the other half when you arrive home from your trip. We agree that Time Travelers, Incorporated, cannot be legally responsible for any injury you sustain at anytime on your trip, or if the trip does not fulfill all your expectations. We provide a service; the adventure is up to you. In other words, if she dies and does not get a second chance, it isn't our fault."

"I understand."

Sam came over to him and looked him in the eye. "But with me there, we can assure you that everything will be done to save her life so that the trip is worth your time and money. I wouldn't want that pretty lady in the picture to do anything but smile. If you can manage Emile's type A personality mixing with yours, she should be one lucky lady."

Stephen smiled for the first time that day. "Do you think so?"

Sam walked away from him and then turned so that Stephen could see his facial expressions clearly. "Time travel is a miracle. Wainwright and I just make the arrangements, but someone higher up pulls the strings. This might have been meant to happen. She may not be able to go to heaven because of this. It will be the most thrilling and unnerving experience of your life. I wouldn't be who I am today without it. But there is something more inside you than the mere desire to save a human life."

"What's that?"

He shook his head. "I can't answer that question. Only Isabella can."

Chapter Eight

It was early morning at the Oaks. Nearly dawn. A misty haze draped the trees like moss. Two men faced each other. Long-barreled pistols were being checked and double checked. The dream was so real that Stephen could make out the smallest details. He was wearing tight breeches and black leather boots. He wore a black jacket the hem of which traveled below his hips. His white silk shirt was accented by a red and white ascot and a gold stick pin. It bore his initials—E. D. He removed his jacket and handed it to Sam Cooper who was also dressed in period clothing. His head was covered with a tall, black hat which he also gave to Sam after placing his gloves inside it. He looked at the pistol in his hand and then at the man who stood opposite him. The man seemed familiar. An unknown man beside him spoke. A count of ten was called. He turned and tried to fire, but the gun refused to work. His chest was pierced by a powerful explosion. Pain. He fell to the ground. The sun became a blur. A doctor—who he seemed to know was Dr. Gayerré—held his hand over the wound above Stephen's heart. The doctor shook his head. There was no point in trying to save his life. He was a dead man. "Tell Isabella that I love her," was the last statement Stephen Templeton would ever make.

Stephen was awakened by his own scream. He ascertained his surroundings quickly. His body was covered with sweat. He had been dreaming, but the fear had been all too real. Isabella's spirit was beside him in an instant.

"I was dreaming. A nightmare. Oh, cher. All this is too much for me. I'm a bit frightened by all I've been told."

Her head was tilted to the side and concern etched her face. "*Yes,*" she said and placed her hand on his forehead.

He looked into her vacuous eyes. "I'll do it though. But the thought of maybe never coming home again frightens me. I was dreaming that I died in a duel." He shivered. "I couldn't see who it was who shot me. Oh God, Isabella. Tell me it won't happen."

Isabella's eyes grew wide. She looked as if she'd say more on the subject if she could. Just then they heard another scream from the next bedroom, and Sam came rushing into Stephen's room.

"Oh, my God, what was that?" asked Sam, bracing himself against the doorframe and pointing towards the guest room.

"I'm sorry. I screamed. Had a nightmare," said Stephen, holding Isabella's hand, giving her his energy to keep her from dissolving.

"No, that's not what I meant. *You* were by my bed staring at me."

"That's impossible. I've been here all the time. Had a bad dream. I died in a duel. You were in the dream too."

He noticed Sam's expression. He was looking at the odd scene before him and unable to utter a word. "By the way, this is Isabella," Stephen said.

Sam smiled and said, "How do you do, miss."

The realization must have struck him that she was not a specter born of imagination. "Oh, my God. Pinch me. Tell me this isn't happening. If you weren't by my bedside, who was?"

"Did *it* say anything?" Stephen said, amused by Sam's reactions. After all, he was used to the ghosts.

"He/it said, 'What are you doing in my home? Go away.' "

Stephen was relieved. "That was Emile. He's here too."

Isabella walked towards Sam. She tilted her head to the side, inspected him, and then smiled.

"She's real, isn't she?" Sam said softly. He reached out to touch her but then stopped.

"Your eyes do not deceive you."

"How can Wainwright sleep through all this?" Sam asked.

"Simple explanation. He isn't supposed to see her or Emile. You are." Stephen rubbed the sleep from his eyes. "I had the dream to remind me to take a second, a friend, and that friend must be you. The dream made me aware of how alone I would be portraying Emile in his world, how much I need to learn, and how hard it will be to protect her. It also reminded me that I might die on this trip. And if I do, someone has to know what happened to me. How it all ended. For my friends and for my parents."

"Why is Emile so against you helping her?"

Stephen swiveled his legs from the bed and stood beside Isabella. "I don't know. Maybe because he misjudged her or didn't love her enough. Wasn't willing to risk it all to help her. I am. I understand my own mortality. And it won't stop me from rescuing her." He took her hand in his and kissed the back of it. "You wouldn't understand, Sam. You're not where I am. You haven't given up. I don't know why I feel that she's the answer to my problems, but she is." He looked at her and smiled. "I'm still going to help you, Isabella," he said, cupping her face with his other hand.

She closed her eyes and kissed the palm of the hand that touched her cheek.

Sam shook his head in disbelief. "Incredible. Amazing. I've never seen anything like this in my whole life. You two are..."

"In love." Stephen gazed into her eyes.

"This is probably a crummy thing to bring up right now, but do you realize that she'll leave if you save her? That you won't even have this if we succeed."

Stephen's eyes teared. He stared at the floor. "Yes, I'm aware of that. That's why I have to do it, Sam. I have to know that I've sent her to a precious, joyful peace. A place I can go some day to be with her. Now she's in limbo, I guess. She belongs nowhere and has nothing. Not a life lived, not an everlasting life to go to. This is what real love is in its purest form, Sam. To sacrifice all you are and have to make life happy for the one you love. The one who loves you in return. See how she looks at me. She knows I'm Stephen Templeton. She knows."

"Sorry about this, Isabella, call me a schmuck, but couldn't she just be...using you?" Sam said.

"You mean seducing me so that I'll do her bidding?" He looked at Sam.

"Something like that."

"You might be right, but it doesn't feel that way to me.

You saw the portrait of Emile. I was her husband. I loved her once upon a past life." He grinned at the phrase. "She was mine, wore my wedding ring, and we consummated that marriage; however, ill-fated it might have been. I'm hers. She knows it. If she was a fallen woman—if she didn't love her husband—then why come back to me? Why send that psychic message to me as I drove past this house? Compel me to stop. Buy the house. Why did I travel all the way from Chicago, when I don't even like the South? I never had the slightest inclination to visit New Orleans or make my home in Vacherie during my sabbatical."

Isabella pointed to Sam's underwear. Sam was immediately embarrassed and placed both hands over his crotch. "This is so damn real," he said.

"She thinks your briefs are funny. I've been wearing the bottoms of my pajamas ever since she first appeared in my room. I admit I've pranced around nude lately, but she's used to me now. Here," he said throwing Sam his robe, "put this on."

Sam laughed. "I'm covering up for a ghost."

She smiled and flirted.

Sam's eyes sparkled with mischief. He chuckled. "She's flirting with me. She's...beautiful. Shit."

Stephen smiled at him. "It's the Southern belle in her. I think she likes you. That'll make it easier for us should you decide to come along on my trip. Just get one thing straight, Cooper."

"What's that?" Sam tilted his head, gave her a wicked grin, and flirted with the specter.

"She's mine."

"Oh, yes, absolutely, no question about that." Sam scissored the palms of his hands across each other and then held the palms open to the air indicating that the field was free from opposition.

"Say good night, Sam, and go back to bed before Wainwright wakes up."

Sam paused. "Sure thing." He turned to go and then swiveled around to look at Isabella again. "You *are* real, aren't you?" She smiled. "Please to meet you, Madam Durel."

Stephen grinned his approval at Sam's politeness.

Stephen took her hands in his. "I'm going back to sleep

now, cher. Thanks for being there when I had the dream. Do you love me?"

"*Yes*," she said.

"Then where's my kiss?" he said.

She leaned against him and let her lips touch his. They were cold. He hadn't expected that. Then she vanished.

The search began after breakfast the next day. Wainwright took the Lexus to the New Orleans's library to do research on the time period and find some maps of the city. Sam started to investigate the house and its surroundings to get a feel for how the plantation would look in 1838. Stephen took the journals he'd found in the safe, and started to read every word in hopes of finding the proper suspects, but hours later, he had only found out that the cholera epidemic of 1832 had taken the lives of Isabella's mother and father. Her maiden name had been Devieux. Dr. Gayerré appeared to have a fondness for Isabella and a genuine love for Emile Durel's family. Emile's father and mother had died during an ill-fated ocean voyage from England. They had been returning from an anniversary holiday in Europe. Their only son had stayed home to care for the plantation. So it seemed as if Emile and Isabella had one thing in common—they were orphans by 1838. Isabella had one living relative—her brother Jean-Pierre—who was married and had one son and one daughter. Stephen supposed that Jean-Pierre had inherited their family's estate because he was the eldest child and the only son.

Sam and Stephen discussed the family situation during lunch.

"Poor kid. Losing her parents and then being stuck with a brother who takes it all and leaves you with next to nothing."

"She might have inherited something. I'm sure there had been a sizable dowry given to Emile on their wedding day. Then, if she inherited something just a few years later... Makes you wonder. Emile must have seemed like a godsend to her. A new home. A new life. A new family. So why do I sense marital discord?"

"It seems that the clues we find only make the mystery harder to solve. Not to change the subject, but we need to get to a costume shop. Shouldn't be hard in the city known for Mardi Gras. We need to be suited up for 1838 when we travel. You say you have some money from the time period?"

"Yes, I have $100,000. Cost me a lot, I can tell you."

"I think we should go through some basic dueling situations since you're having nightmares about them. I'll show you how to load and fire a flintlock pistol and how to fight with a sword. You never know."

"I can fence. I learned it in college. I wasn't too bad either. My uncle and I used to go hunting every fall, too, and I was a decent shot."

"That's a good start. Maybe we can go to that antique store you mentioned earlier and find a pair of dueling pistols."

"I need to learn more about plantation life too. I think this will be a weak area for me," Stephen said.

"I know a little something about hunting, fishing, and farming from my other travels. Just remember that you give the orders—with a heavy hand," said Sam. "I would suspect Emile was like that if he had a thriving plantation."

"That'll be difficult. I abhor slavery. How can I make people work their butts off for me when I know it's wrong?"

"Pay them."

"You're kidding. Are you sure?"

"Many planters made sure that their slaves learned important skills that they used professionally. They were paid for their work and even allowed to make items for other people to sell for personal profit. They saved their money until they could earn enough to buy their freedom and buy some land and a house."

"In New Orleans?"

"Yes, on plantations just like this one."

"So I can pay them."

"Don't listen to him."

Stephen looked at Sam. "Did you hear that?"

"Ah, yeah, I think Emile will be a little upset with your visit. Turning his plantation upside down," said Sam.

Stephen wiped the palm of his hands over his face and looked away. "That's what worries me. I don't want to destroy the life Emile has to live."

"Can't hurt it so much in three months. Might even help

it—like keeping his wife with him for the rest of his time on earth."

"What about all those plagues? Like cholera? Dr. Gayerré's journals describe them in detail."

"Do you understand the diseases?"

"I've studied their causes and symptoms. Can I take my medical bag with me?"

"And all the vitamins and antibiotics you want. What you have in your hands goes back with you."

"I have some jewelry I want to take back to Isabella too."

"Well, if you can wear it or hold it, it will transcend time. Same goes on the return trip. I always bring my brother back a souvenir from my travels. He sells antiques and makes a killing on the items. Some day I'll bring him something so rare, he'll be able to retire from his business for good."

"Doesn't your brother time travel?"

"He does, but lately he seems to want to stay in this century. Had a bad experience in the Middle Ages with Wainwright. Shook him up. He thinks its time to settle down, marry a nice girl from *this* time period, and have kids."

"What about you?"

Sam looked at his hands. His voice softened. "I had a bad experience. I met a nice girl in 1797 who I visited every summer for a long time until I found out I was on a genealogical transfer, and she was my ancestor. I thought I was on a slot transfer, but no such luck. I usually follow my bloodline. This trip will be unique. I can't bump into any Coopers in New Orleans. We never got that far south."

"That you know of."

Sam laughed. His expression lightened. "I suppose you're right, but you have to understand that my ancestors left journals so we have a good idea how far back we go on the family tree."

"So. Why don't *you* find a nice girl and settle down?"

"I don't know. I was so shook up about my 1797 experience that I'm not sure I can love again. May just travel forever."

"Sorry. I didn't mean to be invasive."

"You're just curious, and you have a right to be. You're making a big decision and taking me with you on the adventure.

We'll be inseparable for three months. Compadres. You need to know that if I take off with a coquettish blond for the night, I'll be back the next morning."

Stephen smiled. "You're certain?"

"Yeah," Sam said, grinning. "You can count on it. One night stands are all I'm up for these days."

"Hey, Wainwright *will* be home before nightfall, won't he?"

"He does get carried away in museums and libraries, but I think he'll be home for dinner. Wainwright gets on a lot of people's nerves sometimes, but I'll tell you for a fact that no one knows historical research like he does. He'll have to go back tomorrow, and that's when we'll do our shopping."

Stephen washed the lunch dishes while Sam relaxed on the patio. He started dinner: a pot roast with potatoes and carrots, salad, and store bought chocolate cake for dessert.

Three hours later Wainwright pulled the Lexus behind the mansion and parked it near the patio. Stephen and Sam set the dining room table for dinner while Wainwright placed his discoveries on the library table.

The meal was satisfying, the wine delicious, and the conversation riveting.

Wainwright took them into the library. They sipped their after- dinner coffee and glanced through his findings. He had xeroxed them for Stephen.

"I've discovered information that will help you gel in Emile's world and perhaps solve this mystery," Wainwright said as an introduction to his lecture. "According to all reports, the plantations went through a depression in 1837 so noted in several books as the 'Panic of 1837'. Those who farmed cotton and sugar cane along the Mississippi River were hit hard. I would think that Emile would have been in a fix financially. However, in direct contradiction to his failed financial situation, his wife becomes the belle of New Orleans. Isabella's name pops up on every social record I found. She attended the new St. Charles Theater and was an avid fan of the Théâtre d' Orleans. Not only did this theater have exceptional performances, but it also housed a gambling hall. Operas and plays, concerts and parties. Such a life requires elegant clothes and a hefty bank roll. I've xeroxed off all the information on the theaters in case you have to go there with her."

"Well, at least I can gamble while you watch an opera with her," said Sam.

Wainwright ignored him. "She was invited to every social ball and dinner, assumedly because of her family's distinguished reputation in the city. Her brother, Jean-Pierre, and his wife, Ernestine, were also invited as was Emile Durel, but I don't see his name on the list of party-goers, so he must not have been much of a socializer. Or he wasn't around. He did attend all the Mardi Gras attractions. All this information I found on old microfiche copies of *The Picayune*. It was the most readable old paper. It's possible she owned a box at the opera under her father's name because I can't find Durel's name on the patron list, but I do see Devieux's. I'm going to check out more on that tomorrow. Something else is odd here."

"What's that?"

"All the planters went to New Orleans just after the harvest. They had homes there—or apartments—anyway. This vacation would hit about December. The season ran until early March. Emile and Isabella apparently *traveled* into New Orleans for these events. Very odd. Creole planters used this time to reward themselves for their hard work, shop, party—something Isabella would have looked forward to doing. But by the proof I have here; it looks as if Emile *stayed* on the plantation and only came to town for Mardi Gras. Now, her brother had a residence in town. He hosted parties there. Isabella's original home, as a child, was on the adjoining plantation, just down from this house. You should be able to see it if it's still standing. Her family planted sugar just like the Durels. So, I'd have to assume that Emile and Isabella must have grown up next to each other... known each other as children." He paused and looked at both of them before saying, "Emile's un-Creolelike behavior could be construed as bizarre—perhaps even cruel considering the circumstances."

Stephen smiled. "I guess this means I should pay you, huh?"

Wainwright smiled for the first time. "I'm sure you're good for it. Besides, I'm looking forward to being the caretaker of this lovely old mansion." He flattened the papers in front of Sam and Stephen. "I xeroxed off an 1838 map of the city for you

74

to study. Remember to call Jackson Square the Place D'Armes and get used to the fact that there are only three recognizable buildings there: St. Louis Cathedral, the Presbytère, and the Cabildo. You'll also see three rows of maple trees and look for a fountain, not a statue, in the middle of the square. That should help you get your bearings when you head for the Vieux Carré. I've found you a bank—the Louisiana State Bank—which will be on Royal Street and Conti Streets. I've written the address on the map. This bank was the only one that survived through the Panic of 1837. Since fourteen banks suspended payment in specie, ran short of small bills, and had to issue their own money—which depreciated almost as fast as it was made—you need to get your money into this old established bank—which lasted from 1821 to 1870—as soon as you get there. I don't want you to lose your shirt, and it could make a difference to Emile Durel who's down on his luck now. This depression will be over by 1839, but the planters and people living during this time wouldn't have known that."

"I could set him back on his feet then?" said Stephen.

"Yes, especially if someone you learn to trust in the time period knows it's there. You might want to find something that he's written so that you can practice his signature."

"I do have something that bares his name—Isabella's death certificate."

"Perfect." Wainwright took out another map of the city. "There's even a few railroad trains, probably a trolley sort of thing from the docks: the Pontchartrain which ran from the river to the lake, the New Orleans and Carrollton which went to the suburbs of Carrollton, and the Mexican Gulf Railway that ran from Bayou Terre-Aux-Boeufs. My bet is that you'll want to take a carriage everywhere in town after you travel on your boat from your plantation. You could always walk too."

Stephen shook his head in amazement. It was wonderful having help, and Wainwright was a genius just as Sam had said. "So Emile was worried about money at the same time his wife was a society belle," said Stephen.

"The coins you showed me this morning would have just been minted, but I doubt that Emile had many of them at his home. Probably wrote notes—like our checks."

"Not only do I have a reckless, beautiful wife, a brother-in-law who appears to be snooty and over-bearing, I own a sugar cane plantation that is going down the tubes?"

"I'm guessing of course, but that seems to be the picture portrayed by these records. I'd study these xeroxed copies of the society page soirees and memorize the names of the people with whom she fraternized. Look for repeated names of those who always showed on the dates she did. They're your close acquaintances."

"Could you get any of the legal papers dealing with the Devieux family's will or their obituaries?" said Stephen.

"I could try." He turned to Sam. "You need to find suitable clothing for a rich man, Sam. Not costumes—real style. You two need to wear something for traveling, but I'd find a tailor as soon as you get there. You're going to need tailor-made suits as well as evening clothes."

"So you think we need to 'party' then?" said Sam grinning.

"The murderer must be someone she knows," Wainwright said, sipping his chilled coffee and grimacing. "Someone who had a reason to want her out of the way. Let's face it, there aren't that many motives in the world of crime: jealousy, revenge, wealth, passion. Someone wanted her out of the way quickly. Someone close to her."

"Emile had reason," he said.

Wainwright turned his head away from Stephen's curious look and pretended to be studying his notes. "A beautiful woman on the loose in New Orleans's high society during the antebellum time of double standards, male chauvinism, duels for honor, Catholicism, twisted morality, and purity above all else in a woman and a wife? You said that the antique dealer mentioned her notorious reputation. I'm afraid Emile is the most obvious suspect at this point. If she were committing adultery— and I'm not saying that she was—lavishly spending his money, and ignoring the problems of their failing family plantation, it does look as if he had a motive to get rid of her. There's the issue of no children too. The last in the Durel bloodline might have been worried about that. All speculation on my part, of course. They sure didn't have a close friendship. According to the society page, she was out almost every night—*without* her husband. Looking at it from his point of view, getting rid of Isabella might be considered a smart business move on his part. Don't look at me like that. I don't write history. And you can't judge these people by our modern standards."

Stephen could feel his anger rising—or perhaps it was Emile's. "Speculation only, Wainwright. Doesn't mean a thing."

"Of course not," said Wainwright calmly, "but I think you should know the truth so that you can be better prepared for your trip. This is the age of duels, cruel plantation masters, slavery, honor, family pride, and *submissive* women. Isabella either has a husband who doesn't care what she does or is uncharacteristically independent and assertive *far* ahead of her time period. She's a rebel, to be sure."

"I'll be following her constantly?" Stephen said. He paced the length of the room as he spoke and occasionally walked into the foyer to catch a quick glimpse of Emile's portrait hanging on the wall of the dining room. Was it his imagination or did the man appear to be laughing at him?

"I would. And when you can't, Sam will be."

"What am I getting myself into?" Stephen stood still and looked at Sam.

"Hey," said Sam, "don't get cold feet. You'd be surprised how easily we can bluff our way through this."

"Easy for you to say. You're just my cousin, or old school chum, or something. I have to tame a wayward wife, run a plantation, solve a murder *before* it happens, and go to a bunch of boring plays and operas. Lord!"

"There is one thing to look forward too," said Sam, rising to cross to his new friend.

"What's that?"

"Making love to your wife."

Stephen smiled like a teenager whose love notes have just been read to the class.

"There is one other thing I brought you from my little city trip today." Wainwright handed Sam and Stephen two large paperback books and two compact discs. "You two may need these."

They were French/English dictionaries and *How To Speak French Like A Native* CDs.

"Learn it. No one enters the lives of these two people

without knowing how to speak *fluent* French. It is the language of Emile Durel's heritage."

"Not a problem," said Stephen. "I learned French, German, Spanish, and Latin in college. But thanks for the book anyway, I'll take it with me."

"Good. Being a doctor may help you in another way. Dr. Gayerré is the family friend and physician as well as one of the major physicians at the new Charity Hospital in New Orleans. Thought you might get a kick out of visiting the wards with him. And another thing I think you should be made aware of—disease. There was an epidemic of cholera that killed the Devieuxs in 1832, but Bronze John, or yellow fever, broke out 23 times between 1817 and 1860."

"Mosquitoes."

"Exactly. Twenty-eight thousand one hundred and ninety-two deaths were reported in a 43 year period. The mosquitoes came from the tropics and thrived in the hot wet climate of New Orleans. The people of the city kept cisterns to catch the rainwater, and the insects bred there. This, coupled with unscreened, wide-open windows and no vaccines, made for unhealthy living conditions. Death came quickly."

Stephen slapped Sam on the back. "Well, tomorrow we'll stop in a pharmacy and get some medicine and our shots."

"First French and now shots?" Sam said.

"I have no intention of letting either you, or I, die from a fever I know how to prevent."

"Good thinking, Doc," said Wainwright and smiled at Sam's expression of fear. "Listen, it's getting late and we have a big day planned for tomorrow. In case you hadn't noticed, it's December fifteenth. The solstice will be here soon, and we haven't even sent Jim a notice to look for time holes. I suggest we call it a night and wake early tomorrow."

"You two go ahead. I need to wash the dishes and think about all this information."

Sam winked. "And be alone with Isabella?"

Wainwright raised his right eyebrow and frowned. "What's that supposed to mean?"

Sam tousled Wainwright's hair as he passed him on his way to his bedroom. "You sleep good tonight, Wainwright. Sweet dreams."

"Is there something going on that I'm not privy to?" said Wainwright.

Stephen said nothing and just walked to the kitchen and filled the sink with soapy bubbles.

He smelled roses. "Is that you? Are you wearing perfume tonight or am I starting to get to you?"

She materialized, placed her arms around his back, and then kissed him on his neck. "All this talk bringing back memories?"

"*Yes.*"

"I hope you show me the town when I get back to you."

Then she pulled him away from the dishes and stared into his eyes.

"*I love you, Stephen.*"

His heart burned in his chest as he took her into his arms and smothered her mouth with his lips.

Chapter Nine

Stephen, Sam, and Wainwright headed for the Vieux Carré first thing the next morning. Wainwright planned to stay in the library most of the morning and then head for the Cabildo as well as several other museums and antique stores. Sam and Stephen decided that the Vieux Carré was just the right place to start their search for costumes and the antique items necessary to add the proper look to their new personaes.

The antique store, where Stephen found the ring, welcomed him with open arms. The same clerk waited on him when they asked about dueling pistols. The first pair he showed them was rejected when Sam shook his head and mumbled that they were not old enough. Finally, a set pleased him and was purchased. They cost $15,000.

As they were leaving the store, another man, who had been assigned the task of arranging the antique books they had purchased from Stephen, called to him from the back office.

"Is that you, Dr. Templeton? Aren't you the one who sold us the books from the Durel estates?"

Stephen nodded his head that he was.

"I suppose I should grin at my find and never say a word to you, but since you own Isabella's home, I thought you should know that one of the books you sold us was a fake book cover for her diary. The diary is really of no use to us since you can hardly read it. It was in a hollowed-out copy of a Holy Bible. Since you've been such a good customer to us, I thought you might like to see it. Would you like it back? I seriously doubt that anyone would buy it considering its poor condition. Never know though."

Stephen stammered when he said, "You mean it? You'd give it back to me?"

"You bought the furniture, the coins, the cameo ring, and

the dueling pistols, maybe you'd like to read her own words. At least have a look at it."

Sam pushed Stephen forward.

"Thank you. That's most kind." He held the book as if it were sacred script.

"If you need anything else, you know where to come."

Stephen showed the diary to Sam who opened the door quickly so that they could exit before the man changed his mind or asked for money.

"Do you realize what I have here?" he said when they were back on the street.

"Maybe the answer to many of your questions about Isabella. Maybe it was meant for you to find it. Maybe she wants you to read it."

"Well, I guess she would, but I'm afraid to open it. What if I don't like what it tells me?"

"Then put it in the car for now, and we'll look at it later. Here, let's put these weapons there too."

It took them most of the day to find just the right period costumes, but they purchased tight tan breeches, black frock coats, tan vests, black jackets, silk ascots, ebony boots and top hats, as well as gold cuff links, gloves, and silver tiepins that they found at a small out-of-the way shop in a back section of Bourbon Street. On the way back to the car, they were stopped by one of the street venders—a psychic reader.

"Let me read your future," she said to Stephen. Her jade eyes twinkled.

"No, I don't think so," Stephen said, trying to pass quickly in front of her.

She glared at him. "Don't leave New Orleans without having your cards read."

"I'd rather be surprised," said Stephen.

"Are you sure you mean that?" Sam said.

"Why would I go to all the trouble and expense to time travel this adventure if she's going to tell me how it's all going to turn out?"

"Maybe she can tell you who killed Isabella. That way we'd have a chance at finding the murderer before he strikes."

"And what if she's wrong? We spend the whole time watching one suspect while the other one finishes her off." He waved his hand to dismiss her again because she was shadowing them. "Besides, we have to go to a pharmacist. I need to make up a medical bag, and we both need vaccinations."

"As in *shot*?"

"Several. Oh, come now, Sam, after all your travels you must have taken some medical precautions."

Sam shook his head that he hadn't.

"It's a wonder you're still with us. Do I need anything for the transition?"

"You'll sleep like a baby for several hours after you've landed. Storms cause major headaches so take some aspirin. Oh, yes, one other thing."

"What's that?"

"I'd take something to counteract all known poisons of the day."

"I think I'd better read up on that."

On their way to the car, they passed the Voodoo Museum.

Sam stopped and said, "You know something. New Orleans was a virtual voodoo haven back in those days. Maybe we should peek inside and buy a book on spells or something."

"Why?" Stephen wrinkled his forehead in disapproval. A physician's disinterest with superstition and ancient rituals.

"I don't know; it was just a thought."

They had lunch at a shopping arcade just down from Planet Hollywood and waited for Wainwright.

"It's hard to believe that in just a few days, we'll be in this same city only in the year 1838. This place probably was a field or something," said Sam.

"Take a good look. It may be our last chance to get our bearings before the twenty-second." Then he stood up and walked to the mall's big glass windows. He stared at the Mississippi River and the large boats docked so close to land. "I'm anxious to read her diary."

"Won't Wainwright be surprised at our find?"

As if on cue, Wainwright appeared at the top of the escalator and walked towards them. His face was flushed with excitement, and his satchel was overflowing with papers and books.

"I have so much work to do. We need to go home immediately."

"We've completed our shopping trip successfully with a few surprises thrown in," said Sam. "Stephen found Isabella's diary at the antique store where we found dueling pistols."

Wainwright was impressed enough to raise an eyebrow. "Well, from what I just found out about the Durels and the Devieuxs, I'm sure it will make fascinating reading."

They drove back to the plantation chattering like raindrops on cobble streets until they reached home.

Dinner was nothing more than roast beef sandwiches and leftovers. All three men were excited to show off what they had learned. But it wasn't Wainwright's night for discovery; it was Stephen's. He carefully opened Isabella's diary before their anxious eyes and read aloud from the first torn page he could decipher.

Dearest Diary,   December 16, 1838

All is lost. I can never tell Emile the sorrow and fear I have brought upon myself. How could he understand? Why should he? What has been done can never be undone, and soon I will have no choices left. I have done it all to protect him, to aid him, and he deserves none of it. Pity me, heaven, only because I deserve none. Shame or death? Have I no other choice now? Thank God for Chris, an angel in my hour of need. If only I could speak with Emile. But he avoids me, and it has angered me so that I care not if we ever speak another word to each other again. His name. His home. His honor. His reputation. All this is more important than any problem I could have. Melinda is so strong, so clever, so able to make others do as she wishes. I am too tenderhearted, and it will be my undoing, I fear. I long for my husband's embrace but dare not weaken now. He thinks I hate him. I must for how could I do this to him otherwise.

All would be happier if I were not living. I bring disgrace to everyone. God send me a savior, or I shall commit a graver sin than any I have undertaken thus far.

I don't know how much longer I can live like this.

Isabella

"She's going to kill herself," said Wainwright. "Today is the sixteenth. The anniversary of the letter. On December 16, 1838, Isabella Durel was considering suicide. It explains the blank death certificate. Her husband and her doctor didn't want anyone to know she committed suicide. I think we've solved the mystery."

Sam touched Stephen's shoulder. "Maybe the psychic was wrong about a murder plot—a poisoning. Maybe she deliberately swallowed the fatal mixture."

Stephen threw the diary onto the table and shouted. "*No*, I can't believe it. Why would she ask for a second chance if she..."

"Because she's in limbo. Her religion believes you can't go to heaven if you take your own life," Sam said.

Stephen was forcing back his tears. "No, *no*. She wouldn't."

Wainwright said, "Maybe she couldn't handle the mess she'd made of her life or couldn't control it. She mentions not being as assertive as this Melinda friend of hers."

"Then who is she protecting—aiding?" said Stephen.

"Her husband. She hasn't told him that she's sleeping around because it would hurt his feelings, and now she's got this reputation, and there's nothing she can do about it. 'What's done cannot be undone' she says. Sounds like a woman, with newly awakened guilt feelings about her adulterous lifestyle, who can't deal with the shame. So instead of telling her husband—who obviously doesn't give a damn—and taking his wrath as punishment, she checks out permanently," said Sam. "It does explain the blank space for 'cause of death' on the death certificate. Emile would want her buried with him—his family, and he wouldn't be able to that if it were known that she committed suicide. Their religion would've forbidden it."

"Incredible. I can't believe I never even thought of it," said Stephen.

"Well, why would you want to think that a beautiful lady killed herself?" said Wainwright.

"No, not that. I never thought to look for her grave. Or Emile's. It might have given us a clue."

Sam said as kindly as he could, "Stephen, the case is closed. She was pushed over the brink by her unhappy life and poisoned herself. The entry in her diary is the last one. Sounds like even her girlfriends, Chris and Melinda, weren't able to help her."

"You have no proof," Stephen said viciously. "Stop saying those things about her. She wouldn't do it. You forget that I know her."

Wainwright said, "You know her ghost. A specter who wouldn't want you to know the truth—to think ill of her."

"Talking like a man in love," said Sam. "Thinking with your..."

Emile's voice spoke through Stephen's lips. He grabbed Sam by the shirt, pushed him against a wall, and glared at him. *"Don't you say that. Don't you dare say anything against her."*

Stephen eased his grip on Sam and his own voice returned. "I'm paying for this trip, and I'm the one who'll decide whether we go or not. She wants God to give her a savior on December 16, 1838, and He's going to give her just that on December 22, 1838—me. I'll have two days and three months to give her a husband who will listen, who will understand, who will take action to help her, and who will love her."

"With Emile's personality? Have you thought of how he might have reacted if he'd read this diary page?" Sam said.

"But he didn't. Not then anyway," he said, his body collapsing with a sudden loss of strength "It was lost in the hollow section of a Bible she hid from him. Even I didn't notice it when I was taking the books off the shelves. Clever of her to hide it in the one place he should have found it."

Wainwright reached for Stephen's arm. "Maybe he did."

Stephen dropped into the red leather chair. He covered his face with his hands.

Sam said, "This house has gotten to you. The portrait. The ghost. I admit I saw her too. She's captivating—and very lost. Are you sure you want to risk everything you have—including your sanity—to go back to her?"

Stephen said nothing at first and then finally, "I don't suppose we can find her grave? Do you think they keep church records that far back?"

Wainwright said, "I should think there would be church records. Sure. I bet we can find it. Do you want me to look for you tomorrow?"

"Yes. I'll think about what you said, Sam. I'm sorry I got hostile."

Sam said, "I understand. It's okay. Maybe tomorrow we

could talk more about this, or we could try out the new pistols while Wainwright looks for the Durels' tomb."

Stephen wasn't listening. He took the box holding his costume and the bags filled with accessories, climbed the stairs slowly, and silently went to his room. He knew Wainwright and Sam were going to stay up and discuss all that had transpired, but he didn't care.

As soon as he was in "their" room, he stripped off his clothes and put on the new costume including the hat and boots. He regarded his figure in the full-length mirror. An exact replica of his image appeared beside him in the mirror—Emile Durel's.

Emile raised his right hand to rest on the left side of his chin, and moved his left arm across his chest so that his left hand propped the right arm's elbow. He was scrutinizing—analyzing—Stephen. A wicked grin creased his handsome face.

"Appalling lack of taste. I wouldn't be caught dead in that," said the vision.

Stephen snickered, then began to laugh outright. "Funny you should mention that." He mimicked the ghost's moves.

Emile smoothed his mustache with his long, slender fingers. Then he placed his right hand on his hip and let his weight shift onto his right side. His other arm relaxed at his waistline in a casual manner. He raised one eyebrow and tilted his head to regard Stephen. *"If you're going to purchase the clothes, at least wear them correctly."*

Stephen copied his demeanor. "Did you listen while I read what she wrote?"

Emile began to dissolve. *"I did."*

"Well? Got anything to say? Are we going to do this together or what? Are you with me?" He smoothed his mustache in the same manner as the ghost and then titled his head as Emile had done in his pose.

The vision was nearly gone, but just before it vanished he heard Emile say, *"Save her, Stephen. For God's sake, save her."*

Chapter Ten

Wainwright skipped breakfast and went to town to discover the whereabouts of the Durels' grave. Sam seemed a trifle uncomfortable with his host at breakfast, and Stephen picked up on his mood right away.

"I'm going to finish my coffee in the library and look at the diary. I want to read it again and see whether there's anything else of value on the torn pages. Maybe a name or something."

Sam touched his shoulder as he walked past him. "A word with you. Please."

"Yes?" Stephen said. He didn't like the tone in Sam's voice.

"I don't want you to get the wrong idea from last night's conversation. I'm all for time traveling for whatever reason. I guess I just don't want to see you get hurt if Isabella isn't all she appears to be in her ghostlike form."

"It's difficult to explain, Sam. I keep thinking about what it would be like if I didn't go. How would I feel, say, three months from today? And my answer is—miserable. I have to give it a shot because in my gut I know I can help. Dr. Gayerré's plea to help Emile and his wife, and Isabella's supplication before God for a savior seems like a call from the past to me. The strange draw this house has on me, the odd coincidences, the way pieces of information just seem to drop from heaven right when I need them. Don't you see that I'm supposed to do this for her—and for me?"

"Then I'll contact my brother this morning and give him your exact location. We'll start the search for a portal so that you and I can travel to 1838 New Orleans."

Stephen looked at his new friend. "Do you mean it? You'll go with me?"

"Wainwright thinks too much. He doesn't like to see mysteries go unsolved. It bothers his nicely organized outlook on life. Everything has to make sense to him. And maybe that's his problem. Some things in life have to be searched out by the heart's path not the mind's. Nothing is logical when it comes to your heart. I just thought it would bother you if she was—well, depressed and..."

"You mean going through what I'm going through? No, as a matter of fact, I rather like it. Now, I really understand how she feels. What she's thinking?"

"But what about her reputation? If you find out that she's cheating on her husband?"

Stephen smiled. "She'd be cheating on Emile, not me—and that makes her the ultimate challenge, doesn't it?"

"You're saying that maybe if Emile was a little more like you..."

"And I was a little more like him..."

"The lady would forget whomever it is she thinks she's in love with?"

"I don't know how else to explain it. I love her. I'll do anything I can to save her life. And when it's over, I'll sleep better at night—alone maybe—but comfortable knowing that she's okay."

"And with Emile."

"I can't change that. I can't stay in her time period. But I *can* make it better for her. Besides, I'm beginning to like Emile Durel."

"Until you become him in the flesh. Well, if you've decided. Look at her stuff and then meet me in the backyard for pistol practice."

Stephen wondered what was going through the time traveler's mind.   He went to the library and began his search. He found little in the diary, but the thought that it was hers comforted him. He took the doctor's journal from the foyer desk and looked at it as well. The mystery only became more perplexing to him.

After a fruit salad lunch, he and Sam fired some shots with the antique dueling pistols until Stephen felt comfortable with his grip on the butt and the firing mechanism.

"I sure hope I don't have to kill anyone with this," he

said.

"Precautionary measure only. Now, let's talk with my brother while you look over the contract and write us a check."

"This is really going to happen, isn't it?" Stephen said.

"Let's just hope Jim can find you a good spot. I hope the Mississippi River isn't the only portal in town."

"Leave it to me to be the only person who has to leave by way of a burlesque house on Bourbon Street."

Sam's lips curled into a wicked grin. "Well that might not be so bad after all. Wainwright would shit bricks waiting for our return. That might be something to see. Old Wainwright watching tits while we sneak out the front door in our 1838 clothes."

They sat down near the computer, and Stephen watched as Sam logged on. Jim's screen name popped up on the newly formatted Buddy List, so he sent him an instant message. Sam told his brother that the matter was settled, and that Stephen had signed the contract and given them the down payment. He explained where they were geographically, and Jim went to work. The two men drank another pot of coffee and waited.

Jim's instant message jingled after a half an hour. "I have several portals. You'll have to tell me which one is nearest to you."

"Shoot. I'm going with him so keep that in mind. Gotta be a strong connection," wrote Sam. "Two in one."

"I have one in a swamp close to New Orleans," Jim wrote.

"I don't think so."

"I have one on Bourbon Street in some place called The Pink Pussycat."

Stephen and Sam looked at each other and laughed. "No, I better not. Try again, little brother."

"I have one at the Gallier House in the Vieux Carré."

Stephen shook his head. "That's like a museum now, and we'd have to break in."

"Can you find anything that isn't a building that belongs to someone other than our client?"

"Let me look. There's one at the dock of the Durel Plantation. Near you, I think."

It occurred to them that they had never told Jim the

original name of the plantation only the address.

"Duh! We're staying at the Durel Plantation. Sorry."

":-P!!!!! Thanks a lot, Bro. Well, the dock is close to the water and there's a portal right under it in the mud. I should think that if you stand on or near the dock, you would fly."

"It'll do."

"Hey, you leaving December 22 then?" Jim wrote.

"Yeah, what do you want me to bring ya back, kid?" wrote Sam.

"*You* in one piece."

"Bought a classy pair of dueling pistols yesterday on Royal Street."

"Yeah? How much you pay?"

Sam told him, and he responded, "ROFL. You got fleeced. How about bringing me back the real McCoy?"

"Is that all you want?"

"Well, some coins from 1838 might be nice."

Stephen said, "Tell him we'll send him a few right now."

Sam relayed the message.

"How's Wainwright doing? He mad because he isn't going?"

"You know Wainwright. Got the location and gotta go."

"Right. Take care and don't have too much fun, Bro."

"Will do. See ya in three months." The screen went blank.

Stephen said, "Three months? That seems like such a long time."

"You'll be surprised how fast it'll go. You better start making up some good lies for your family and your therapist. Ones Wainwright can uphold while you're gone. And pray no emergencies come up while you're out of town. Tropical islands work nicely as a vacation spot unless you have a mother who must know the phone number of your hotel. Good luck. I'm going to look over Wainwright's research and start memorizing the names of all those places I'm supposed to know. Practice my French. Oh, yeah, got any ideas whom I should be?"

"A distant cousin from France?" Stephen suggested.

"Might just work at that."

He left Stephen alone.

"He believes in us. He has to," Stephen said to the air.

90

A cool breeze chilled his cheek. "I know. You're getting anxious. You should have told me you were depressed before you died. Or at least the psychic should have. Threw me bad, Isabella."

The chill moved all around him. "I understand. It isn't something I would want someone to know about me either. Guess we're more alike than I thought. Both getting pushed around. But not anymore."

He joined Sam in the library and began reading the hundreds of papers left on the large table by the research professional. Sam had a portable CD player hooked by earphones to his head and was saying things like, "Je suis votre cousin."

The last days before they left flew by speedily. Wainwright did find the Durel grave site, and all three made a visit. It was a bittersweet discovery. Stephen was moved to see what remained of his beloved. "Emile lived thirty years after she did and obviously never married again. He must have loved Isabella very much."

Sam said, "Or was fed up enough with her not to try his luck again."

Stephen ignored the comment and placed a white rose in front of her tomb. He wiped away his tears before the other men could see that he was crying.

On the day before they left Sam memorized all the maps and *The Picayune* clippings while Stephen prepared his gifts for Isabella, his money, and his medical bag. Sam had brought an old tapestry bag with him from home, so he filled it with dueling pistols, research papers, maps and anything else he thought might help. Stephen gave himself and Sam various vaccines, a flu shot, and stocked up on aspirin, vitamins, antibiotic creams, pills, and an emergency first aid kit. He studied all his medical book data on poisons and made sure any possible antidote was in his bag. But in actuality, the only thing he could really do was get the poison out of her system by making her vomit. He didn't have a 1998 hospital near their plantation or a 911 number to call for assistance.

He prepared long and complicated stories about where he

was going for three months and sent e-mail messages to his family and his therapist. He received urgent messages from both of them to not leave for such an extended trip. He never answered them. What could he say? He was leaving and there was no point in pretending that it would be safe.

He wrote checks ahead of time to all his creditors so that Wainwright could mail them on the appropriate dates. He placed all of his money in one checking account so that all the checks would clear without any interference. He then explained to Wainwright how to take care of the house and water his plants.

On their final night, Sam and Stephen dressed in their costumes and feasted on a sumptuous repast that Stephen had prepared earlier. He did his best Emile imitation during their meal to convince both Sam and Wainwright that he could pull off the switch.

"I hope she comes to see me off tonight," he said nervously. "If all goes well I'll be holding the real Isabella in my arms tomorrow morning."

"And never seeing the ghost upon your return," said Wainwright who was silenced when he saw Sam dart a puzzled look his way. "Hey, look, the idea that you two are going to leave me all alone in a haunted house is making me a little nervous."

Sam gave him an 1830s cavalier smirk and raised his eyebrow in a show of disdain. "With your luck with women, Wainwright, she'll hide in the closet until Doc comes home."

Stephen hurried into the conversation with, "Not to worry, Wainwright. She won't hurt or scare you. She's not like that."

"But her husband is another matter," added Sam grinning as he sipped his brandy.

"You're a real joy, Cooper," said Wainwright.

They drank heavily until twelve o'clock when they walked in somber fashion towards the pier.

The night wore a mystical veil, and there was a hint of unidentified perfume in the air. It was as dark as the waters of the Mississippi, and Stephen couldn't see so much as his hand before his face. Several times he tested his footing to see whether he was about to fall into the river. He glanced often towards the house to see whether she was watching him. She was nowhere.

"Got all you need, Doc?" Sam said, interrupting his thoughts.

"Yes. Do you have the maps and dueling pistols?"

"In my bag. You got our money?"

"And the medical bag, the necklace, and the ring."

"Well, then," said Wainwright. "I guess all we have to do is wait until the solstice hits. It might be a good idea for you to face each other and grasp onto one another with your free hand. I'm not saying it will happen exactly at twelve. Sometimes it comes much later—two in the morning generally although a great deal depends on where you are located on the earth's surface."

Sam and Stephen did the best they could with their hands filled with luggage and the awkward and confining new clothes.

"I'm a little frightened," Stephen admitted. "Where is she?"

Stephen looked one last time at the house and noticed a light in the master bedroom window. It had to be her because he hadn't left any light on there.

"Isabella! Look, she's there," said Stephen pointing. "Come to say good bye to me."

Sam and Wainwright looked at the second floor window.

"Cool," said Sam, restraining a sudden impulse to wave to her.

"Shit," said Wainwright, lowering his head and kicking the mud with his right foot.

Just then the two travelers were thrown into the time tunnel. It felt as if a tornado had swallowed them whole and hurled them through an unknown vortex filled with shadows. Stephen heard the same whirring sounds one hears in the middle of a blizzard and felt a sudden nausea come over him. Sam cried out with joy—like someone in the front seat of a roller coaster ride that had just hit the peak of its highest hill.

"Hold onto my hand," he said, breathing hard. "Think 1838."

The circular motion of the tunnel stopped and when Stephen looked around he was right where he had been only minutes ago.

"It didn't work. We're still here," he said.

Sam touched his shoulder and pointed to the river. Same

sky, same moon, same breeze, same season, but with a big difference. A boat had just docked, and two black men, holding a lantern high above the ground, were helping a lady in a long, velvet cape from its deck.

Stephen cleared his throat. "Isabella?" he said. He tried to see her in the dim light, but she seemed only a vision in a black cape.

She spun around to face him. First, she was anxious, then frightened, and finally angry. "What are you doing here, Emile? Spying on me?" she said in French.

It started to rain. Stephen gulped, and his mouth went dry. All the anticipation, and now he was tongue-tied.

The beauty regarded Sam with a cruel look. She placed her hands on her hips and tilted her head to the side. "Who's this?"

"Your cousin, fair one, from France," Sam said, kicking the tapestry bag aside so that she wouldn't notice it. He spoke with her in French, "That is to say, your cousin by marriage. The pleasure is all mine, dear Isabella," Sam cooed so smoothly an iceberg could have melted on his lips. He then took her gloved hand and kissed it, never allowing his glance to waver from her eyes.

Stephen was glad he'd brought the seasoned traveler along for he was still reeling from the time transition and felt awkward, sick, tired, and disoriented all at once.

She smiled despite her anger. "Well, cousin, you must not stay out so late on a Louisiana evening or is it morning, I'm never quite sure," she said shooting daggers from her eyes at Stephen. "What can you mean by standing out on the docks at such an hour and in such dreadful weather?"

Emile forced Stephen's mouth to function. He tried to think of something to say. "And what, may I ask, brings you home at such a disreputable time, mon cher?"

"The opera was late," she said yawning, "and I am very tired. Much too tired to banter words with you. Bonsoir." With that said she sauntered like a peacock past them, floated across the yard, and strutted up the stone path and into her house.

Sam and Stephen watched her. Sam gave a low whistle.

"You got your work cut out for you this time, Doc."

Stephen stared at him and then at the freshly painted,

glowing with richness and life, Durel Plantation. His home no longer in ruins or in need of his touch. It was gorgeous, and he was its new master. Everything he saw, even Isabella, made him proud to be Emile Durel. For Isabella was exactly like her home. Proud, beautiful, colorful, regal, and brimming with life and passion.

"Good Lord, you've done it," he said to Sam grasping his satchel.

"We've done it. You doubted? Slumber awaits us. Leave her for tomorrow. I'm about to crash." Sam picked up his bag.

They walked across the grounds towards the door and were greeted respectfully by the servants. This felt odd to Stephen who decided that the best way to learn about his new world was to keep his mouth shut and listen. A petite, young slave girl with light golden skin, a gentle voice, and her dark hair covered by a blue turban, came to him and asked whether she should prepare the guest bedroom for Samuel. She spoke with him in flawless French, but never raised her eyes to meet his. Stephen simply said, "Oui."

He almost cried when he saw the interior of the house—the way it should have always looked—the way he would make it look when he returned in the year 1999. It was painted grand, royal French blue and antique gold, not green as he had made the colors of the rooms. He would discard the drapes when he returned and alter the interior of the house to fit this French design. He cursed himself. Stupid, of course, it would be French colors. Fleur-de-lis. He should have known. Then he realized how humorous it was to be thinking about refurbishing the old house when he had just been part of the most miraculous experience he had ever lived through.

Isabella was removing her evening wrap and handed it to the slave girl when he tried to catch her glance. She was wearing the same golden gown that she had worn in the portrait without the necklace or any ring but her wedding ring on her hand. This surprised him. A night at the opera and not a speck of jewelry on her satiny skin. Her hair was piled high on her lovely head in perfect ringlets, her long graceful neck begged to be kissed, her red lips were so desirable, her eyes were alight with life and mischief, her cheeks burned crimson with flushed excitement, her skin glowed with good health, and her voice was both commanding and feminine. In short, she was the living, breathing, and very passionate, Isabella Durel. It was all Stephen could do to contain his passion for her.

"Welcome to Durel Plantation, Cousin," she said to Sam while deliberately ignoring Stephen. "You have a name?"

"This is ...Samuel, Isabella," stammered Stephen.

"Samuel? You must be joking. A Durel? Well, welcome, Samuel. It's late, and we shall get to know one another better tomorrow. Anna," she called to the slave girl who had spoken to Stephen when he first entered the house, "see that our cousin is made comfortable." She gave Stephen one last quick look. *"Samuel?"*

"An American name my cousin teases me with, mon cher. My name is Evan Durel."

Isabella gave a curt smile. "Emile, always one for a laugh," she scoffed, then said hastily, "Hurry, Anna, the man has just arrived, and he is tired."

Anna never looked up at any of them. Her eyes stared at the floor. "Yes, ma'am," was all she said.

His wife began to ascend the stairway.

"Isabella?" Stephen said.

"What?" she called back, refusing to turn and look at him.

He bit the inside of his lower lip. "Nothing. Sorry. Have a good night's sleep." It didn't make him feel powerful to speak so to her.

Emile came to him in a flash, faster than the Gemini Effect could have stopped him.

He raced up the stairs, two steps at a time, grabbed Isabella's wrist, and turned her around sharply. She scowled at him.

"Let me go," she spat at him between clenched teeth.

"Not before my good night kiss, mon cher," said Stephen, but with Emile's stern voice.

Before Stephen could stop himself, he had Isabella in his arms and was kissing her roughly on the mouth, far fiercer than Stephen would have dared. She stared at him as if he were a ghost.

"What's come over you?" Her eyes opened wide with surprise and then closed coolly. "Is it your cousin's visit?" she whispered, with vengeance underlying her tone. Her lips were burning. He could smell the heat of her temper rising. Her skin was hot to the touch. She smelled of roses. Nothing like the kiss her spirit had given him at home. This woman was fire, and he wanted her—now.

"You wish to play the lord and master of this house for your kin? Well," she forced his hand from hers, "command your slaves—not me." And with that she dashed into her room, by way of the master bedroom suite, and slammed the door behind her.

"Nice going, Doc," mumbled Sam as he was lead into his bedroom by Anna. "'Night."

Stephen ambled towards the location of the master bedroom of his 1998 home and was astonished to find a lovely, fully decorated room so stunning that it took his breath away. He had refurbished this room from the torn original wallpaper. Or so he thought. Now he was to enjoy the beauty of Emile's bedroom the way it should have looked. Facing him was a grand dark mahogany bed with a French blue swag with gold fringe and a fleur-de-lis pattern draping the canopy positioned above a velvet blue coverlet and several, huge, fluffy pillows. This was a king's bedroom. The furniture was finely upholstered, rich looking, and made from dark heavy wood. The walls were painted, not papered, with a pale blue tint and accented with white trim around all the doors. So, he'd wasted his time on some other owner's wallpaper design when all he'd had to do was paint the room.

His night clothes had been laid out for him on the royal blue bed cover that had been turned down for him.

He dropped his satchel on the floor next to the bed. A different maid was warming the sheets with a brass warming pan filled with hot coals from the fireplace in his room. She had been startled by his entrance but did not look up at him and nodded her head as she exited.

He was glad to be home even if it were another time period's domicile. It was still the home he had purchased a month ago—just newer. And it didn't feel strange to strip off his clothes, throw them on the chair nearest his bed, put on the silk nightshirt with the embroidered "E. D." on its shoulder, slip between the freshly warmed sheets, and rest his head upon the mountains of goose-down pillows. He was tired and not much in the mood for any investigations, adventures, or lengthy conversations. Sam had told him that transitions weakened you for a time, and he'd been right; Stephen felt as if he'd been hit by a baseball bat.

He reminded himself that Isabella's ghost wouldn't come to him tonight. Before he closed his eyes, he smiled at the door separating himself from his wife. Separate rooms? That would have to change.

The real Isabella slumbered in the room next to his—no ghost—and he had three months to open that door and correct the situation.

Chapter Eleven

Stephen's room faced the north section of the house, so the sun did not awaken him—a tap on the door did. "Excuse me, master. Do you want your breakfast served in your room or in the dining room? Master Evan asked me to see whether you were awake?"

"I'll have breakfast with him in the dining room," he said. "If I can figure out how to shave and dress myself," he wanted to add.

"May I bring in your hot water and shave you then, master?"

As soon as I find the chamber pot—ah—there it is, he wanted to say to her. "Wait," he said instead. "I'll call you when I'm ready." He guessed that she would stand there dutifully waiting until he did so. He hopped out of bed and deciphered how to use the small porcelain pot used as a toilet. Then he threw on the crimson velvet, initialized robe which was dangling on a chair beside his bed and called for her to enter.

Anna poured the hot water into a large china bowl. He washed his face with the soap she gave him and dried it with the soft; linen towel she offered him. She looked quizzically at him when he dried his face, so he rubbed some of the soap back onto his cheeks so that she could shave him. This was an impromptu adventure, and he had to pull it off successfully or they'd find something odd with Emile Durel. He'd already made the mistake of calling Sam by his real—American—name. But who would have thought that the simplest morning ritual would have been his first *major* problem? He thought of his wonderful shower back home and fantasized about the hot, steamy water pouring over his head.

He sat on one of the embroidered chairs while she used a straight razor to cut away his beard from his skin. "Wouldn't be good to get this girl angry," he told himself.

She wet his hair and combed it forward. The natural wave of his hair thwarted her attempts. He might have been overreacting due to his paranoia at taking another man's place in time, but he thought she noticed the difference. She said nothing to him if she did. What could she possibly think? The truth wouldn't cross this uneducated, 1838 slave girl's mind. It amused him to imagine what she might be thinking about the new curl at the nape of his neck. It bounced back every time she tried to flatten it into place.

She arranged his clothes on his bed after she'd made it for him while he was drying his face. He thanked the Divine that she had done this, as he had no clue what to wear for a day of ordering people about on this farm.

After she left, he took the soap and washcloth and gave himself a sponge bath. He was feeling *time tunnel lag*. He was awake but not really cognizant of all that was around him. Sluggish. Trancey. After his bath, he stood and stared at his new underclothes and day suit. Men's fashions weren't all that troublesome to determine since pants were pants no matter the time period, shirts the same except for the lack of buttons on this one, vests and belts went the same place, jackets were worn over the vest and shirt, stockings were worn on the toes, and boots were pulled onto the feet in the same fashion as they were in 1998. A blue, silk cravat around the neck finished the look. And the best discovery of all was that Emile's clothes fit him *almost* to perfection. He should have been taller and bigger than an 1838 sugar cane plantation owner, but he wasn't. Emile must have been huge in comparison with his friends because Stephen was a lean but strongly built man of just under six feet. Emile must have done some heavy labor to make his arms and legs strong enough to fit into these clothes. Little by little, he was learning all about the man who would share everything with him for three months.

The new Master Durel walked over to Emile's bureau. He glanced over the items on the top of the mirrored dresser. There was a small, black velvet box lying on the top of the bureau. It was worn around the edges indicating there might be an heirloom inside. He opened it immediately. It held a gold pocket watch, and chain—the one he guessed Emile had hidden in his vest pocket for the portrait. There was engraving inside the lid. It was an endearment from one of his forefathers. It stated—in French—that the watch was an heirloom to be passed down through countless generations of Durels. He attached it to his vest and slipped it into its pocket.

The 1998 costume still sat on the chair where he had thrown it the night before. Maybe he wouldn't wear it home. He might just take an original suit back with him.

He stared at himself in the full-length mirror that sat in the corner of his room. He looked so much like the portrait of Emile it was scary. He smoothed down his mustache with his long fingers, smiled approvingly, turned around to see whether he looked all right from the back, and sauntered out of his room. His first thoughts were of Isabella.

Anna passed him at the top of the staircase so he called to her. "Is your mistress awake?" he said to her, while checking the time on the watch. It was seven-thirty in the morning.

The girl said soberly, "No, master."

"Well, when she awakens, tell her I'd like to see her downstairs promptly. For breakfast."

Anna almost made the fatal mistake of looking up and into his face, so surprised was she at his comment. Stephen perceived the spontaneous look of shock indicative of just how empty a relationship the Durels must have had. Can't even have breakfast with each other first thing in the morning?

He remembered that Sam was waiting for him, and his stomach was growling its emptiness to him, so he hurried down the stairway and into the foyer, then turned left and entered the dining room. Sam was staring out of the open window which showed the plantation and the slaves' quarters.

Stephen joined him. "One of the first things I'm going to do is rebuild those houses." Stephen looked at Sam and smiled. "I may not be able to free them without destroying Emile's life, but I can make damn sure they are treated well—and paid. Thanks for the idea."

"You do as you please. You're the new master here at Durel Plantation even if only for three months. Are you hungry? I've already eaten," said Sam, filling a second plate of food.

"I could eat a whole cow," said Stephen.

"Time travel makes me ravenous," Sam said. "Sleep well?" he said.

"Like a king in a king's bedroom," said Stephen.

"Woke at five-thirty, or thereabouts, and decided to check out the downstairs area—get a drink of water or some fruit. No sooner had I set foot in this room, than three servants rushed to meet my needs and ask whether I'd like something to eat. I'll warn you right now that I'm an early riser. I told Anna that we were going into town today on business, and to lay out your day suit so that you wouldn't be confused about the *costume du jour*."

Stephen took a blue china plate and helped himself to the ham, scrambled eggs, and hot biscuits that sat on matching china platters on the side table. He poured coffee into the same china cups he used back home and sat across from Sam at the dining room table.

"I asked Anna to tell Isabella to come down for breakfast. She seemed confused," said Stephen.

"Since I'm the guest, I could get the girl to tell me all about the routine here. It seems that Emile is always up early and off to his plantation chores. Isabella, who is generally late from her evenings out, and gets to bed only hours before dawn, sleeps in and takes her tiny breakfast in her room while she gets ready for her chores. She's supposed to be up with the servants, open the pantry, decide the cook's menu, and discuss the domestic slaves' chores for the day. When she's out late like last night and can't rise for breakfast, she gives the cook—Nora—enough food from the pantry for breakfast before she leaves for town. I guess there was an argument between Emile and Isabella about that last night before she left for town. Nothing was said during the argument last night about a visitor. So, everyone is probably gossiping about me today." Sam smiled. "Oh, well. Once Isabella finally rises, she works a long, hard day. At least one day a week, she goes to town to shop or visit with her friend, Melinda. She usually brings a small gift back for Anna and Nora. Isabella makes their clothes for them and tries to liven up their garb by bringing home lace or frills to decorate their dresses. The girl made no comment about the setup, nor did she hide any of the facts. This is the way it is here in their home. I couldn't read how she felt about Isabella or her husband."

"When does she visit Chris?"

"Apparently, the servants know nothing about a Chris, but Melinda has visited the plantation on several occasions so they know her."

Just then a wiry, gaunt man with unkempt brown hair and pale blue eyes came into the room. He smelled of horse dung and unwashed clothes. Stephen assumed it was his overseer. The game was getting more difficult by the minute.

"Excusez moi, monsieur," he said.

Stephen feigned disapproval at being interrupted during his breakfast and their conversation and said, "Yes? What do you need?" he said, using a bitter tone in his voice.

"I was just wondering if you were going to ride. If you wanted your horse saddled so that you could look over the fields. You will want to check the cane. I think it's safe to assume that we have taken all that we can from this crop. It will need to be replanted—this is the fourth year, after all."

"I suspected as much," said Stephen glibly, having no idea what the man was talking about. "I won't ride today. I'm going to town. Can you handle things without me?"

"Oui, monsieur, you know I can."

Stephen wanted to hug him, he was so relieved. He was expecting a drunken, evil swine like the ones from popular fiction, but was delighted to find the man quite pleasant and business like.

"I'm taking care of some important business matters today that will put our financial worries to rest once and for all. We'll have the money for that new crop of cane."

The man grinned, took off his planter's hat, and wiped his forehead with a handkerchief he'd found in his pocket. Stephen could tell that this worker was not treated as an inferior by Emile and had been entrusted with great responsibility on the plantation.

Stephen added, "I wish to speak with the skilled laborers tomorrow morning out back by the cabins. I'm referring to the slave artisans. Also, I want the slaves' quarters rebuilt with sturdy wood sides and tin roofs. See that each one has its own hearth too. Let me know what supplies you think I might need to purchase for the job. Now leave us."

"I can order the supplies from up the river if you want

me to," he said.

"Then do so and let me know how much it will cost."

The man looked at Stephen as if Emile had been leveled a hard blow to the head then dashed out to do his employer's bidding.

"Emile having a fit inside you?" Sam said, as he consumed another hot, buttery biscuit.

Stephen laughed. "Not yet. Maybe he's still asleep. Not ready for this complete transformation. But he did make me attack her last night—on the stairway. Not my style, I can assure you."

"I was wondering about that. I think we need to travel to New Orleans *alone* today. Get the lay of the land without your wife tagging along."

"She'll not like that at all. I'm sure she'll want to shop while we do our banking."

"Tell her to get a Christmas feast prepared. It's only a few days away. Say that you want to buy her something in the way of a Christmas gift. We can find her something at one of the shops and have it wrapped in a pretty gift box. Maybe a bonnet. Rhett bought one for Scarlett, and she loved it."

"We're not in the Civil War time period—antebellum—remember," said Stephen.

Sam shrugged his shoulders and gave him his lopsided smile. "I think women loved hats and bonnets all during the Victorian time period. Either that or jewelry. Goes across time—women and jewelry."

"I have the bow necklace and the cameo ring, but I think I'll wait on that. We'll say that we're opening a business together—our own joint account. That you have a bank note which we're taking to be transferred into New Orlean's coinage and placed in the bank. The story will work with the bank manager, at least."

"An account little Isabella can't touch," Sam said grinning.

"Right. I'll find her something to wear with that gold dress as a Christmas gift. She looks naked without jewels at a time when men showed off their wealth by covering their wives with it. I want her to look beautiful—more beautiful than any other woman in all New Orleans," Stephen said.

"Not too much in love with her, are you?" said Sam.

"Completely insane about the woman." Stephen laughed and went back to the table for seconds on the eggs. His nutritional breakfast of a bowl of oatmeal and a bagel was replaced by this buffet which satisfied his uncharacteristic hunger.

"Sure didn't look too depressed last night when she yelled at you, did she?" Sam said.

"Just a cover, Sam, trust me. I'll unlock her secrets—with your help."

"Don't forget that we have to be careful with her around Christmas Eve."

"Right. Neither one of us will leave her alone. I'll make sure the holiday is especially happy. Perhaps, one present isn't enough. Old Emile might have been too frugal in the past. Bills, he did well, but a lady needs to know that her man thinks about her when he's away and shows it with a present. Too bad we can't have a Christmas tree like in our time. My Mom'll be upset that I'm not home in Chicago for the holidays. I gave them their gifts on Thanksgiving when I was there. Told them not to open them until Christmas. Mom'll be playing with the bow all Christmas Eve."

Sam looked at the ceiling as if trying to recall something. "Jim and I have our own holiday traditions—far away from the portal cabin we own. We lost our folks a while back, so it's just us now."

"My parents celebrate for a week. Mom'll cook and bake as if an entire army is coming to dinner. Dad'll complain about the fat content and the calories—like a good doctor should—and then eat them anyway."

There was a lengthy pause in the conversation while a small attack of homesickness ran its course.

"I wonder how Isabella will react when she finds out she can't go today?" said Sam finally.

"Can't go where?' said the irate and freshly awakened Isabella. She stood with her hands bracing the door frame in a crimson velvet, initialized robe and wearing a voluminous pink and white nightgown underneath it. The robe was tied with a red velvet sash with gold tassels at the tips. Her hair fell around her shoulders, drifted like satin ribbons down her back, and floated all the way passed her waist. Stephen thought she looked like an angry angel.

"Not taking me where? What are your plans, gentlemen? I'll not stay on this god forsaken farm while you gallivant all over town."

Stephen smiled and looked at Sam. "I'm afraid you must stay here, mon cher, and do your chores. I've promised Evan a tremendous banquet for Christmas Day, and I want you to take charge of it. He's used to my uncle's magnificent holiday dinners that go on for a full week."

She folded her arms across her chest. "Really? Is that what you want? I thought you hated big dinners and religious feasts. 'Social occasions are so boring,' were your exact words, as I recall. And while we're on the subject of uncles—why have you never mentioned this one to me?"

"You see, cousin," interjected Sam, "one branch of the Durel family tree resides on a country estate in the vineyards of France. We make wine. I'm afraid I haven't been to Louisiana on very many visits. Not as I should have, I fear. Since his parents' deaths, we haven't had much time for such visits—until this month. Now, I'm anxious to help my cousin in his time of need—financially, of course."

Her voice softened. "You're going to help us?"

"That was my intent."

"Forgive me for my rudeness last night. I was not in the proper mood to greet a guest."

"My fault entirely. I should have stayed in town another night and arrived this morning, but I was in such a hurry to see Emile. After all, I've never met his beautiful wife."

She looked at her husband, and Stephen's heart melted. "You asked for me to come to breakfast?" she said none too sweetly.

"I wanted to tell you that I'll be gone all day. Evan and I are going to town. We have some financial matters to attend to."

"Why can't I come with you? I'm sure I can construct the beginnings of a Christmas dinner with a few simple words to Nora. We still have a few days before Christmas. I'd love to visit the shops."

It was difficult for Stephen to say no to those large, sad eyes.

"Well," he said gently, "Evan is in a passion to find a good tailor, and I thought I might have some clothes made as well. Evening clothes."

It was as if a viper had suddenly curled at her feet. "A tailor? Evening clothes? Why would you need evening clothes?" She tried to regain her composure.

Sam said, "My fault there as well, I'm afraid. I so love the theater and concerts and the rich exciting night life that New Orleans promises, that I rather placed it upon Emile to take me to some evening entertainment while I am here."

She blushed. "It's the most terrifyingly wonderful city in the world."

"That's what I've heard." Sam and Isabella stared at each other for a brief second. She smiled.

"You mean to gamble?" she said.

"But of course...*and more*," he said, and winked at her to show what he meant by *and more*.

She diverted her focus back to her husband's face for assurance that he would never attend a performance himself. "You don't mean you'll go, as well?"

Stephen shrugged his shoulders, "Why not? I can't let my cousin loose on the town without a proper chaperone."

She hesitated for only a moment. "Well...my family has a box at the Théâtre de Orleans, and you're both welcome to attend with my family. My brother and sister-in-law aren't always there—she's quite provincial. Sometimes Jean-Pierre goes by himself. They wouldn't mind if you and Emile came with me, I'm sure."

"That's most charitable of your family," said Sam.

"Emile has told you, no doubt, that my mother and father died during the cholera epidemic several years ago. It's just my brother and me now."

"Allow me to extend my condolences."

"Thank you." She walked over to her husband and tilted her head in the exact same manner as the ghost had when she looked at Sam's shorts. "Why can't I go with you today? I promise to stay out of the way."

Stephen wanted to tell her she could go anywhere she wanted to, but reminded himself that he had to remain firm on some things if he were to help her. He cupped her face in both of his hands, let his fingers work around her slender neck to check for lumps or swollen areas, tilted her head back to look for any problems in her skin tone, oddities in her breathing, or obstructions or bruises at the base of her neck, and then, with true adoration, he gazed—as well as examined—her brown eyes.

"Not today, mon cher." His initial diagnosis was that his wife was healthy and strong but completely exhausted. He planned on continuing the spot examinations as often as he could.

She stared in amazement at him but didn't move a muscle. He leaned towards the side of her face and kissed her cheek tenderly. When he moved his head away, her eyes were filled with tears. Her hands shook. He took a hold of one of them and noted that they were red, swollen, bruised and cut. She withdrew her hands from his and looked away. Her lower lip trembled. Isabella Durel was suffering from nervous exhaustion, stress, emotional trauma, and tremendous anxiety. She could hide it from the slaves, but not from her new doctor.

"You can't be with me when I pick out your Christmas gift," he said to her gently. His first prescription for his new patient was huge quantities of TLC.

"Christmas gift? Why would you buy me something?" Her hands shook again. "We've never done that before."

"There are many things we haven't done before, but that's going to change. Evan's aid will get us through this difficult time. I know I've been harsh about your spending sprees, always yelling about the cost of everything lately, but I had to. We were in a financial disaster. I need you to be patient with me—with our livelihood. Do you understand?"

She reached for the handkerchief that hid in the open slash pocket of her robe. She tried to hide her tears and used the linen cloth to whisk them away. Her lips quivered as she turned her back on Stephen. Sam moved to her other side and was examining her as if she were lying under a microscope. She was trapped between the two men.

"I was wondering if we might ask Dr. Gayerré to Christmas dinner, Isabella?" said Stephen.

Her voice shook. "Do as you wish. You'll see him in town, I suppose."

The notion struck him that he had no idea what the good doctor looked like.

She moved towards the china cups to pour herself some coffee.

"Ah...Isabella, do you suppose he'll be at the Charity Hospital today?"

It took every ounce of control for her to hold the cup. She took a quick sip of the hot chicory blend and kept her face away from their curious stares. "You know he takes his turn between the hours of noon and four."

Stephen smiled at Sam and sighed. "Yes, of course, he does. Silly of me not to remember."

"Must you buy me something for Christmas?" she said, as if she didn't want anything—or rather didn't deserve anything.

"Why not?" he said.

"It's just that...I have nothing for you."

Stephen relaxed. He moved towards her, took her cup, set it down on the table, and held her hands in his. She winced. "Of course you do, you're here with me and that's a gift in and of itself."

Her voice grew cold in an instant. She moved away from him. "I must change now. Forgive me, gentlemen, but I would not wish to keep you from your busy day." She stormed out of the room.

Sam said, "Whoa, what was that was all about?"

"If I knew the answer to that question, I wouldn't have spent all that money traveling to 1838."

"Not what we expected."

"Complete contradiction. Did you see her hands? She's depressed and right on the edge. What in hell caused it? There are times when I want to console her, and times when I want to..."

"She seems to like me well enough," said Sam, smiling as if he'd won some important victory that needed to be recorded in a book somewhere.

"But she doesn't like her husband very much, that's for sure." Stephen looked at the walls of the dining room as if they could tell him the answer. It was then that he realized that her portrait...and Emile's...were missing from the house.

"Not to worry," he said smiling, "she's in good hands now."

Chapter Twelve

As soon as they left the boat and walked towards the Place D'Armes, Sam unfolded the xerox copy of the map he'd hidden under his vest. "To the right and down a few blocks, then make a left," he said.

"I hope no one sees that paper," said Stephen, darting nervous glances around the street.

"Why is everyone staring at us, or is it just my initial paranoia?" said Sam.

"I think Isabella gave us a clue when she brought up the fact that Emile *never* goes to town. Do you think you can find the Charity Hospital? Man, this will be tricky when people I'm supposed to know start greeting me."

"Wainwright's maps are very detailed. We shouldn't get lost."

They traveled down Royal Street until they saw the modest Louisiana State Bank building. They entered and were greeted by a plump, balding man with a bad cold.

"May I help you, gentlemen?" asked the man, sniffling into his handkerchief.

"My name is Emile Durel and this is my cousin, Evan. I'm here to open a business account. Can you accommodate us?"

"Of course, I've heard of you, monsieur. Please step into my office." They did as he asked and sat down in the straight-backed, wooden chairs in his office. "Your wife not with you today?"

"You know my wife?"

"But, of course, monsieur. Who in town does not know Madame Durel? She was in just the other day to alter an account she has with us. One her father opened for her many years ago."

"Oh? Interesting. Was she placing money in the account?"

"She didn't tell you? Odd. She closed her account after ten years. I assumed it had something to do with this terrible panic we're going through. But now that you're here that cannot be."

"As a matter of fact, my cousin and I are opening a new business account, and I was hoping you could handle a large sum of money for us."

"How much might that be?"

Stephen told him. Sam smiled and played with the hilt of the walking stick he'd found in the foyer of the Durel home.

"Your cousin has been a timely blessing to you, I think. He's from..."

"France."

"My, my, do tell. Family still in France?

"Emile's great-grandfather was quite a rebel," said Sam.

"I see. Well, I can handle all the paperwork for you. Ah, do you have the money with you?"

"Yes, but I hope you don't mind that we exchanged a bank note into new coins." Stephen opened the large leather bag, the same bag in which the antique store had placed them on the day he had purchased them in 1998.

The man took one look at the coins, reached for a linen handkerchief from his pant's pocket, and wiped his forehead.

"Not at all. I'll just be a minute." He waddled out of the room.

"I wonder why Isabella closed her account?" said Stephen.

"Sounds desperate to me. I'll bring it up at dinner tonight."

They signed the necessary paperwork; gave the man the money; smoked cigars; sipped one, small glass of brandy each; and then left the man to his business.

"You sure we couldn't stop in at a small café and have some coffee? I'm beginning to like the chicory."

"Seems to be a restaurant at the end of this street, but I was wondering if we could go to the Charity Hospital first. I'm anxious to meet Dr. Gayerré. It's on Canal Street."

"Yes, I suppose that's our second order of business today. But we did learn one thing, Isabella had an account with her father's money in it and it's been emptied."

111

"Think she's spending it on frills?"

"You know something, Doc." He stopped walking and looked at Stephen. "Gut reaction here. She doesn't seem the type. I know she has this facade of social bustle and pride, but those tears in her eyes spoke another message."

"Yeah, I was wondering about that too."

A man tipped his hat to Stephen. "Bonjour, Emile, nice to see you in town."

"Nice to see you too," said Stephen, and then adding under his breath, "whoever the hell you are."

It wasn't difficult to find the huge hospital because the building was almost a block long. They passed around the fence and the small trees until they found the steps and walked into the front door of the hospital. Things were just as busy as they'd been at Cook County General Hospital. It brought back pleasant memories.

"This will be trickier than I thought," said Sam.

Stephen only smiled and said, "We're on my turf now."

They entered the hallway of the hospital. It smelled of soap and sickness. "Not in too bad a shape for what it's gone through," said Stephen. "Let me handle this." He spoke with a man who was rushing into an amphitheater. "Excuse me, sir, could you tell me where I could find Dr. Gayerré?"

The man waved at them to follow him. "He's giving a lecture in the amphitheater right now. He should be nearly finished."

The amphitheater was modest with rows of seats and a small stage with a podium. They saw Dr. Gayerré at the lectern. He was not a thin man but not plump either. The crown of his head was bald. His face was long and angular. His eyes appeared to be blue, but it was hard to judge from the distance. He was about five feet seven and must have weighed approximately one hundred and sixty pounds. He was wearing small glasses which miraculously sat on the bridge of his nose without any support. His voice was low but audible enough in the echo chamber where new doctors listened to every word he said and hastily scribbled notes.

Stephen was entranced. This was his world, and he couldn't participate. People were dying in these wards. He had the knowledge that could end their suffering. He wanted to reconnoiter every face, study every patient's illness, and chat for hours with these new doctors about his favorite topic—saving people's lives. Only hours ago he had stumbled through a discussion with a foreman who ran a plantation he knew nothing about, and now he stood in the middle of history in the making and was powerless to do what he could do better than any of them—heal the sick. He focused on the good doctor's words.

"Here we have the sick wards, crowded with patients of every age and sex, of every color, speaking every language imaginable. We have every type of disease, every gradation of injury from a simple cold to malignant vomito, from a sprained ankle to a compound fracture. It is your duty to make a careful analysis of every condition. Your duty is to keep this hospital clean, and your patients bathed so disease cannot spread. I have lived through several epidemics, gentlemen, and I believe that cleanliness is a must to hold back the spread of infection. I know it seems difficult to accomplish when one has so many patients, but I beseech you to do the best you can. We treat thousands of patients in this hospital each year, and I am proud to boast that we have the reputation of being the best-run hospital in the country."

It was the end of his lecture, and the audience applauded. "After Christmas, my lecture will be on the evils—*not the benefits*—of blood letting." This started a raucous chorus of comments, but the old doctor only grinned and waved his hands that it must wait until another time.

Suddenly, Dr. Gayerré saw Stephen in the crowd. "Emile!"

He ran over to the two men. "I'm so glad to see you. What brings you to town? Where's Isabella?" Then he turned to Sam. "I've not had the pleasure."

"You've no idea how happy I am to see you." And that statement was truer than the old man could have ever guessed. "This is my cousin, Evan, from France who came to rescue us from our financial distress by going into business with me."

"What? Well, pleased to meet you. Good timing. Did you hear my speech?"

"Yes, the end of it rather. Quite good. I'd go on about the blood letting. I just happen to feel you're right in your assumption that it's a detriment rather than an aid to the patient's life."

Dr. Gayerré smiled as if it were amusing that Emile should be discussing something a planter knew nothing about. "I have to speak with you privately," he said.

"You can say anything in front of Evan," Stephen said.

"Does this new flow of money mean that you've changed your mind on the matter we discussed on December first at your home?"

"Ah—what might that have been?"

"I don't give a damn what I pledged to your father, Emile, I'll not be a party to it. I've had nightmares about it every night since our discussion. I only went along with your plans to calm your temper. You were in such a state."

"What might those plans have been?" Stephen said.

He whispered to him privately, but Sam leaned over to hear.

"Why your plans to poison poor Isabella. Pray God you have forgotten it all. Just a temper tantrum, correct?"

"I told you that I would murder my wife?" Stephen was shocked and showed it.

The doctor regarded his friend. "Yes, when I was having dinner and stayed the night. It didn't seem like an act to me."

Stephen placed his arm affectionately around the old man. Now Dr. Gayerré's supplication to God made sense. *Change his mind and her heart.*

"Did I say that I would *kill* Isabella?"

"In complete and horrific detail. This is the first I've had to speak with you on the matter since that night. I'd hoped you'd changed your mind. I know the woman is a handful, but there are ways to tame a wayward wife."

"Monsieur, I assure you; I have no intentions of poisoning my wife. Such a thing will never happen while I live as her husband. I'm sorry if I said such a thing, for it was an evil thought, and should never have entered my mind."

Gayerré smiled expansively. "I knew you were just having one of your fits. You could never hurt her. You love her so, don't you? You two can work things out, I'm sure."

"Of course we can. I came to ask you whether you would like to have dinner with us on Christmas Day?"

"You're having a feast for the holidays?" he said.

"Is that so odd?"

"It's just that you've never done so before. Yes, I will join you—happily. And bring a gift for your wife. Your very healthy and *living* wife."

Stephen shook his head in affirmation. "I'll leave you to your chores and see you on Christmas Eve. Might as well spend the night. I'll send the boat for you."

"Ah, since the loss of my Ellie, I so miss the big meals for religious holidays. What a pleasure. I shall be more than happy to spend this day with you, Isabella, and your cousin—Evan, is it?"

"Yes," said Sam, "Evan."

As he traipsed off to his chores, Sam and Stephen stared blankly at each other.

"Good Lord," said Stephen, looking at the marble floor of the newly built hospital. "Emile was going to kill his wife, and the doctor—a man sworn to heal the sick—was going to assist him."

"It explains the..."

"Yeah, yeah, I know," Stephen said irritably, "it explains the blank space on the death certificate. Shit!" He looked at Sam and then shook his head in despair. "Good Lord, Emile, what could you have been thinking?"

Chapter Thirteen

Stephen walked quietly by Sam's side for a block or so. Disappointment was settling in again, and he'd promised himself that he would stay true to his vision of Isabella's plight no matter what he learned about her, but the thought that her husband had planned to kill her on Christmas broke his resolve. To top it off, the man who loved her like a father, had agreed to assist in some fashion, if only to sign the death certificate. Stephen felt light headed.

"Are you all right, Stephen?" Sam said.

Stephen stopped and placed his hand, momentarily, to his forehead. He closed his eyes from the sunlight—his mind from the truth. "So much to digest all at once. The information is coming faster than I'd expected. I'm still suffering from the effects of the time tunnel experience. What could she have done to make him despise her so much that he would want to *murder* her? I was just beginning to like Emile. We're one. Oh, my God."

"Want an honest answer?" Sam said.

Stephen looked at him, and his lips curled into a disapproving smirk. "Not really. Let's get that cup of coffee, and maybe we can try to figure it all out."

One block past Camp Street, they found a huge building with three stories of, what appeared to be, offices or apartments and had a delicious aroma of dark rich coffee coming from inside it.

Sam grinned. "We've found a mall. Starbuck's coffee awaits." He frowned. "It looks American though."

Stephen rolled his eyes upwards. "You do have a way about you, don't you? I've never met anyone so full of adventure. At this point, I don't care if the place is Hindu."

They walked into the door at the Magazine Street entrance and saw an unusual sight. The large center of the building's roof was glass. This dome must have been used primarily to separate the two sections of the block-long arcade. You could see right up to the sky, like a skylight, very much like the modern malls about which Sam had joked. There were people rushing from office to office. Mostly men. One or two ladies exited the restaurants, but the general gender seemed to weigh heavily on the masculine side. Right next to the entrance, was a grand coffeehouse, and Sam laughed out loud when he saw it. "See, I told you."

They sauntered into the restaurant with the elegance Sam had acquired from years of time traveling, and the dignity Stephen had inherited from Emile. A mâitrè d' moved like a ballroom dancer towards them.

"May I seat you gentleman, or would you rather be served in the billiards room?"

"This will do nicely," said Stephen, and then followed the man.

They sat on plain, wooden chairs at a small table. The menu was in French.

"I hope you can read this," Sam said.

"Don't worry. This I can do."

He ordered coffee and some French pastry for both of them and shook his head in disgust when the waiter was out of earshot.

"This is too much for me, Sam."

Sam lowered his voice and there was a caring, sensitive tone to it when he said, "It's just beginning. We still need to find a tailor and a gift for Isabella." He glanced warily at Stephen. "Provided you still want to do that."

Stephen was bewildered that Sam might suggest that he'd changed his mind about his love for Isabella, but of course, he'd shown it in his expression earlier, and it wasn't Sam's fault if he'd noticed it. "I do. I'm sure she has a good reason for all of this. No wonder she's so depressed. Married to that bastard."

Sam raised his hand to his chin and mumbled, "Don't look now, but some man is looking our way with a concerned and familiar look. He will join us in a few minutes, unless I miss my bet."

The man came over expeditiously and asked tersely, "Where's my sister?" He had dark brown hair, almost black, which curled around his face dramatically. His face was as handsome as Isabella's was beautiful. He was dressed more elegantly than Sam and Stephen and had an 'old money' feel about him, but he wasn't old himself. Not much older than Stephen. He was shorter and not as well-built. The first thing you noticed about the man, besides his enormous brown eyes and oval face, was his hands. He used them in the same way a duelist uses a saber, cutting the air with gestures much as a man might swing a fencing foil.

Stephen hoped that the sister in question was Isabella and not some mistress whose honor this person before him would have to avenge.

"Jean-Pierre, how nice to see you," Stephen said, taking the risk of looking foolish. "Isabella is at home preparing for a Christmas feast which you and your family are welcome to join. Unless you and Ernestine have other plans."

The man was irritated. "You *know* we do. I'm in town for the season as you well know. Can't get all the way up the river at this time. The children are such a handful these days. Thank God for the servants. Did I tell you that one of my slaves tried to run last week? Caught her up the river. Had to beat her in front of the others. What else could I do? Stupid of them to run. I sold her son last month, and she probably was trying to find him. He was my son, too, but I had to please Ernestine who whined so; I had to get rid of him." He looked at Sam curiously.

Stephen bit the lower inside of his lip, gritted his teeth to keep from screaming at the man, and took the cue. "Allow me to introduce my cousin, Evan. This is my brother-in-law, Jean-Pierre Devieux. Isabella's brother."

The brother looked towards the ceiling. "Who wishes he'd never been cursed with such as she for kin. Nice to meet you. Welcome to our city." He shook Sam's proffered hand.

"Nice to meet you," said Sam. "Your sister is utterly charming. She's taken the liberty to invite me to join you and your wife at the opera some evening. I'm here from France to join Emile in a mutually beneficial business venture, you understand. Thought it might be nice to see the night life of 'the city that care forgot.' "

The muscles in Jean-Pierre's face relaxed. He almost smiled. "I'm pleased to offer you the hospitality of my family's box in the hopes that Emile will come as well. Why don't you take a house in town, Emile, mon Dieu?"

Stephen smiled. "I'm thinking about it. I was wondering if you might recommend a tailor to my cousin and me so that I might look more sociable at these events. We need some evening clothes."

Jean-Pierre's manner lightened. "Finally, you see reason. My tailor, of course, is Monsieur Gatou. He has a small shop on Royal Street just behind St. Louis's church. I believe it is 125 Royal Street. You don't mind if I sit with you two for a moment?"

"He's good?" said Sam, as he moved his chair over to accommodate Jean-Pierre. "Well, of course, he must be, look at the cut of your vest and coat."

"My family has been going to him for years. His wife is a seamstress who made clothes for Isabella until she was seventeen." He ordered a coffee.

Stephen took a chance. "Then she made the golden gown for my wife. I thought as much. It looked French."

Jean-Pierre's hand waved in the air dismissing the gown Isabella treasured. "That rag. Sacrilege to say such a thing. Dear Emile, how little you know. French? Perhaps, but not from Gatou's house. I know things are not going well for you, but couldn't you afford to buy her something new? She wears it to almost every social event. Ernestine offered her some of her own gowns, but Isabella is so stubborn about such things. And well, they aren't the same size, and it would be such a bother to alter them down for Isabella."

Jean-Pierre's attitude was making Stephen's blood boil.

"Isabella looks like a queen in it," he said, and stared at anything he could so as not to look at the man.

Jean-Pierre removed his hat and placed it on their table. "Oh, let's face it, Emile, you're too much of a recluse," he said, while slowly taking off his gloves and placing them inside the crown of his tall hat. "You never come to anything but Mardi Gras. How would you know what the well-dressed people of New Orleans are wearing these days? It's very pretty on her, and quite elegant, but I doubt that it's a French gown, and definitely

119

not from the House of Gatou."

Stephen wanted to say, "You pompous little ass. How dare you insult your own sister in this manner. Just because you have most of Daddy's money, you needn't act so superior." But he didn't.

Coffee was served. Stephen noticed Sam's careful gaze. He was watching everything, taking it all in, not just as a spectator, but as a detective would.

Suddenly, a very pretty blonde with enormous blue eyes, a beautiful face, high cheekbones, and wearing a pink and lace dress that would make stale fudge melt, smiled at Sam from across the room. She sat alone at a table, ordered something that was brought in a china pot, and commenced sipping tea. She leaned her body over the table and rested her elbows on it, bending her bodice in their direction.

"Zut," exclaimed Jean-Pierre, "let's hope she doesn't come over here. Don't acknowledge her whatever you do," he said to Sam.

Sam didn't wave, but he did return her smile. "Why? Is she single?"

"Worse. Married to money and age," said Jean-Pierre. "Well, you should introduce her to Evan some time...when I'm not around."

Sam took the hint from Stephen. "Why not now?"

"Because Isabella's bound to introduce you to her at the opera, or sooner, and I cannot tolerate the woman. How my sister could be friends with that tramp is beyond me? In the restaurant—unescorted. What can she be thinking?"

He swallowed one sip of the coffee, took up his gloves and hat, and moved his chair away from the edge of the table. "Well, thank you for the coffee, the conversation, and the introduction. I'm off to do business. It's just down the hallway. Thought I'd stop by for a cup of coffee before I had to sit for hours. I'm heartily glad I could speak with you today, Emile. Sorry about Christmas, but there's still that dinner party I'm having in January at our house in the Vieux Carré. You and Evan should attend with my sister." He tipped his hat and walked away.

"So *that's* Melinda?" said Sam. "Not bad. Not bad at all."

Stephen grimaced at the implied meaning of the remark.

Chapter Fourteen

"Don't let him get you down, Doc," said Sam, still eying the obvious flirt whose blue eyes sparkled with mischief.

Stephen seemed pleased by the new information yet also angered by the conversation with Jean-Pierre. He could tell that Sam's mind was not on the mystery but on this new lady.

"Okay. If she isn't spending the money on gowns, is wearing a 'rag' to the opera—so says Jean-Pierre—where's the money going?" He tried to bring Sam back to the problem at hand.

"Do you really think that's Melinda? Wonder how old her husband is?"

"*Sam!*" said Stephen stiffly.

"Right. Isabella," he said, turning to face Stephen. "You said you wanted to buy her a Christmas gift. We could ask Melinda where she gets her jewelry."

"You're going to do this, aren't you?" said Stephen.

Sam moved his chair, tossed his linen napkin onto the table, walked briskly away from his coffee, away from the table, away from Stephen, and away from the mystery. "Oh, yeah," Stephen heard him say.

Stephen spoke aloud but under his breath, "What about discrimination? What about etiquette of the time period? What about history, formal Victorian introductions, manners, *morality?* What about all the things you time travel guys are supposed to stand for?"

He watched as Melinda blushed and arched her back so that her bosom bloomed before the Frenchman.

"Gone. All gone. Lost in the lady's eyes." He noticed how lovely her bodice looked in the 1838 dress. "Eyes? Whatever.

Now, what the hell am I supposed to do without my *cousin*?"

The waiter smiled and asked him whether he might like another coffee and more pastry. "Why not?" he said. He called to the man just before he was out of earshot. "Do you know of any jewelry stores on Magazine Street or in the arcade?"

"Something for Madame Durel?" he said, his eyes twinkling like an expensive diamond ring.

Stephen was attentive immediately. "You know my wife?"

The waiter said, "Naturellement. She's in here all the time with her friends. Enjoying coffee and conversation for hours. If you don't mind my saying so, monsieur, your wife is quite lovely, and it's a joy to watch her laugh and chat with her many companions."

Stephen had hit a gold mine. "Yes, yes, of course, she is very happy when in the presence of her friends. She's here a great deal, then?"

"Oh, yes, she helps Madame Chabonnais on her many shopping excursions." And then, he wiggled his eyebrows. An amazing feat with those full dark, heavy eyebrows of his. This waiter had information Stephen needed to hear. Isabella was no depressed vixen as far as this man was concerned. He thought her charming and—happy. In one quick comment, he'd dispelled Stephen's doubts.

"I'm turning into a first-rate detective, after all," he thought to himself.

One look at the figure of his companion in deep conversation with the grinning and giggling blonde made him decide to continue his interrogation of the waiter.

"With her friends? That would be Madame Chabonnais and Chris..."

The waiter seemed puzzled. "Do you mean Christopher Fairchild, the British actor? Yes, he is so comical. He makes me laugh with his expressions. One of the best actors I've ever seen. Madame Durel gave me a ticket to see him perform at the Théâtre de Orleans once. She's quite generous. He was in a comedy, a—vaudeville, I believe." The man was lost in his tale. "Not Shakespeare. Not this time. There were so many twists in the plot that I became lost, but I laughed until I thought I would fall out of my seat. I enjoyed myself immensely. Let me get your coffee for you, monsieur."

The waiter was gone in a flash. Stephen took the brief moment to plan his next series of questions. So, the ever-loving Chris, of whom she was so fond, was an actor, not a lady friend after all. It explained why 'Chris,' Christopher, had never been to the plantation. The dynamic trio—Isabella, Melinda, and Christopher—'haunted' the arcade daily, laughing and shopping. And if he remembered the way she had phrased it in her diary, Chris was the favored of the two—the most helpful. Was he then the mysterious lover? To a depressed woman, a charming, funny actor might I have been the healing salve she desperately needed. Stephen hated Christopher Fairchild instantly.

"She is *so* amusing," said Sam upon returning to his chair and his cold cup of coffee.

Stephen sipped his hot, steamy beverage and waited for the verdict.

"Totally mesmerizing, I can tell you," Sam continued.

"I gather things went well with the fair Melinda?"

"Her husband is very ill, and she wasn't overly upset about that fact. She didn't want to talk about her friend—my cousin-in-law—at all. She did ask why you were in town without your wife, and if I were married. She'd never heard of the French Durels. She seemed quite surprised. She showed a little interest in the fact that I was saving your plantation. It doesn't bother her to come by herself to the arcade as her husband often suggests she go out without him since he can't accompany her. He sounds very unselfish to me. She often sips tea or coffee here while munching on sweet treats like honey cakes and chocolate. She adores chocolate. She thinks I have beautiful, blue eyes."

Stephen stared at him before saying, "Figures."

"She would rather be with her friend today, but Isabella isn't planning on coming to town until Friday evening."

"You uncovered a great deal. And she can't be with Chris today either because *he* has a matinee or an early evening performance."

"What?"

"The fabulous Chris is an actor. Famous by reputation and English by birthright. *Not* a female friend."

Sam raised an eyebrow. "Whoa. So, this *could* be the

heart throb we're looking for. How did you find this out?"

"The waiter is a fan of Isabella and Chris's. It seems that Mr. Fairchild must be the light in Isabella's; otherwise, dreary existence. But, I did find out that Isabella is rather charitable and well loved by everyone who knows her. So, I'm not sure where this bad rep is coming from. She goes shopping with Melinda and Chris, but if we're to believe her brother, isn't buying anything."

The waiter interrupted. "If I were buying something special for my wife, Monsieur Durel, I'd visit the jewelry store around the corner. All the wealthy gentlemen go there."

"Thank you so much," said Stephen. Then he turned to Sam, "I think I need to talk to you far from the lovely Melinda's ears as well as find a gift for Isabella. Let's go."

They stood up to leave. Sam smiled one last time at Melinda who winked coquettishly. They exited the restaurant and headed for the street.

"You're perturbed with me?" said Sam after a long pause.

"No. I just have so much on my mind right now. We need to go all the way back to Royal Street to find that tailor, and it's such a long way from here. But the jewelry store is around the corner. I haven't a clue what to buy her."

"I wouldn't worry about that. Something will catch your eye."

They continued walking and greeting people as they enjoyed the fair day and cool Southern breeze.

"But," Sam said lightly, "we have learned a lot today."

"Maybe too much. We'll have to find a way to assimilate it all when we get home."

The manager was pleased to see any customer come through the door. Times were obviously sparse for him as well, for he greeted them with almost too much excitement.

"I'm looking for a nice gift for my wife."

"Monsieur Durel, how nice to see you again," said the small, thin man with the strange, skinny mustache and beard.

What might Emile purchase for her? Had he ever given her anything Stephen owned? Was it the diamond bow necklace, the cameo ring, or both?

"A nice brooch? How about a hair ornament?"

"Nothing of that sort," replied Stephen, with a wave of his hand. "I'm looking for something truly spectacular to give Isabella for Christmas. Have anything in diamonds and gold?"

The man produced a gorgeous, golden necklace with one large and very lovely diamond, probably one full carat in weight, at its center. But its design was too simplistic, and Stephen wasn't looking for something unable to be seen by all New Orleans.

"This won't do at all. Haven't you something with more diamonds? Something that would compliment her gown when she goes to the theater?"

"Well, monsieur, I do have a very special piece with ear baubles to match, but it's rather expensive." The subtext screaming, 'How can you afford this when you are destitute?' "Would you like to see it?" he said.

Stephen nodded his head that he would. Sam spoke over his shoulder and too low to be heard by the salesman, "She'll just sell it in a week."

"Shush, no, she won't."

The man returned with a treasure. It was feminine and extraordinary and meant for a unique woman. A woman like Isabella. It was a necklace made with delicate grape vines of individual strands of strong, thin gold, filigreed like ancient scripted letters, and with diamonds, like stars, encrusted at various places on the shiny scroll. It would drape, like gossamer lace, across the nape of her neck, tickling her skin seductively, like the long and slender fingers of a lover. Graceful. Elegant. And without asking the price for the item, Stephen said that he would purchase it. He wanted to see the earrings that were less ostentatious but breathtaking none the less. "Wrap it up with ribbons."

"Sir, with all due respect, these items are valued at over three hundred dollars a piece."

Stephen almost laughed at the absurd and old-fashioned price tag. It was so much money then, he thought, and with the depression happening all around New Orleans, an incredulous sum to ask from a down-trodden planter. But Dr. Stephen Templeton could afford it—and more.

"Would you take my bank note for it?" said Stephen.

"What bank?" he asked. It was an intelligently asked

question.

"Louisiana State Bank."

The man smiled too broadly. "Well, of course, Monsieur Durel. The ear bobs as well?"

"They will look lovely on Isabella, don't you think, dear cousin?"

"But, of course. Allow me to buy her them for her."

"Well, if you insist."

"You do take cash?" said Sam. A nice gesture on Sam's part considering it would be Stephen's money.

"Of course, monsieur. I'll wrap them for you. They will look lovely on your wife. She is very beautiful, if you don't mind my saying so."

"Yes, she is. Quite beautiful," said Stephen.

They paid for the diamonds, drank another glass of brandy each, told the man they would be back another time, and to have a nice holiday. He smiled expansively, and said that he would most certainly have a wonderful holiday.

The next shop to discover was the House of Gatou where Stephen planned to speak with his new tailor, and the woman who had known Isabella since she was a child. It was a tiny shop, rather difficult to find, and with a barely distinguishable sign.

When Stephen walked into the shop, a bell chimed above his head. The shop was orderly and neat which made Stephen think that the back room was where the real work was done.

"Good day, Monsieur Gatou," Stephen said, taking his hat into his hand and bowing in much the same way he assumed Emile would have done. "My name is Emile Durel. You design suits for my brother-in-law, Jean- Pierre Devieux," he stated matter-of-factly, as if he expected to be received with the utmost respect because of the introduction.

"This is my cousin, Evan, and we are looking for a new wardrobe and some evening clothes. Something fashionable and elegant. We will be attending the opera, and, of course, if you have any ideas for Mardi Gras. I believe you once made dresses for my wife, Isabella."

The tailor smiled. "Monsieur Durel, how wonderful to meet you at last. Your cousin's visit has prompted this desire, no doubt?"

"Quite. And besides, I have missed socializing with my

wife these past years. It isn't fair for me to make her go to these soirees alone even if I am busy with the work of our plantation. Been selfish for far too long."

The man nodded his head as if he understood completely.

"Farming can get rather boring after a while. I want your wife to make something special for Isabella. For the opera. For Mardi Gras. If that's possible."

His wife emerged from the back room. "Isabella?" She smiled at the sound of her former client's name. "I still have her measurements, but she has not come to me for so long. I miss her. What would you like me to make for her?" Her hands worked and reworked a ribbon sash for a dress she was making, and it looked as if she were nervous, but Stephen couldn't tell since it might have been something her hands did continually when she spoke with customers.

"A gown worthy of the Queen of France," he said. "Some design you've been saving for someone special. And a costume for Mardi Gras. There's that dinner party at her brother's; she'll need something for that."

"But her costume must match yours, Emile. What will you be?" said Sam.

"Have you any ideas?" Stephen said, making sure he was duly excited about the festival as Wainwright had told him he should be. "This will be your first festival with us. We should all go as someone truly magnificent."

"I think you should be a pirate," said Sam, as Monsieur Gatou sized him for his new suit.

"A pirate?"

Madame Gatou giggled. "Jean La Fitte?"

"Yes, Jean La Fitte will do nicely. I've recently discovered that women find pirates quite irresistible," said Sam.

"Very well then. And what will you be, cousin?"

"I should think I will be...a...a...knight in shining armor. Well, not armor. Maybe a tunic."

Monsieur Gatou took Emile's measurements. His wife showed Emile patterns of her one-of-a-kind gowns. He thought one looked like the perfect match for Isabella's personality. The seamstress could make the dress in a gold satin material with a smooth veil over skirt.

"This shell, over the skirt, would be made of a sparkly

material which will glisten when the theater lights shine upon it," she told him.

"It will match the diamonds," said Sam. Both tailors looked at each other.

Stephen said, "How soon can you have the gown ready for her first fitting?"

"Well," she said hesitantly, "I could have the bodice finished by next Saturday. I need to see whether she's put on weight. I doubt that she has. Still. This is a busy season, you understand." She was hedging.

Stephen caught her meaning. "I'll double the fee for making the dress if you can get it to her in two weeks."

"I'll see what I can do, monsieur," she said and then ran back into the sewing room.

"Are you and your cousin attending the theater next Friday—for the opening of Monsieur Fairchild's play? The one he wrote and directed?"

"Oh...I'm sure my wife will want to attend." He took a risk. "They are such good friends, I believe. Monsieur Fairchild and Isabella."

The man never batted an eyelash or changed his position in the least. "She comes in with him sometimes when he buys his suits. He takes her suggestions very seriously." He was deep in thought. Probably wondering how to design a suit for the tall cousin from France.

Stephen searched for something unusual in the man's demeanor when he spoke about Christopher to Isabella's husband. It looked as if the relationship between the actor and Emile's wife were either platonic, or an affair known to so many people that Monsieur Gatou might assume that her husband knew about it and didn't care. And the thought that it might be the latter bothered him tremendously.

Obviously, the actor respected her opinion. She laughed in the actor's presence. At his stories, at his speech, at him. He amused her. Made her happy. And her husband could do none of these things. Emile would not get high ratings on giving his wife much of a life, but maybe he wasn't supposed to in *his* time period. Maybe he was going about this all wrong. He was shifting 1998 ideas of equality, love, and friendship onto a Creole slave owner with a prearranged marriage to a woman who

128

was only living in his house to give him heirs.

Stephen felt a pinch. "Oh, so sorry, monsieur," said the tailor. "I will have your suits ready in two weeks."

"Well, cousin, I think it's time we headed homeward."

The tailor asked, "The costumes, monsieur? Would you like me to draw up a sketch for you?"

"Thank you. Make the colors to match all three outfits."

The tailor gave them his calling card, as if they needed one now, and bid them farewell. Just as they were leaving, a handsome, young man of strong but slender build, with hair the color of tarnished gold, and eyes as blue as a blue jay's feathers, pushed rudely past them.

"Excusez moi, monsieur," said the man. And then in English, "Forgive me." The man rushed past them, then froze in his tracks, turned so that he could regard Stephen, and stared at him. An oddly awkward moment.

Stephen returned the look into the man's eyes. It seemed as if the time tunnel had swallowed him entirely, and he was back home in a fraction of the time it took to travel. The young man was an exact replica of the new surgeon who'd asked if he could lighten Stephen's workload by helping him in his clinic once or twice a week. It was this same man who had taken Stephen's patients so that he could leave on his sabbatical. Stephen wanted to say hello to him, to thank him for being there for him when he was emotionally stressed, and to ask how Mrs. Olmstead's difficult pregnancy was going. But it wasn't that young doctor at all. It was a golden-haired Anglo in a French-speaking world who had the audacity to buy suits in an elite men's shop. And Emile would not have spoken to him or even made eye contact with such a man.

"Ah, bonjour, Monsieur Chesterfield," said the tailor. "Your suit is ready for your second fitting. Just let me get it."

The young man mumbled something in reply, but he did not look at anyone except Stephen. His eyes were cool, icy blue, just as they had been when they'd covered the sheet over their last surgical failure. Cold. Detached. Impersonal. Riveting. He had rested his hand on Stephen's shaking shoulder and told Stephen to take a break—he would finish—would speak to the man's widow for him. How he'd envied his new partner's ability to handle the cherished patient's—*friend's*—death with such composure!

Stephen smiled at how much the man looked like his new partner and thought, "I never expected this. But, I suppose it makes sense. If I lived before, why not others I know? Wonder who'll pop up in this one? They say you hang out with the same souls in every lifetime. Wonder if my father is anywhere around?"

He couldn't wait to speak with Sam privately.

Chapter Fifteen

The sun was setting beyond the waves of the Mississippi River, slipping into the horizon as a pocket watch slips into a man's vest pocket, as the small boat drifted easily back to the dock in front of the Durel Plantation.

"Let's sum up what we've learned so far," said Sam. "The gorgeous golden gown, which we saw in the portrait at home, is a rag according to her brother. Isabella never goes shopping except to help her *friends* purchase clothing but doesn't buy anything for herself. So, where is the money going? She has two major friends: Christopher, an amusing actor; and Melinda, a big-time flirt who's married unhappily to an old coot. Dr. Gayerré was pulled into Emile's plot to poison Isabella on Christmas, which he refused to do, but initially stated that he would. Her brother seems to hate her, but likes Emile; yet cared enough to tell you to buy her some decent clothes. Emile seems to be respected all over town. Isabella is well known by nearly everyone, and the people who know her love her. The real people in her life want to strangle the life out of her. Why? She's a mystery."

"But Emile isn't," stated Stephen. "Upset about finances and thinking his wife is every bit the flirt and social butterfly her pal, Melinda, is, he plots to rid himself of a woman who is frivolously spending his money and too much of her time in New Orleans's society. She is, but she isn't, and he doesn't seem to know any of the real truth. He probably doesn't care for her association with Christopher because she enjoys his company more than she does her husband's. I don't think she's having an affair with the actor because their friendship is too public. But if what she wrote in her diary is true, she is definitely fond of him. Maybe more so than she is of Melinda. She said that Melinda is strong-willed, but comments that Chris is the shoulder she cries on. Emile has never liked going to social affairs as Wainwright discerned, but enjoys the Mardi Gras, as he also guessed. Most people are astonished that Emile came to town today, and that he has a cousin in France. And most people respect his family's name. I noted no snickers behind our backs to indicate that his wife has made him the cuckold husband we feared he might be. The tailor didn't bat an eyelash when I brought up Chris's name."

"She's wearing none of the jewelry she should own from the look of her portrait, bursts into tears if you are kind to her in any fashion, and is rude beyond belief, when pressed on anything dealing with her social life. She obviously hates her husband."

"Gee, thanks," said Stephen.

Sam grinned. "Well, seriously, look at her face. You touched her cheek to give her a kiss, and she recoiled. You mentioned going to the opera with her, and it was as if a tarantula had just settled on her arm. She didn't want you to buy her any gifts and seemed astonished that you were going too anyway. Turning down something most women would go crazy to get."

"The more I learn; the more puzzling this whole marriage becomes."

"And it doesn't look as if you're going to get laid, either."

Stephen titled his head in Sam's direction and raised his eyebrow. "I beg your pardon. I didn't come all this way for that. Don't turn my noble deed into something vulgar."

"She can't stand for you to touch her, Doc."

A devilish grin played across his lips. "I'll get there, and not because I lust after her, either. Because I love her. And I'm going to prove it to her."

Sam threw his hands into the air as if he were worshiping the sun.
"Ah, Isabella can't be bought by diamonds and dresses."

"That's just the start. I'm going to solve her problems; something old Chris hasn't the power to do. And when she realizes how much I love her, she'll give herself to me willingly."

"I wouldn't bet the plantation on it," said Sam.

They walked into the house expecting the warm smell of hot food, and they were not denied. On the dining room table was a delicious dinner of fried ham, sweet potatoes, corn, cake, fresh-baked cornbread, wine, and coffee. But there was no Isabella waiting for them.

"Anna," Stephen said to the slave who had just taken his hat and gloves. "Where's your mistress?"

"She bids you and your cousin good night. She's already eaten her supper and has retired to her room for the evening."

When Anna left, Stephen said, "That's not good. She's negligent in her duties as hostess to Emile's family. Deliberately snubbing us. Giving me no chance to discuss my day's activities with her, or ask her about our dinner party on the twenty-fifth. How can she refuse her husband's wishes like this? Ignore the chance to get to know his kin who has just arrived from France and is going to save her lifestyle? What *can* the woman be thinking?" Stephen's face flushed with obvious anger.

Sam said, "Well, she might be thinking of what to write in her diary right now, as she swallows that small vial of poison she has hidden in her dresser drawer."

"Good Lord!" Stephen raced up the stairs.

He didn't knock but burst through the bedroom doorway unannounced. Isabella looked up from her journal, and the look on her face was one of abject terror.

"Are you mad?" she said, after calming herself and placing her pen in the divet of the silver tray.

"Why aren't you downstairs waiting for us? I have much I would like to discuss with you. Evan desires your presence." He stood tall and bold in the door frame. His arms were crossed over his chest, his jaw firm and fixed, and his legs were straddled wide apart as if he could keep her from fleeing for her life by just standing so.

Her eyes narrowed into cruel slits. "How *dare* you enter my room without knocking first."

"I am your husband, this is my house, and I can go anywhere—do anything—I wish." It occurred to him that he had said practically the same thing to Isabella's ghost. The thought

133

amused him so much that his demeanor extenuated.

"You gave me this room and told me that you would always call to me before entering. You are behaving like a country boar rather than the gentleman I married. I cannot ascertain this odd change that has come over you, but whatever it is, I hope you're cured of it soon. I became bored waiting for you. How could you expect otherwise?"

She returned to her writing, but he noted that her hand was shaking too much to pick up the pen. She merely looked at her book covetously, pretending as if her glance towards her diary was enough to dispense with her husband's wrath.

"Writing in your diary?" he said.

She grabbed her pen and turned towards him. Her eyes went wide, and for a moment, Stephen thought she might lance him with the tip of the writing utensil.

"How could you possibly know about my diary? I have never shown it to you. Have you been searching my room? Am I no longer mistress in my own home? Must I beg for a little privacy, as well?"

A surge of anger rose in his chest. His mouth opened, and Emile's words came out. *"Never take that tone with me again, Isabella."*

The words stung the air.

Stephen continued but with Emile's thoughts and voice. *"We have a guest downstairs, and you will put on your dress and entertain him. Do you hear me?"*

"No."

"You try my patience."

"When you have the time to notice me, which isn't often, you order me about as if I were one of the slaves. Perhaps that is customary behavior for other men and their wives, but I will *not* have it. If you wish to speak with me, there are seven days and nights to do so. You're only interested in your farm and inventing ridiculous excuses for staying home when we've been asked out. This place is lonely, and boring—a forsaken island—and I am *tired* of staying here and waiting for you to return only to see you take off with your kin leaving me desolate again. I am the only planter's wife whose household has not retired to the city for a rest after the harvest. You keep me isolated like a prisoner here, far from the city life that I love. It is all well for you to travel to France anytime you please, but when you return, and I ask nothing more than to travel to town with you, you prevent me with some stupid excuse. Guests? Now, as if overnight, you want to be the perfect host...and I am supposed to play your devoted wife, n'est ce pas? The wife whom you've shown little or no interest in up till now. Well. I shall *not* be ordered about like a servant. If you'd been home earlier, when the food was fresh and hot from the fire, I'd have been there to dine with you. I'm not about to sit around all night and stare at the burning candles while you frolic with your *cousin* in town."

The word "cousin" had been said so strongly that Stephen conceived the idea that she was slightly jealous of Sam. Then he rationalized that she had every right to be. After all, Emile had refused to accompany her to town when she'd wanted to go, and then in walks this cousin from France, and he's ready to jump on the first boat to the Place D'Armes. He had to think of a righteous retort. She had sounded her bitterness with such emotion that it was more an explosion of betrayal and pain than the words of a nagging wife. She had brewed a hatred for Emile that spanned several years. Now Stephen and Emile, were getting the brunt of it. Emile remained mercifully quiet during her outburst. It was up to Stephen to counter and soothe the deep wound somebody had cut into Isabella's heart. His plan to be gentle with her had flown out the window.

"As *you* do," he said, challenging her. "I have no idea where you are half the time when you go out. Gone during the afternoons and then out again in the evenings until the wee hours of the morning. What could occupy my wife's time so much that she has no time for her chores—or her husband's bed?"

She went pale and then blushed. He'd guessed correctly that she hadn't warmed the sheets of the master's bed for many months—maybe years.

He continued, "Such a saucy tongue to give your husband. You've spent too much time with Melinda," he said. And then added, "And Christopher. They've tutored you to behave impudently to the man who provides you with a roof over your head."

"What do you know about Chris?" she said, with a protective edge in her voice.

He thought of how Emile would walk as he swaggered like a rooster into the room and closer to her chair. "I pique your interest, do I? I've learned about your little actor friend. So amusing. So charming. Been invited to his play Friday, and we're going. I want you to introduce him to me after the show. Quite the Anglo celebrity, I'm told. I'm sure he'll be happy to meet your husband. And will Melinda's spouse be there, or is he too old to hear the words from the stage? What can you be thinking, Isabella? Appearing unescorted save by an actor and a friend in the Vieux Carré? A woman friend with a questionable reputation, or so I've been told by your brother. And a British actor. Good Lord. Don't you know what we do to Yankee buzzards, mon cher? What about your reputation? Ours? We're Creole. You seem to have forgotten the line is firmly drawn between the Anglos and the French and Spanish settlers. How can you tarnish yourself by even being close to one of them? I wager he doesn't even speak French."

"You *have* been spying on me? How dare you. And he speaks perfect French."

He saw tears in her eyes. Chris was a nerve not to be toyed with.

He closed his eyes as if he were in pain. He pushed Emile's personality from his mind because Emile wanted to accuse her of more than fraternizing with Americans. Emile's tone wouldn't help him gain his heart's desire. "What should *I* say to her now? Stephen not Emile?" he wondered.

He touched his forehead with his index finger, as if gaining control of his temper, and with a soft, comforting voice, he said, "Please, Isabella, I would like you to join my cousin and me. I realize I've been remiss in so many ways in the past, but I plan to change all that. Evan seeks the pleasure of your company, and he's traveled such a long distance to be with us. I'm sorry if I've been too busy to care for you as I should."

He bent towards her, offered his hand so that she might rise from her chair and face him, and then held her fragile, white hands between his. They were rough, calloused, bruised, and the skin was dark red and dry. He had touched them briefly before but hadn't realized how horrible they really looked earlier. The knowledge surprised and saddened him. He involuntarily checked her pulse. It was racing. Close to the edge and highly charged emotionally, he warned himself to be careful with her. She pulled her hands from his grasp and rose to face him.

"Don't be afraid." He touched her cheek with the back of his fingers and angled his face close to hers. "And don't leave me," he whispered into her ear.

She cocked her head to the side just as the ghost had done. "What an odd thing to say. What's come over you? You're not yourself."

He wanted to say, "You've got that right, sister." But, instead, he took her into his arms. She fought him, but he held firmly onto her tiny waist. He looked into her beautiful, brown eyes, that had just been oil paint on canvas before, but now danced and sparkled with spirit and emotion. She stared deeply into his. What was she looking for? What did she expect to see? The muscles in her face weakened. Her lips parted. He felt her body relax against his. "Thata girl," he said to himself. "Take it slow." A soft gasp came from somewhere deep in her soul.

He tilted his head, and slowly moved his mouth close to her cheek. Gently he pressed his lips against hers. It was an unpretentious kiss, full of tenderness not passion. He wanted to see what her reaction would be too such a velvet embrace. Sam had said that she wouldn't let him touch her, and he had to prove the time traveler was wrong. The mystery of the woman intensified. What he was holding was untapped, untrained fire. He'd sensed it before, but it was obvious now. Her breathing became erratic. Once again, she tried to push him away from her...but not too roughly, he noticed. No one had ever taken the time to make love to her. Her reactions told him so.

"Will you come downstairs, Isabella?" His voice was a hushed endearment, not a question or a command at all.

She looked at him for some time as if she were pondering her next move. Her voice turned to honey. There were tears in her eyes. "Yes."

He had waited all day to hear his ghost's only spoken word come from this woman's lips. It was a start.

Chapter Sixteen

Isabella sat quietly and watched as Sam and Stephen ate. Stephen could swear he heard her thoughts clicking inside her head. What was she thinking about right now? Who is this man? What's happened to Emile? Maybe he really likes this cousin?

Stephen smiled at Sam's comments to Isabella while they sipped coffee in the parlor. Questioning, interrogating, a perfect blend of innocent query and shadowy clues. She answered like an automaton, in the ghost's style of "yes's" and "no's." What was she hiding from her husband?

"Will you play for us, mon cher?" Stephen asked when the lag between her responses grew too lengthy. She nodded her head, walked straight to the instrument, which was exactly where it had resided in 1998, opened its lid, and began playing as if she thoroughly enjoyed the music. Eyes closed. Her body swayed gently while her arms and finger performed the task of playing each note perfectly. But her songs were all sad, melancholy, and dark. Sam glanced at Stephen often, and the subtext behind his look read, "My God, she's maudlin."

"Isabella," Stephen said too quickly not to hide the fact that he couldn't bear another 'dirge.' "I spoke with your brother today."

"Yes," she said, closing the lid of the musical instrument and rising.

"I asked him to join us for our dinner and he refused—plans of his own."

She looked at her hands. "Yes," she said.

"He told me of a dinner party he's having. That we're

invited to. You never mentioned it to me."

"I thought you wouldn't want to attend."

"Do you?" Stephen said.

"If you wish. It doesn't matter to me. It would be nice to go but..."

"But what?" he interrupted.

"Ernestine is obtuse and insulting, and her children—our niece and nephew—spoiled and willful. I detest them. I'm sure their guests will be...amusing." Then she dropped the front. "They will be droll, boring, selfish, obnoxious, and with way too high an opinion of themselves."

Sam grinned from ear to ear, and the sparkle returned to his eyes.

"Are you bothered because your friends will not be invited?" Stephen said.

"Melinda will be asked only because her husband, Etienne, is rich and Creole, and because she is Catholic and speaks French...but not Christopher. Now that you've heard his name, I suppose you must know that he's a very talented actor. Jean-Pierre would never ask him to his party although he's accepted into the finest American homes and reputed to be the greatest living actor the world has ever known." Obviously, she would protect this man to her grave. The bond between them was amazing. Her eyes moistened, her lips quivered, her hands nervously grasped each other, and she repeatedly licked her lips to moisten them as she spoke. Was she hurt on Chris's behalf? Stephen was jealous.

"Then do you wish to go and spend some time with Melinda, or ignore your brother to satisfy your friendship with Christopher?"

The space between her eyes relaxed. Her eyes opened wide. Her whole body went limp. Stephen wondered if it were because he had asked for her opinion on the matter. A Creole gentleman never asked his wife for her opinion on anything but domestic matters. He should have reprimanded her for having the friendship. Emile would have, but Stephen would never find the murderer that way.

"Well...I...wouldn't want your cousin to miss a social event of such magnitude."

Sam said, "It doesn't matter to me, cousin. It's up to

you."

She tilted her head and raised her chin. The move was inherently symbolic. She thought for a while and then said, "I prefer not to attend."

"Then we won't." He stared at her evenly. "You may leave us now."

He wanted to ask her if she'd sleep with him tonight, but thought that might be rushing things beyond plausibility.

She walked over to Sam, bent to his cheek, and gave him a small kiss. "Bonsoir, Evan."

"Bonsoir, Isabella," he said, in a voice heavy with tender emotion. Even Stephen could see that Sam was sensitive to her amazing sadness and appalling gall.

Stephen watched her every move. This was the woman who had said she wasn't as assertive as Melinda? In one day she had quarreled, grouched, complained, snarled, hissed, and made demands which would never have entered the mind of a normal Victorian-Southern-Creole belle. Like a wise king, Stephen had made the boundaries clear to her, and, for Stephen, under the circumstances of his affection for the woman, it was quite therapeutic. He loved her enough to keep her from destroying her life. His total commitment to Isabella's happiness was making him take charge of their lives in a positive way. In short, he was learning to be assertive and yet retain the qualities that had made him the most beloved and respected physician at Cook County General Hospital. Kind and solid Dr. Templeton was, once again, fighting for someone's life. And no one would stop him from saving hers—not even Isabella.

She walked over to Stephen and bent to give him his kiss. She hesitated slightly, her face and lips just above him. Then she kissed him gently on the lips. "Bonsoir, mon cher," she said to him.

His body reacted simultaneously. How long could he wait?

"Au revoir," he said to her after clearing his throat.

She left the room, and when she was out of earshot, Sam said, "Damn, I wanted to go to that dinner party. Melinda will be there."

"Let's go easy with her right now. Remember, she's supposed to die on the twenty-fifth. Don't push her."

"You're right, of course. What was all that upstairs tonight? You get into a fight with her?"

"We had a...confrontation...which I won with a kiss."

"So, we're up to close encounters of the first kind?" Stephen couldn't help grinning with satisfaction.

"Something like that. You know what, Sam? She has no idea what passion and love are all about?"

"You mean the adulterous, flirty, Isabella..."

"Is as cool as ice. At least she is right now."

"That sure runs parallel to all that we've heard."

"I told you they were rumors."

"Really? What about the look in her eyes when you mentioned Christopher?"

The comment unsettled him. "I don't quite know how to read that yet, but I'm working on it. Well, I think we've accomplished a great deal for our first day, don't you? Tomorrow morning I have a date with destiny."

"The slaves?"

"I can't stand this part of the adventure. How can I? Everything inside me recoils. It's one thing to read about it in history books, but it's quite another when you are living it—watching it in action. I knew I was coming back to this, and I decided to face it for her sake, but what can I do that won't change Emile's life, but could encourage a better one for these people? I want Anna to look at me—to smile when she says hello to me. I want Nora to wait in the dining room until I tell her how delicious her dinner is. And most of all, friend, I want to go down to those cabins," he motioned out of the window, "unlock the bolts we saw on those cabin doors, and set them free. But I can't. I would destroy history, Emile's existence, Isabella's legacy, and maybe get them both killed by the other planters for doing so."

"I have a few ideas."

Stephen turned to regard his friend. "And so do I. Being able to write Emile's name will be enormously helpful." Without warning, Stephen fell to the floor in agony. A bolt of pain flashed through his head.

"What's the matter?" shouted Sam, rushing to his side.

"My head. Oh, God, my head," he cried, holding onto his temples with his hands and completely helpless to do anything but moan in agony.

Anna must have heard the cries and hurried into the room, anxious for her master. "Is it one of your headaches, master?"

Sam said, "Do you have something for it?"

"The medicine is in the pantry, and Missy has the keys."

"Go and get the keys."

Isabella hadn't completely disrobed when she heard of her husband's anguish. "Is it the headache?" she said to Anna, as she flew down the stairs and into the room. "I'll get the laudanum."

Stephen whispered to Sam, "Just get me some of the Advil I have in my medicine bag upstairs."

Before Sam could do that, Isabella had returned with the bottle of laudanum.

"Six drops should do it. It worked before," said Isabella, measuring out the medicine and pouring it onto Stephen's lips. He calmed down partially because he didn't want her to give him anymore of the drug.

"Lie down on the settee, mon cher," she said, with an air of true concern.

Sam helped Stephen onto the small, red velvet couch. "Get some water, Anna."

"I'll be all right. Just let me stay quiet for a while."

"Are you sure? The argument. You always get this way when you are tempered."

He took her hand in his. "Thank you for the medicine. Now you go up to bed." He winced in pain. She looked at him as if she thought she shouldn't leave him. "Go on. I have Evan here if I need anything."

She parted her lips to say something and then nodded her head and slowly walked out of the room.

"Damn," said Stephen.

"No storm. It can't be a change in atmosphere."

"I feel like someone just hit me with a lead pipe."

"Emile?"

He shook his head. "I think so. The moment I said I could sign his name to any document I wish. But she did say that he gets them whenever he's tempered. Wasn't expecting to take on any of his physical maladies."

Anna came back with some cool water in a cup. He drank the liquid, thanked her, and dismissed her by telling her not to come to his room in the morning, but to attend to her mistress for she had a busy day ahead of her. Then he turned to Sam.

"Help me to bed before I start to hallucinate. Good Lord."

"Think he had high blood pressure or migraines?"

"Maybe...or...it's just that the man inside me knows I'm about to irreparably change his life."

"We learned something else too. Since Isabella holds the household keys, she also has access to strong, and potentially fatal, drugs." He helped Stephen to the steps.

"Can you imagine giving someone laudanum with no clue as to how much to give, or what it might do if taken incorrectly? This is appalling," he said, steadying himself on the banister.

"No, this is 1838, Dr. Templeton." Sam bade him good night at the door to his bedroom.

His headache subsided after taking off the binding clothes and donning his nightshirt. He was seeing stars and flashes of light, and it was making him nauseous. He walked over to the windows, which were made to look like miniature French doors, and opened them. Then he moved out onto the porch. The air was cool and eased the burning behind his eyes. A small breeze tossed the limbs of the trees. The pleasant perfume of Palmer violets permeated the darkness. He stared at the moon, and the tall, majestic oaks that arched the path to their front door. Then he heard it; the song of the night of the South—of its heart, its soul, and its sorrow. It was something to be proud of if nothing else; a tiny, almost-invisible emblem of New Orleans, whose song could be heard above every other sound.

A mockingbird perched on a twisted branch of the oak tree and sang a song of hope. It seemed to be singing only for Stephen. Its melody would help him through every day of his three-month stay.

The pain in his head disappeared.

"I'm here," he said to the bird. "I'm really here. Do you know any love songs?"

Chapter Seventeen

Stephen wanted to examine the library without anyone's knowledge, so he rose early, washed and shaved himself with the toiletries Anna had left for him in his room, chose his clothing from his wardrobe, and tiptoed downstairs. "*My* library," he thought to himself. "Will it be the same?"

Most of the servants were asleep, and even the mockingbird had decided to stifle his morning call. He shut the French doors behind him and secured them at the top of the door. He found it amusing to see how new and clean the very books he'd pieced together and sold to the antique store were. He took a few down from the shelves and opened them. There weren't many. He didn't expect to find her diary. It would be in her room. He hoped to find the safe, however. It was there. Sturdy and new. And he couldn't pry this one apart to open it either.

"Okay, Emile, help me out here. It's ours, after all." There was just a small keyhole. He looked all around the safe and finally spotted a tiny key hiding on the shelf next to the safe. The key fit, and he opened the door to the safe immediately. "Thank you," he said to his other half.

There were documents, wills, deeds, two small portraits of whom he assumed to be Emile's parents, and letters tied in a blue ribbon. He took the letters and shut the door to the safe.

Finding a high-back, leather chair near the window, he placed a splinter of wood in the hot embers of the fireplace, lit the candle nearest him with it's flame, and made himself comfortable.

They were love letters from Emile to Isabella, and he

wondered who had decided to save them. "Now we're getting somewhere," he said aloud.

Emile and Isabella apparently had been childhood friends. Their parents had celebrated holidays, as well as suffered the good and bad times of farming together. It seemed as if the three, Jean-Pierre, Emile, and Isabella, had been tutored by the same man a certain Frenchman by the name of Monsieur Dumont. The teacher was the subject of several sentences in one of the letters. He'd been quite scholarly and taught them mathematics, music, art, dance, and literature. There were remarks about dancing in the one letter. Isabella and Emile apparently heated up a dance floor when they were together at parties. According to one sentence, Emile promised to never dance with anyone except her, and begged her to keep her dance card clear for him alone. The Devieuxs and the Durels must have been very progressive. The letters spanned many years with no break, although Emile complained about not hearing from her while he was in Paris in 1827. He wrote to her anyway. One of Stephen's favorite letters began:

> Mon cher, mon amie,
>
> I am at a loss to understand why you have neglected answering my letters. Have you no further affection for me than to treat me with such unwarranted contempt? My heart breaks. This morning I, once again, searched my mail for a letter from you; but, alas, there were none. My sweet Isabella! I must speak with your father when I return home, but I am obliged to hear if you will accept my suit before I ask. I have documents from France as to my character as a businessman, and scholar, and affidavits to attest to my morality. You must know how I love you. How this separation is my greatest agony! I send to you this fan of the highest and most expensive quality and design for I know none other will catch your eye or heart, as proof that I mean to marry you, and that I love no other woman but you. My father wrote to me that he would speak with your father before my homecoming next month. I will lay my fortunes at your feet, mon coeur, and remain faithful to you alone for the rest of my life. Je t'adore. I cannot live without you. I desire you with all my heart. Just thinking about you, with your form so far from my arms, keeps me awake at night. Write to me, mon cher.
>
> Everlasting in love and honor,

Emile

"Ah, the French," said Stephen grinning. "You sly, old dog, Emile. So, you *do* love her, don't you? *Everlastingly.*"

And there was more. Emile had been away from the plantation two years in a row on business after they were married. He sent only letters rather than come home to help his wife with the incredible responsibility of running the whole sugar cane plantation with no one but an overseer who wouldn't listen to her. Stephen found sentences where Emile responded to her bitter claims. He told her, in no uncertain terms, that he couldn't come home no matter how much she needed him, but she continued to write faithfully, pleading with him to come home.

Mon Coeur,

If I could, I would be on the next ship home. I trust your judgment entirely for you have brought in the harvest on your own before, having learned to do so by my side when first we planted our new seedlings. It grieves me that the slaves are so troublesome, but you do have the luxury of having more than most from your father's inheritance. Think of poor Jean-Pierre having to work his plantation with 20 less slaves! Well, he won the homestead, after all. Take consolation in the fact that I will be home by November and bring with me the prettiest gowns from France any wife could wish for. I send you this bonnet, which I am told is all the rage for ladies here in France, as a sign of my eternal gratitude.

Je t'adore,

Emile

"The *bastard*," said Stephen out loud. "She's killing herself trying to run his father's plantation alone, and all he sends her is a *bonnet*. I'm beginning to see her side, Emile. Did you see those hands of hers—so rough—so bruised? Why didn't you come home and help her? France could have managed without you," he said to the spirit of Emile, "but she needed you, and you weren't there for her."

There was a tiny knock on the French doors. He cursed himself for speaking aloud, and, perhaps waking the household.

"Yes?" he said.

It was Anna. "Do you want something, master?" she said in a soft, sleepy voice.

He put away the letters, closed and locked the door of the

safe, and then covered it up with books.

"I'd like some coffee, Anna," he answered, before opening the door.

She looked appealingly innocent and sweet, rubbing the sleep from her eyes, half raising her head and then remembering to look down. "I'll put some on the hearth. Anything else?"

He wanted a bowl of oatmeal and a bagel smothered in jam. "Do you have any preserves?"

"Yes, but Missy has the key to the pantry. Should I awaken her?"

"Why not? Make me some toast—ah—you know chunks of bread placed over the fire and smothered with butter and preserves."

For once she shot him a quick look and emitted an unavoidable giggle she tried to cover with the palm of her hand. "I know how to make toast, master. Would you like some of the cornbread left from last night's meal?"

"Yes. Tell Nora to make ham and eggs for my wife and cousin. A big breakfast." He shook his head. "Why am I so hungry?" he said, half to himself.

"Your headache. The medicine. You always get this way after your sickness. I better get your coffee fast."

She couldn't have been more than twenty-two. Not poorly treated either, for she seemed to have a spirit he wouldn't have suspected from a slave. She was dressed in a fashionably made, hand-stitched dress of homespun cloth, which looked as if it had been created exclusively for her. Isabella must have used her own dress patterns to make the girl's clothes. No one else had anything like it. Obviously Anna was Isabella's favorite.

As he waited for his wife and cousin to join him, he thought about what he wanted to accomplish that day. Only then did it occur to him that it was December 23.

Sam, who had remarked earlier on his inherent need to rise early, had slept in. Isabella came downstairs in her dressing gown. She was so beautiful that she looked even better when she was half-asleep. She swished past him, after a curt good morning, and went to the pantry to get the day's food supplies. The cook, Nora, followed her. They returned with their arms filled.

"Will strawberry preserves suit you?" she questioned

him, as she raced into the kitchen. "I had no idea you liked my preserves so much, or I would have left one jar out so that you could make yourself something to eat. Up before us all, Emile?"

He couldn't resist watching her hustle down the hallway. Her hips swayed back and forth in her gown. The hem of her nightgown swished along the wooden floorboards. His wife. Rushing on his behalf.

"Come back when you're done," he said.

She turned and stared at him. She placed her hands on her hips in defiance. "And when might that be, mon homme? Midnight? You wanted a Christmas feast. Do you think they grow on oak trees? I'll be busy all day." He didn't reply for she was gone immediately after offering her retort.

Sam joined him in the dining room for coffee while they waited for breakfast to be served.

"I got into the safe and read his letters to her. I wonder who saved them. So far, I've seen nothing but personal notes and legal documents—no jewelry. I didn't have time to read everything. One told of their relationship before their marriage, and another one told of what it's been like since then."

He told Sam everything while Isabella was well out of earshot. The hot, delicious food was served when she returned, and the two men ate as if they'd been fasting for a month.

Sam whispered to Stephen, "Whatever you do, don't sell the cook."

"I thought I might do the baking myself, if it pleases you?" she said. It was a question, and it puzzled Stephen. She twisted her hands as she spoke.

"You may if it pleases *you*, mon cher."

"It has been some time since I've tasted the sweet treats my mother used to make for Christmas, and I have all of her recipes. You so enjoyed your mother's holiday specials too. I've found her recipes in the pantry. Nora has created some special dishes of her own. Because we're having guests, I thought we might demonstrate what a fine cook we have here on our plantation."

"Good Lord," he thought to himself, "Mom's found me."

"My favorite?"

She blushed and looked to the floor. "I will make my new recipe for rice pudding and let you sample it tonight. It will take most of the day. Are you riding this morning?"

"Evan and I will speak with the overseer this morning."

The look she gave him when he said that stopped all further speech.

"There's another problem?"

"He does as he pleases, my husband, as I have already informed you, and refuses to listen to anything I have to say on any matter pertaining to our farm. He needlessly whips the slaves in your name, and tells me that you alone give him his orders. I hate the man. I know you didn't tell him to beat our slaves. You wouldn't have said that. But since your return to Durel, you've said nothing to him in my defense."

"Forgive me, Isabella. I'll have a talk with him today. I don't plan on traveling back to France, so that may help matters."

She gave him a quick look when he said that.

"I'll need him to run the place in our absence."

She tilted her head as if she weren't sure she'd heard him correctly, "Absence?"

"After Christmas we're moving to the St. Louis Hotel until I can purchase, or rent, a home for the season. We'll take the domestic slaves with us. Evan and I will find a suitable residence while you enjoy your friend's visits and purchase theater tickets for us. Now, are you quite sure you don't want to go to your brother's dinner ball? I've assigned all your dress designs to Madame Gatou, who, I understand, is an old friend of your family?"

Her eyes went wide, and her lips trembled. Her skin lost its color. "We're moving to town for the winter?"

"The weather is rainy and cold here, and you're correct about this place being depressing. You yourself said that Evan might see New Orleans on his stay with us. What better way to do that than to move there like the other planters?"

"Your head still hurts some?" she said.

Sam caught his chuckle in his napkin.

"Actually, I feel fine this morning—a bit hungry—for so many things," he said, shooting a knowing look Sam's way. He was sad about leaving the one connection he had with his real life in 1998—the plantation that was his only link to both time periods. It was a sacrifice he would gladly make if it brought a

149

smile back to her pretty face, but it hadn't—yet.

First she blushed, and then she smiled, then frowned, then made a comment that it would be such a bother to move, and so he said, "We'll just stay at the hotel then. You won't have to lift a finger. A wonderful vacation for you. One I think you deserve." And then, she started to cry and ran from the room.

"Well, now you've done it. You made her cry," said Sam.

"Will I ever understand women?"

"She's not the average female. Isabella's a different breed all together."

"Do you know how to ride a horse?"

Sam's face went white. "Ah...well...I tried to ride one in Aruba. Been traveling mostly to the colonial time period where I walked beside my horse as much as I could. If it isn't too high-spirited a mount, I might be all right. I really need to take riding lessons one of these days."

"We won't be steeplechasing, just trotting around the farm."

"Then, I think I can manage."

They finished their breakfast and called for their horses. The boy, who brought the two quarter horses, looked as if he'd been beaten to a pulp. One eye was completely closed from swelling, his cheek was enlarged, and his lip was cut. "Tell the overseer I wish to see him immediately."

When the boy was out of earshot, Stephen said, "That bastard!"

"This part won't be easy, will it?" said Sam.

"I hope Emile is outraged, too, or I'm in for another headache."

The overseer came promptly.

"There are some things I wish repaired on the estate while I'm wintering in town. First, I want to see the slave quarters fixed like I told you yesterday. Secondly, I will draw you a design of a screen, rather like cheesecloth for straining, fitted to a frame, which I want made to fit *all* the windows and doors. Place the material on square wooden frames so that they fit each window and archway perfectly. Nail them to every opening in both the main and slave houses too. When you have that done, I want you to make the same style of screen, but attach this one to the rim of a broken barrel, and place it over the cistern. I want the cook to boil all water that is served in this house. *No one* drinks directly from the cistern. Cool the boiled water in jars and place them in the cooling pits, cover them, and see that they're kept free from mosquitoes. These screens should keep pests, rats, and other rodents from coming into the house or falling into the cistern. We need to keep mosquitoes out of our drinking water and from coming into the house. Have the domestic slaves help with the boiling of the water. No one on this plantation drinks from the cistern, and no one lives in a house with no screens. I hope I've made myself clear on this issue. I should think you'll have that job completed upon my return. Evan and I will come out to the farm occasionally to see whether you need any help with this project. Furthermore, my wife is my partner and my mouthpiece. She's been raised on a sugar plantation and is a co-owner of this one. I never want to hear that you have disobeyed her orders again. If there is trouble with a slave, bring it to my attention immediately, no one is whipped on this farm by you or anyone else. Do I make myself clear?"

The man was about to protest and so was Emile. Stephen pushed the notions, and his inner voice, aside. "Every skilled laborer is to be paid for his work upon completion of each task. When he has received $20.00, he may have his freedom. They have to prove to me that they've saved enough money to start a new life. Tell the men that. They may also hire out their skills to other planters if they wish. If you are trustworthy and complete these tasks that I have given you, I will double your wages and build you a better house. If you break one of the rules I have mentioned this day, on that day, you will be given leave to seek employment elsewhere, and I shall find a new overseer. I will look at the account books today and bring them up-to-date. My cousin is now my partner, so anything he tells you, you will obey without question. Do you have anything to say?"

"Only that when you are not here, the slaves are rebellious, lazy, and complain of ailments I do not think they have just to get out of work. They are insubordinate to your wife, so I put them in their place for there has been too much slave rebellion as of late in Louisiana."

"I thank you for your honesty. I will not be leaving again except for our brief seasons in town. I think my new improvements might make it easier for you. Is there a particular troublemaker in the lot?"

"Yes. Terence."

"A skilled man?"

"No, a field hand."

"Has he some intelligence?"

"Probably."

"Could he learn a skill?"

"He's good at building things."

"Then put him to work as one of the skilled laborers under the contract I will write for them and make legal by my own signature. Have him rebuild the cabins with the other construction workers. If he wants his freedom, this is a perfect way to earn it. Who knows, if he helps with the screens too, he may have enough to leave soon."

"Forgive me, monsieur, if the men earn their freedom, they will leave us, and then what will we do?"

"My hunch is that they may stay to earn even more money so that they can build a home in town or start a farm of their own. But if they do leave...then...I suppose we'll just...buy more slaves." It was difficult for Stephen to speak the words.

"You are planning to stay in town for the whole season then?"

"That's correct," Stephen said.

"Would you be able to stop by the St. Louis Hotel? We could use a few more slaves to work in the fields, and I'm sure the auctions will be held there during your visit. Would you be able to bring home some new servants for the household, too? We could sure use the help."

Stephen shot a quick glance towards Sam and cursed his stupidity. The one hotel he should have avoided would now be his home for several months.

"I'll look into that," Stephen's hands tightened on the reins of his horse to keep from screaming at the man. How could he stay in the hotel that held the most famous of New Orleans's auction arenas? The cries from the sellers would haunt him for the rest of his life. He wondered if Isabella's ghost appreciated what he was going through on her account. Then he looked up to the second balcony and saw her.

"Dressed already, mon cher?" he called to her.

"Yes, might I ride with you?" she said.

"We would be honored. Hurry." He turned to his overseer. "Have the boy bring her horse?"

She took to the saddle and clicked her tongue to the roof of her mouth to command the horse. "Where are we going?" Her face was flushed with excitement. She looked at him with clear expectations. She wanted to race.

"Just around the plantation. Do you wish to choose the route?"

"May I? I haven't seen that section of tall trees, where we used to play pirates, since you left for France. I don't like to ride that far...leaving the house unattended for so long."

Pirates? Perhaps Sam's idea of his Mardi Gras costume was a stroke of genius. "I thought you were going to bake today," he said.

The wind blew some loose strands of hair from the tight chignon at the back of her head to the front of her face. She tried to return it to its pinned spot, but it wouldn't stay. "Oh that, I can bake later. I told Nora to make the cornbread and muffins without me. I'll make the rice pudding later."

She was smiling. He was entranced with the childlike, whimsical expression on her face. It was such a pleasure to see her smile.

"I could always best you in a race." It was the challenge of a thirteen-year-old girl, and it tempted the little boy who still lived inside his heart.

"Not today, mon cher. Evan needs to get his riding legs back from so long out of the saddle, and I want to *show* him the plantation, not race him around it." He let her lead the way because it combined his desire to let her have her way in a few things, and erased the problem that he didn't know his way around his own farm.

He felt a sharp push on his back. He sat up straight immediately and felt the inside of his thighs press harder on the sides of the horse. Emile was telling him to how to ride *his* horse.

As they trotted along, she began the conversation with, "I heard what you said to him from my window. Those are good ideas. Are they yours or Evan's?"

"Mine. I'm pleased you appreciate my plans," he said,

153

trying to keep his horse close to hers. Sam was having some trouble with his steed and lingered behind whispering curses into the beast's ears.

He had to force himself not to worry about his time-traveling companion's angst, so that he could speak with his wife.

"Things going well for Christmas dinner? I wish we had more guests coming." It was a stupid topic to pick since they'd already discussed it, but he had no idea what to say to her.

"We have so few friends. If it is your common practice to ignore your friends' invitations, they soon stop inviting you."

She didn't waste time getting to the fight of the day.

"I suppose you're right," he said cautiously. "I'm going to change all that."

"And when your cousin has gone back to France, resume it, n'est ce pas?" She was good at raising a man's blood pressure.

"Isabella," he said calmly. "I plan on changing every aspect of our life here on our plantation. This is *our* land, and the product we make here is something of which I am quite proud. It has made us wealthy in the past, and it will again."

"But I am not allowed to touch the funds?"

"As of late, you've shown an odd interest in money. I'm confused about many aspects of your spending habits."

"How so?"

"The money is gone, but there's nothing to show for it. Nothing. Where is it, Isabella?"

She hesitated, playing with the reins of her horse and turning to see whether Sam was all right. But she was stalling, and you didn't have to be much of a detective to figure that out.

"Well, are you going to answer me?" he said.

"I have household expenses."

"Not that many. I shall check the books today. What items should I look for? Which ones cost us our whole lifestyle?"

Her horse slowed its pace, and her chin dropped to her chest. "I spent the money on clothes. I've told you that. Selfish of me, I know, but I've been so depressed with the loss of my parents and your abandonment."

So she called his business trips *abandonment*. Well, it

was.

"You have purchased nothing new in months. Jean-Pierre told me so, and the Gatous confirmed it. Are you investing in Christopher's plays?"

Her right hand flew into the air as if she were swatting an irritating insect from her head. "Why all the questions? You make me feel like a suspect in some crime." The stray hair flew about her face.

"Some people might think of it as theft, when money disappears, and there are no receipts to support its withdrawal from a bank account or from our safe. I see no new equipment, no new slaves, and the overseer hasn't mentioned any problems which would warrant such extravagant expenditures."

"I thought we were going to have a pleasant ride," she said.

"I thought you wanted a husband to talk to. Or do you only want one who tells you what you want to hear? Takes you to plays and parties. Someone to tell you how clever, talented, and beautiful you are. To show you a good time and never mention the dirt between his fingers from his hard work, or the redness of his wife's hands from placing ham shoulders into brine so that they can be corned. Maybe you spent the money on gloves so that Melinda wouldn't notice that the skin has been torn from your hands from hours spent at salting pork. Delicate fingers that ache at night from the hours you spend sewing socks and clothes for everyone on this plantation." He thanked Wainwright for his research, and briefly wondered if the ghost were entertaining him back at his house.

"My father's slaves help with that."

"I know, but you can't deny you do most of the domestic chores without their help. We don't have that many slaves in the household to do all the mandatory labor. Most of them have been engaged with the harvest work, and you've been busy putting up foodstuffs in the pantry without them. You've complained so often to me in your letters about it, that you cannot contradict your story now."

She started to cry. Oh, Lord, thought Stephen, don't let her cry again.

"The darkness comes over me sometimes," she said, as tears rolled down her cheeks. Her voice was weak. The fire was gone. "I feel so sad all the time. I think I would like to die rather than go on. I've lost all hope of happiness."

"Don't ever feel that way," he said, not wanting to mention the fact that she had artfully sidestepped his question. "I'm never going to leave you. We're going to have a life together. It'll work, you'll see. Things will be happier, I swear."

"Yeow," cried Sam, as he slipped off his horse.

Stephen thought, "They told me that they knew how to do everything in the past lifetimes, so why doesn't he know how to ride that silly horse?"

"Are you all right, cousin?" he said.

"Fine, fine," Sam said in an unconvincing tone, while trying to put himself back onto the saddle. Thankfully the poor horse remained still and waited for him.

"Will he be all right?" she asked. Then when Sam was back on his horse and smiling again she said, "Why did you suddenly decide to change your mind about moving into town for the season? You always said that it was a waste of time and money when we had a perfectly good home here."

"But that was...ah...before I went to France and realized how lonely you must be with no one but the servants to talk to. You miss Melinda. She's your one good friend."

"She introduced me to Chris. I began enjoying the theater. It's such a joy to go there. The lights of the beautiful homes. The after-theater parties and the conversation. I've been educated, as have you and my brother, and conversation here rotates around food, giving birth, and sickness. I become bored. Melinda and Chris are interesting and funny. What else can I do for entertainment? I have only a few books to read. Melinda gives me her old ones."

"What sort of books has she given you?" he said, having no idea why he asked the question.

"Books about romance—love."

"You like that sort of thing?"

"Not really, but it's all I have, and I'll read anything I can get my hands on," she said.

He thought of the library. How many of those tomes were romance novels? How many would have been her private property? She had loved them, as an outlet for her despair, and he had heartlessly sold them as trash. How would he have known? So that was why the journal had been buried in with the books. They had *all* been hers. Now they sat in an antique store on Royal Street in New Orleans—and he wanted them all back now.

He stopped talking and took a moment to view the grounds. It was a huge plantation, stretching hundreds of acres to the south. It would take over fifty workers just to cut and gather the cane, and, no doubt, another fifty to process it. The grass was bright green and there were small, yellow flowers, possibly buttercups, covering the grass. It would be snowing in Chicago right now, but here, on River Road, it seemed like spring.

"Do you mind the holiday festivities?" he said to her, after a reflective moment. "You seemed a bit put-out about it when first I mentioned it."

"I was shocked that's all. It was so unlike you to suggest it. Our families always made such a grand time of Christmas, but since your parent's death, you haven't been interested in celebrations. You aren't usually home for Christmas, and when you are, we never give gifts or entertain."

Stephen heaved a sigh. "You're a real charmer, Emile," he said to his alter ego. "No wonder you've had such trouble with your wife. I'd escape to town too."

"What do you do on Christmas, mon cher, without me?" he said. He could actually feel the pain in her heart.

She hesitated and then fought the resurfacing tears. "I won't go to my brother's for it's too sad to see Ernestine and her brood all making merry, and me feeling like an impotent, old-maid aunt as they open their gifts. They always make sure I have a gift, but I can't help feeling it's something Ernestine doesn't want and has wrapped in linen so that I'll have a present to open. Last year it was a brooch which I've never worn."

She paused before going on. "Perhaps, I should wear it though. It was my only gift last year. I keep it in my jewelry box and look at it from time to time. It *is* rather pretty. A blue stone at the center of a circle of silver with odd writing engraved around it. I'm not sure what the words say, but she meant well in giving it to me. She wants me to visit more and talk with her, but..." She took a moment to ease the heaviness in her heart before saying, "Most of the time I stay at home, read from the

Bible to the servants, and then go to my room and cry. It's lonely without you on any given day, but your absence is especially felt on Christmas. There are no children." Her right hand covered her eyes in one rapid movement.

He didn't know what to say to her. Emile didn't appear to be the type to go to France and leave his wife unless it was something important. He could bet the man was at least loyal to his love. He thought he could feel a deep sadness inside their shared egos.

"You know it was business—for our benefit."

"I know," she said, "but I wish this place would burn to the ground, and the sugar cane plants rot in the dirt." Her voice did not hide her bitterness.

"Don't even think such a thing."

"I'd rather live in a shack than live alone another day."

Stephen felt tears welling in his eyes. Her passion, tenderness, loss, and enmity were incredible. How could he not empathize?

"Do you want a family? Is that what you're missing?"

"We talked about that before you left. I told you how afraid I was. That hasn't changed."

"You're healthy, strong, active, nothing will happen."

"That's what they said to Tillie when she brought her baby into the world. I watched her bleed to death. I was just five. She was like a mother to me, and was the only mistress to our father, or so Jean-Pierre told me later."

"That doesn't mean it will happen to you. Dr. Gayerré is a fine physician, and I'll take you to him when it's your time—or bring him here. He would do that for us. No midwife, if that's what you want."

She mused, "I don't know. I'll think about it. I better ride back without you."

"I'll go back with you. Evan and I will study the books while you bake. I want all to be in readiness for our vacation. Plus, I want this to be the best Christmas you've ever had. I do have something special for you and so does Evan. And, it isn't a brooch."

She smiled suddenly. "Do you really mean that I may have new gowns?"

"You have your first fitting Saturday."

"The play is Friday. I suppose I'll wear the gold gown."

"Have you nothing else?"

"Why? It's from France. Don't you like it?" she said defensively.

"Yes, of course, it's lovely." She wanted him to think it cost a fortune, so why should he spoil her story. Especially since it would give away how much he knew.

"Wear whatever you wish," he said. "The woman who wears it is fairer than any gown ever made."

She looked at him, pursed her lips trying to hide her grin, and said nothing as they galloped back to the house.

Chapter Eighteen

After a hasty lunch, Sam and Stephen retired to the small business office by the kitchen and searched the papers in Emile's desk. The account books were orderly and neat which indicated that Emile was a thorough businessman. They read like a personal journal of the man's life. By checking over all the books in the desk, it appeared as if he'd followed in his father's footsteps. Emile had taken control of the business before his parent's death. He'd survived the hurricane, and the sinking ship, because he couldn't get away from the farm when they wanted to visit France. They'd retired from plantation work, leaving it to their son; unfortunately, they never had a chance to enjoy their freedom.

They had died during the harvest by the notation in the books. Their deaths were subtracted from the monthly sum by the way of Emile purchasing a tomb for them. There were adjustments made, also, after he inherited the entire plantation. It all belonged to Emile and Isabella. The two of them should have owned the richest plantation on River Road.

Emile's marriage was even indicated in the ledger. September 20, 1831. He and Isabella had been married seven years ago on this very plantation. He had given the priest a healthy donation to St. Louis's Cathedral for services rendered. There'd been a reception of sorts, and her dowry was mentioned. He'd received the twenty slaves as Isabella's inheritance upon her parents' deaths—which happened just two years later—and $20,000 as a dowry. Several pieces of furniture, the harpsichord, her own bedroom furniture, and some china also came with the beautiful Isabella. This was a rich dowry by any time period's standards.

"She was the only daughter, I'll bet. Jean-Pierre got the homestead and would have brought in some money when he married Ernestine. I sure hope Emile didn't marry her for the money, though it would have been tempting," mused Sam.

"According to the letters I read, he appeared to love her. He even asked her approval to 'woo' her. He was very anxious to make her his wife. And, he was established by that time, having concluded his studies in France."

"No doubt. His parents die a year before his suit is accepted, so he has more than most to offer. And here's this cute, little neighbor girl with a dowry like none other. He'd have it all if he could win her heart," said Sam.

"It must have taken some time to do that by the look of these dates. Wonder why she played hard to get? They weren't strangers. But for some reason, just after they're married, he starts making trips to France leaving her here all alone to manage their plantation. What's wrong?"

"He's not getting any."

Stephen looked at Sam in amazement.

"His wife isn't getting the job done in bed, and there are no heirs," Sam said, flipping to the final page and looking at the last column of numbers.

"Who do you suppose handled the accounts while Emile was out of town?" Stephen said.

"It had to be her."

"Why?" said Stephen.

"Almost $5,000 has been subtracted in only six months."

"You're kidding." Stephen had been reading the household itinerary. He came over to the table to look at the book.

Sam gave a low whistle. "I should think Emile would be angry. Not a single notation next to any withdrawal." Sam stared at Stephen. "She runs his finances into a hole while he's away, gives him attitude when he's home, never sleeps with him, runs around with Anglos, gets a reputation as a wanton flirt, refuses to give him any children, and spends all their hard-earned money on—who knows what—leaving them practically broke. Not a very nice picture, Doc."

"The question is—why?"

"Did you talk to her about the money?" Sam said.

"Yep, and she used the same old story—she's had gowns to buy and domestic expenses. She was in a fit when I made any inquiry, cried buckets, tried to push me into a verbal battle that was off the topic, or sidestepped the issue entirely by bringing up her loneliness and abandonment. So far, she hasn't told me the truth."

"Oh, come on," he said, throwing the book down onto the desk in disgust. "She lives out here in no-man's-land. They don't even have mail order catalogs, QVC, or charge cards to max out. What's she hiding?"

"She's secretly buying her own plantation?" Stephen said.

"Funny," said Sam.

"She's backing a political candidate for president."

"A Creole? Get real."

Stephen said, "She's giving huge sums to the Sisters of Jambalaya, and the Lord has told her that her deeds will be rewarded in heaven provided she says nothing to anyone about it."

"In your weirdness, you may have hit upon something. The church. Or maybe someone she knows who's in trouble. She's covering for someone."

"Melinda? Chris?" Stephen put the list down on a chair and turned to study Sam's expression.

Sam said, "We don't know them very well yet. Melinda seems to have it all. And I mean that in every way a man can mean it. But Chris could use her money to back his plays, and she *is* defensive about him—almost guilt-tripping about it."

"Jean-Pierre seems to have *his* plantation under control, so he wouldn't be borrowing any money she'd be embarrassed about mentioning to her husband. You're right about Melinda. I think her husband would give her money for almost anything she wanted—trophy wife kinda thing. But the way she acts when we mention Chris. It must be him."

"So, he might be eliminated as a suspect if this is true. Why kill the golden goose? Do you think we'll get her to agree to go to that dinner at her brother's? It might help if we could meet everyone she knows all at once. Watch her reactions to everyone and visa versa."

"Everyone she knows except for Chris, who we'll meet this Friday. Wonder if his play is worth $5,000?"

"We'll soon find out. Tomorrow is Christmas Eve, don't forget. Not trying to press the matter, Doc, but you better have her in the master bedroom by that time."

"My pleasure. I found out why the lady is cold. She's frightened of childbirth. I'll have to be careful with her. Don't want to rush her. I won't ask her for something she doesn't want to give, but there's nothing wrong with sleeping together."

"I told you, you weren't going to get laid," Sam said.

"Oh that will happen in time. I'm in no hurry."

"Like hell you're not. You have three months. Please to remember, Doctorsan."

Stephen smiled wickedly and said, "How's your butt, Mr. Time- Traveling Man?"

"I won't be sitting for some time, thank you." He grinned.

"So, who checks her room, you or me?"

Sam put the books back in the desk. "Me. You get her into your bed Christmas Eve, and I'll read the famous diary and look for tiny vials."

"You won't hold anything back, will you?"

"Can't. You're my partner. The whole truth and nothing but the truth."

"I'd love to see what those rotting pages said, but I think I'd lose it if she's told Dear Diary about another man."

"That's why I'm here. By the way, if she's telling you the truth about being frightened about childbirth, which makes a lot of sense given the time period, it does prove one other little detail."

"Which is?"

"She isn't sleeping with anyone *else* either."

Stephen smiled.

Stephen watched as Isabella, Nora, Anna, and the others worked like driven demons to get everything prepared for the holiday. There seemed little class distinction in the cookhouse.

163

Nora would mumble to Isabella that she might want to use more cinnamon in the pudding, and Isabella would mention that the cornbread didn't look ready to take from the hearth oven. Anna would comment that the fire wasn't hot enough for tonight's stew. Then she would order one of the boys to fetch more wood.

There didn't seem to be any bond between them though. Isabella was still the mistress of the house, and that fact was never forgotten by the servants. But 'their' plantation home was about to be viewed by a guest, and the 'community' at Durel Plantation was ready to show Dr. Gayerré their finest. He watched as Anna polished the silver, dusted the china, and wiped the crystal clean with a pride of ownership he wouldn't have expected. Unified yet separate. Womanly pride. Isabella made the best rice pudding, and Nora knew how to make the finest meats, desserts, custards, and muffins on River Road. Anna made the dining room shine until the crystal sparkled like diamonds.

Diamonds? Stephen had almost forgotten his gift for his wife. He took one of the linen napkins from the china closet and went to his room— the only place he could be himself. He took out his medical bag and inspected the items he'd brought with him. Her gift was there too. He didn't like the way the man had packaged the diamond necklace, so, he rewrapped it inside the white, linen cloth. He went to her sewing room and found some red, satin ribbon and tied it around the present. He put it back in the medical bag and under the bed for safekeeping.

It occurred to him that he'd not had time to inspect all Emile's personal items. The closet had coats, jackets, vests, pants, and shirts. The bureau drawer had linen nightshirts, cravats, and toiletries. On the top of the bureau, near the mirror, he discovered a small glove box that had escaped his view before. On first sight, it looked like a fake drawer designed for decoration purposes only. He opened it with the key that was already in the lock.

Whatever was in there was no big secret, but could be made secure if the key were taken and hidden elsewhere. He'd transferred into Emile's body at two in the morning. Emile would have probably been asleep, and the only one in his room, so he'd left it unlocked. The drawer held fine, kid-leather, white gloves and a variety of expensive-looking cravat pins, but further in the back of the drawer, was a small vial. Stephen took the odd-looking, green glass bottle with its tiny, cork top, opened it carefully, and sniffed at its contents. Then he placed his finger on the top of the bottle, tipped it gently, touched the liquid to his tongue, and spat it out quickly. It was arsenic.

Chapter Nineteen

They spent the evening in the usual way save that dinner was later than normal and a sampling of what was to come Christmas Day. Her rice pudding was sinfully delicious. Emile pressured him to eat huge quantities, and he did so trying hard not to think of the word 'cholesterol.' Isabella joined them in the library/parlor. She played and sang her melancholy songs. Sam finally yawned and said that he was tired and ready for bed. Then he whispered to Stephen, "With those songs, I'll wager she spent the money on the Sisters of Jambalaya, for sure."

Isabella moved towards her husband to give him her customary kiss when he grabbed her hand and said, "Isabella. I understand your fears, but..." He stood to make his point more emphatic by placing himself within inches of her face. "I want you to stay with me—in my bed—from now on."

"What?" she said, her eyebrows wrinkling with concern.

"You may use your room as much as you wish during the day, but I'd like you to sleep with me at night. I won't try to make love to you, if you don't wish it. But a husband has some rights, I should think, and this is certainly one of them."

"Just sleep—near you?"

"That's right."

"Mother and Father did not sleep together."

"That's the way they wished it, but it's not the way I want to live. I want you near me. I can't sleep without you."

"I will obey you in all things, Emile."

"Hmmm," thought Stephen. He watched her ascend the stairs. "Wonder what I said that was right?"

True to her word, she came to him after he knocked on her door that he was changed and ready. He opened the balcony door a little so that the cool night air could come through. The mockingbird was singing a much happier song than Isabella had learned.

She was dressed in a thin, white cotton nightgown with a ruffle top that buttoned all the way to her neck. Her hair was down and long enough to mark her waistline. Standing there like that, she resembled the ghost a bit. Her skin smelled as if she had bathed in roses. The rose scent she had worn even as a spirit. He took her in his arms and kissed her. He noticed that she'd rubbed some ointment onto her hands, and they looked much better and felt softer to the touch.

"Thank you for coming," he said.

She smiled. "You seem so different. What's come over you?"

He motioned that she should sit on the bed. "When I was away, I realized how much I missed you and my home. I transferred all of my business dealings to another man. He will represent me and write to me frequently. I'm trying to finalize my holdings in Paris. Whenever I travel, I can't help thinking, sometimes, about my parents and how they died. We had a bad storm one night at sea that I failed to mention to you. I thought about you, alone, waiting for me, and me not returning. You'd begged me to return to you. What if I never did? It made me realize how important our life is. I don't want to risk it again."

He sat next to her, and took her face in his hands as he had done the first morning at breakfast. "I know you have fears. So do I. I don't want to lose you, Isabella." He had a vision of the ghost next to his bed at home. "Oh, I never want you to leave me. Promise."

"I promise," she said softly.

"Then get under the covers, and we can hold each other until we fall asleep."

She did as he asked, and he held her so that her head fell gently onto his chest. He could feel her body close to him, and it encouraged his manhood to stiffen with excitement. No woman had ever made him hunger this much. Desire was a delicious ache fueled by months of fasting for his soul's sake. No women, he had told himself, until he was well, until the stress was gone, until his heart was healed. But this was Isabella, sweet vision of a man's erotic dream, and she was alive, close enough to take, and wrapping her small feet around his calves with no apparent idea of how she was affecting him.

The cotton nightgown couldn't cover the heat of her skin. Her breathing, soft and low, made the hair on his neck stand on end. He could feel her breasts-soft, round, full, malleable, next to his arm, and ready for his touch. He could feel her nipples grow hard; her hands touched the flat muscles of his stomach. He bent her head back so that he could kiss her. His legs automatically moved to separate hers, but he kept them from doing so.

His left arm arched around her body and moved so that her hips would relax against the mattress. Her hair smelled like fresh honeysuckle. Her body's rose scent was overpowering his judgment, for, what had been a simple fragrance before had now become intoxicating by her skin's heat. She had placed the cream all over her body. Why? If she didn't want to make love to him, why had she made herself ready for it? There was an added scent that even she could not mask with perfume. Her body, like his, was ready for love's natural course. Her lips parted. She closed her eyes. He kissed her again.

"Do you want me?" he said.

"I don't know. I'm frightened. You promised—just sleep."

"Yes, just sleep."

"*Take her now, you fool.*"

He should have guessed that Emile would interfere.

"When she asks for it," he whispered.

"What did you say?"

"I said that I would only make love to you," he said, tasting her neck with the tip of his tongue and running it up and down seductively until she giggled, "when you ask for it."

Her hand touched the muscles of his thigh, gently letting it trail upwards. "You seem so much *stronger* than you did before your trip to France."

His manhood reacted in accordance with her touch, and he was wondering how on earth he was going to force it to behave. His lips went dry, and his tongue felt thick and heavy in his mouth.

"Have you any idea how much I want you right now? Please. If you insist on celibacy...I really must protest."

"You want me?" She said it as if she were shocked by his comment.

"Yes. I do. With all my body, heart, and mind. I want to make love to you all night long and be too weary to wake in the morning."

"Emile," she said, removing her hand.

He took her in his arms and pulled her body under his.

"You wouldn't," she said.

"*Take her—for the both of us—for the love of God—if you are a man.*"

"Not unless you ask for it."

His right hand went beneath her gown and touched her left breast. He squeezed its nipple until she moaned. Her mouth went wide in that moment, and his tongue lanced her lips. They were full, fleshy, and swollen. He bit the lower one to make his point, as he squeezed with his hand again.

"Not until you tell me you *want* me," he said.

His left hand tugged at her nightgown's hem, pulling it up towards her hips. His hand parted her legs like a knife, and then turned the movement into a smooth, soft, soothing, rhythmic massage. She relaxed. He took her hand and made it touch his manhood. In the sliver of moonlight that peeked through the white lace curtains, he could see her eyes widen. And when they did, he pushed her legs apart with just one hand. He moved his fingers into her satiny skin, and she closed her eyes. She was slowly submitting to her own passion.

His jaw was fixed, his lips tight, his intent callous, his position perfect. Inside his head he was thinking, "Why not? It will be a perfect remedy for my stress-filled id. I've come a long way, spent a lot of money, and I should not be denied anything I wish. Certainly not her."

"I'm afraid," she said. "This is so different from the other times, Emile."

"Is it?" How would he know?

She kissed him. Her lips were fire. Her flame matched his. They were the same. She wiggled and squirmed so close to his swollen manhood that it was all he could do to keep from ripping the nightgown from her —that beautiful, luscious body of hers—and piercing the wet heat of her womanhood until *he* was satisfied. Her fingers took his manhood in her hands and touched it so gently that he thought he would explode. Then she unbuttoned the bodice of her nightgown, pulled it over her head, cuddled next to him, placed his hardness on her thigh, and stroked it with her fingers.

He refused to stop touching her even though she was making it difficult by lying on her side. She cried out in ecstasy, and her body arched and then went limp. Her hand stopped moving against his swollen manhood. The sound was hungry, healthy, and long overdo. But she still hadn't said the words, and he had promised, though that promise might have been lost with their first embrace and was a moot issue now.

He took her breasts in his hands and kissed, fondled, and tasted the skin of each one, then his tongue continued down her stomach. He held her tightly against his body until tears fell from his eyes. This was his vision in the night. A real woman—not a ghost—not a dream. Warm skin, sweet lips, her breath against his neck, her words whispered softly into his ear—alive. He'd traveled through time to be with her. "I want you so much. I love you so much."

"What did you say?"

"I said I *love* you. I have since we were children. I will forever. Nothing will change that."

She cried. "I've waited seven years for you to say those words to me again. The way you used to before your business meant more to you than I do." She looked into his eyes and smiled. "I want you. I do. I'm just afraid of so many things."

The way she said the phrase made him think that she meant more than being afraid of giving birth to an heir. He stopped every movement. "Like what?" he said.

"I don't want to talk about it."

"We must have no secrets between us, mon cher. You can tell me anything. I'm your husband."

"I can't. Please, just hold me."

"I want to make love to you. How can I if you're keeping things from me? I can satisfy you sexually in many ways, but I'd sooner make love to you. Intimate, heartfelt, passionate love. It's been a long time since I, we, well, France and all."

"Yes, I understand. I want to make love to you too. You seem, well, more loving and tender tonight. Maybe the help from your cousin has eased your burdens."

"Are you hiding something from me?"

She took his hand and placed it in the soft space between

her legs, that niche that had given her so much pleasure only minutes before. "Don't talk now. We'll have time to talk later." She removed her hand and ran it gently down his cheek. What a way to change the subject!

"Emile," she said, smiling up at him as she gazed into his eyes. "It is good to have you home."

He moved on top of her and slipped into her body. "Talk all you want to later, Stephen," he told himself, "but *not* now."

The moonlight danced across the bedroom; its brightness streaming through the lacy curtains and piercing the night's shadows. Her body glistened in its silver radiance. He stared at her face with his every move. He had no intention of missing anything she did. At first, he was so anxious that he almost exploded too rapidly, so he focused on what he wanted to accomplish, changed his pace to a slow-rocking gesticulation of his hips, and watched her face. She closed her eyes, parted her lips, tilted her head backwards on the pillow, and exposed her neck for his caress. He kissed her and let his tongue slide down her neck, feeling her quickening pulse on his lips. Life. Heat.

He moved her legs wide apart with his feet. Every part of his body was alive and tingling with excitement. The sensation was beyond reality, beyond fantasy. Isabella's body undulated beneath his. Her hips tried to move with his rhythm—tried to reach up to meet his. Her skin's perfume became increasingly erotic. Her mouth was open; her lips moist and luscious. He could feel the perspiration running from her breasts across her stomach, and he could feel his own on his back. The cool air from the open door touched and aroused his flesh. Adding to the sensuality of a delicious Southern breeze, her long, dark hair became a third party in their embrace, as it randomly tickled their arms and thighs.

"All night, cher."

"No," she said, but instead of a denial, it was more the cry of a tiny animal begging for affection.

"Yes," he said. "I'm going to eat you alive until there is nothing left of you." He bit her neck passionately, and she laughed.

She opened her eyes. "I wasn't aware—of—" She closed them.

"What?"

"How hungry I was!" She moved him over to his side. "What do you want?"

"To look at you, to touch you, to smell your skin, to trace the muscles here." She moved her fingers across his arms and stomach. Then her hand reached around his neck, and she pulled his face towards her lips. She kissed him with such intensity, he could barely catch his breath. Her body was wet; her skin glowed in the moonlight.

"Lie down," he said.

She complied. He moved his body inside hers again, rocked slowly, then with force, until she cried out again with a spasm of pleasure. He found his own delight was a blend of sexual satisfaction as well as emotional joy.

His mind cleared until only she remained there—other problems flew from his thoughts. She took hold of his heart. Those big ovals of brown sadness, underneath those long, dark lashes, were looking at him with so much trust, just as they had in this very bedroom in 1998. He wouldn't let her down. She'd wedged herself into the center of his soul. Nothing else mattered but Isabella. Not home, not family or friends, not the hospital, not Sam, nothing. Logic was gone. Rational thought, a joke. Only the two of them existed on the earth. Together for all eternity. From one lifetime to another. Past death. "I'm going to make it. She's just what I need—have needed—for so long. Her fire can heal me," he thought to himself as he collapsed by her side.

"Are you all right?" she said.

"Yes. And you?"

She grinned. "More than all right. It's funny." She curled beside his body, cuddled into his arms, and put hers around his chest. "I mean this with all due respect, mon mari," she whispered sweetly, "but if I didn't know better, I could swear I'd just made love to a total stranger."

He squeezed his eyelids shut, grimaced, and, so that he wouldn't laugh, pressed his lips tightly together. He kissed her on her forehead. "You ain't seen nothing yet," he said to himself.

Chapter Twenty

It was Christmas Eve, and daylight brightened the master's bedroom. Isabella awakened beside him. He wasn't fully awake, but he could tell she was tossing and turning near him. She was doing everything in her power to awaken her husband short of calling to him by name. She hummed, whistled softly, stretched, yawned, then rose and walked to the balcony. Stephen rolled over, realized where he was, what had happened last night, and saw her leaning on the balcony railing. He tossed aside the bed quilt and sheets, threw on his robe, and joined her. He came up behind her and folded her into his arms. Together they watched the sun rise over the old, oak trees. She turned in his arms and looked up into his face. She smiled and then stood on her toes to kiss his lips. He was in heaven. His dream finally coming true. The mockingbird sang a love song from his branch. Isabella heard him and sang a soft, little song for him to repeat.

"What's that melody?" Stephen asked.

She regarded his expression. "A tune I learned from Tillie when I was very small, before she died." She sang: "When we do meet again, when we do meet again, when we do meet again, t'will be no more to part." She smiled at him. "Brother Billy, fare you well, Brother Billy, fare you well, We'll sing hallelujah, when we do meet again."

"When we do meet again," he sang after her.

She laughed. "That's right. Now who's the mockingbird?"

"Are you hungry?"

"Yes," she said, putting her arms around him and resting her head on his chest, "for you."

"That can be arranged." He scooped her into his arms, walked back into the room, and tossed her body onto the bed. She giggled like a little girl.

"You wouldn't."

"Eat you alive, mon petite croissant? Mais oui."

She laughed. "I have a household to run."

"I don't have a damn thing to do today...except ravage my wife."

"But I do."

"I am the master of this house and you are my wife, which means what I say counts, and you have to do everything I want you to do." He had to admit that he liked the sound of that last statement.

She played with the curl at the back of his head. "Do you want food on the table when Dr. Gayerré arrives tonight? Because if you do, I have to do my chores. We've been baking for two days in between cooking our everyday meals. There is so much to be done today."

He sighed and rolled on his back. "Very well. I guess I can wait until tonight."

She sat on the edge of the bed and said, "Haven't you had enough?"

He pulled her to his body and crushed her with a rough embrace. "I'll never get enough of you."

She touched his cheek with her index finger. "Emile." She looked as if she were about to cry. "I..."

"What?"

She moved away from him and stood up suddenly. "Nothing." She hurried into her room. He stayed on his bed to enjoy the moment and ponder her odd behavior. The mockingbird sang her song back to her, even though she wasn't there to hear it.

"That's it, Mr. Bird, sing your heart out," he said aloud. "I want to sing too: 'Ain't to proud to beg, Isabella,' " he sang softly and in a slow, smooth melody uncharacteristic of the real number. His eyes were rimmed with tears. "Please don't leave me now." He didn't sing the last part, just spoke the words. "Oh, how I love you, mon cher. How happy you've made me!"

They sat at the big table to have breakfast together, and Stephen couldn't resist kissing Isabella's cheek in front of Sam, just so that she would blush and show the look of love on her face. Glowing. Bright. Happy.

Sam coughed and said, "Dr. Gayerré is coming tonight, n'est ce pas?"

"Oui," said Isabella. "To travel on Christmas Day would be too dismal. I have to rush out to the cookhouse to see to tonight's meal. But, if you would like to ride later, and my sewing is done, I'd love to join you."

"I will anxiously await that trip," said Sam.

She blushed, curtsied, and departed.

"All things went well, I assume?" Sam said.

"Better than I could have hoped. Oh, Sam, I love her so much."

"Then I'm happy for the both of you. Since your mind is elsewhere, I'll hunt for clues."

"I'm not that bad, am I? I can still think."

"Things have changed. Your mind is elsewhere. On a long awaited honeymoon. It's a good thing I'm here. How did Emile react to the whole thing last night?"

"He tried to tell me how to handle her, how to force his will on her, but I just ignored him."

"Excellent. Keep doing that. Oh, and by the way, something occurred to me this morning. Do you know how to dance?"

"A little. Yes, I see. The ball at Jean-Pierre's? I've had so many things on my mind, but the thought that Emile was tutored in music, art, and *dance* has made me wonder exactly how I'm going to pull this one off."

Sam held up his index finger to help him make his point. He looked so much like an Evan Durel at that moment that it was difficult for Stephen to think of him as Sam Cooper. "This may surprise you, but on one of my trips years before I joined the company, I did a general transfer as a professional dancer in Spain. My partner was a hot-blooded Spanish woman, and—oh baby—did I learn to dance. Latin. Tango." He closed his eyes, apparently savoring the memory of the lady.

"Well, I know how to do a basic waltz—nothing fancy."

"I'll make you a deal. I'll show you some tricky dance steps, if you'll show me the way to stay on my horse."

"Deal."

During the morning, they waltzed secretly in the library. They promised to continue rehearsing every day even after they moved into town. Just before lunch, Stephen gave Sam riding lessons. They rode inside the huge stable so that no one noticed what they were doing. A scowl from Stephen sent anyone curious about their activities rushing for cover.

Some of the domestic slaves kept busy with cooking and the general housekeeping for the Christmas meal, while others packed for the move to New Orleans. The field hands ran errands for the skilled laborers who were building the cabins and the screens.

Sam and Stephen had plenty of time to talk and enjoy their second full day on Durel Plantation. Isabella came to the courtyard for the afternoon ride, and this time all three enjoyed their promenade around the plantation.

The entire staff of excited servants greeted Dr. Gayerré when he entered the house late in the afternoon. He told stories at dinner that made Isabella laugh. They weren't particularly amusing tales which made it all the more obvious how much she needed this social atmosphere. The men went to the library for brandy and cigars after their meal, and Isabella made another trip to the cookhouse, fed the slaves for the evening, and then went to bed.

"Have I missed something or has the mood in this house changed considerably?" said Dr. Gayerré, while pouring himself a snifter of brandy.

"Is it so?" Stephen asked, slicing the tip from his cigar.

Sam smiled. "Must be *my* presence."

Gayerré laughed. "Undoubtedly. I think that I should tell you that, after we spoke December first, I did a little investigating on my own. I hope you don't mind. I didn't want to mention anything to you until I had evidence to corroborate my story."

Stephen smiled and gave a good-humored wink at Sam. "Not at all. What have you learned?"

"That Isabella may have many secrets, but her reputation has been unjustly tainted by her association with Melinda Chabonnais and that Anglo actor."

"Unjustly tainted? I see. Guilt by association."

"Precisely. Are you attending the grand opening of his play Friday? Half of New Orleans will be there. That Fairchild fellow has put a great deal of money into this play of his," said the good doctor.

"Christopher Fairchild is a good friend of Isabella's, so naturally we'll attend. I wonder if he's really as good as she says he is."

"Supposedly." He sat in one of the more comfortable leather chairs and stared at Stephen for some time before saying, "Why do you allow her to be friends with an unmarried male actor? I thought you were upset with her friendships with other men."

How could he answer when he had no idea what Emile had said to this man that evening? "Sometimes, Isabella stays at Melinda's home when I'm away. She became friends with Fairchild through her. Apparently, the relationship has been good therapy for her chronic melancholy, even if it has proven somewhat scandalous. She's told me about her meetings with the two. She hides nothing about their relationship from me. This leads me to believe that there's nothing wrong with their friendship. I know that it isn't proper behavior for a married Creole lady, and mistress of a plantation, but under the circumstances, and considering the nature and personality of my wife, I see nothing wrong with it—now. I think this town is too full of wagging tongues who have nothing better to do in a day but discuss the life of a neighbor. Bored aristocrats, no doubt jealous of Isabella's beauty, intelligence, compassionate nature, and fire."

"Are you sure you've had no blow to the head recently?" Then he laughed off the comment. "What a change, Emile! What has happened between you and Isabella? I am beside myself with joy at this miracle. And am I glad to hear you speak so highly of the woman who was prohecied to be a handful on the day of her birth."

He laughed at some private memory before continuing. "The gossips have much to say about Chris and Melinda though. They say he's flattering Melinda because he wants both her and her husband's money. Her husband is on his deathbed. I'm his physician and find myself perplexed by his malaise. He's about my age, not much older, and I have no idea how to diagnose his condition."

Stephen felt the professional urge to quiz him on the subject, commiserate on the patient's symptoms, and help this colleague cure the man. "How so?" he said.

"He has nothing wrong with him. Not as far as I can see anyway. He complains of a stomach ailment, has diarrhea, and vomits for an hour or so; then he's fine and can eat whatever he wishes. He's himself for a few days, maybe weeks, and then falls ill again. It isn't Bronze John."

Stephen wanted to ask for a battery of tests to be run beginning with some blood work, but he couldn't. Emile Durel wasn't a doctor, so Stephen did nothing but shake his head remorsefully.

The doctor continued. "Anyway, she's a beauty. Melinda that is. All men have eyes for her. One poor actor shan't win her heart. How did Isabella ever become friends with her?"

He looked towards the ceiling for some sort of a clue or sign as to how to answer the question. This would be a grand time for Emile to respond for him—but there was no help. "Childhood, I guess."

"Has Melinda chosen a second husband then?" questioned Sam eagerly.

"Rumor has it that she can't wait for her husband to leave this earth because she's heated over some fair-haired Yankee. Wants the money and the new man. The thought of her running two Creole plantations with an Anglo husband is the talk of the town. You know she's done virtually nothing with her parent's plantation. But the story is that the Yank doesn't want her. I don't know who he is. Poor Fairchild is getting nowhere. Friendship only. Can't imagine Jean-Pierre not in a boil over his sister's all-to-public relationship with these two Americans."

Sam interrupted Gayerré's thoughts. "I find Melinda quite attractive," he said.

"Very well, bachelor, toss your hat in the ring and see what happens. But watch yourself. She's a demon in feminine form, if you know what I mean—honey to the eye, vinegar to the heart."

"Then Christopher Fairchild is in *love* with Melinda?"

Gayerré studied the dying tip of his cigar. Sam relit it for the old man with a piece of kindling from the fire. Stephen poured his guest more brandy. "That's what I've heard."

Stephen felt a huge boulder rise from his shoulders. If

all that the doctor heard was correct, then Isabella was, indeed, Fairchild's friend—period. Chris after Melinda, Melinda after someone else, and Isabella just along for the excitement.

"Isabella looks stunning," said Dr. Gayerré so quickly that Sam and Stephen were simultaneously pulled from their thoughts.

"Yes, she's happy about our leaving for the season. We're moving to town the day after Christmas. Staying at the St. Louis Hotel. I think I'll look for a house."

"Really. Well, that's excellent. Good for you. Now you can come and visit me sometime."

"Anytime. Have you been invited to the Devieux ball in January?"

"But, of course Jean Pierre wouldn't think of leaving me out since I've helped deliver both of his children and watched over his mother and father through their final hours. You weren't home when they died were you, Emile?"

"Ah, no. No, I wasn't," he said, hoping he was correct on this important issue.

"Isabella's heart was broken, you know. You away, Jean-Pierre expecting his first born, and her own parents wasting away before her eyes. And, of course, the threat that anyone in the household—including an expectant Ernestine—might catch the disease. As a matter of fact, it was the first time I ever saw Jean-Pierre overwhelmed with any emotion besides greed. I know he's your brother-in-law, but I can't say as how I like him much. Sorry."

"Quite all right. There are times when I feel as you do on the subject."

Dr. Gayerré laughed. "Can't choose your relatives, eh?"

Stephen glanced towards Sam who was listening intently to everything the man had to say.

"I'm afraid it's been a long day for me, and I must turn in for the night, if you'll both oblige me," said Stephen.

"Quite. I'll stay up with your cousin."

Sam took the hint. "Actually, I was heading to bed myself."

"Well, well, I guess Christmas Day will start early for all of us."

They said good night and went upstairs. The doctor was to

stay in Isabella's room.

Stephen crept into their bedroom hoping not to awaken his wife, tiptoed over to the bed, and kissed her on the cheek. She was awake.

"Oh, Emile, I feel awful."

Stephen was instantly alert. December twenty-fifth was only an hour away. "What's wrong?"

"I feel sick to my stomach." Her body was wet with perspiration, and she had been vomiting in his white porcelain wash basin. Why hadn't she summoned someone? He examined the discharge—noted the color. Poison. There was no time to waste. He picked her up in his arms and hurried down the stairway and out to the cookhouse. The slaves woke to his anguished cries for help and so did Sam and Dr. Gayerré.

"How can you be so sure it's not a little dinner discomfort?" asked Gayerré.

"I'm not taking any chances. Get me some milk, Nora, cream." It was all that he had to use on an unknown poison. It would have to do. Nora ran to the large, covered pit where there was still some cream left from their evening coffee. He poured it into Isabella's mouth. She sputtered and coughed, then wretched up the poison.

"Her pulse is weak. She didn't cry for help, but she's vomited in the basin in our room. It must have just come over her in the last few minutes."

"What could it have been? Dear God," said Gayerré. "Get me some laudanum from the pantry, Nora."

Stephen stopped her with his voice. "No, I don't have the keys with me, and I want her to vomit up whatever she ate or drank that made her sick. Evan, assist me."

Sam and Stephen held her in their arms and lifted her up so that she would be awake and nauseous enough to vomit, or in some other way, purge her body of the poison. It was life or death for her now, and he could no longer pretend he didn't know what to do when standing next to the antique physician.

Her gown was wet, she was shivering, so Stephen ordered her robe to be brought. Anna ran to fetch it.

"Every minute counts now, Evan."

"Tell me what to do," whispered Sam.

He confided to Sam, "Can't pump her stomach, but we'll

180

have to get the poison out of her before it destroys any organs or gets into her blood system." Then he said in a louder voice, "Water, Nora. We need milk, cream, *water.* And *sugar.* Something that I think we should have plenty of."

Isabella wretched again, moaned weakly, and collapsed in their arms.

"Good girl. Keep that up and your stomach won't be sick anymore."

"Emile, you didn't..." said Gayerré, touching Stephen's arm.

"How could you even think it? But she might have swallowed something harmful...by accident."

She fell to the ground, and the two men lifted her again. "Let's get her upstairs." He and Sam helped her on with her robe and up to the master bedroom. She felt like a limp, rag doll in their arms.

"December 25. My God," Sam said.

"I know. I'll stay up with her tonight."

"We all will."

Hours dragged by, but the three men refused to leave her side as she slept. She'd awaken once in awhile, vomit, sweat, and sleep. Stephen sponged her body with a wet cloth. When she was conscious, he mixed warm water and sugar in a cup and managed to get it down her throat. Eventually her pulse became normal, and the fever seemed to subside. She looked at the three men beside her bed and gave them a weak smile.

"What's wrong with all of you?" she said.

"You were sick, mon cher," Stephen said, as he gently pulled her hair from her face. "We've been up all night helping you. We were very frightened. How do you feel?"

"Hungry. May I have some bread?"

He called to Anna who ran for Nora. He touched her cheek with his hand. "I thought I'd lost you."

"Was I that bad?"

"Let's just say that you'll be on a very plain diet tomorrow."

"You amaze me, Emile. Where did you learn to treat this stomach condition of hers?" said Gayerré.

Stephen looked at Sam, who shrugged his shoulders sheepishly. "One of the men I do business with in France...is a physician...such as yourself. One of our business associates became ill when we were dining out, and this is the method he used to save his life. I'll never forget it."

"Do tell. I'll have to remember this technique. Cream, is it?"

"Well," Stephen hesitated before answering because milk was not the antidote for all poisons, "milk or cream. Makes them vomit. They have to get it out of their system before any damage is done." He had no choice but to give his answer based on Emile Durel's limited education on the subject.

"Hmmph, well, I'll leave her to your capable care. I'm going to bed."

Sam left with the doctor. He and Isabella were finally alone in their bedroom.

"What did you have to eat? Did you drink anything?"

"You saw what I ate and drank. The same as you."

He held onto her tightly. "Isabella, please, stay close to me from now on. Don't leave my side. Hold me all night. I won't sleep until I know you're all right. All night. Hear me? I'm here."

She slept soundly the rest of the night, and when dawn broke through the clouds, Stephen and she were fast asleep in each other's arms.

No one wanted to rise in haste on that festive morning everyone had so anxiously anticipated. When Anna knocked tentatively on their door, he told her to let everyone sleep in but to tell Nora she could start preparing breakfast. He dressed quickly in just his shirt and pants, deciding to bathe after breakfast.

He took Isabella's keys, went to the pantry, ordered Nora to take what she needed for breakfast, locked the door again, and went back to their room. As he passed her, he told Anna to bring a pot of coffee with two cups to his room. Then he stood on the balcony alone and watched for the mockingbird while waiting for the coffee. Eventually the bird arrived and sang 'good morning' to him.

"Merry Christmas, little guy. Are you going to miss me when I go to town?"

The bird tilted his head to the side and sang again. He heard a knock on their door. It was Anna with the coffee. He opened the door and took the tray from her.

"Missy better?"

He smiled. "Yes, thank you for your help last night." He shut the door with his foot after taking the tray from her.

Isabella moaned, stretched, smiled, sat up, and vomited.

"That's my girl. Brought you something that's sure to make you feel worse and better all at the same time. Smell." He put the tray on one of the small, piecrust tables, and poured two cups of coffee. He took one over to her and waved the hot, steamy, chicory-filled coffee under her nose. She smiled again. He handed her the cup, and she sipped at it cautiously.

It occurred to him that he had changed history last night. Here it was eight o'clock, December 25, 1838, and Isabella Durel was alive. The death certificate would change. He was amazed that he'd altered history, and just stared at her, probably giving the impression that he'd never seen anyone drink hot coffee before.

"Why are you staring at me?" she queried.

"What happened last night frightened me. I'm amazed that you're still with us this morning. You didn't...drink anything...evil last night did you?"

"Of course not. I kept waiting for you to come to bed, but how you men talk on so! I packed a little, tried to find my Christmas gift, brushed my hair, changed into my prettiest nightgown for you, ran some of that rose cream you like so much over my hands and arms, mended a rip in the hem of my gold gown that I hadn't noticed before, and then gave up waiting and tried to sleep. Nothing out of the ordinary."

His eyes went instinctively to the place where he'd hidden his traveling bag, but it didn't seem to have been moved from under the bed.

A devilish grin crossed his face. "Tried to find your Christmas gift, did you? I thought you didn't want one?"

"Well...you said you were going to get me one anyway, so I peeked around to see whether I could find it." She sipped her coffee and looked so much like a lost orphan that he inwardly chuckled at her.

"Close your eyes," he said. She looked suspicious at

183

first, and then did as she was told. He took the cup of coffee out of her hands, and placed it on a nightstand before she spilled any of it. He took the gift from his bag and placed it in her hands. She opened her eyes when he gave her the order.

"What is it?" she said.

"One sure way to find out...open it."

She unraveled the red ribbon and folded back the linen as if it surrounded the crown jewels. It gratified him to see her cherish the present in such a manner. He was glad he hadn't listened to her that first morning.

She opened the velvet box, and her eyes went wide. "Oh, Emile, it's beautiful! It must have cost a fortune."

Stephen had a nasty flashback of Sam's comment that she might sell it the day after.

"Put it on." He helped her fasten it around her neck. The diamonds were of the finest quality, and they sparkled despite the dim light. The gold strands glistened against her skin. He found her hand mirror and let her gaze upon her reflection. "Look at yourself."

Her eyes were rimmed with dark circles from her night of sickness. Her lips were dry and trembled a bit when she drank her coffee. Her pallor was 'ghostly,' and its paleness reminded him of the spirit who used to say 'good morning' to him in 1998. So far he'd witnessed a tempered wife having never seen the vulnerable sweetness of Isabella's soul—the woman he'd grown to love. Thank God they'd saved her. And mostly, thank God for Emile's alibi.

Now he knew unquestioningly that Emile Durel hadn't poisoned his wife on Christmas Eve. If he *had* thought about it, Stephen had changed his mind. He'd hadn't been given any cognitive clue that she was in trouble, nor had there been an emotional trigger for him to complete Emile's original plan. Emile had been unaware of the situation—silent. He could be eliminated as a suspect, and that thought eased Stephen's mind considerably.

"Come here, beautiful, I want to hold you."

She cuddled in his arms. "Do you like the necklace?" he asked.

"Yes, I shall wear it to breakfast, provided I'm allowed to eat, Doctor."

He was stunned by her reply. "Doctor?"

"You healed me last night, not Gayerré. You and Evan. And the other night...well...that was more splendid than a thousand trips to New Orleans all wrapped up in one." She began to cry against his nightshirt. "Oh, Emile, I was so sick last night. Don't let it happen again."

He held on to her and let her drain the emotional 'poison' out of her system. He kissed her forehead. Something magical was happening. Despite all that could possibly be foretold by Time Travelers Incorporated, even they didn't understand that an intimate bond might expose—without any clue as to why it might happen—a psychic revelation of another spirit from the future inside the physical body of the man from the past.

Isabella knew, but didn't understand why she knew, that this man was more than just her husband. She could have no possible understanding of time transference; but, she had called him 'Doctor' and she'd been right. A jest about the way he'd helped her, a cute retort, a new nickname, but correct nonetheless. Her husband was both planter and doctor, a passionate as well as a sensitive lover, and as aggressive as he was compassionate. Quite a combination considering the time period. This is what Isabella knew inside her heart even if the idea could never have entered her intellectual mind as a scientific possibility. It wasn't a scientific possibility. It was a metaphysical reality. It was supernatural, beyond comprehension, mystical, and—way cool.

"Some hot rice cereal, I think. With cream and sugar," he said.

"Am I strong enough to get up?"

He took her into his arms and carried her downstairs. "Probably not."

Sam and Dr. Gayerré were feasting on bacon, eggs, hot cakes, cornbread, and hot coffee. He worried that the smell of the food would make Isabella nauseous.

"Do you feel all right, cher?"

"Put me down on one of the couches, and I'll see if I can eat something."

A bowl of cereal was brought for her. They put some cream on the top of it, a little molasses to sweeten it. She took her spoon and gingerly ate some of the bland mixture.

"Slowly," he said.

Sam said, "Feeling better, cousin?"

She looked at Sam and licked the sugary spoon clean of the cereal. "I think so. I don't know yet."

"Nice baubles around your neck, cousin," he said. "When you are finished with the cereal, I have something for you too."

She placed the bowl on the floor, and said, "I'm finished." She saw Stephen's look. "Well, it...needs cooling."

Sam came over to her, reached into his inside vest pocket, and handed her the tiny package.

She opened the present hastily. "The earrings to match? How lovely!"

The two men helped her put them on.

"What do you think, Dr. Gayerré? Am I not the most beautiful lady wearing diamonds to breakfast?"

"You have no idea how happy I am to see you this day." He looked at Stephen. "Merry Christmas, dear."

"I must get up and see to the servants, or we shall have no meat for our Christmas dinner. Everything else is cooked, covered with linen cloth, and sitting in the pantry."

"It can wait. I think you'll have to take it easy today if you want to be healthy enough to travel tomorrow. Of course, if you aren't, we can wait a few days."

"But, then we'll miss Chris's play."

"I think, under the circumstances, your health is more important than his play. Eat your cereal; it's getting cold. I want to see if it stays down."

She nodded her head obediently, and Stephen took a plate and helped himself to the hot food on the sideboard.

"I can't begin to tell you how much it means to me to have somewhere to go on Christmas Day. Thank you for inviting me, Emile," said the doctor.

"It does my heart good to see a family of sorts in my home on a holiday. My wife and cousin—and our family friend. Merry Christmas."

"I have a small gift for Isabella too. Such a gracious hostess must have a reward." Gayerré took from his vest pocket a small box. "Here," he said, handing it to her, "something just for you.

Inside was an oval-shaped, gold locket.

"It's very pretty. Whose picture shall I have placed inside?" She looked at Stephen. "Mon mari, I think, and on the other side..."

"How about me?" said Sam.

"Of course." They all laughed. "I shall see to it immediately. If I can find portraits of both of you." Her strength weakened after breakfast, and she slept on the couch with a quilt draped over her while the men took walks and conversed.

About three in the afternoon, Dr. Gayerré went to his room to take a nap.

"Let's check on the servants and then discuss this new information," said Sam,

"Right."

They had their horses brought to them, and then rode far away from curious eyes.

"Merry Christmas, indeed," said Sam.

"I don't understand why we weren't alerted. I had no idea."

"Well, why would you? You knew *you* weren't going to kill her, and, originally, Emile was our prime suspect. Or Isabella herself, if she decided to kill herself."

Stephen said, "And any of those possibilities might have been present in the original scenario. But when we transferred, we changed all that. She even called me doctor this morning and made a cute comment that she felt she had made love to a total stranger the night before."

"Bet that made Emile real happy."

"He's been dormant ever since she and I made love. Not a word."

"Maybe he's compliant with the odd turn of events considering you helped him get what he probably wanted more than anything else in the world—to have sex with his wife."

"Could be. So, what went wrong?" He told Sam everything she had said about her activities before the incident.

"I suppose we shouldn't leave her alone even now."

"No, I should think not. And it's going to be hell when we get to New Orleans and have virtually no control over her comings and goings. I can't very well tell her that someone wants her dead. She'd want to know why, and I haven't the answer."

"Maybe it's something we've overlooked, or she thought too unimportant to mention to you."

"Well, she was very weak when I questioned her. I read that book on poisons and that helped me save her life, but I've no clue what she took. I do know that it couldn't have been a very large dose of whatever it was."

"How so?"

"Most poisons work within a half an hour and leave you weak for some time even if you are thorough enough in getting the poison out of the victim's body. I'm truthfully surprised she's with us. I wonder if we should postpone the trip for a few days. It might be too much for her. I should let her rest."

"You tell her you plan on missing Chris's play. I'll run for cover."

Stephen grinned. "Okay. We'll take a few of the domestic slaves and just the clothes and toiletries we need, then buy the rest when we get there. I've got to get her away from the attempted murder scene. Something tells me it'll help."

Sam stared at his reins for a few moments before saying, "Christmas 1838. I wonder if my brother made a big meal or just had turkey Lean Cuisine. We don't usually travel without each other around Christmas. I'll have to make it up to him by buying him something worth a small fortune. At least Isabella liked her gift."

"I was surprised. She was so excited. Like a little girl with a new doll."

"Man, I gotta tell you this," said Sam. "She's getting to me. There's something about her that just creeps right into your heart. Don't get me wrong; I've no intention of putting the moves on her, or anything like that, but it's spooky how she makes you feel."

"I know exactly what you mean. It's her spirit. There's something incredibly vulnerable beneath that tough Creole veneer. And once you catch a glimpse of it, it's hard to forget. She needs us now. We're the only ones who can find this murderer in time to save her life. One attempt thwarted. Will there be another? I have learned one thing, however, from being with her for two nights."

"Yes?"

"She's definitely hiding something she feels guilty about—can't quite confess. Unless I miss my bet, she's frightened about how I'll react to it. She can't bring herself to tell me even though I think she wants to."

"And you think the answer is in New Orleans?"

"It *has* to be."

"But nothing from New Orleans was here last night."

"The mystery can be answered there. Someone can send death to her from far away. Emile has realized his fears about his wife are ungrounded; that she's loyal to her vows, and unbelievably sexual when treated with an ounce of affection. He's just waiting to find out what we'll learn next, so that he can make his next move. I wouldn't want to be in his path, when he uncovers the answer."

"Do you think he has a nasty temper?"

"I didn't get a chance to tell you that I found arsenic in his glove drawer the other day. I didn't know how to handle the situation. It had to be his. But Emile could never hurt his wife."

Sam gave him a curious look.

"Just a gut feeling I have. I spoke with his spirit right before we time-traveled. He told me to save her. He wouldn't have done that if he'd been the murderer. It just has to be someone else."

"What manner of man is he?"

"I think he's strong, passionate, physical, aggressive, intelligent, devilish, aristocratic, and in a great deal of personal pain. I'm hoping he has a nicer side."

"Personal pain?" said Sam.

"The man's heartbroken. I can feel it here," he said, tapping his finger to his chest. "And the pain here," he said, tapping his finger to the spot on his head where he'd had the severe headache. "Because of this miracle, we're all healing."

"Something magical always happens, my friend."

"Let's get back to *our* girl before she needs her doctor again."

They returned to the house, gave their horses to the stable boy, wished 'Merry Christmas' to the worried slaves, and headed for the slumbering Isabella. She was still asleep on the fainting couch, so Stephen came up to her quietly and kissed her on the cheek. "You alright, mon cher?"

She opened her eyes and smiled. "I'm hungry for dinner. Is everything ready?"

"Absolument. I have to wake Dr. Gayerré. Do you want me to help you into your dress?"

"No, call to Anna and have her help me. You give orders to Nora and the others."

Anna came upon request, gave her mistress a worried look, and helped her up the stairs.

Isabella called back to him, "I won't be long. I want to wear the gold gown with my new jewelry. You change too. This is our first Christmas together since the year after we were married, and I want it to be special."

The slaves lit candles in all the rooms to add a religious touch to the holiday atmosphere. It did his heart good to see how beautiful his home appeared in this romantic glow. Stephen called to the house slaves who gathered around the table for a small Christian service to thank God for the gift of His Son's birth, and for taking care of Isabella when she was sick. Nora sang one stanza of a slave song which thanked God for his bounty. Dinner was served.

Isabella suggested that Nora and Anna serve the slaves their dinner since she was too weak to do so, and they told her that they'd be pleased to help her. She ate like a sparrow, judiciously tasting everything before trying to place it on her sick stomach. Dr. Gayerré was in rare form, discussing all the gossip from town, and carefully leaving out anything about Chris or Melinda.

When they'd finished Isabella's rice pudding dessert, they retired to the library where Isabella summoned the strength to play hymns on the harpsichord. The mood was as festive as it could be. They discussed their plans for the next day, and Dr. Gayerré told them that he'd be pleased to help them move to the hotel. His help would be unnecessary, but Stephen didn't have the heart to tell him that he thought the man might not be physically capable of helping in any way but to drive them crazy with his continuous repartee. Stephen told him that the three of them appreciated the offer, but that they could manage without burdening such a busy man.

Night closed with a reminder of the holiday, and the

meaning of God's love and goodness in saving Isabella's life. Stephen remembered the doctor's plea and Isabella's prayer. Obviously the Almighty's hand was on their lives, and this encouraged Stephen.

She wanted to wear her diamonds to bed. Stephen told her that they might cut her skin or keep her from sleeping, and that she needed to have a good night's sleep.

"Are you sure you're up for this move?" he asked.

"I want to go, so I'll make myself go. I can rest at the hotel. You know, even as excited as I am about this move, I think, maybe, I'll miss it here. Funny, isn't it? Can't wait to leave, and suddenly sorry to go."

"I think that's normal. Any time you get homesick, we'll come home."

She cuddled into his side. "You don't like this, do you? It isn't like you to want this social business."

"You and Evan want to go, and so it's my job to make you both happy."

She kissed him. "Am I too sick to make love?"

"That's up to you."

"Then make love to me tonight. Please."

She didn't have to ask a second time. He took her into his arms, whispered how much he loved her, and then took his time making long, slow love to his wife.

Chapter Twenty-One

Isabella did her best to prove herself fit to travel the next morning, and Dr. Gayerré helped somewhat. The two servants, Nora and Anna, needed to be shown what to take and how to pack all of it. The overseer had to be given the keys to the pantry so that the second-best cook could prepare food for the staff while they were gone. The boat was made ready for their trip. They took two men, Cicero and Nathan, to handle the river ride and move them by carriage to the St. Louis Hotel.

Isabella was excited and animated all the way down the Mississippi River. She pointed to areas that she fancied and showed them the various plantations on River Road, explaining in lengthy detail about the people who lived there. Stories that Emile would have heard a thousand times over but would have patiently listened too anyway. When they arrived at the mouth of the river, they had to restrain her lest she take to land before they'd docked.

Her skin was still very pale, and Stephen knew she was much sicker than she let on. Cicero called for a carriage, and they moved themselves and their baggage to the rig. Dr. Gayerré found a driver to take him home. He promised to call on them in a few days.

Stephen noted Nora's and Anna's excitement about being in town and seeing all the beautifully dressed ladies and gentlemen, as well as the prostitutes and sailors parading through the Place D'Armes.

"That woman has such a fit of feathers 'round her shoulders. Looks like a wild bird or something," said Nora in disgust. She was a roundish, stocky woman with a mind of her own and a powerful sense of humor. Anna, who was much younger, was slender and pretty in comparison with this woman who couldn't be more than thirty-years old but looked a great deal older.

"No homespun dress," Anna reported. "Not much of a dress at all. And such a color. *We'd* never wear something like that on the streets of a big city such as this one."

Isabella looked at Anna and then at Nora. "You can wear my gowns after Madame Gatou makes me new ones. Then you won't have to wear homespun either," said Isabella in a matter-of-fact manner.

"Ain't nothing wrong with our clothes," said Nora. "You cut them out, and we all sewed them good."

"I know, but I want you to have something nice to wear when you travel in town with me."

They passed a lady with a shocking bonnet so tall they all thought she might teeter over if the wind blew.

"That's *some* hat," said Nora. "Bows and ribbons all the way down her back. Lawd, have mercy. Some folks just have to show off, don't they?"

Sam laughed at Nora's butchered French phrases. "You want a hat like that, Nora?" he said to her.

She shook her head. "No cause to own something that big 'cept to go to church—or show off."

"Oh, we'll be going to church quite a bit now that we're near St. Louis's Cathedral. Father and Mother loved to go to service there. And I haven't been to confession for some time."

Sam shot a look at Stephen and grinned.

"This Sunday, we'll all go," she said, expecting no one to disagree.

Stephen went pale, and Sam cleared his throat. Neither was Catholic, nor did they know any of the procedures a good French Creole gentleman would have been taught.

"Church?" asked Sam.

"Don't you want to go with me?" she said, turning her head around to see his expression.

"I'm not much of a churchgoer. May I bow out of this one?"

Stephen gave him a facial expression that's meaning said it wasn't fair for Sam to leave his client stranded in a pew with no idea how to behave.

"Certainly not, *dear* cousin," said Stephen. "A family that prays together..."

"Besides, Jean-Pierre has our family's pew, and we can

all sit together: the children, Evan, Ernestine, and, of course, we'll take Anna and Nora."

"Been some time since I was in the house of the Lord," said Nora.

"Well, your soul is my responsibility, and one I take very seriously. So, if you both want hats to wear, we shall buy you hats. Not quite so high, Nora, but a nice bonnet just the same. Your head must be covered in the cathedral. And I insist on you wearing my dresses once I get my new clothes. We'll alter them to fit. We won't look like planters from the country then."

"I'm thinking of looking for a house," remarked Stephen, changing the subject. "We need a townhouse to live in during the season. Evan and I will start searching tomorrow. Would you like to come with us?"

"I'm still feeling the effects of my illness, and think I shall stay put until the performance Friday night," she said.

"Won't you, at least, let Melinda know you're in town? Maybe she can come and cheer you up at the hotel while we're gone," said Sam.

"But of course. I think I might just have to surprise dear Chris though. He won't know that I'm in town until after his performance. There are parties afterwards. Might we go?"

Stephen said, "If you feel up to it. Don't forget we have the fitting Saturday and next week we have Jean-Pierre's soirée."

"Ernestine will be by to welcome me to town, I'm sure. I must send a letter to my brother and let him know I'm here. He'll be so surprised."

"Remember your condition. I prefer you to be with me as often as you can manage—in the hotel room or anywhere else."

"Yes, I want to go all over this town with you...but..." she looked at her gloved hands and not into his eyes.

"What?"

"Won't I have some free time to be with Melinda and Chris?"

"I can understand your need to be with your friends, but I would like to get to know them first, and hope I might be included from time to time."

"It's just gossip and shopping," she said, trying to get

him to change his mind.

"Evan wants to get to know your friends too—especially Melinda. And if Chris is as good an actor as you say he is, I suppose I can, at least, have lunch with him."

She seemed surprised by his statement. "You'll meet him Friday night. I'll have to get more tickets."

"I'll send Anna to get them. You can handle that, can't you, Anna?"

"Yes, master," she said, but he could tell she was afraid to go alone.

"Oh, that's alright, Anna, you don't have to. Evan and I can manage the tickets tomorrow. You stay with your mistress and fetch her what she needs."

Nora said, "Ha! Can't have cooking like we have at home."

"You might be surprised," said Sam, turning to regard Isabella. "But until you're better, we'll have to eat lightly. Nothing spicy."

Stephen had a flash of inspiration. "You don't have to contact Jean-Pierre by letter. We've rented the rig for the day, so we might as well get unpacked, and take a trip over to see his family and wish them a Merry Christmas."

She thought it over before saying, "I think a visit is a splendid idea. I'll have Anna and Nora unpack for us. Then we'll visit. It'll be time for their midday meal, but I don't think they'll mind. No guest is ever turned away from dinner at the Devieux house. Traditional hospitality, always."

They took a suite of rooms at the St. Louis Hotel and paid for two weeks' rent. Bellhops took their luggage up the circular stairway much to the pleasure of their servants. Their rooms were lavishly decorated, and Isabella cooed with pleasure over every aspect of its finery.

Nathan joined them an hour later and informed them that the boat was safely docked and payment made so that it could remain there. Isabella changed into another gown, and then Cicero took them to Jean-Pierre's.

Stephen recognized the townhouse. He'd walked past it a few times on his shopping trips to Royal Street. It was opulent compared to other buildings nearby.

They were ushered into the home by a black man who recognized Isabella and whose gray hair precluded that he'd probably known her most of her life.

"Hello, Artemus. Will you tell my brother we've come for a visit?"

The butler grinned and hurried to find the family. Isabella took Nora and Anna into the parlor and settled herself comfortably by the fireplace.

Stephen nodded to Sam that they should do a little investigating. The room they were in had a retractable wooden doorway that separated it from the dining room. On the left side of the foyer was a room that appeared to be the master bedroom. There was a hallway that stretched from the foyer back to the end of the house, and a stairway Stephen thought would have led to more bedrooms. This placement of the master bedroom at the front of the house was very odd. The windows in this room were covered with shutters and little light came through. Behind this room was a lounge with a small fainting couch, a tall boudoir, and a small chair. The next room was a nursery. Beyond that was what appeared to be a bathroom with a tub, drains, and pretty, Dutch-blue tiles. Stephen wanted to move in right away. Sponge baths could never compare to a good soak in hot water.

They discovered the family sitting in wicker chairs on a stone patio enclosed by French doors. The butler had just relayed the message when the two men entered.

Jean-Pierre seemed elated to see him. "Emile, how good of you to visit." He gave him an enthusiastic handshake. "You're here just in time for dinner. Where's my sister?" When told she was in the parlor, he hurried out of the patio flanked by Ernestine and her two children.

The man seemed so different in this domestic setting compared to the way he had acted at the coffee shop. He was animated, and energetic and full of the passion of life his sister displayed so often. Jean-Pierre was every bit as handsome as his sister was beautiful. With the same oval face, long lashes, and big brown eyes, he would have been able to charm any woman. He was not as tall as Sam or Stephen and not as strongly built either. More the businessman than Emile, he didn't appear to have ever done any physical labor except ride his horse. Where Emile wore a healthy tan, Jean's complexion was rather pale.

Beige was the correct term for Ernestine's complexion.

The words fat and beige came to mind the moment you saw her. Her face was round and merry looking, but she wasn't ugly. Her nose was short, and her eyes were round and lacking spirit. There was pink in her cheeks, and her blue eyes could have twinkled if they'd been happy, or intelligent, but they weren't either. You couldn't compare her to Isabella. She was a different breed of woman altogether. She must have weighed 225 pounds. When she stood up to follow her husband, Stephen realized, for the first time, that she was pregnant.

Her fashion sense matched her dull, expressionless face. She couldn't sew like Isabella. The children were dressed in homespun with poorly woven fabric. This was in direct contradiction to Jean-Pierre's tailor-made clothes. Maybe, thought Stephen, he considered domestic clothing her responsibility, but for the public eye, and for formal wear, he had to have their clothes made because this woman had no idea how to do the complicated stitches required to make a suit or a ballgown.

Yet he had made a comment about his sister's gold gown being a rag. Apparently, he and his sister must be dressed like royalty, but Ernestine and her children must not be considered worthy of the same treatment. Or maybe he was just trying to be an irritating brother-in-law. Odd how you can learn so much about people and relationships by just observing their clothing, thought Stephen.

Jean-Pierre hugged Isabella, ordered her slaves to go to the kitchen and help his people make refreshments, and introduced his family to Sam. Then he ordered one of his slaves, the nanny, to take the children back to the patio. He and Ernestine sat in high-back chairs and offered their guests candy and cordials.

"So finally, you have decided to come to town for the season. This is marvelous. Ernestine has missed you so much, Isabella. You can gossip and shop together."

Stephen smiled inwardly, remembering Isabella's comments about Ernestine being obtuse.

"Oh," said Ernestine, "I'm sure I would be boring company for such a high-spirited, cultured sister-in-law, Jean."

Stephen regarded the woman with renewed respect.

"However," continued Ernestine, "if you would like to come to tea tomorrow, I shall have cakes made for us, and we can talk. I want to get your opinion on my son's education. He'll be ready for school soon. Should we find a good tutor or send him away for schooling elsewhere? I hate to see him leave home; he's so young. And our daughter will need to spend time with her aunt, of course. Surely Jean-Pierre has told you that I'm expecting another child in three weeks." She smiled, but her eyes welled with tears.

Jean-Pierre fidgeted as if he was uneasy about the fact that he'd never mentioned his wife's pregnancy to his sister or brother-in-law. "And what a Christmas present she'll be for you, Isabella, *if* it's a girl."

"Whatever can you mean?" said Isabella.

"If we are blessed with a son, he will, naturally, be my pride and joy, but if it's a girl, I'm giving her to you so that you might enjoy the comforts of motherhood. I mean, after seven years, what's a man to think? I cannot have you unhappy, sister. A woman needs a baby, and, heaven knows, I don't need the expense of another girl right now. Ernestine may have many more, I think, but you seem to fear the ordeal of childbirth. So, I have decided to make my dear sister as happy as her mother was with us. We're family. She'd be your niece, so now she'll be your daughter too. Someone has to look out for your well-being." He tried to soften the comment by smiling at his brother-in-law, but Stephen still wanted to punch him in that smug face of his.

"You can't mean it?" said Isabella, but she wasn't surprised either.

"I have told Ernestine how I feel on the subject, and she understands. Don't you, Ernestine?"

"Yes, of course, Jean-Pierre. I want you to be happy and fulfilled, my dear sister." Her eyes told a different story. "Do you have someone who can be a wet nurse for her?"

"I suppose..." said Isabella, trying in vain to think of something to say.

"Surely you can find one. You have over forty slaves. One of them must be 'knocked up.' You can't keep the dry wood near the flame without raising a spark."

"She'd be Devieux blood," said Ernestine. "I've even

sewn some clothes for her, and I have some hand-me-downs that you can use until you have time to make some."

Stephen said, "The offer is very kind, Jean-Pierre, but totally unnecessary. I shall start my own family when Isabella feels ready. If we choose not to, then that is our wish. Thank you, Ernestine, for being so generous, but truly, your sacrifice isn't necessary."

"Don't be ridiculous, Emile. Think of the hours of joy you might offer your wife with her own niece to raise. I understand your fears, Isabella. Tillie and all; it was horrid to watch. I'll never understand why mother didn't call for Dr. Gayerré. Tillie might have been saved, and heaven knows we could have used her. How she could cook and sew! This way, you won't have to go through the pains of labor, yet still enjoy the happiness only a child can give you."

Ernestine spoke. "I want you to have my little girl. Jean's offer is very generous." She said it as if she'd been tutored to say those exact words, but her heart was breaking. "You can take her when you go back to the plantation in late February. It isn't as if I'll never see her again, now, is it?"

This was more barbaric than anything Stephen could think of. It wasn't kindhearted. They weren't worried about Isabella's happiness. Jean-Pierre was making a business transaction that benefited *his* life only. It was obvious Ernestine didn't want to part with her child but had no options. She wasn't being afforded any more respect than one of Jean's slaves. Human life, to this man, was something to be bought and sold or given as gifts. A daughter was an added expense. There was a dowry to think about when she could marry, and he already had one girl to worry about on that score. Jean-Pierre was the head of his family and expected to be obeyed, but he was telling Emile what to do as well, and Emile and Stephen didn't like it one bit.

"*I don't want your child,*" said Emile. "*How dare you presume to tell my wife and I what to do about planning a family. I am insulted, sir, but since you are kin, I shall overlook your appalling lack of judgment and ethics. Come, Isabella, we shan't stay here a moment longer, nor shall we break bread in your brother's house.*"

Stephen said to himself, "Way to go, Emile!"

Ernestine's eyes opened wide, and Jean-Pierre looked as

if he had just swallowed hot coals. "I meant no disrespect; I was just being helpful."

"You were just trying to run all of our lives as you run your slaves'. You presume to tell your wife she must give up a child she has carried these nine months taking no notice of the grief in her eyes. You presume to tell my wife when and how she shall become a mother. And, what I find most alarming of all, you presume to tell me when I shall have an heir, when I shall become a father, what sex my child shall be, and how I shall raise your offspring for you. Anna, Nora, we are leaving. Get our hats."

Isabella was shocked, but a tiny smile brightened her countenance. The three women raced down the hallway. Sam followed, displaying the proper amount of outrage as was befitting a good cousin from the Durel family who had been wronged on his cousin's behalf.

"I meant no discourtesy, I swear. Please. We see so little of both of you," said Jean-Pierre, trying to stop their exit.

"And you'll see a damn sight less of us from now on. Isabella, to the carriage."

"Please, Emile, accept my apology. I did not mean to anger you. On my parent's grave, I meant no disrespect. Stay to dinner."

Stephen glared at the man. *"If my wife and I think to come back to this home, it will be for your party. Hopefully, by then, you will have a better regard for my family than what you have shown to us this day. Good day, Ernestine. And Merry Christmas."* He slammed the door behind them.

They found Nathan and Cicero waiting for them at the sidewalk with the rented carriage, hurried into the cab, and ordered the men to take them back to the hotel. Isabella never questioned her husband. He couldn't tell whether she was impressed or humiliated. Her husband had just defended her bruised feelings. There might have been some brotherly regard shown in this offer, but the fact that neither woman's feelings on the subject had been taken into account, had Emile boiling. Considering the time period, and the chauvinistic manner of most Creole gentlemen of 1838, Emile was either progressive, or learning something from his 1998 alter ego.

Sam and Stephen left the women to rest in the hotel room and went for coffee at Bank's Arcade.

"I've never seen anything like it," said Sam.

"Was he something! I'm glad I didn't have to make up the dialogue myself. He has such flair."

Melinda walked into the coffee shop while they were conversing. Her favorite color must have been pink, for again, she was decked in ribbons and lace and the brightest pink a modest woman could dare wear. She made no attempt to hide the fact that she recognized them and came over to their table. She did not look at Sam. Her stare was directed at Stephen. The fact unnerved him. She tilted her head coquettishly and smiled like a vixen. "In town again, without your wife?"

"Melinda Chabonnais, so pleased to meet you at last. You shall be happy to know that my wife is with me and staying at the St. Louis Hotel. I'm sure she'll want to see you as soon as you're able."

She glanced at Sam and smiled again. "And this is your charming cousin, Evan. We've met."

"My pleasure," said Sam.

"May I sit with you gentlemen?" Like a coiled serpent spreading itself in the sun, she slithered into the chair opposite them. The waiter came running to take her order, and Melinda ordered tea and honey cakes.

"So at last, you've come for the season, charming. Isabella will be so happy." The look in her eyes showed a vague interest in Isabella's pleasure and an all-to-active regard for her own. One sort of stimulation specifically, Stephen wagered. She was playing the part of a wealthy lady from New Orleans, but trilling each word in unconscious imitation of another sort of woman who threw beads from balconies.

"I'll be by soon to see how she is."

Stephen said, "She's not well. She was very sick the other night."

"Really," she said, knitting her brows briefly so as not to add an untimely wrinkle. "Is it something catchy?"

"I don't think so."

"I'll find her more of that rose-scented body cream she likes so much. I gave her a gift of it for her last birthday, and she hardly ever uses it. Still, I'll buy her some perfume too.

That should cheer her up. So," she purred, "what's it like in Paris these days? Wicked?" The question was directed towards Sam.

"Ah...as it always is," Sam said.

"I remember it very well. Half my gowns are from Paris. New Orlean's clothing is so provincial." She leaned over to stir honey into her tea and to show both men her ample bosom. "The bodices here are so suffocatingly prudish, don't you think?"

If it is possible for a man to drool invisibly, Sam was doing just that. Stephen thought of going home immediately and making love to his wife. Especially when Melinda accidentally, or on purpose, let her satin slippered foot slide up his calf. She was blonde, buxom, and beautiful, and so obvious it was an immediate turn-off for Stephen. She wasn't even in Isabella's league. It was sad to think that Isabella admired her so much, and here she was trying to seduce her best friend's husband and cousin with no care which one followed her to a hotel room.

"French fashion doesn't suit me," he said. "I prefer the more modest styles. It's less obvious and more ladylike."

She flinched and sat back in her chair. "What's wrong with Isabella?"

"She took sick Christmas Eve. We thought we might lose her. But she's all right now. Thank God."

"I see. Then she won't be attending Chris's play?"

"She wouldn't miss it for the world. Nor would my cousin and I."

"You're going? Will wonders never cease. I have my own box." She smiled at Sam. "You may join me there if the play becomes too tedious for you."

"I wouldn't leave my family."

"I'll be alone. In need of companionship."

"Well," said Sam, "then, I suppose I could wander over after intermission." There was a huge, symbolic viper pit right in front of Sam, and Stephen watched his new friend hover on its edge.

She took his hand after she sipped her tea. Her tongue ran across her lips to wipe the honey from them. "Maybe afterwards, you and I could get to know each other better."

"Maybe so. Won't your husband be attending with you?"

She laughed. "Of course not, silly, he's very ill, or haven't you heard?" Her cheeks crinkled in a suppressed smirk. "He hasn't been out of the house in months."

She looked again at Stephen. "I do hope you come to visit me while you're in town. Isabella will show you where I live." Her hand grazed Stephen's. "Anyway, I'll be over to see her after I shop for that fragrance. I just love buying things for her. She gets *so* excited when I give her anything that it's such a thrill to buy her gifts."

The subtext was that Isabella was in such dire need, that she made a big deal over any *little* thing anyone gave her. Even attention. Melinda was so spoiled and pampered that it seemed reasonable to assume she got anything and anyone she wanted.

"I do hope that exclusive shop is open today. She likes the rose scent, though heaven knows, I've offered to have an individual fragrance made for her. I have several made-to-order fragrances. Can you smell this one?" She leaned her open bodice over for Stephen to catch the scent, and a heady aroma of strong, spicy, and sickeningly sweet cologne hit his sinuses and made him sneeze. "Different from roses, isn't it?"

"Yes, but I like the rose fragrance. She wore it for me the other night. I thank you for buying it for her."

Melinda's mouth gaped. "She finally used it? Really. Whatever for?" She giggled as if she knew that Emile and Isabella had no sex life.

"Perhaps, she wanted to please me. You have good taste, Melinda, I loved it. Though Isabella is so beautiful, she could wear vinegar and still be incredibly appealing. As her friend, I'm sure you know that, though."

"Isabella is unbelievably attractive in a homespun sort of way. But surely, a man who spends time in France every year must like a bit of *pastry* instead of cornbread once in a while."

Stephen almost choked on his coffee.

"I mean." She leaned very close to him, and her satin-covered breast touched his arm. "The French have such unusually exciting morals when it comes to making love, n'est ce pas? Any time you want to remember some of your nicer French evenings, just send me a note."

She looked at Sam, and the invitation was for him as well. "I like Frenchmen. Alone or in a pair. It makes no difference to me."

She moved her foot up his calf again. "I'll be alone Friday evening while Isabella supports Chris in his artistic endeavors. She's so loyal," she said, rolling her eyes as if it were a third-rate joke and giggling. "If you get bored, I have a room at the St. Louis Hotel. If we time it right, we'll be back for the final curtain, and she'll never know."

"I would not leave my wife, Melinda." He made his voice as cold as he could.

"Pity. But Evan could."

Sam surprised Stephen when he said, "I wouldn't leave my cousin on such an important night."

"C'est la vie." She targeted Sam with her gaze. "Amour? Maintenant?"

Sam didn't answer.

"Non? Voulez-vous couchez avec moi, ce soir?"

"Pas ce soir," said Sam.

She shrugged her shoulders, but showed no defeat. She rested her coffee cup on the saucer and stood up to leave. She regarded Stephen one more time. "Remember my offer, Emile. It can be our little secret. After all, friends should share everything, n'est ce pas?"

She left.

"Good Lord in heaven," said Stephen.

"Incredible vixen," said Sam.

"I thought you liked her."

"I like a challenge. Where's the game in this? She might as well strip and spread her legs right here on the table. From the sounds of it, it wouldn't be the first time. I think we're learning a lot about New Orleans today."

"How *could* she? Her best friend's husband. With a bachelor right here waiting for her, yet she comes on to me."

"Kinky too."

"Both of us? At the same time. During intermission," said Stephen.

"And she sure doesn't think much of Isabella's ability to keep her husband satisfied."

"She probably knows that we haven't been sleeping together for seven years. Close friends do talk about stuff like that. So, you aren't going to let her lead you into sin?"

"And get a disease? Are you kidding? Be another notch on the old hotel room bed post? Ernestine has more appeal, and that's saying something," said Sam.

"So, what's the deal here? Melinda is a tramp, and my wife is supposed to be one too? They're as different as night and day. I'm not sure I understand what Isabella sees in this person."

"Well, she's rich and spends her money on her friends. She's got a sort of glamour about her, and she probably pays for the tickets to the theater, or else sleeps with the impresario, or something, to get them. Her husband never tells her she can't spend or do as she pleases. So I suppose she's available as a friend unlike the other women Isabella knows who have children to raise and households to run."

"There's a point. Ernestine made a comment she didn't have time to go shopping with Isabella, and if you're looking for excitement, Melinda must draw it to her like a magnet. The plantation life Isabella has is lonely without a husband or a close female neighbor to chat with. Can you see Ernestine and Isabella trying to converse?" said Stephen.

"No."

"Precisely."

"Things are certainly starting to heat up around here."

"I'll say. Brother dearest wants to run everyone's life. Ernestine wants to love her children instead of cruising the town with her husband. And Melinda just wants to have fun with no regard as to whom it might hurt. That lady is lethal."

They looked at each other and let the thought grow.

"I want my wife," said Stephen. "Let's blow this taco stand."

"I'm right behind you."

Chapter Twenty-Two

The Théâtre d'Orleans was alive with lights and activity. They'd arrived early so that they could have dinner in one of the supper rooms. Stephen promised Isabella that he would purchase a box for the Durel family. This pleased his wife. She was filled with energy and enthusiasm about Chris's performance.

She kept saying, "Of course, I shouldn't tell you so much about the play, or I'll spoil it for you. It's just that Chris has told me all about it, and I think New Orleans will be delighted when they see it. Oh, Emile, I'm so excited that you and Evan are here with me tonight. Look at everyone noticing."

She was correct on that account. All New Orleans was aghast at the sight of Isabella Durel, not flanked by Melinda, but with two charming gentlemen at her side. The gossip mill rotated with the news that Emile Durel had finally revealed himself for more than just the Mardi Gras, and that he was interested in witnessing the play her Anglo friend had produced. They probably wondered who the man was beside the couple, but then, it wouldn't be New Orleans if the good citizens hadn't already heard from the banker, the waiter, the jeweler, or the tailor, not to mention the Devieux family and Melinda.

Isabella was talking with a friend, so Sam and Stephen moved to the side of the lobby, just out of earshot, but close for her to see them.

Completely unaware of where to go, Sam pulled out his Wainwright notes and the xerox copy of the theater's original blueprints from his inside jacket pocket. "Damn that Wainwright's good. Okay," he said, reading from the copy. "There are two tiers of boxes here, and, from the look of this blueprint, we might just as well ask where the supper rooms are because I don't see them specifically marked on this design. Notation from Wainwright: this is the first home of the Grand

Opera in America—yippee." He twirled his index finger in the air. "Though the plays were primarily performed in French, they did allow some English plays to be produced here. Well, I guess. In the 1820s, John Davis brought singers and musicians from France to perform here, and the place started jumping. Ah ha, what do I spot here? Those gambling rooms he mentioned are just down those stairs." He smiled and looked at Stephen.

"You wouldn't leave Isabella to play poker," said Stephen.

"I'm not much of a theater person, and if this play gets as boring as I'll bet it's going to get, I shall depart while she is enthralled with his majesty's performance and see if I can win plane fare home."

He raised his hands to defend himself against Stephen's shocked expression. "Joking. Ha ha. Time travel humor. Besides, where there are money and cards, there are men; and where there are men, there's conversation. And where there is conversation..."

"There are clues to solve the mystery."

"Right. Okay, let's ask this guy where our supper room is so that we can get to the main event of the evening—Chris's play."

They returned to Isabella who noticed Melinda and hurried to her side leaving them alone once again. The two men followed slowly, hoping, in vain, to go unnoticed, but their luck ran out right away. Isabella looked gorgeous in her gold gown, but like a pauper next to Melinda's opulent, satin, Parisian gown of pink and white frills with a bodice so low everyone would be making bets all night long that sooner or later her nipples were going to be revealed. She was unescorted, and, by the glint in her eye, hoping it wouldn't take long until someone joined her in her private box. She was, by far, the finest-dressed woman in the place.

American styles were plain even for formal wear in 1838. The quality of the material was more important. Creole dress was rich and beautiful because of the imported material. Melinda,however, stood out because her fashion was notably French by cut and design, expensive because of the cloth used, and was daring styling even for New Orleans.

"I'm famished," Sam said.

Melinda's shoulder drooped, which made her bow slip, which dropped the gown's bodice so that she was forced to replace it with her dainty, gloved fingers. A twist of the body showed off her waist and shifted her neckline tantalizingly close to his arm. She flirted, tilted her head, and laughed, but her mind was as dense as a newly installed drain pipe. In the ear—out the mouth. If Isabella were looking for intelligent conversation, Melinda Chabonnais was not the book of knowledge. However, if you were looking for gossip and girl talk, there was no one better to spend a day with.

"Do you have a box?" she asked. "Are you sitting with Jean-Pierre? I hear his wife in labor tonight. Can you believe it? Another little pig- faced brat. I'm sure he'll be here tonight though. Who would miss all this excitement to stay at home and hear a woman's screaming and wailing?"

Isabella paused and stared at her friend before saying, "She's my sister-in-law, Melinda."

Melinda turned to her but didn't look at her. She was flirting, and she wasn't going to let Isabella interrupt her. "Don't worry, dear, I won't hold that against you."

"We're dining first," said Stephen.

"Oh," she whispered close to his ear, "then you can say you fell asleep because of the delicious food and the wine instead of the boring plot."

He wanted to answer, "How would you know? You haven't the intellect to understand the jokes." He was beginning to like old Chris, and wasn't sure why. Melinda was supposed to be his friend too, and, yet, here she was ripping his endeavors to shreds. Assuming Emile hated the theater, she was trying to make points with her best friend's husband by stabbing her other friend in the back. If Isabella and Chris had worked on this play together, it might be worth the price of admission to see it. Melinda must have yawned and asked for more tea when they brought up the subject of lines and plot twists.

"Did you see my necklace?" Isabella inquired, pathetically trying to get her friend's attention. "It's a gift from Emile. And the earrings are from my cousin, Evan."

Melinda regarded the new baubles. "Dazzling. Simply dazzling. And how they bring that gold gown back to life. They're beautiful." She fingered one of the earrings and winked at Sam.

"Men with such good taste are hard to find."

Sam coughed into his handkerchief. Stephen was beginning to understand that this was Sam's way of suppressing laughter. Sam motioned to a nearby usher and asked him where their supper room was.

Stephen took his wife's arm. "Well, we have to go now, Melinda. Nice chatting with you."

"Later," said Sam.

Isabella looked at Sam and then at Stephen. "Is something going on that I'm not privy too?" Stephen remembered that Wainwright had used those exact words when he and Sam had discussed the ghost. He patted her hand and smiled.

"We saw Melinda at the coffee shop the other afternoon," said Stephen.

"That's right," said Sam.

"Oh? And how did that go?"

"How do you think it went? You know her better than I do."

She answered without hesitation. "She tried to seduce Evan."

"Precisely," he said, without mentioning that she'd also tried to seduce him as well.

Just as they'd seated themselves comfortably in the curtained room, ordered food and wine, and were beginning to relax, a comical face parted the curtains. It had to be Chris. He was round-faced, cherry-cheeked, thin and wiry, and covered with hideous, waxy makeup.

"Good God," Isabella said, "you frightened me."

"Who the hell is this?" Chris asked, smiling and motioning to the two men with his shoulder.

"This is my husband, Chris, and our Durel cousin from France, Evan."

"Pleased to meet you," said Sam and Stephen together as they offered their hands.

Chris gave them a strong handshake. "I committed a grand sin to find you. An actor should never appear in costume, or stage makeup, in the lobby, but I risked it all for you, my lovely Isabella. All for you, and here you sit with two handsome gentlemen."

He sashayed his way into their room and pulled the

curtains together behind him. "Good God, what's that around your neck? Did you attack a pirate?"

She giggled. "No, silly, this is a gift from my husband. The earrings are a gift from Evan. Why are you here? It's almost curtain."

He grabbed her hand dramatically. "Hang the curtain, it's you I must see." He waited. "Get it. *Hang* the curtain."

Sam laughed in spite of himself and looked as if he regretted it. It wasn't the line; it was the man. A fast-moving, fast-talking charmer who had charisma to spare, a quick wit, and boundless energy. Isabella chuckled at the bad joke.

"Go away, we're eating," she said, motioning for him to leave with a wave of her gloved hand.

"Oh?" he said, dropping into an empty seat, "anything for me?"

"No, you have to entertain us. Now go backstage."

"Very well, but I just want to say one thing to your husband—whom *I've* never met."

"Yes?" said Stephen, giving him an Emile Durel-raised eyebrow.

"Don't believe everything you hear about me; I wrote most of the dialogue myself. Oh, and this too, I'm madly in love with your wife so shove off." He playfully pretended to nibble her neck amorously, and she laughed and tried to push him away.

Stephen grinned. Isabella shook her head in apparent fear that Stephen might not understand Chris's strange sense of humor. But Dr. Stephen Templeton had seen a few stand-up comedians in his day, so he took no more offense to the activity than if Robin Williams were attacking his wife.

"I hope this is a comedy we're seeing tonight, or we're in for a rough time. I may go and gamble with you," he whispered to Sam.

"I must fly, or is that I must flee; no that can't be right because who would want a flea? Kiss me, my darling, for good luck."

"No, I don't want to get that hideous makeup on me. Now get backstage."

"Oh, sure, now that your husband has returned from France just toss me to the wayside. Poof. Gone." Fake sobbing and put-upon wailing. "Don't worry about me, Issy, I'll manage." More over acting and then a big grin.

"Issy?" thought Stephen. He was initially appalled by the nickname until he saw her face light up with joy. She was radiant.

Chris took her hand and spoke gently to her. The smile was gone. "I heard you were ill? Why, Issy? Why were you sick?"

"I'm all right now. It was some virus, or, I ate something bad."

"I'll personally see that everything you eat here tonight is untainted."

The waiter came through the curtain with the wine as if on cue. "Hold, servant, stay, I say." He spoke like a Shakespearean actor playing Mark Anthony. "Let me taste that wine before my lady doth drink its heady liquid."

The man shrugged his shoulders, popped the cork, opened the bottle, and poured a glass of wine for Chris. The actor sipped it cautiously. Then he dropped the glass; seized his throat, his eyes looking as if they were going to pop out of their sockets; he gasped; cringed; and fell 'dead' on the floor. The waiter grinned. A momentary pause for effect. Then the actor rose in one swift movement and said, "Perhaps I should try another glass."

"Oh, stop it," cried Isabella. "Go to the stage and make us all laugh."

He knelt beside her. "Oh, how I love it when you order me about. I'm off," he said and was gone.

"He's got that right," Sam said to Stephen. They both laughed at Sam's comment, and Isabella gave them a questioning look.

"Nothing, beloved, nothing at all. Just enjoying the wine." He toasted her with his glass and then drank.

"You can't help but like him, though," said Sam quietly so that she wouldn't hear his remarks.

"Let's not invite him to tea soon," said Stephen.

They indulged themselves with a seven-course meal while the play's first act created the major plot scenario. It wasn't a unique British farce, as far as Stephen was concerned; but to these people, and considering what they were used to, it was quite amusing.

The story revolved around an aged husband whose young

wife was cheating on him with several men, hiding them in various parts of the house, and calling them *servants* if he discovered one. The doltish husband never caught on, stretching incredulity to the ultimate limit. No matter how obvious the situation or what romantic interlude she seemed to be undertaking at the time he entered the room, he missed it. Chris played the husband to perfection.

"Wonder where he got the plot?" said Sam.

"Don't go there," Stephen said.

In the second act, the unsuspecting husband decides to have a bit of fun himself with one of the new maids, whom it turns out, is one of his wife's lovers in drag trying to escape without being discovered. Sam was laughing so hard Stephen thought he might get indigestion. Isabella frequently dabbed at her eyes with her napkin for she could not stop laughing at her friend's ability to charm the audience with his writing and acting.

In the third act, the wife finally decides to get rid of the old geezer and marry one of her lovers, but she's afraid she might not win any money in the divorce. So she asks the lover, who had tried to be a woman earlier, to pretend he was having an affair with the husband so that she could divorce him on the grounds of infidelity. The problem arises when the disgruntled lover learns that she is not going to run away with *him* but another, and chooses to not uphold his part of the bargain and leaves. The lover's sister comes to call on the lady to find out if the rumors of her brother's illicit affair with a married woman are true, and the old husband falls madly in love with her thinking that she is the 'maid.'

The major plot twist arrives when she decides she really loves the old fellow, because he treats her so well, and tells him of his wife's reputed duplicity. He divorces his wife, leaving her without a penny but with the man who really loves her, and marries the pretty, young sister. Curtain. Chris's character wins.

"We must go backstage," she said.

"If you insist. Are we attending the after-play party?" said Stephen.

"I suppose for a little while, yes. But I'm still rather weak from my recent illness. The move to town was exhausting.

We'll stay long enough to say hello to everyone. I wonder if there's any news about Ernestine?"

Stephen wondered at the change in Isabella's attitude towards her sister-in-law.

"We said that we wouldn't go back to the house."

"I know. Still, she might be in need of comfort," she said.

"We can stop by the house when your brother's not home, if you want."

"I could send Anna over to help her. I don't really need her right now. It would be a gift."

"I think she has all the servants she needs. How about another sort of gift? A new gown, personally created by Madame Gatou?"

"Yes, perhaps," Isabella said, as if she wished to drop the subject.

The stage was surrounded with excited members of the audience. Stephen could see Melinda gushing around Chris as if it were somehow her success not his.

Isabella moved up the steps and towards her friend, but Sam and Stephen stayed in the audience area and waited for her.

"His play was good. *He* was good." said Sam. "I noticed real concern on his part when he spoke with Isabella about her illness, didn't you?"

Stephen said, "Too bad Melinda didn't show the same concern."

"Isabella's health wasn't a major concern that day. She had to make her points with us. That was all she cared about. And, I thought she was hot. Poor Isabella had to mention her new gifts to her best friend, but Chris noticed them right away. Your wife has only one true friend, as far as I can see. I think we need to talk to this man."

"And tell him what?"

Sam looked at Stephen. "I think we need to tell him that she's in danger. That it's time to tell us all that he knows about her—including her little secrets."

Stephen wasn't sure. "Do you think he'll talk to her husband?"

"I think he'd cut his right arm off for her. We should at least get to know him better. Warm him into our confidence."

"All right. It's time to divide and conquer. The best way I know for two detectives to get the most information. You take Melinda, and I'll take Chris."

Sam groaned. "Do I have to?"

"She's hot for you, man," said Stephen. "Dazzle her with your Cooper charm."

"What I'll do for a beautiful woman! Okay, I'll go up there and ask her to dinner and brace myself to be raped."

"It won't be that bad."

Sam waved to her when she looked his way. Melinda winked and blew him a kiss.

"And I'll invite Chris to—lunch—isn't that what you're supposed to do in the theater world? Invite them to lunch?"

"I think so. What are you going to use as a reason? I mean, to have a conversation with him without Isabella around."

"I'm not sure." Stephen thought for a moment. "Wait a minute. I'll say I'm interested in backing his next play."

"That'll work." Sam looked at Melinda again. "Well, into the lion's den". Might as well get started."

Stephen put his hand on Sam's shoulder. "Does it help if I tell you that I'm very impressed with Time Travelers, Incorporated, right now?"

Sam looked at Stephen and smiled. "Yeah, it does."

Chris saw Isabella making her way towards him and almost knocked Melinda over trying to help her onto the stage.

They overheard his conversation with her. "Did you like it?"

"It was wonderful. You should be so proud, Chris. You wrote it, directed it, and starred in it."

"I couldn't have done it without your support." He kissed her cheek.

"So," said Chris to Stephen, "what did you think, Emile?"

"Very entertaining. I thought Evan would have heart failure because he was laughing so hard."

Isabella smiled at her husband and took his hand.

"The party is at my present residence on the hill. Isabella knows where it is. Wait for me there."

The crowd was too much for her. She was glad to get out of the theater and into a carriage. She took them to the house where they were greeted by an English butler.

"Are you sure you want to do this, Emile, Evan? We're on the American side of town. They'll be Yankees everywhere. Perhaps, we shouldn't."

Stephen pondered at her sudden lack of interest in the social life she had told him she loved more than family, pride, and financial security.

"Won't there be other Creoles?"

"Not many. Probably just us. I never think about it much because I'm alone all the time. It's changed now that the two of you are with me. I don't want to embarrass you both."

"It's up to you. He's your friend. If you want to stay, we'll stay. If you want to go home, we'll stop at a nice restaurant and have a pastry and coffee to celebrate."

"Oh, I *can't* leave him. It's his big night, and he would be so hurt."

"Then we'll stay."

Emile made Stephen's mustache twitch. He touched it with his fingers.

The butler offered them drinks, and they waited in the parlor of the grand house, retelling the jokes of the play and making comments about Chris's acting and that of his co-stars'.

Chris came home about a half an hour later, with his fans following him. He moved through the hallway searching for Isabella. Stephen noticed fleetingly the same tall, blond man who resembled the new surgeon at Cook County General Hospital. The man had crossed his path again, and now Stephen's curiosity was aroused.

He was devilishly handsome with golden, blonde hair; a healthy, tanned complexion; clear, sparkling blue eyes; a long face with high cheekbones. He demonstrated an unwavering self-confidence, and stood tall and proud like Emile. This man was the only one Stephen had met so far who was equal to Emile Durel in physical strength—and arrogance.

The mystery man moved across the room with the fluid grace of a panther stalking his prey. Stephen presumed that the man's arms were powerful and lean under his finely tailored jacket and vest. His fingers were long, perfectly shaped talons that gracefully opened to receive a crystal goblet of champagne, twisted elegantly to hold a lady's hand as he kissed it, and swayed in animation when he talked. He wasn't an actor. What was especially dazzling about this Yankee gentleman was his smile. He could steal meat from a pack of wolves with that smile. His face, eyes, and deportment became brilliant when he acknowledged someone he liked. His eyes were crystal chandeliers of light shaded by dramatic brows that outlined his perfectly chiseled cheekbones. And more than one woman noticed.

"Help yourself to champagne and food," said Chris.

Sam sauntered Melinda's way exhibiting a sexy smirk. It caught her attention. He took her hand and kissed it, then offered to fetch her some champagne. The look in her eyes registered victory over at least one Durel. She smiled at Isabella who seemed docile, quiet, and shy all of a sudden.

"All right, everyone," announced Chris. "I have another surprise for you this evening. Follow me into the library."

Upon entering the room, Stephen noticed a white sheet covering what appeared to be a wooden frame.

"My good friends, I was able to accomplish tonight's success because of one person's undying faith in my abilities. And to honor this person, I have created her likeness on canvas. Poor artist that I am, I mean to flatter her, and hope she will be pleased with my efforts." He glanced at Isabella and then pulled the sheet from the portrait. It was the picture Stephen had found in the attic. Isabella's portrait with the gold gown, the bow necklace, the white rose, and the cameo ring. Chris had painted it for her. He wondered how it had found its way to Durel Plantation.

It was an incredible discovery for Stephen. Déjà vue at its finest. He now knew who the artist was, that the art work would have been revealed posthumously, and that Emile must have had it brought to the house *after* her death. Such an action on her husband's part reaffirmed his devotion and the fact that he must have spoken to Chris after her death. At the funeral perhaps. She never viewed the portrait that haunted her home for over a century after her death. How wonderfully changed everything was now. Isabella had been kept alive to view Chris's surprise only because Stephen had traveled back through time.

Isabella was shocked by the portrait. Everyone gasped at the beautiful rendition which gazed at them from the wall. Then they applauded. Isabella blushed. "It's wonderful. But, how could you have done it. I never sat for you," she said.

The mystery man spoke, "You've done a great service to us all with your oil paints, Fairchild. But no matter how beautiful the work of art, it pales in comparison with the original."

Stephen was unnerved by the man's comment. He was flattering her. Why shouldn't he be allowed to make an ingratiating remark to Isabella, but it made Stephen jealous, and it was an agreed-upon emotion based on some instinct he shared with Emile.

Isabella blushed again, something Stephen thought he'd never see outside of their bedroom. She dropped her chin to her chest and refused to look up. She didn't respond as a lady should to a gentleman's compliment. Her fingers touched the canvas.

Chris said softly, "Do you really like it, Issy?"

She looked at him, and her eyes glistened with adoration. He showed similar affection to his muse, for apparently that was what she was to him.

"This rendition is the highest compliment anyone can make to a woman. My wife is an inspiration to everyone she meets. Chris, this is splendid work, indeed. Would you allow me to purchase it so that I may display it in our home?" asked Stephen.

Everyone in the room gazed in bewilderment at the husband who'd never been by his wife's side before this. Curiosity and anxious gossips speculated in covert whispers.

Chris toasted Emile with his champagne glass. "Buy my painting? No. It will be my gift to both of you. I can never begin to repay her. When you return to Durel Plantation, I will see that you have it. But until then, I wish to see her beauty every time I enter this room."

"How did you ever find the time to paint it while working on the play?" said Isabella.

"I started it a year ago, Issy. I've worked on it off and on since then. It's yours."

She hugged Chris.

The mystery man said, "A toast to Chris's fine performance tonight, his enchanting portrait, and the lovely lady who inspires men to...dream."

Everyone joined in the toast. Isabella lifted her glass hesitantly. She turned and looked at the mystery man. They glared at each other for a long moment. He tilted his chin towards her, lifted his glass in a salute, smiled knowingly, and sipped.

Stephen wanted to walk up to the man and say, "Okay, pal. You want to tell me what this is all about?" But instead, he watched her every move. He could tell that her respiration had increased, and that she looked as if she had just locked eyes with a scorpion.

Stephen was able to intercept the host in the hallway.

"Might I have a word with you?"

Chris motioned to a place away from everyone's notice.

"I would like to donate a large sum of money for your next production. I think you have tremendous talent. You obviously care for my wife a great deal, and the sentiment is returned, I think. It would make me happy to make her friend happy. Would you be interested?"

"Forgive me if I appear surprised by your proposal. I'd heard that you don't usually support your wife or her hobbies. Apparently, you've been misrepresented to me."

"I'm a businessman, and, because of that, I have to be away from home a great deal. But in my absence, you have kept Isabella from the depths of loneliness and depression. For that, I am most grateful. Now that I'm home, I want to make it up to her and repay you for being her friend."

"In that case, I would be most interested in your generous offer of assistance. We could meet next week—say on Tuesday at noon."

"Pick a place where we can talk privately."

"I'll send word to your hotel," said Chris.

"Very good. Thank you again for the more than generous gift of her portrait. You did a splendid job. It will out last us all." Stephen had played the scene perfectly. It looked as if he were offering a gift to match Chris's, and this seemed the appropriate thing for a husband to do.

He found Sam leaning against the wall of the dining room. "I have a dinner date with Melinda Tuesday evening in some private little restaurant that has curtained rooms—hint, hint," said Sam.

"Good for you. And I have a luncheon date with Chris."

"Looks like things are looking up—except for Hercules over there."

"Hercules?" said Stephen.

"Yeah, he sort of looks like a blonde demigod, don't you think?"

Stephen pressed his lips together in irritation, and said, "Thanks a lot, Sam. If I weren't feeling jealous before, I am now."

"Oops. Oh, well. She isn't interested in his sparkling, blue-eyed charm that he keeps tossing her way, so I don't think you have anything to worry about—yet. Let's go back to the hotel."

They bid farewell to the host and headed for the door.

"Bonsoir, Isabella," said the mystery man, who was leaning against the parlor door frame and looking exceedingly confident.

Isabella didn't respond to him in any fashion nor did Evan or Emile Durel.

Chapter Twenty-Three

Isabella was a tigress when they made love that night. Begging for what she wanted and harmlessly biting his skin, she found ecstasy easily and wantonly asked for more. She wanted to be taught all that he knew. To be told how much he loved her. To feel his hands on her body, caressing her breasts. To savor every inch of his anatomy.

She massaged his back and chest with her fingers, using the same gentle, but firm technique she had used on the piano keys. She did whatever he asked without hesitation. It almost seemed as if she took personal pleasure in teasing him into his orgasm. She would allow him to enter her body, then push him away, and then roll over so that she could lay her head on his chest. Then she would kiss his lips and face while running her fingers through his dark hair. She would demand that he stop every movement—right when he felt the most passionate—and thereby slow their pace.

"Why are you doing this to me?" he asked.

"I want us to take our time; I want to feel everything. It's so wonderful to ache for something you desire with every part of your being and then deny yourself. Sweet torture swells into rapture, like a perfectly written piece of music. Yes, I want you to be passionate, but not so fast that I can't savor every moment of it. I've waited and dreamed what it might be like to make love to you, and I want the tender beauty of it to last." She put her arms around his neck and motioned with her hands that she wanted him to kiss her breasts.

"You're a wonderful lover, Emile," she said.

The moment she said the name, something happened inside Stephen. He pulled her arms down from his neck and pinned them roughly onto the mattress.

She looked into his eyes. "Why? I want to touch you."

"*I want you. No more seduction; no more sweet torture,*

mon cher; I want all of you."

Her body arched under his forceful attack and writhed beneath his.

"No, that's too rough." She tried to free her arms.

"Je t'adore, mon cher. Mon coeur. Mon amour."

"Emile? No...please."

His body pressed into hers with a savage fierceness that matched her earlier feline performance.

"You do not make the rules, mon cher." He bit her neck and then kissed the spot. *"Sweet beyond words. I must have all of you."*

"Nothing like being in a ménage à trois with your former self and your wife," thought Stephen.

Emile forced her into submission. He took the lead in all things. She could not move, to fight, or to make love to him. He didn't want her to. He wanted to devour her. Stephen felt it in so many ways and couldn't fight the man's spirit on this one—it was far too delicious. His body yearned for his wife to give all of herself to him. It was more than making love—much more.

He paused. *"Trust me."*

"I'm afraid."

"Of what? Climbing to a greater height of passion than you have ever known? You are so beautiful. I love you so much."

He pressed his body further into hers. Rocking with more rhythm and no sensitivity at all. Only hunger. He took an almost sadistic delight in taking charge of their lovemaking. It was masculine dominance at its best. Raw, ravenous, and relentless. And all the time, Stephen was delicately kissing her cheek, eyes, lips, and neck with overt tenderness. One half of his torso was gyrating spasmodically into her body, delivering her beauty up as a sacrifice to his animal lust; and the other half was showing her the affection she needed. What she must be thinking—if she was thinking at all at the moment.

Her mouth moved towards his. Her tongue searched for his lips. There was a low, feline sound. Nothing left for her now but to feed his craving and, in so doing, drink water from the same well.

"Let my arms go, Emile."

"No."

"Please."

"*Pourquoi?*"

"I want to put my arms around your body, so that you'll be close to me. I want to hold you. Feel you against me as if we were one being."

He freed her arms, and she clung to him, digging her fingernails into his back. Her head curled into the nap of his neck. She sighed with joy. Emile made no sound and simply continued burying himself into her soft flesh.

Her body went limp, complacent, docile. She moaned and whispered into his ear, "Take all I have to give. Take all of me."

She buried her face into his neck and kissed him until it seemed she was no longer breathing. The two of them were living with one heart and one body—joined physically and emotionally. He would have to keep them alive by breathing for both of them, so close was the union.

"Swallow me whole until there is nothing left of me," was her submissive reply to his touch. "I want you to lead. I will follow you. I trust you to make me happy. Tell me where to move, how to please you. Close my eyes and waltz to your rhythm, sway my body so that it moves with yours. I have lost myself in you."

"*And everything in the world is you, Isabella.*"

She began to cry. Her tears fell on his neck.

"*Come with me, cher,*" he said.

He moved faster and pressed his hips forward into hers. Her legs parted. Her abdomen lifted to meet his. The movement brought on a more fevered eroticism on Emile's part. She collapsed under his body. He pushed deeper into hers until she cried out, and they both rode the wave of ecstasy together.

Stephen's head felt dizzy, and he collapsed on to her body. She held him close to her breasts, let her fingers play with his hair, and sighed. She coiled next to him like a tiny kitten.

"I never in my life thought it could be like this. Never this wonderful," she said.

Stephen said truthfully, "Neither did I."

And then, Emile said, "*Mon coeur, you are my angel, my delight. You are not of this earth. You come from some sphere far beyond—beyond what men may know of reality. How can I begin to tell you what you mean to me? Life would have no meaning if you were not by my side. I cannot conceive of leaving you again. Promise me you will never leave me."*

"You want a second chance at love? I'll never leave you if you promise to stay with me always."

"I swear."

He touched the side of her face with the back of his fingers. His eyes filled with tears, and he felt a burning inside his chest.

"I lost you that night. I had to go on without you. Have you any idea how miserable—lonely—distraught I was? Sometimes you don't know what you have until it's taken from you. And then it's too late. I was angry with you. Horribly angry. I shall never be so again. I said things I should never have said. I'm sorry. In God's name, I am sorry. I shall make it up to you until my last dying breath."

"It was just a little disagreement." She said, obviously thinking that he was apologizing for the fight they'd had in her bedroom. Stephen knew what Emile meant though. An apology long overdo.

"I should have taken the time to ask, discover, query about your life and your friends. Instead, I made hasty judgments and came to ridiculous conclusions. I should have trusted you. My wife. I should have trusted you."

She held him in her arms. "Don't talk now." She kissed his forehead. "Hold me."

"I love you, Isabella," said Stephen.

"I love you, mon coeur," said Emile.

"And I love you," said Isabella smiling.

It was difficult for Stephen to awaken his "sleeping beauty" the next day. He washed and dressed in one of the other rooms so that he wouldn't disturb her. He could hear snoring from Sam's room, so he let him sleep in. "Mr. Early Riser. Right," he said in a low voice.

Anna and Nora woke immediately and asked what they could do to help him.

"Get ready to go have breakfast."

The two women seemed surprised by the statement.

"Just us?" said Nora.

"We'll bring back something for your mistress and Evan. Let her sleep; she's healing."

The ladies were dressed in a flash, and Nora chattered all the way down the stairs, through the lobby, and onto the street. Nora led them to a restaurant one block from the hotel.

"How do you know they have good food?" he said in response to Nora's prattle.

"My nose." She pointed her chubby finger to her nose. "I can smell, can't I? A good cook can smell another good cook's handiwork."

"I guess I can't argue with your nose," he said.

They were immediately segregated the moment they entered the restaurant. One waiter moved the girls to a back room, while Stephen was ushered to a table at the front of the dining room by another. Before the girls left his side, he told them to order anything they wanted. Nora replied that it was her duty to sample a bit of everything so that she could duplicate the recipe back home.

Stephen felt lonely sitting by himself with no one to talk to. He mused at the treatment of his servants, and how it would have been nice to hear Nora's witty comments while he drank his coffee. He ordered country ham, eggs, pancakes, coffee, and a dozen sweet rolls to go.

When he was finished eating, he asked the waiter to call for his servants. He paid the bill, and they left the restaurant.

"I don't suppose I could teach their cook to make any better pancakes," said Nora, patting her stomach in appreciation of the fine meal.

"I suppose we need to stop by a hat shop and find you two better bonnets."

"Hats! Lawd, have mercy, we got us a regular gentleman now, Anna. And I jes' happened to spy me a real fancy hat shop yesterday when we was taking our walk with Missy."

Stephen grinned. "Well, then," he said, "lead the way, ladies."

Nora ran so fast he thought he'd explode after the large breakfast he'd just finished. When they entered the shop, the woman who owned it lifted her nose into the air and spoke French to both women. His two servants wouldn't have dared to respond to her and looked to Stephen for support. The woman told them to leave. But when Stephen spoke with her in brisk French that they were with him, and that he wanted to purchase three of her finest hats, she smiled and became solicitous. While Anna marveled at a yellow hat with bows that looked very nice with her lighter complexion, Nora found a brilliant cranberry-colored one with ribbons, and Stephen looked for a hat for his wife.

"Whatcha think, massa?" Nora showed off her choice.

"Remember your mistress wants you to wear these hats to church. I think the yellow one is very nice, Anna, but that berry-colored one..."

"Well, how 'bout this here blue one." She pointed to a dark blue hat with lace around its brim.

He watched as she tied its ribbon under her chin. "Quite suitable. Now, I have to find Isabella one."

"For your wife?" said the proprietor.

"Yes, she won't like just any ordinary hat."

"You would like to see the ones I have recently received from Paris?"

He smiled. "By all means."

He looked at twenty-four bonnets before he found a pretty brown hat, with burnt orange trim, and small feathers stitched into its brim.

"I'll take all of these and this cream-colored one with the blue trim."

She was swift in placing the hats in boxes and adding up his bill. As they walked away from the shop, Nora said, "Missy, gonna love dem hats. She sure do like New Orleans, don't she?"

"She loves it here. I want her to be happy."

"Well, she sure gonna be happy this morning. What with the hats and the sweet rolls and the..." She started to giggle uncontrollably.

Anna hushed her with, "You mustn't say it, Nora."

She laughed. "Well, how'm I suppose to not know?"

Stephen understood.

"Well, I doesn't have to say it, I can see it. One happy lady des days, thas fer sure. And a happy mistress makes for a happy Nora. That woman can be a damn sight too cranky when you ain't home, massa. Needs to stay outta my cookhouse."

Anna tried to quiet her again.

"Well, I hope to change all that. I hope we can have a family and make Durel Plantation a good place for everyone to live."

"Nora lives too much in the cookhouse, massa, so she doesn't know when to talk and when to shut up." Anna darted a fierce look Nora's way.

He laughed at the two of them as they scowled over their social roles' distinctiveness.

"I'd like to see her fix a meal without me," Nora said.

"No one can cook like you, Nora, I'll vouch for that," said Stephen.

"Why even Massa Jean asked me to leave the plantation and come cook for him after he ate my gumbo."

"Sneaky devil," said Stephen.

"You wouldn't sell me to him, would you? Heard he's meaner than a crocodile."

"No, Nora, I would never sell—you—to anyone."

Sam and Isabella were dressed and waiting for them in the hotel room.

"Where have you three been?" inquired Sam.

"Shopping. Rolls for breakfast and hats for m'lady."

"For me?" she said.

"I hope you like them."

Sam started to eat the rolls while Isabella modeled her new bonnets. She liked both, but favored the cream and blue one. "I have the sweetest husband," she said, and kissed him hard on the lips for the gift. Sam gave him a "I-told-you-the-hats-would-work" look.

"Well, do you feel ready for your fitting today?"

Sam cried out, "Oh, that's right the fitting. Well, that's good. I'm getting tired of these clothes."

He noted a sudden change in his wife. Isabella ate the sweet rolls in silence and slowly dressed for the day. It was as if someone had closed the drapes on the sunshine.

The Gatou family was waiting for them.

"I've chosen a gown that I think you will like, Madame," said Madame Gatou stiffly. "It's a new pattern which I designed from a French one. Your husband seemed to like it."

Madame Gatou showed the gown to Isabella while Stephen and Sam were moved to another room at the back of the shop.

He heard Isabella say, "It's the grandest gown I've ever seen. When can I wear it? Well, to Jean-Pierre's if we're still going."

"We'll go," called Stephen from the other room. "This fits quite well," he said to Gatou. "I need formal togs and five more in the same style but with different colors and vests."

"Mais oui," said the tailor.

Sam made a few adjustments on his and then ordered more of the same. They asked about their Mardi Gras costumes while they put on their original suits.

"Do you want to see ours?" Stephen called to Isabella who was in a small dressing room with Madame Gatou.

"What are you going to be?" she called back to him. "I have to pick one too."

Monsieur Gatou showed Sam's knight costume first. A brave warrior from the Middle Ages wouldn't be caught dead in this costume, but a Creole gentleman and bachelor trying to impress a lady would make headway with it. It looked striking on Sam.

"All you need is a sword," said Stephen.

"And yours, monsieur," said the tailor.

The pirate costume wouldn't frighten anybody, but women would fall in love with the man wearing it simply by its design. Stephen wondered if Emile would be shocked. The black shirt had voluminous sleeves and two slashes—made with scarlet material—running down the sides of the sleeves. The slashes gave the impression that there was another shirt underneath the black one. Stephen liked it immensely. The big, open shirt made his bare chest look even more powerful. The black pants were snug and showed the muscular line of his strong legs. A four-inch, red satin sash, with fringe at its hem, cinched his waist and dangled below his hips. There was a black, three-cornered hat with a matching red band and feather. The feather was long enough to drape dramatically behind his head. All he needed were boots. The tailor mentioned where he might look for appropriate ones to match the costume.

"Take it out and show it to my wife," said Stephen.

"It's a wonderful costume, mon cher," said Isabella.

When Stephen and Sam were finished, they returned to the front of the shop.

"Now for Isabella," said Gatou. "My wife and I took the liberty of designing a Spanish lady's costume to match yours. It's made of the same red satin as the sash of your costume and has black lace over it, a black waistband, black lace shawl, and the side of the heavy skirt is slit for dancing and walking. There's a comb and a black veil too, if you want it. Both costumes have masks to match. What do you think, Isabella? Do you like it?" He held up the costume for her.

"I think we should be the best dressed threesome at Mardi Gras this year."

"Should I have muskets, a sword, or something with this costume?" said Stephen.

"How about an eye patch?" said Sam.

Stephen winced and shook his head.

"A long-barreled pistol might be nice as long as you don't plan on using it," said the middle-aged man laughing. "Perhaps a saber at your side. Still with the huge crowd around you that might not be safe for anyone. Besides, you'll be so busy dancing and having a good time that those props might get in the way."

"I guess you're right. Isabella? Do you want anything else? Order whatever you need. How soon can you have this delivered to the St. Louis Hotel?"

"The suits will be done tomorrow as will her gown. Now that my wife has her measurements, she can start making more dresses, say, fifteen to start with?"

Isabella gasped. "I don't need..."

"That will be fine," said Stephen. "You don't need us to come back then, do you?"

"I think Isabella might need to come back a few more times for fittings. Say two weeks from Tuesday?"

"I thought you said that all you needed were her measurements?" Stephen said.

"We do, but women's fashions, especially new patterns from France, need to be fitted so that they may flatter the lady's figure to best advantage."

"I see. Well, cher, I think you, Anna, and Nora may have to make that trip without me. I'm sorry."

Isabella gave Gatou an angry look, and neither Sam nor Stephen missed it.

"Can't Madame see me in my hotel room? It would be easier," she said.

"My wife is getting too old to go to the customer's home, and we work better when we have our material at hand. The shop is best."

Sam and Stephen stared at each other and tried to read the other's thought, for the expression on Isabella's face resembled the one she had worn the night they'd met her at the dock.

"I will have these delivered to your hotel by tomorrow afternoon." Gatou read the bill to Stephen who paid in cash.

"Merci, Monsieur Durel. A pleasure doing business with you."

Isabella walked through the door, letting it bang shut behind her. The Gatous disappeared.

Stephen said, "What do you suppose that's all about?"

Sam said, "I don't know, but she sure is angry."

"I have my lunch and you have your—dinner date—tomorrow. I think one of us needs to get some answers. Isabella should have been happy to see her 'old childhood seamstress' today. Even Madame Gatou made no attempt to rekindle fond memories with her former customer. I thought she would be delighted to bring up the 'good old days' when Issy was only a teenager in need of dress for the social. She liked the clothes, but she wasn't talking about the past with either one of them. What gives?"

"You think she kept quiet because of the recent death of her parents?"

"That's a possibility. Maybe Isabella and her mother always came in together. There was her question as to why Gatou couldn't come to her hotel room for the fitting."

"That was how the rich would have had it back then. Maybe she just expected the old treatment and was mad when she was refused."

They looked at each other and paused to decipher the whole scene.

"There's more to that look of hers," said Stephen.

"Much more," said Sam.

Chapter Twenty-Four

Chris pointed to the salmon as being the best item on the menu to order, and so Stephen ordered it even though he was too nervous to eat anything. He had so much to ask the actor but was afraid of frightening the man from being open with him. He had to monitor the conversation judiciously.

"I'll take your word for it then," he said.

"You won't be disappointed." The actor's demeanor became businesslike immediately, almost as if he'd always hoped for this meeting so that he could state his opinion on a few things. "Forgive me for being so blunt, but I always like to get down to the point, if you don't mind."

"That is the best way to be."

"Isabella is a beautiful woman. Why do you leave her alone so that other men can lust after her?"

Stephen wiped his mouth with the linen cloth before answering. "Talk about being blunt," thought Stephen.

"Are you saying that you're attracted to my wife?"

"Of course. Every man in New Orleans is, but I desire her friendship above all else, and so I keep that in mind every time my thoughts run to her eyes, voice, and body."

"I appreciate that. She's quite fond of you, and I'd hate to see your relationship end."

"Precisely. So my question again. Why do you leave her alone?"

"I have to do business away from our home. It's expected that a plantation wife will take care of the family farm while her husband is away. You understand little of the work of a sugar cane planter, Fairchild."

"You just explained it rather well."

"My wife is as intelligent as she is beautiful—as you know—and   plantation life is too stifling for her, I fear. She has become bored and depressed. It appears that she's come to town

230

to find excitement—without me. That will all change soon."

"How so?"

"I'm concluding my business affairs in France, so that I will never have to leave her again. We're buying a home in the French Quarter, so that we can rest and enjoy the fruits of our labor. As a matter of fact, my cousin and I have found a nice home on Bourbon Street between Conti and St. Louis. Do you know the one?"

"Yes, they say that it was vacated recently, so you should get a good deal on that one. That's quite a home for just a vacation."

"It has crossed my mind to sell the plantation." The headache returned, but Stephen reached into his vest pocket, took out two Advil, and swallowed them unobtrusively with water while massaging his temples until the pain went away.

"Are you all right? Can I get you something?"

"I'll be fine. Had too much champagne after dinner last night. So, you see, I have her best interests at the heart of my plans."

"Then make her happy, for God's sake. She's the joy of my life and has been so damn depressed I thought she might kill herself. And it's all your fault."

"Well, the comical fellow has a determined side after all," thought Stephen.

"All you need to know, Monsieur Fairchild, is that I adore my wife and support her in all matters. And she loves me. Any more questions?"

He grinned. "How much do you want to invest?"

Stephen laughed aloud. "How much do you need?"

"She said your cousin, Evan, has aided your financial distress?"

"That's right."

"How about five hundred dollars?"

"I can make you a bank note, and you can cash it today."

"Which bank?"

Stephen chuckled. "The Louisiana State Bank."

"Good and don't let Issy near it."

"Why do you say that?"

The actor realized that he'd said something he shouldn't have. "Ah, well, you know how she is with money."

"Yes, I've found that out, but what I don't know is where it all goes."

"Clothes?"

"Uh-uh, try again."

Chris wouldn't meet his gaze. It told him a great deal.

"But surely her gowns..." said the actor.

"What do you know about the gowns? They aren't tailored, and she didn't buy them. You should know that because you and she shop together. How does she get them—Melinda?"

"How should I know?" Chris was playing with his napkin, twirling it between his fingers as if it were a woman's braid.

Stephen grew angry with Chris's evasiveness. He was hurting from his Emile migraine and losing his patience with the actor. He said, "Look. You want to be blunt about my personal life and talk about my wife's sadness and depression, blaming it all on me, but the moment I ask you a direct question that would help me understand my wife better you lock the door. It works both ways, Fairchild. Maybe this whole idea of lunching with my wife's best friend was a mistake. Maybe we should just forget the whole investment idea too. You want more than friendship from Isabella Durel, that's the way of it, isn't it?"

"I'm sorry. You're correct. Forgive me. I'm in love with your wife and terribly jealous of you. I wish you had left for France and never returned. I don't have the financial means to give her what she needs, or I would have taken her from you. I need her laughter, her beauty, her smile. I need her for my art. She's my muse."

"I thought Melinda was the woman of your dreams?"

He laughed. "Who told you that?"

"Ah, I'd rather not say."

"Melinda is a treasure chest full of gold, but not very bright."

"But if her husband departed for the world beyond, you'd marry her?"

"Of course, I'd be a fool not to. She's beautiful and very rich. There isn't a single man in New Orleans who hasn't made a bid for her. But, she can't compare to Isabella. Melinda knows it too. Surely, you must realize that Melinda Chabonnais is a *social outcast*, Durel."

"Ah, well, I'd guessed that."

"Naturally. She's part-Creole and part-American which is a total embarrassment right there, isn't it? How she managed to seduce that old Creole fool isn't too hard to guess. He's buried five already and was looking for a young wife. At twenty she was over ripe, if you know what I mean. Her parents were willing to give the old fool a handsome dowry if he'd make her legitimate in the eyes of the Creole families. But, you and I know that will never happen. Her Daddy owned one of the better plantations, so Chabonnais took the scandal and the money hoping to get an heir at fifty-one years of age. She didn't want to marry the old man, but her parents told her that this was the only way she could get into the *tradition*—and the old man could take good care of her. She'd want for nothing. I mean, she would own two plantations, and with money as tight as it is right now, no one will turn her away from the front, or back door, so to speak. I heard that her parents moved to Charleston. She's presently selling both plantations—one to a family from Virginia whose soil gave out on them and who can pay top dollar—and the other to a neighbor because he wants more land. She likes the mansion they own in the city, because it's beautifully decorated, and she's close to all the excitement."

"Her husband isn't well?"

"God, no, he probably won't make it through the summer."

"Rumor has it that she's hastening the gentleman along. Is that true?"

"I wouldn't put anything past her. Marie Laveau is one of her best sources for that sort of thing."

Stephen remembered the voodoo shop Sam had wanted to see the day they shopped for dueling pistols.

"What does she get there?"

"She likes to get her fortune told by the young hairdresser. Supposed to come true. Marie has already told her that she'll marry another, a younger man, soon. So, who knows if she also purchased something from the woman to help Chanbonnais along death's path? There are also aphrodisiacs for sale there—love potions. She drinks them. She and her husband never have sex, so it can't be for him, if you know what I mean. I've made it clear that I'm available, but alas, I fear I'm not her

233

type. She has her eye set on one man. Such a love potion might bring her what she wants."

"And who might that one man be?"

"Ah, look, lunch. I do hope you like this. Isabella doesn't like the salmon much."

"You dine together often here?"

"As often as I can. I love her company. If people talk, that's your fault, and that's exactly what I've told her. If you aren't going to give her a life, she best reach out and take one. You only live once."

Stephen was going to tell him that wasn't necessarily true and that he was living proof of it, but he didn't want to argue with a man who seemed agitated at the moment.

"My cousin finds Melinda very attractive."

"Well, he's more her type than I am, it would seem."

So her type was tall, handsome, brownish-blonde hair, blue eyes, experienced, and with a wicked smile.

"Still, I'll give him a run for his money, if he makes a move. If I can't have Isabella, I might as well marry for money."

Stephen felt the boldness of Emile rise inside him. *"You're not Isabella's type anyway,"* said Emile.

Chris took a bite of the salmon. "This is delicious. Allow me to buy lunch. What did you say?"

"Ah, I can see why this isn't Isabella's favorite type of fish, but it seems quite good—so far. Where does my wife spend our money, if she isn't spending it on gowns?"

"Why don't you ask her?"

"Because I'd rather ask you."

"I don't know."

"You're lying."

Chris stopped eating. "I don't feel comfortable telling other people's stories."

"Really? You just told me all about Melinda, and she's your friend, isn't she? My wife has been trailing around New Orleans's society in a gown her brother calls a rag and isn't wearing the necklace or the ring that you depicted in your portrait. They've just disappeared." He took a dangerous risk. "I was able to buy them back, however. She doesn't know I have them."

The man lost his appetite for salmon. "Where did you find them?"

"No matter, they were sold, and I bought them back for her, though I haven't given them to her yet. Well? Do you know why she's been spending a fortune with nothing to show for it?"

He dabbed his mouth with his napkin and settled back into the chair. "She doesn't spend it on clothes. I give her the gowns."

"Why? How? Do you have the money to buy her gowns?"

"I make enough to live comfortably, but not enough to purchase a friend's gowns. I have many patrons. I rent my home from an American who lives in Europe now."

"Does my wife invest in your plays?"

"No. The gowns are former costumes from our plays. The costume designer is very kind to both of us and takes the loveliest gowns from a performance, changes some of the details so that they are unrecognizable, and then she wears them to the plays or the parties she, Melinda, and I go to. You have to understand something, Durel, I couldn't write or perform without her. I wasn't doing well in Britain despite my press in *The Picayune*. My plays were considered mediocre, and my acting couldn't match others whose family names had given them a career boost. I moved here three years ago and met Melinda who introduced me to Isabella. I began writing again and, suddenly, there was magic in everything I touched. Fame, fortune, and great reviews. Everything I dreamed of came true—and it wasn't Melinda who inspired me; it was Isabella. I owe her my career. I'd do anything to make her happy. And, forgive me for saying so, if anything ever happened to you, I'd drop my suit for Melinda in a heartbeat and spend the rest of my life wooing Isabella until she broke down and accepted my proposal. And I'd do that if she were the poorest girl in town."

"God forbid such a horrid union!" said Emile.

"Did you say something?" said Chris.

"Ah, no, I was chewing. I can see why Isabella doesn't like this salmon, God forbid I should order it again. Horrid. Continue."

"Oh, I'm sorry I suggested it."

"That's all right. You were saying?"

"So, when she mentioned to me that she hadn't a thing but homespun to wear to an opera Melinda was in a passion for us to see, I came up with a way to help her out. Now, it seems that she has you to buy her pretty things. It's about time. I've spent three years hating you."

"Well, that's direct," Stephen thought to himself. "I spent one month hating you, but now I don't have to."

"But now you don't have to," Stephen said aloud.

The actor smiled. "No, now I don't have to. You've saved her life."

Stephen grinned. "And the painting made her smile. *You* make her smile."

"Then we have no quarrel with each other?"

"Not unless you're trying to poison me or something, so that you can have my wife."

"What the heck, go for broke," he thought, as he deciphered the man's reaction.

"It wouldn't matter, Emile. She isn't in love with me. Despite how you've treated her, this angel in human form loves you. You better understand it before it's too late."

"Too late for what?"

"I've said too much as it is. Don't tell Isabella I told you about the gowns."

"I won't, but please, if you know anything more that can help me return my wife's health and happiness to her, tell me."

He looked at his pocket watch. "Look at the time. I must run, or I shall be late for rehearsal. Thank you so much for the investment. I'll pay the bill at the door. Enjoy the rest of your lunch."

"When will we speak again?"

"Melinda has tickets to another opera. Are you going? Because I'm attending with her, and we could talk then."

"If that's what Isabella wishes, then we'll go."

"Tell your cousin good luck with Melinda."

Stephen thought that was an odd statement for Melinda's suitor to make but finished his coffee and pondered all that the man had said. He was keeping her secret for her, but why?

Sam said, "So, we go to this exclusive little restaurant and get placed in this curtained back-room-kinda thing where no one can see whether you're getting laid or not. She orders oysters, gourmet shit, and gallons of wine. I offered to pay, but oh, no, she wanted to *treat me*. So, I'm thinking, 'okay, baby, treat-me time is near, and I'm going to have to deliver.' "

"Seems far superior to my lunch. Go on, I'm listening."

The two were practicing their waltzing while Isabella was shopping with Melinda. Sam had promised to teach Stephen how to tango later. They glided around the room, pretending to follow nonexistent music.

"There's a fainting couch in the room, and we have to sit on it to eat. She's got this Paris original on, and when she takes off the lacy top part, her breasts are completely exposed. Pretty, soft, creamy white, with—"

"The story, please. Cut the graphics," Stephen said.

"All right. No, you lift on the second step and come down on the third. Don't dip with your knees; just drop down, and that gives it the glide. So, anyway, she's reclining on this couch after the order has been sent to the kitchen, and we've tasted the wine. Not to be disturbed for quite a while she tells them, right? Knock on the door first before entering is the message to the waiter. I'm thinking, so even if she's dumb, she's cute, and she's here."

"I understand," Stephen said.

"So, she smiles this sexy little come-on look at me. She asks me if I'd take off her shoe; it hurts her foot. I do this. Then she reaches into her bag, takes out this tiny vial, and pours its contents into both our drinks. She tells me it's an aphrodisiac. Okay, I'll buy the woman isn't going to poison us, but then Dr. Gayerré said that she was a serpent, right?"

"Yes." It was difficult to dance with Sam when he was animated like this.

"You have to lead the lady. Isabella will take over if you don't have control."

"Yes. Go on."

"So, I start to massage her foot," Sam said, "and when she closes her eyes to moan about how good it feels, I dump the drink in a nearby plant."

"Good move."

"I'm not that thirsty. So, then she opens her eyes. No, no, lift on the second. Make it graceful. That's it. She pulls up her stockinged foot and proceeds to place it right in my *crotch*."

"Uh-huh," Stephen said, without missing a beat of the dance.

"She smiles and massages my..."

"I get the picture."

"Okay, I'm thinking forget the food, right? I lean over her gorgeous body, wrapped in this ultra sexy dress, and kiss her. She's like a fish. Her lips are so cold. The friend in my pocket doesn't care, so I move to her breasts. I make some sort of seductive statement about eating her pretty nipples for the entree, and she freezes up."

"What?"

"I move onto kiss her breast and put my hand on it, and she pushes me away and sits up. She says to me, 'Who told you you could do that?' So I say, 'You did by the choice of gowns you wore tonight, and the nice massage you just gave my active friend. Ah, and there's the matter of the aphrodisiac. It's working overtime right now. How about yours?' She stumbles around for something to say, and then tells me that she has to eat first. I'm not pleased, but then I was there for information anyway, so I said that I could wait. Right! She puts on her jacket like she's cold."

"So after you eat dinner, she's the dessert?"

"*No*. Promenade to the left now. She goes into this lengthy tale about her childhood, and how she was snubbed by two worlds because she wasn't exactly Creole and not exactly American. I'm thinking to myself, 'Who cares? You're gorgeous.' After dessert; they bring champagne. We talk some more; only this time it's about her life with her husband. A real cute thing to bring up when you want to get laid by some guy, right? He can't satisfy her but gives her everything she wants. I'm thinking again, 'Who cares? Money can't buy you love. Come here and let me show you what I've learned on my travels to Asia 1200 a.d.' "

"This is getting boring," said Stephen, and then noticed the hurt expression on Sam's face. "Oh, I didn't mean *your story*—the dancing. Sorry. Can't we try the tango?"

Sam stopped his story long enough to return to his role as

dance instructor. "Now we have two forms of tango; Argentinean, which I don't think you can pick up in a few short lessons, and American which you could probably manage. The music is the same. We have no way of telling which one Isabella and Emile knows, so I'm going to say that the easier steps will just have to do. If she questions you, just say that you learned it in France, and that she should just follow you. Do you remember how I told you to remember the rhythm?"

"T-A-N-G-O?" said Stephen.

"Fred Astaire would be so proud of you."

"Thanks."

"The tango is the dance of passion, seduction, fire and ice. It represents all that is good and bad in life. It's ancient and never loses its charm. It's about a man wanting a woman with all that's in him, and a woman who appears to not want the man at first...but...she teases and flirts with him, giving the man the impression that she...hey, this is beginning to sound like my date!"

They moved into the first few steps, and then Stephen swung Sam to a side promenade. He tripped on his own foot. "Maybe you should stick with the waltz," said Sam. "The tango is hard to learn on such short notice, but your waltz is pretty good."

Stephen threw up his hands in anguish. "Isabella told me how much she *loves* to tango with me; how we had such a great time last year *tangoing* at the Mardi Gras Ball."

"I'll take care of her tangoing; you take care of her waltz."

"I still want to know how to do it. Continue."

They redid the first four steps. "There's no point in tangoing with Melinda. She can't 'dance' if you know what I mean. She continued whining about never getting laid by her old man, and I'm trying to get my hand around her back so that I can touch her breast. Finally, I just can't take it anymore, so I push her onto the couch, take off my jacket, and start making love to her. Hand right up the inside of her thigh. She starts to cry like a little girl. 'How dare you?' she says. Now, I'm furious. I ask her why she invited me to a private supper if she didn't want to play. Oysters and aphrodisiacs—come on. She goes into this fairytale thing about how she wants to be in love with the man

239

before she makes love to him. I tell her I've been hit with Cupid's arrow."

Sam pushed against Stephen, forcing him to move backwards, but Stephen faltered. "This is where the lady slips her right knee between your leg, so you lean backwards and turn your face towards hers—she'll look away. If you don't bend further than that—you're going to be in big trouble."

"Gotcha."

"She says that she isn't in love with me. *Now* she knows this; *before* she didn't. Then she confesses there's this American guy she's hot for; who won't have anything to do with her. Like I'm really interested in this after I've swallowed all these oysters. I guess he hangs with their crowd a lot. Her husband doesn't know that she's in love with the guy or that he's in her circle of friends. The guy wants nothing to do with her, though she's tried to get him into her bed for some time. She's told him that when her husband dies, she'll have a fortune."

"She will. She has two estates worth of cash coming in soon."

"So apparently, Mr. Heart throb has told her he'll come near her when hell freezes over. Apparently, he knows more about women than I do. She thinks that if she has tons of money to offer him, he'll change his mind. So the big question is, why invite me to dinner and offer what she isn't willing to give?"

"And the answer is?"

"Even though I'm Creole and he's American, I look a lot like this guy. Cute, considering that Sam Cooper isn't Creole by any stretch of the imagination. I tell her that we could pretend. I have no shame now. I just want that luscious body of hers. I've lost my senses at this point."

"Why doesn't this guy want her? She's pretty and rich. Not a bad combination."

"I asked her that, and she says that he's in love with someone else. And that's the end of my big date with Melinda. She pays the bill, and I tell her not to call me again. End of a fruitless evening."

"Ah, but it was fruitful. You found out that Melinda isn't as hot as we thought. I found out that she's nothing to New Orleans's society but a bank account. You found out that there's a guy in town who won't sleep with her for love *or* money. We also see a powerful motive for her to bump off her husband. With the information given to us by Dr. Gayerré, I'd say that it's safe to assume that she's poisoning the old man. She frequents a voodoo queen for fortunes and potions. One is an aphrodisiac; the other is, perhaps, a poison. The woman seems capable of murder. That's quite a lot to learn. I found out that Chris adores Isabella, supplies her with hand-me-down costumes for her gowns, thinks she's the answer to his dying career, paints portraits of her from memory, *would* marry Melinda for her money, and wishes I were in my grave."

"That means we have two people who think in terms of terminating husbands—but not wives?" said Sam, stopping the tango mid-lunge.

"We know that there are two people who have access to poison. Marie Laveau could just as easily make a vial for Chris as well as for Melinda."

"There's that matter of Emile's vial of arsenic. Where did he get a hold of that?"

"Unless it was a gift from..." Stephen said.

"Oh, my God!" said Sam.

"What? What?"

"What if someone gave it to Isabella—as a *friendly* gift of poison so that she could kill herself—or as an aphrodisiac to stimulate her libido in *his* favor—or..."

"As a poison so that she could kill her husband to be with someone else?"

The two time travelers stared at each other for a long time without speaking.

Sam said, "New thought. Why would she keep it in *his* bureau where he would find it?"

"Good point," said Stephen. "Dumb place to hide a murder weapon. And, besides, even Chris told me that she adores Emile even though he's a bastard."

"Then Emile bought it himself to kill his wife."

"Maybe. Unless your theory of being given a love potion, which is really a death potion, is true. She might have placed it in the room so that she could pour it into her, or his, glass if and when they ever got to make love again," said Stephen.

"She wouldn't tell *you* that she drank it. It might be embarrassing to tell a husband that you wanted a little boost to get by. So, she drinks it for a good night of love making because someone has told her that it works great, but it's a poison instead, and she gets sick," said Sam.

"Nice work. That means it might have been an accident. The vials were mixed up. And, then again, someone could have lied to her and told her that it was one thing, when it was really another."

"If this 'friend' tried to help her have fun, and then there was a mistake, that means Mr. Chabonnais's poison was replaced by a love potion. That should have made for an interesting evening for Melinda. If it were on purpose, we still have no *motive* for killing Isabella. Melinda *likes* her friendship with her legit Creole friend," said Sam.

"And Chris doesn't seem the type to harm a fly—too artistic and sensitive despite his threat. So, if it were an accident, then there'll be no more attempts to end her life," said Stephen.

Melinda, Isabella, Nora, and Anna walked into the room without knocking. Stephen was glad that they'd just stopped the tango lesson.

"Bonjour, tout le monde," sang Isabella. "Melinda and I have been very naughty."

Nora shook her head and said to Stephen, "Wait 'til you see the bill."

Isabella's face was radiant. "Melinda took me to this voodoo lady who read my fortune with a deck of cards." Her expressions were lively and full of mischief and enthusiasm.

"That's nice, cher," Stephen said. "What did she say?"

Isabella placed her packages in Anna's hands and ran over to Stephen. She threw her arms around his neck and kissed him hard on the lips. "It was a pack of lies."

"Oh, now, don't be too sure, Issy," said Melinda, as she set her own packages on one of the chairs.

Isabella looked into Stephen's eyes. "She said that a handsome stranger from a way up north would travel a great distance to be with me. Be drawn to me by some romantically hypnotic trance. I would fall madly in love with him. Isn't that silly? A Northerner. Father and Mother would roll over in their graves. Besides, I couldn't fall in love with another man; I'm madly in love with you. She said that I came very close to

242

death, but that my guardian angel was looking out for me and saved me. What an imagination she must have that Marie Laveau! Now, I'm going into the next room with the girls and model all of my new hats for you and Evan, and you must tell me what you think of them. If you don't like them, I'll take them all back. Oh, Evan," she called back as she left the room, "I bought some new books that you can read first if you want to."

"Why does she need more hats?" said Stephen.

She and Melinda walked toward the next room with Anna and Nora close at hand. Melinda turned to give Sam an icy glare and then shut the door on them.

Sam said to the closed door, "Oh, right, now *I'm* the villain." He turned to Stephen to say, "I told you we should have gone into that voodoo store that day."

Stephen crossed his arms over his chest and sighed. "Thanks for reminding me."

Chapter Twenty-Five

Stephen and Sam purchased the home on Chartres Street, and the three of them spent several days buying furniture for it. He tried to find chairs, sofas, and tables that resembled the same style he'd chosen for his refurbishment of Durel Plantation. It was his own personal way to touch 1998.

Isabella found the new home suitable with the proviso that she could keep the furniture there and not have to move it back to the plantation, which was the custom when a planter traveled to town for the season. Sam made the comment that he wouldn't be moving anything back to the farm unless they got a very large U-Haul, and she laughed at the joke without getting it.

It took them only two days to settle in their new home since everything was ordered new and delivered. Nora and Anna traveled to the marketplace and retrieved supplies for the cookhouse. Isabella, Sam, and Stephen unpacked their own bags while they were gone. Sam and Stephen were careful to hide their 1998 traveling bags in a locked closet in the guest bedroom.

Nora announced that the cookhouse was better than the one back home, because it was much closer to the main building. Anna said that the stairway was easier to maneuver, and that the dining room looked fit for a king. Cicero and Nathan so liked the fact that they had a carriage house within inches of the patio, that Stephen bought a rig and horse for their city adventuring. There was a second floor inhabiting warm, cozy rooms that allowed the domestic slaves to live in the same building with their masters. Each apartment had its own fireplace so that the servants could cook their meals in the privacy of their own room. The garden was a delight for any Creole lady. Isabella pointed out the different flowers in her new garden, acknowledging that the last mistress had superb taste.

Isabella and Stephen made love the first night they were

in their new home.

"I take it that you like the idea of purchasing the townhouse. You didn't at first," he said, afterwards.

She said, "I was wrong. This is wonderful. Especially the luxurious master bedroom." She kissed him.

"How did you get to be such a wanton little vixen?" he said with a grin.

Her hand massaged his thigh. "I must have had a good tutor."

He kissed her nose.

"I don't know," she mused. "The hotel was nice too. No one had to worry about cooking or cleaning. The whole day was completely free to do as one pleased. A vacation home is no vacation for the girls and me."

"We don't have to dine in. We can still go out to eat if you want to."

"Can we dine in—here?" she teased, kissing his neck and burying herself under the sheets. "Right here in our four-poster bed?"

He kissed the top of her head. "Every day, mon cher, if that's what you wish."

And so, once again, Dr. Stephen Templeton set up a new home with the help of Isabella Durel.

It appeared that Jean-Pierre's party was the most fashionable if you wanted to welcome 1839 into existence in style. Isabella was resplendent in her new gown, and the diamond necklace matched it perfectly, just as Stephen had hoped. They had their new carriage brought to the front of the house, and rode in style to the Devieux home. They wondered at the reception they would get, for they hadn't spoken to Jean or Ernestine since the disagreement. They needn't have worried.

"Ernestine is upstairs and hoping you'll come to look at little Robert. Named after our father, of course," said Jean-Pierre.

Stephen gave him points for not bringing up the other day's discussion. He seemed overjoyed at the prospects of having a new son.

"You go without me, cher. Lady's talk."

Isabella couldn't wait to see her new nephew. How things had changed! The unhappy and lonely aunt had now become the picture of familial pride.

"I'll give Ernestine our gift."

"And convey my happiness to her," said Stephen.

"You two come with me," said Jean-Pierre. "In my study. Let's have a snifter of brandy and smoke some good Cuban cigars I had especially ordered for the christening. It is next Saturday, if you'll be so kind as to come."

He poured them the drinks and helped them prepare their cigars for a fine smoke. The two Durel cousins sat down comfortably in two, high-back leather chairs.

Jean-Pierre started the conversation with, "Listen. I want to apologize for what I said the other day. I was not trying to insult you or Isabella. Forgive me. I'm certainly glad you came tonight, for I wasn't sure how to handle my apology. I saw you in church last Sunday for Mass, but it didn't seem a fitting place for airing the topic. Did I see a smile on my sister's face that day? Everyone in town is talking about the play, the portrait, and Monsieur and Madame Durel's new-found financial security which comes so fast on the heels of a visiting cousin from France. You are making my sister very happy, Emile. The house you purchased is one of the oldest and most talked about homes in all New Orleans. Excellent choice. By the way, they say it's haunted, but then they say that about every old house here."

Stephen thought, "Just what I need—another ghost."

Jean-Pierre continued, "Granted, I think it's highly irrational for you to be seen in the presence of Anglos, going to Anglo plays, and chit-chatting with Yankee buzzards, but, as I have stated before, and well you know it for you grew up with her too, Isabella is a handful and will get her way no matter how she does it or what *traditions* she destroys. Is that a smile I see on your face, as well?"

"Your sister has made me a happy man, and I am very much in love with her. That is why I was hurt by your comment the other day. She has been melancholy for months, and I didn't want her to think about our childlessness. But she's over it now, and I hope to keep her that way."

"Then I shall offer you something quite unique, and I hope

you will accept it as a peace offering."

He called into the hallway and a pretty, slave girl came into the room.

"This is Marisa. I just purchased her from a wealthy family in North Carolina. She is educated and ready to start work immediately as a domestic slave. She's yours."

The girl looked at the floor, never once making eye contact with Stephen.

"This is a very generous offer, but I must risk insulting your generosity by saying no. I do not wish more slaves."

"She's pretty."

Stephen shook his head.

"Very well, you can go back to helping the cook, Marisa." The girl left. "I just bought her at the slave auction yesterday. I was surprised that I didn't see you there. She's such a treat to look at, and I'm in need of a new mistress. That last one ran off, as I told you, and I had to beat her. Ruined my interest, of course, so I had to sell her. We had a son too."

Sam coughed, and it wasn't to hide a giggle this time.

"You know, Father gave you most of the good ones when you and Isabella married. And when he died, she got our best domestic slaves; Anna, Nora, Nathan, Cicero, just to mention a few. I can't tell you how much I miss Nora, the best cook in New Orleans. Any day you tire of her, let me know, and I'll buy her back from you."

"That will never happen."

"Still, you're missing something not taking a mistress. You have the prettiest girls too."

"I'm not being critical of what you feel is your due, but I have no intention of touching another woman. I love my wife. I would not soil our relationship with another woman's affections."

"You think Ernestine doesn't know? Of course she does. What can she say about it? Nothing. My father and his father and their father before them all had wives and mistresses. Most of their octaroons lived in town, but some of their slave girls lived right alongside the rest of the family. More natural that way. The plantation should be a family, a community, where everyone gains something—especially the master. After all, everyone's survival is in his hands. Quite a burden, you know.

Don't you agree, Evan?"

"Ah, well, I go along with my cousin. I haven't been lucky enough to start a family."

"That can't be. You've found no woman of your own?"

"Ah, well, I was in love with a nice girl named Abby once but, ah, she married another man. I've been broken-hearted ever since."

"Not natural for a man to hold back his basic instincts and pleasures. The lovelies are there for the asking. Take the one that pleases you to be your mistress and marry the one with money. I came into much wealth when I married my wife. But then you know that, Emile." He smiled.

Stephen shook his head and sent circles of smoke into the air from his cigar.

Jean-Pierre turned to Sam. "Emile, here, married for *love*. Prettiest girl in all New Orleans, my sister. Devieuxs are handsome people, n'est ce pas?"

Sam nodded his head.

"I remember when we were young. How you loved Isabella! Did he ever tell you the story about the peaches?"

Sam said that he couldn't remember hearing it, and Stephen lifted his shoulders in frustration when Jean-Pierre turned away for a second.

"We had had a rough lesson with Monsieur Dumont that day and had been scolded for being lazy. I went to ride my horse, and asked Emile if he'd like to go with me. He said that he wanted to talk with Isabella. Well, I was young and thought that was a fool thing to do—sisters being such an irritation. Ah me, I forget, what was it she told you?"

Emile spoke through Stephen's lips, *"She told me that she wasn't in the mood for walking around the garden with a boy. She said that she wanted to play pirates. She loved pirate stories and read the romances every chance she could—especially when her father might not find her doing so and throw them away."*

"Yes, that's right. You two were so much younger than I. I was through with that sort of thing by then. Horses and wenches were more to my taste. And I knew which slave cabin to go to for relief. That Eva would come up to me and smile so cute saying that she knew how to please her young master. Mother would have a fit if she knew what was going on." He paused to remember Eva before saying, "But you two went off to play pirates."

"I had to promise her that she could be a pirate, or she wouldn't spend any time with me. I told her that girls' couldn't be pirates, and she cried. So I reached into the bag of food my mammy always gave me when I went to your house for my lessons and took out two of the finest peaches any girl ever saw. I offered them to her. She stopped crying, ate one of the peaches, motioned that I should have the other one with her, and then did a surprising thing—she kissed me. I'll never forget it. I think I fell in love with her that day."

"That's right, now I remember. She came running back into the house and told the entire household, 'That boy has the nicest peaches. He gave them to me, so I kissed him and let him play with me.' It took Father a few moments to understand what Isabella meant. Her innocent look proclaimed her lack of discretion in choosing her words—that your actions were harmless. How my father laughed, but I thought my mother would haul your butt to the river and drown the last of the Durels in the muddy Mississippi."

"I remember," said Emile, whose voice was heavy with emotion.

Isabella burst into the room with her new nephew covered in a warm, white blanket. "Oh, look, Emile, Evan, isn't he the sweetest baby you've ever seen?"

Sam looked at the wrinkly face and smiled. "He's a Devieux for sure."

"How can you tell?" she said.

The baby yawned in his aunt's comforting arms.

"His mouth is never closed," said Sam.

Even Jean-Pierre laughed at the joke. Isabella scowled and then smiled. The family scene was interrupted by the guests' arrival. Isabella took the baby upstairs. Melinda and her husband were the first to enter. Stephen looked at Sam who blushed.

"Oh, shit," said Sam.

The man was the complete opposite of what they'd expected. He walked with no cane for his back was straight, and his feet firmly planted on the floor. His gate was slow but not wobbly. He had a full head of gray hair which was parted to the side. His face was lined with age, but it displayed intelligence and personality. His smile was warm but sophisticated. He wasn't particularly tall, and his light build gave the impression he might be younger than one would expect—say in his late fifties. His eyes were the color of clear lake water. He didn't limp or cough, or breath heavily. He stayed in one place, moved a few steps once in awhile, and kept his hands behind his back, like Dr. Gayerré did, rather than gesture when he spoke.

Melinda was prudent and quiet next to him but gave a few fervent looks towards Sam. She was playing the proper Creole wife. It was almost psychotic the way she could be such a vixen one day and a demure kitten the next. The real Melinda? Who knew her? Isabella maybe.

Sam whispered to Stephen, "Who would have guessed that this is the same woman who tried to seduce me the other night."

Stephen said, "Amazing."

They ate a seven-course meal in the dining room, and then the slaves moved all the furniture so that the guests could dance to the quartet that arrived at nine o'clock. They danced for several hours and then the quartet left. The crowd gathered as the time approached midnight. They cheered when the clock chimed its twelfth note.

"Just think, it'll be 1999 at home, and we just brought in 1839," Sam said.

The women stayed in the dining room/parlor to listen to a skinny soprano try to sing, while Isabella accompanied her on the harpsichord. The gentlemen retired to the patio for a smoke and brandy. Dr. Gayerré had arrived late because of an emergency at the hospital, but he joined the men on the patio after checking on his two patients upstairs in the nursery.

Melinda's husband was there and many other Creole aristocrats, but tonight there was no Chris. The mystery man was made conspicuous, in Stephen's mind, by his absence. The general conversation was about whether Texas should be a free or slave state. Everyone in the room agreed that it should be just as Louisiana—slave. They discussed the recent debacle in Texas, and how they'd assisted the cause with money and supplies. Stephen feigned interest.

"I read in the *Bulletin* that that Yankee, Thomas Banks, will place his arcade up for bid at a public lottery this year. I never go there myself, but I know you do Jean-Pierre, and *your* wife likes the coffee shop, doesn't she, Monsieur Chabonnais?" one of the men said, gesturing towards Melinda's husband.

Chabonnais did not answer at first.

"Putting the arcade up for sale so soon. Why, it's only five-years old," said Jean-Pierre.

"Yes, you're correct, Monsieur Bernard. Melinda likes to treat her friends thereafter they've been shopping," said Chabonnais.

Stephen said, "We just purchased a new home in town."

The men looked at him in bewilderment. He had dared to change the subject. Stephen was feeling left out and had thought he'd add something to the conversation.

"Oh, yes, good idea," said Monsieur De Buys. "At last, Isabella may enjoy the season without traveling back to the homestead all the time.

The men looked at each other and smiled. De Buys continued, "Still, it's odd that you do this so soon after our last conversation. I could have sworn you told us that you would never buy a townhouse, for you loathed parties and the theater. The change seems rather sudden."

"Yes, the conversation was rather emotional, as I remember," added another man. "We told you about the rumors concerning Isabella, and you stormed out of Jean-Pierre's house like a madman. Several of us feared for Isabella's life by the look on your face. Now, you're the model husband and she the model wife. It is, indeed, comforting to see, but how did it happen? You told us that she'd ruined your family's name with her adventures."

Stephen smiled. "How did I convey that sentiment to you exactly?"

"Isabella is a Devieux first and a Durel second. Her adventures are noted by every Creole in this city. She's been seen in town without an escort, spends much time with Yankee peasants, goes to the theater without her husband, reads too many books, discusses the contents in detail with our wives and sisters, and has been known to make abolitionist statements from time to time, born from Northern literature such as that one notably entitled *An Appeal to the Christian Women of the South* which she's recently read and let my wife borrow. How could you let her say such things? Why, my wife saw her exiting Marie Laveau's house just the other day. The voodoo woman? Emile."

"Now, now, you gentlemen speak of a time long passed. Our women are very modern now. I enjoy that aspect of the 1800s. Why should we hold to the old ways when there's so much new about our city? Isabella is a kind and generous woman who cannot be expected to follow ancient dictates," said Chabonnais. "I'm married to an Anglo/Creole woman by choice, don't forget, and she's my wife's best friend. They shop, gossip, and go to the theater *together*. Perfectly harmless. I'm pleased she finds such an interest in my wife's friendship. Melinda is the one who enjoys the witch woman's association, not Isabella. She likes to have her fortune read, and Emile's wife tags along. Such silliness. Isabella doesn't believe in such things but humors her friend. She told me so when she stopped by our house for tea the other day. A saner, more intelligent woman I've never met. I'm happy Madame Durel visits my home so much and spends time with my lonely wife. Melinda has so few friends."

Sam coughed.

Bernard said, "That Fairchild's a friend of theirs as well. Astonishing lack of good taste. I can tell you what they would've done in the old days with a wife who refused to be discreet and obedient."

"What was that?" said Stephen.

Bernard gave him a wicked smile. "Let's just say that she would become very ill suddenly of some rare disease and die the next day."

Stephen flinched.

"I love my wife," he said. His heart was pounding hard against his chest. His emotions strangled his words. How could they speak of a man's life partner like that?

"She's lively, intelligent, passionate, and my days would be long and sad without her," Stephen said. "I can't believe you mean that you would murder your wife for reading books, being curious, or finding a friend outside the tradition."

"It's your family's name she's tarnished. Everyone assumes there's more to the scandals. But then, we have already discussed some of those."

Sam said, "Do you have proof to support your accusations?"

"No, of course not, but people say..."

"Many things which are not true," Sam said, interrupting the man. "Probably more than half. Isabella may be a rebel, but she's an honest and faithful wife."

One by one the men regarded each other and tried to hide their amusement.

"Do you suppose they'll have carriages again for the Mardi Gras parade? I so liked that idea. I know how much you love the festival, Emile. Have you a costume already? I'm sure you have," said William, trying to change the subject.

"So, Durel, rumor has it that your cousin has invested heavily in your sugar cane business. Is that so?" said Bernard.

"He has indeed."

"And Isabella's creditors paid in full, I see?" said Vignaud.

"Whatever do you mean by that remark?" said Sam.

"I might be interested in purchasing Bank's Arcade," Jean-Pierre said, trying to change the subject again, but it was of no use. "How much do you suppose they'll want?"

Vignaud smiled and then pounced. "You might as well know your wife's latest scandal. At the end of last month, Isabella was seen in a lengthy discussion at Bank's Arcade with a handsome Yankee by the name of Anthony Chesterfield. He lives on the third floor in an apartment he rents there. Whatever do you suppose she's discussing with *him*? The theater? Oh, no that cannot be. She speaks with *Christopher Fairchild* on *that* subject."

Chabonnais said, "That is all we shall hear on this subject."

"But why? When you came home from France, Emile, you were enraged when you heard that your wife's name had been blackened by every Creole wife in New Orleans. You fumed over every detail we suggested. The beautiful Isabella running all over New Orleans with any man—or Anglo—who caught her eye. Spending the family's money as if there were no end to the well."

"My wife is faithful to me," said Stephen, but the news about the fair-haired Yankee had shocked him.

"Enough," said Jean-Pierre. "This is my house, and

Isabella is my sister. How dare you soil our family's name in such a manner! You've had too much to drink, Vignaud. Apologize immediately or meet me on the field of honor. Which is it to be?"

Stephen was amazed at Jean-Pierre's valor.

The man backed down immediately. "Forgive me, Jean. You are correct. My manners do me a disservice. Please accept my apologies. You are correct, Evan. I have no proof and have only heard rumors that she had a fight with Chesterfield. I never witnessed it with my own eyes. Forgive me, Emile, I should have realized that you and your wife are happy again. Too much wine. I retract my statement and beg your forgiveness."

"This night was meant for joy and pleasure, not hatred and accusations. I have a new son upstairs sleeping. We are meant to celebrate his new life and our new year."

"You are right," Bernard said. "Still, if our wives continue reading this abolitionist garbage, they may think it a good idea to free all our slaves. I'd like to see them do their chores without them. But then the fairer sex is none too bright anyway. Their emotions give sway to all intelligent thought. Religious zealots come around while we're traveling on business and feed them their ideas about morality. They should mind their own business. Taking food from our mouths. Northern idealism based on their own greed, for they're the ones who sold us the slaves. Let the North farm the way it wants and leave us alone. My wife has been reading all their literature as well as attending these religious assemblies. She asked me the other day if we could *pay* our slaves a small stipend. Can you imagine?"

"You've been away too long when they start talking that way," said Vignaud. "The black man has a roof over his head and food in his belly. Better than they had before. All we are asking from them is a portion of work to help build a life. My wife sews all their clothes, takes care of them when they are sick, teaches them about God, and, generally, takes as good a care of them as she does our children."

"These northern values are causing such a stir. Some of the slaves have dared to run off, or even rebel, against their master's—especially when the owner is away doing business—because they have listened to these preachers. A warning to you all, there are trouble makers on every plantation. Find them fast before it's too late, and you come home one night and find your house burned to the ground."

"That's not a problem at our plantation," said Jean-Pierre. "Most of the domestic slaves have their own rooms in the main house. Almost seems like they're members of our family. When my Evie died last year, the whole family was devastated. Just cut open her foot one day when she was carrying something from the kitchen, took sick, and was gone a few days later. Odd. We buried her next to the family's vault."

"My wife complains constantly about them. Sometimes, I think they're more bother than they're worth," said Bernard.

"I couldn't manage without mine. What about you, Emile?" said Vignaud.

He could not answer because he had no idea how Emile felt about the subject, and he surely must have mentioned his ideas to these gentlemen at other times. Besides, he was still in shock over the man's comment about Anthony Chesterfield and Isabella. He remembered Gatou saying 'Good morning, Monsieur Chesterfield,' to the mystery man. So that was why he had saluted Isabella and Chris. He knew her. He was embarrassing her in a public setting before her husband, her cousin, and two of her best friends. No wonder she was so quiet that night. Blushing. Why had they argued at the arcade? Why was there a hint of romance surrounding the two? Was this the terrible secret she hid from him? Why she refused to open to him completely? Had he, at last, found the truth about her liaisons in town? Was his trust in her unfounded? The answers made a difference to Dr. Templeton. His own sanity depended on it. Had his perception been faulty from the very beginning? Had the ghost truly seduced him into believing a lie? Was he so much in love that he couldn't see the truth? He could feel the white hot anger rise in his throat, and his chest ached. It was as if someone had cut open his heart; the pain was so intense. His mind was reeling from a jealous fever aggravated by the man's callous disregard for Jean's, Emile's, and Evan's feelings. He wondered why Emile seemed quiet about the statement so lightly made, but he had learned why Emile might have thought about murdering his wife. He felt the same tension in his body right now. One little lady had plenty of explaining to do. Their love might be true, but if based on deception, it was a lie. He felt dizzy, but tried to remain cognizant of the conversation.

"Ah," said Chabonnais, "honey cakes." The new slave girl offered them coffee and honey cakes. "Thank you, don't mind if I do. Now, don't give me that look, Gayerré. My wife makes these for me occasionally, and they're a harmless vice."

"Melinda bakes—in the cookhouse—with your slaves?" said Bernard, laughing.

The old man smiled. "She makes them just for me. How can I resist such devotion? Come to tea and you shall find Sophie's pastries, *but* for *me*, honey cakes made from the rich honey that comes from our own beehives. Melinda has many talents. You should see her garden."

Sam coughed.

"Isabella's playing has ceased," said Gayerré. "Perhaps, we should join the ladies."

They agreed and moved towards the dining room.

Sam spoke with Stephen privately in the hallway. "Well, what do you think about that man's comments about Anthony Chesterfield?"

"He's 'Hercules,' Sam." Stephen gave free rein to his anger now that no one could see him.

"The mystery man?"

"Remember that first day, when we were at Gatou's?" he said pacing. "The guy who came in the doorway and almost ran us over was the one at Chris's party. And Monsieur Gatou said, 'Good morning, Monsieur *Chesterfield.*'"

"Yes, I remember now. So, we see a connection." He looked at Stephen's face. "She isn't having an affair with him, Stephen. You've got to know that by now. Don't let Emile go over the top. I'll stick close."

His arms ripped the air around them as if he were tearing his clothes from his body. "So, why didn't she tell me that she had angry words with a Yankee? Is she in some sort of trouble? Who is he to her? Why keep secrets from the man she loves?"

"Don't be angry with her. Remember the time period is so different from ours. You heard what that man said these guys do to scandalous females in the family tradition. Maybe she's afraid to tell you. I'm sure there's a logical explanation."

"There can be *no* logical explanation for lies. I asked her to tell me if something were bothering her, and she froze. Several times she almost told me—I could see the concern in her eyes—but, she didn't trust me enough to say it. I sensed she was hiding something."

"And you're jealous, aren't you?"

"Why would I be jealous?"

"Because Anthony is every woman's dream lover in human form."

"Yeah...well...they argued for some reason, so it must not be good between them."

"Do you think she might have broken off with her lover after you came home from France, and they argued about it?"

"Anthony Chesterfield is *not* Isabella's lover; let's just get that straight right off. I told you that when I kissed her, she was cold. She had no idea how to please a man that first time we made love."

"Then why did he toast to her beauty at Chris's party, and why did he stare longingly at the woman whose face was in the portrait? She may not be in love with him, but *he's* in love with her."

Stephen's expression lightened. "Melinda."

"What about her?"

"The gossips said that Melinda is in love with a Yankee who refuses to have anything to do with her. Perhaps, because he is in love with..."

"Your wife? You think Chesterfield is the man Melinda has the hots for. The reason she didn't satisfy my needs the other night?"

"Going with my gut here. Yes."

"The reason Isabella wasn't sure she wanted to go to Chris's party, but agreed to come to this one was..."

"Chesterfield wouldn't be here, but he would be there. And her husband would be with her for the first time, and it might be too much pressure for her."

"How could an Anglo get close to Isabella? I mean you saw where the Devieux's live."

"I don't know the answer to that one. But I do know one thing."

"What's that?"

"We're going to do some serious talking with one

brunette when we get home."

They walked into the dining room. Most of the guests were preparing to leave. Isabella came to sit by her husband and fondly kissed his cheek. She looked at his face.

"Did you have a nice time with the gentlemen, mon cher?"

"Lovely," he said, biting the inside of his cheek to keep from screaming his outrage at her.

"Would you like to go now? You seem upset."

"We'll stay for a while. I would not risk offending your brother by departing so soon. But, we need to discuss something when we get home."

She seemed to read his meaning, frowned, and wouldn't speak. She reached for his hand, and, after a second, he dropped her touch. He saw tears in her eyes. It did nothing in the way of healing his pain, and he felt no pity for her.

Chapter Twenty-Six

Jean-Pierre rescued her discarded hand, kissed it, and smiled sweetly at her. "Isabella, my sweet sister, I would like to show you what your dear niece made for you today. Evan, Emile, would you come, as well."

Isabella's manner changed. She suspected something. "You would leave your guests?" she said.

"They're leaving. And there is still wine for those who choose to stay. They shall be fine. Upstairs, Isabella!"

The four ascended the stairway, went into one of the guest bedrooms, where Jean-Pierre closed the door behind them. His French was fast, clipped, and breathtakingly emotional. It was the opposite of the demure manner the host displayed before his friends downstairs.

"Who is Anthony Chesterfield?"

Stephen was amazed, and, he had to admit, somewhat grateful. It showed that her brother knew nothing about the situation and would represent Emile's sentiments on the subject.

"I...I..." She looked at Stephen and then at Sam. "He's an Anglo."

"Go on."

"What's to say? He's part of Chris's circle of friends."

"Not good enough. Why did you argue with him in a public setting?"

"Who told you that I did?"

"Don't play games, Isabella. I've had enough of your adventures for a lifetime and know you well enough to decipher when you're hiding something. My last party was ruined by the gossip that you were disgracing our family's good name, now must I hear this, as well? Who is he?"

She looked at Stephen whose expression was cut in stone.

"Why are you lying to me, cher?" Stephen said.

"He's a friend...from my past."

"And how did you meet him?" said Jean-Pierre.

"He is Monsieur and Madame Gatou's ward, adopted son. When mother and I went to town, she would always stop and have a dress made for both of us. It was our special treat. The Gatou's had a seamstress there by the name of Dominique Mercier who became enamored with a Yankee politician who came to Louisiana on business many years ago. They fell in love, had an affair, and she became pregnant with Tony."

The name bothered him. It was too familiar, too cute.

"So, why didn't they fire her on the spot?" said Jean-Pierre.

"They couldn't. They had no child of their own and fell in love with her little blonde boy. She would have had but one way to make a living if they'd abandoned her. She died a few years later when Tony was four—right about the time Mother and I began stopping there for our yearly visit. Tony and I became friends in much the same manner Emile and I did."

"Go on. There has to me more, sister."

"Well, you know how I always dreamed of Emile asking me to be his wife. But when I was eighteen, Emile was in France studying, you had just married Ernestine and were in Europe on your wedding trip, and Father and Mother were busy with the plantation. No one took much notice of me or what I was doing. Father had a habit of giving me money to buy anything I wanted so that I wouldn't pester him, especially on the seasonal trip to New Orleans. So, as most young girls do, I spent my money on gowns and the theater. Tony was now old enough to take an interest in me, and, without my parents' consent, I started meeting him at the dances."

"Mon Dieu! This is a nightmare. Mother never knew? Zut!"

Isabella continued, "I met Melinda there. She was having an affair with Monsieur Chabonnais at the time. We met at Gatou's too. She was twenty. I found her behavior extravagant and appealing—so mature. It defied the staid-old traditions I had long outgrown. The three of us would talk at Gatous for hours. Tony fell in love with me and...I with him. That was why I stopped writing letters to you, Emile."

She couldn't look at Stephen. "I was eighteen and you were just hinting at romantic intentions then. But a young wayward girl, such as myself, sometimes gets overwhelmed by the flattering words of a...liar."

Emile said, *"He took advantage of your innocence?"*

"I guess you could say that, yes. Father and Mother didn't know. Then one day he asked me to marry him. I thought I was in love, so I said yes. I knew that my parents would not give their consent, so we were married by a priest in the cathedral."

Stephen felt Emile's disappointment—his bitterness and rage. *"This cannot be. I loved you. I told you that I would come home and marry you. I promised you. Is our marriage a lie?"*

"No, my love. After the marriage, Tony wanted me to return home and tell my parents what we'd done so that they would understand that everything was legal, and that he should be allowed in the family with open arms. He said that he had no money to start a life with, and that I should make my parents give us some. His manner bothered me for it seemed unlike the romantic gentleman I thought I was in love with."

"I wager Father was beside himself with rage when you told him."

"This isn't easy for me to tell you, brother. I have kept this secret for many years. Though it is a great relief to be unburdened with this confession, I wonder what destruction my admission might create." She looked at Stephen. "I do so love you, Emile."

"Continue."

"Our marriage was never consummated, but I longed to be his wife because I thought he loved me. It was a lie. I finally told my father. I thought he would kill both of us."

"What did he do?" said Jean-Pierre.

"He went to the priest and forced him to annul the marriage or be reprimanded by a higher order for marrying two people without the girl's parents' consent. He did so."

"And how did Monsieur Chesterfield react to this loss?"

"We had an argument, and he ran away to Texas to fight in the war for freedom there. He said that he would rather fight and die for people's freedom rather than to live an hour without my love. He made me feel guilty, because he said that I'd betrayed him."

"Oh, brother," whispered Sam.

"At that time, Emile had sent his letter asking me to

consider marrying him. I told my father not to push me into anything yet, for I was so wounded by Tony's betrayal. Father told me that if I didn't marry soon, I would never have a family. He was worried that Emile would find out that I'd fallen in love with someone else and been married. He told me that I had committed a heinous sin in doing so, and that no decent man would have me if they knew. That thought was with me always. But," she looked at Stephen for pity, "I always cared for you, Emile. I made a mistake. My heart overruled my head. And Melinda would go on and on about Tony while she was marrying Chabonnais. She was in love with Tony, but Tony loved me. So, she agreed to marry Chabonnais out of desperation, and never gave up on winning Tony back with her wealth—provided he ever came back from Texas. I suspected he wouldn't. I was wrong."

"And what is your relationship with him now?" said Sam.

She stared at Stephen. "You and I were quite happy when we were first married. Then you went to France. Tony came back and saw me in town shopping with Melinda. I had no husband to prove to him that I was happily married. He warned me that he would soil my good name and ruin my marriage if I did not..."

"What?" Stephen said.

"At first, he said that it was for the cause of liberty that I should give him money. The fight was still brewing in Texas at the time. He wanted money from both Melinda and me. When that was no longer a good reason, he changed his story to one that required me to help *him* get a start in a new business venture. His liberty, so to speak. He also tried to charm me again, but by now, I had learned how shallow he was."

"You paid him?" said Stephen.

She was sobbing now. Her hands covered her face to hide her shame. "I had no choice. He threatened to tell Emile about our marriage. And then, when he had broken our marital trust, he would lie and tell my husband that we were still in love and having an illicit affair. If Emile believed the first truth, he knew it would be easy to destroy my marriage with other lies. Emile would never believe a word I said after he knew the truth. So, I paid him. I had to meet him at Gatou's, or at the theater, to give him the money. I wanted nothing to do with him, but I was frightened. I became melancholy. I thought of killing myself. I was squandering away our money, but dared not tell you or Jean about it. Chris had the costume designer remake gowns for me because I had no money to purchase them, and I needed them to meet Tony so that I could give him the money."

"You gave money to this swine. Without coming to me for help? What's a brother for, Isabella?"

"I was afraid you would challenge him, and then I might lose you too, Jean. I had to take into consideration the welfare of Ernestine and the children. It was my problem, and I was the only one who could solve it."

"But you only made it worse. You gave into him."

"I realize that now. I was so confused and frightened. Oh, Emile, you have no idea how often I wanted to tell you! I was afraid that you would throw me out of your house, hate me, or kill me if you knew. I was lonely, dejected, and so unhappy. I needed you, and you were in France. You never seemed to stay with me long enough for me to tell you the truth."

"So, he's still taking our money?" said Stephen.

"No, when we were losing so much money, I broke off with him. I told him that I could no longer make the payments, and he would have to use Melinda's wealth from now on. He said that he would tell you about our past, and lie to you about our present relationship. I thought of killing myself. Chris knows all about it and tried to comfort me. He would go to Gatou's with me. Have the gowns made for me. He told me to tell you about the situation, and that if you threw me out, I was supposed to go and live with him. He would take care of me. But I didn't want to leave you, Emile. I love you. It took me some time to realize that. I have always loved you—since we were children. A girl can sometimes be swayed by a sweet-talking charmer, but not anymore. Our argument was his fault. I had sent him a letter telling him that I had no more money and would not pay him any more. He saw Melinda and me at Bank's Arcade. He was rude to me, so we argued. But I swear to you, brother that I never dishonored our name, or that of my husband's. I will swear on our parent's grave to that effect."

"So be it. There is only one thing I can do now."

"I think you are right. I'm with you in this, brother," said Jean-Pierre.

"When I am done with Monsieur Chesterfield, he will have no need of any woman—neither you nor Melinda. Did the man say that he was on the third floor of Bank's, Jean?"

"I believe so."

"Then let's bring in this new year and new life with the proper termination of last year's problem."

Isabella stopped Stephen as he moved towards the door. "Please, no. I couldn't bear to lose you."

"You had your chance to tell me the truth and save my family's name and money. You gave it to this man. The choice was yours, and you chose to dishonor me."

"No, only to save our love."

"By ruining everything my family lived and died for."

"Don't go to him, Emile. Please. Evan, don't let him do this. Jean-Pierre?"

"Not now, Isabella," said Jean, in a soothing tone. "You must let men do as they must."

She stopped Stephen by putting her hands on his chest and then tried to place her arms around his neck. "Please."

"Do you beg for Tony's life or mine? One cannot be too sure at this point."

She pulled away from him. "How can you doubt me, Emile? I was frightened. I didn't know what to do."

"You had good reason to be frightened, Isabella. I shall be staying at the hotel with my cousin from now on. Enjoy your new home, mon cher. You will stay there from now on. You love New Orleans so much—stay here—alone. When I return to Durel Plantation, you shall not be by my side. Keep Anna and Nora, for the rest shall stay with me."

She looked toward Jean-Pierre with a pleading expression.

"Do not come to me for assistance, sister. What could you have been thinking when you married that peasant?"

She dropped to the floor and sobbed. Her voice was weak. Her heart broken. Her will to live gone. "I wasn't thinking. Don't you understand?"

"Enjoy your stay in town this season, mon cher."

Stephen wanted to go to her, tell her that he understood, but Emile was a man on a mission. And Emile was the stronger component right now because Stephen's heart was broken too, his will defeated. His mind understood, but his soul wanted vengeance. There had been so many opportunities to doubt her in the past, and he had survived them all with blind faith and unconditional love. Trusting his own instincts had carried him through every situation.

Sam turned to regard the pathetic woman sobbing uncontrollably.

"Isabella," Sam said.

Emile stopped him from going to her with, *"Now, Evan."*

Ernestine came running into the room. She still wore her nightgown and seemed weak but determined to get pass the men. Stephen waited for a second in the doorway to see what would happen.

"What has happened? Why are you crying?" she asked.

"Leave her alone, Ernestine," said Jean-Pierre.

Ernestine defied her husband by cradling Isabella in her arms, as if she were her own child. She regarded her husband with a scornful look.

Isabella Durel clung to her sister-in-law while she watched the man she loved shut the door on their relationship.

Cicero raced the carriage to the Bank's Arcade building even though Emile and Jean-Pierre doubted that they would find the man in his apartment.

"I'll find the man if it takes all night," said Emile.

But it didn't. Having no idea which apartment belonged to Tony Chesterfield, they went to the downstairs area to look in the gambling rooms, where they found him playing poker with four gentlemen. Gambling with money that did not belong to him and that was supposed to be for his 'new business.' He must have known that Isabella would never see him here, or guess how he was using her money.

Emile was incensed, and making sure that he didn't say too much in anger, he called him out.

"Are you, Monsieur Chesterfield?"

The man was surprised. Obviously, if he were being confronted by Isabella's husband it could only mean one thing—Isabella had told her husband the truth. Emile had trapped him in front of his peers.

"I am Anthony Chesterfield," he said, placing his cards face down on the table.

"Sir," Emile said and slapped him across the face with his glove. *"You have insulted the Durel and Devieux family names. You have taken advantage of the kind generosity of my dear wife, and for that, sir, you are a villain. You have robbed my family of money, sir; therefore, you are a thief. You are a coward and an opportunist who has finally met his match. My brother-in-law will be my second, and my cousin will be in touch with you in two days."*

Tony stood to face the assault. "I have no quarrel with you, Durel."

"But I have one with you. If you are a man, you will meet me on the field of honor at the Oaks in four days. Justice will be served."

"How can it be served if I kill you?"

"Who shall die is in the hands of God. Will you meet my challenge?"

A self-satisfied grin creased his lips. He was putting on the cavalier attitude for his friends, but Stephen could see that it was false. "I welcome the challenge, and the chance to finish you off once and for all."

Sam grabbed Tony by the lapels of his tailor-made jacket, raised him off the ground a bit, dropped him, and then gave him an uppercut to the right jaw. Tony fell to the ground, nursing a bruised, or possibly dislocated, jawbone.

Sam said, "We'll see about that, you bastard."

The three men walked away from the gentlemen's gambling parlor feeling somewhat vindicated.

"Will you return to my home with me?" said Jean-Pierre.

"Not tonight. I have to find a room.

"Do you really mean that you'll leave my sister for good?"

Jean-Pierre showed a sensitivity on the subject that Stephen hadn't expected. It was comforting to see that he really was concerned about his sister's happiness.

"I do, indeed," said Emile.

Jean-Pierre paused, looked at the ground for a moment, and then at his brother-in-law. "I'll find my own way. She may still be there with Ernestine. I'll see that she finds a way home."

"The carriage is hers. She can find her own way home. Take my man with you."

Jean-Pierre clasped Emile's arm at the elbow as a sign of farewell. "Bonsoir, Emile. We shall finish him off together."

"Bien. Au revoir."

As soon as his brother-in-law was out of sight, Emile faded.

"Okay, now what?" said Sam.

Stephen raised his hands to his temples and cried out, "I can't take this anymore, Sam! What the hell am I doing? Emile is taking over. Isabella can't be alone right now with a murderer out there looking to kill her and with neither of us nearby to watch over her."

"Emile's having a jealous fit inside you, that's all, but we should've known this would happen. I mean, sooner or later the truth would come out."

"You have no idea how much I wanted to go to her, but I felt such pain. Headache and heartache both. Doubly intense. He's hurting. We're hurting."

Sam touched Stephen's shoulder. "I'll stay with her."

"Will you? Comfort her. I'm afraid that this might set her up for a suicide attempt. She was so happy."

"I think it's about time you had a talk with your alter ego."

"That should be interesting. I'm disappointed too, but I still understand what happened. Emile's a proud man. I feel his soul inside my body, our body. Even though he still loves her, he won't return to her."

"Yes, he will. Just give him time. Talk to him. In your head—or something. We have more important things to worry about besides his love life."

"Yeah. I'm about to duel a man who may very well kill me—us."

"I doubt that Emile will let you hold the gun, so don't worry. Good thing I brought those pistols. Maybe a bottle of whiskey and a long night of soul searching with your best friend will help," Sam said.

"You're my best friend, next to Isabella."

"I meant Emile."

"I'll be at the St. Louis Hotel. Take care of her. We have to keep history at bay or this whole trip is a waste of time and money."

"I'll do my best. What's a cousin for anyway?"

"Tell her not to worry. Tell her that I still love her—that Emile is just out of his mind with jealousy, but that he'll get over it. Don't let her be sad."

"I'll take care of Issy; you take care of Emile."

"Come to my hotel tomorrow early in the morning, and we'll talk—have breakfast together—something."

"I better get a rig and get back to Jean-Pierre's. And you—find the answers in the shadows, pal. It's what it's all about."

They parted. Stephen walked to the hotel, and found that he could have his old suite of rooms back, though the clerk seemed curious as to why he would have the need of it.

He opened the door to his room, lit the light nearest the door, and dropped his body into a chair.

"All right, Emile, it's show time."

He rubbed his eyes, looked at the ceiling, as if trying to guess what to say, then stood up and walked into the bedroom. He stared in silence at the decor. At the center of the room, was a full-length mirror. He'd talked with Emile via the mirror in 1998. It seemed the only way to speak to his dark side.

"Emile! I want you to listen and listen good. I've had enough of your interference in our lives."

"*I might say the same thing,*" said the voice in his head.

Stephen smiled. It was working. "She's the woman of your dreams, your life, your hopes, and she loves you. Are you an ass hole or what?"

A long pause and then, "*I am hurt beyond words.*"

"Well, get over it! You called the man out. What more do you want?"

"*To kill him and to hurt her.*"

"Oh, shit. Emile. She was young and romantic. You were out of town. It's your own fault that you didn't propose to her before you left for France. You knew she was the only girl for you. She got a crush on this guy, and let's face it, he's a good con artist. So, she's weak. At last, we see that she is, not as tough as she pretends to be and is very vulnerable. That vulnerability is rather appealing, don't you think? You were angry when she was running the show. Now when she needs your help because she's got herself into heavy trouble she can't handle, instead of being her knight in shining armor, and her savior, you're acting like a damn fool."

"*I want revenge.*"

"And you're going to get it, okay? But don't take it out on her, take it out on *him.* Has it ever occurred to you that he might kill *you* ? Then he gets your money, your life, and your wife. What else can she do but go to him if you're killed? She gets the plantation and the townhouse. This guy's going to move right in. Real bright, Emile. The last of the Durels gets iced. Tony wins it all. Just what he's been waiting for since she was eighteen. Isabella in his bed and the family's money in his pocket. Just picture Durel Plantation being run by this Anglo 'cause you have no heirs, pal."

"*She wouldn't marry him after he killed her husband.*"

"And why the hell not? One: you kicked her out of your life. Two: you challenged him, not the other way around. Three: she'll have your estate after your death, but we both know she can't run it by herself. Four: she asked for forgiveness from a man who's treated her like shit in the first place, and he refused her. If she tries to run that farm, she'll need help, if she doesn't get it, she'll sell it. Either way, she gets the dough. Five: *our* Isabella won't stay celibate for a lifetime. And if it's a choice between Chris and lover boy, she will pick Tony. Not right away, of course, because she knows he's a cad, but eventually, her passionate nature will force her to give in to his charms. And let's not forget the tiny possibility that if you die, Jean-Pierre has to take up the challenge and try to avenge your death. What if Tony kills him too? Ernestine and Isabella become wealthy widows. What about his children?"

"*She'll not go to him.*"

"Did it ever occur to you that after that little display of temper of yours tonight, she might not want *you* back?"

"*What?*"

"You were so mean to her. You always have to have your own way, don't you?"

"*She betrayed me.*"

"No, she didn't. She fell prey to a handsome con artist and blackmailer while you were at school in France. Summer-vacation-kinda-crush thing. So, why didn't you tell her you loved her—that there was no other woman on the planet for you?"

"I was frightened she wouldn't accept me."

"She made a mistake at a tender and impressionable age. She wasn't totally sure of your intentions. In walks Mr. Macho-man. She gets a little crush which blossoms into stupidity. Daddy steps in and fixes it for her and for you. She loses her parents a few years later and now has only you for comfort. Then guess what happens—you *leave* her. Macho-man returns. The guy has some major issues about being left as an orphan and seeing all these rich Creoles come and go from his adoptive parents' shop he decides he wants a piece of the pie. Then he sees Isabella and wants a piece of that too."

"Really, Stephen. Must you be so crude?"

"Hey, I'm just telling the truth. You know how she affects people. You aren't around anymore, and Tony sneaks back into town. Lonely wife? It's not a new story line. He's blackmailing her to keep *you* from killing her. What other option does she have? Lose the only family she has? Lose the man who's abandoned her and whom she still loves? Lose her life when her hot-headed Creole husband finds out about all of her lies? The lies Daddy instructed her to tell, no less. Have Tony destroy the only thing she has left to live for?"

"Well, now, I hadn't looked at it like that."

"Well, you've got to, pal, or you lose it all. I could live without my money. Life is more than that. She was right in your loving arms the other night. Hungry, passionate, submissive, vulnerable, and, oh, baby, is she in love. Makes Juliet look like a rookie. You saw her struck down by the poison. Why don't you just finish her off like you wanted to, 'cause you've done a nice job on her tonight?"

Stephen's voice was loud and fierce. He didn't care who heard him. Everything that had bothered him for seven years was pouring out of his soul. It felt wonderful. "All that *bull shit* the other night, when you were making love to her, about how you can't live without her—every night was hell without her—yadda yadda yadda. Just talk, Emile?"

There was a long pause. So long, in fact, that Stephen was afraid he'd lost Emile.

"No, it was not simply words. She's my life."

Stephen smiled. "And we still have her, Emile. Just let me talk to her. In short—butt out! I'm trying to save your life too, you know. I appreciate your help on the riding and the history stuff, but when it comes to saving your life and hers, you gotta *butt out*—stay out of my way—or you're going to get all of us killed."

"I do appreciate the chance to alter my life for the better. And I do thank you for all that you're doing."

"It isn't for you alone. It's for us. Karma and all that crap. I have to be healed too. Somehow, this is for me, you, *and* Isabella. But if you keep having these temper fits, giving me these headaches, everything I'm trying to do will be ruined."

"You want me to 'butt out'?"

"Well...not entirely...but let me handle the tricky parts and be there to help me when I'm in trouble. I do need you. We're one. You just need to understand that what happens to you makes a difference to *my* life as well as yours."

"I do not understand all this."

"It's all right. I don't have a handle on all of it myself. I need you, and you need me, but she needs both of us. Dr. Gayerré asked God to change your mind and her heart in his journal. Isabella asked for a savior in her diary. We're answering the prayers of two people you care about very much."

"I see your point. Forgive me."

"No problem. You and I are blood, spirit, mind, and flesh. I don't mind any of that *except* when you start putting words in my mouth. *That* I mind."

"I won't do it again."

"It's all right if I don't know how to answer a question—like the 'peaches' thing. That's cool when you do that intervention stuff when I'm tongue-tied for something to say." He decided to lighten the mood. "And to be perfectly honest, I've never had sex like this in my life."

"The French passion?"

"You gonna tell me that if all goes well at the Oaks you can live with the thought that this woman is in New Orleans, all alone, while you rot on that plantation without her in your bed every night? Some English actor kissing her hand and proposing marriage to her? Remember, she's depressed and *he* makes her laugh. Time goes by—sooner or later—divorce-city. She's rebel enough to defy her religion on this one. We both know she's independent and hot-headed enough to go against the Creole tradition. It's her nature. Why should she uphold the proud family tradition when you and Jean-Pierre have thrown her out of it? She will want to be happy and hang the cost."

"But the money she threw away was my family's money too."

"I know, I know, but, money isn't everything. She's the only family you have now, Emile."

"I've been a hot-headed fool."

"Don't be too hard on yourself. I know how you feel. You're just a man in love, and you were raised with this value system thing about family, name, honor, etcetera. If it makes you feel any better, I'm upset too. I was glad Evan punched him, and I'll be there for you at the Oaks. I'm sworn to save lives, though, not to take them, so you run the show there, because I can't."

"I understand."

"Then you'll stay out of my thoughts when it comes to this relationship?"

"Yes," said Emile. *"Do I have to stay out of her bed, as well?"*

"Well...I don't suppose *that's* a problem. She seems to like it."

"I've been such a monster to her."

"You're just an old-fashioned guy with old-fashioned ways. She's a very modern girl. Enjoy it. Trust me, the women in my time can't compare to her, or I'd be married by now. You're very lucky."

"I'm lucky because you're here to help me. I shall repay you, Stephen. You are generous beyond words to come all this way, and at such expense, to help total strangers."

"Not strangers, Emile. We're the same."

"The duel?"

"I'm not thrilled with the prospect, but it goes on as planned. I want revenge too. She lied to us for a reason, and that was wrong of her, but this man will pay for what he's done to all of us. She will not go back to Gatou's either. Now that I see where that's heading, I understand why she was so upset about having that fitting."

"You are a very intelligent and compassionate man, Dr. Templeton."

"Look in the mirror, Emile Durel; we're one and the same."

Emile and his headache faded. Stephen collapsed on the bed. Every aspect of his emotional pain was gone. He was reborn. Complete relaxation. Release of all emotions. Joy. Satisfaction. Sanity. Sweet, sweet sleep.

Chapter Twenty-Seven

Stephen was awakened by Sam's knock on the door and his name being called. Because his sleep had been so sudden, he was still in his clothes and able to answer the door immediately.

"All right. All right. What's the matter?"

"It's Isabella. She's hysterical. Won't sleep, eat. It's awful. I hope you and Emile settled things last night because she needs you."

"What happened?"

"I consoled her at Jean-Pierre's before we headed home, and she seemed to be okay about you maybe coming back and all that. We got home, and Nora and Anna helped her out of her clothes and into bed. She called to me, and I came in and sat beside her. She was bad off so I stuck close. She'd cry, then she'd be okay, and then she'd cry again. Finally, she told me to leave her, that she'd be all right. I told her to call me if she needed me, that I'd be in the next room. She knows you challenged Tony. She's depressed; I can't say what she might do. I know she didn't sleep all night. You've got to come back."

Stephen paid his hotel bill at the desk, and they drove the rig as fast as they could to Emile's new townhouse.

"Where is she?" he said, as he raced into the house and up the stairs.

Nora said, "Thank goodness. She's been calling for you all night long. Don't know what you two been fussing over, and it ain't none of my She's as pale as a ghost."
business, but I shore hope you're fixing to stay. She's as pale as a ghost."

That thought unnerved him.

He walked into their bedroom, and Emile kept quiet.

"Isabella?"

She turned her head on the pillow. "Emile?" She held out her arms to him.

He sat on the bed beside her. "Are you all right?"

"If you say you're here to stay with me, I am."

"I was upset and foolish."

"You promised never to leave my side."

"I know."

"You won't leave? Go back home without me?"

He held her close to his chest. "This is the only home I know."

"I'm so sorry, Emile! I broke your trust. I should have told you from the first, but Father told me to keep quiet on the matter, and I obeyed him because I didn't want to lose you. Then when Tony came back, I was trapped. If I told you about him, then I would have to admit that I hadn't been truthful with you from the start. Then it would have been easy for Tony to lie to you about me. You might have believed him. I tried to tell you back at the plantation, but I was frightened of how you might react. I've made such a mess of things."

"It's all right. I understand. I didn't at first, but I do now."

She pulled away from him so that she could see his face. "Then you'll not duel Tony?"

"Ah...I'm afraid I can't change that." He wiped away a tear from her cheek. "Jean-Pierre is to be my second."

"God, no, what have I done?"

"You were used, that's all. He preyed upon your innocence. Someone has to teach him a lesson."

She held onto him. "You can't. He might kill you or Jean-Pierre. Then he wins it all and destroys what little happiness I have."

"And if I kill him?"

"Then I'll feel responsible for his death since I agreed to marry him once and gave him money instead of sending him away as I should have. If I had been more aggressive with him when he returned to New Orleans, none of this would have happened. My weakness is our undoing."

"It is no longer in your hands, cher."

She looked into his eyes. "Please."

"It's too late. What was done in the past cannot be undone." He stroked her hair gently. "Everything will be all right, Isabella, you'll see."

She held on to him and whispered in his ears. "Promise me?"

Sam came into the room. "I'll see to it that nothing happens to Emile, Isabella. My word as a gentleman and a cousin."

Stephen found it difficult to console her when he was not comfortable with shooting a man. He knew Emile would handle the situation for him, but somehow that thought didn't make him feel any better. He held onto the reality that sobbed in his arms, closed his eyes, and found peace.

The next few days were not easy ones. Sam was sent to retrieve the clothes from Gatou's and tell the couple that the Durel and Devieux family would not be returning to their shop. He cleaned the dueling pistols, making them ready for their debut.

Melinda came to the house to console her friend. Her presence surprised the time travelers. Nora and Anna stayed quiet and did their chores without complaining or causing any problems for their mistress. Chris came by to sit with Isabella and talk privately with Emile.

"I'm sorry about not telling you all that I knew on this subject, but Issy told me to keep it a secret. It would have been wrong for me to interfere when I'd been asked to keep her secret. It's an awkward situation to be in. On one hand, I'm delighted that this dirty secret is at last out in the open. One less burden to trouble her. But the duel, that's another matter. For Issy's sake, I pray you make peace with this man before it's too late," said Chris. "He was her past; you are her future. Neither should be tarnished. Tony's proven how low he can sink, and she realizes that he's not her savior—you are."

"I can't forgive him for insulting two households. We've been through so much in the last five years. He chose to take advantage of that. To bleed her for what she could not change. I only thank God that her father had the marriage annulled so quickly. But how torn she must have been—and for so long."

"I wouldn't say I'm close with Tony, but he is in my social circle. I know him fairly well, and I don't like him much after what he's done to Issy. But I will tell you what I *do* know.

His friend, Jonathan Connally, will be his second. Both men are fine shots. They'll pick pistols. Tony's told all of his friends that he can overpower you on the field. Just talk, though. He's a coward. Went to fight the war in Texas or so he says, but I doubt that he saw any action. Just tells people that was what he did those years he lived away from the city."

Chris smiled before he continued, "Concentrate on his every move. Now that I've discovered what sort of man you are, Emile, I hate to see anyone get hurt. I'll stay with Issy that day."

"If you wish."

"Good luck. I mean that sincerely. She loves you. No one can make her happy but you."

Stephen could see that the man was speaking the truth. "Thank you for saying so. Coming from you that means a great deal to me."

"Her eyes can't lie. The truth is there."

Isabella and Stephen spent the day before the duel together. Conversation was at a minimum. They allowed no guests into their home. Isabella cried and trembled at turns and ate very little. He knew she was in emotional pain, and he wanted to tell her that he probably wouldn't die because he was a time traveler, but he couldn't be sure of anything right now. He had changed time. He was equally worried about Jean-Pierre who would never have fought this duel in his lifetime and queried why Tony's life had to be altered too.

"The Domino Effect," he said to himself. "A new one for Time Travelers, Incorporated. Push one thing out of its place and all the other ones fall too."

But then maybe Tony deserved to pay the price for blackmail and manipulation. The only answer he could find to this challenge was a spiritual one. Gayerré had prayed that God would intervene in their lives— "change his mind and her heart" he had written in his diary. Perhaps it was God's justice, after all. Even the Almighty thought that Isabella deserved a second chance. The thought comforted Stephen that and the reminder that Emile would be there to play out the scene.

Isabella was in a panic the morning he left with Sam and Jean-Pierre. He gave strict orders to Nathan not to be swayed by her pleas to follow them to the Oaks. Chris came just as Stephen was leaving, in order to keep Isabella from holding him back. She begged him not to go, so he kissed her and told her that he would be home for lunch.

It was a misty morning, and the light green of the trees at the Oaks blended with the fog which draped the scene like moss. It was just as Stephen had dreamed it.

Suddenly, he was very frightened of dying. He wondered if he would see his own father again. If life were to suddenly end, how would his friends and family know? Who would tell the staff at the hospital that Dr. Stephen Templeton had died in a duel in 1839?

Jonathan Connally and Sam came together to talk. Dr. Gayerré read the rules of the duel, and they both agreed to them. Sam loaded the pistol and handed it to Stephen.

"It worked perfectly when I used it this morning. Don't worry. Emile will be there," he said.

"Do you take back the words you spoke with Anthony Chesterfield?" said Dr. Gayerré.

"No. He has insulted the Durels and the Devieuxs by his behavior with their daughter and my wife."

"Very well. Turn your back on each other, walk ten paces, then turn and face each other. When I drop this white linen handkerchief, fire."

Stephen's hands were shaking. He felt Emile's solid grip on the butt of the pistol.

"It's my turn."

The comment eased Stephen's mind. He counted ten paces, but when he turned, he heard a horse whinny. It was Isabella, Chris, and Nathan in the rig. "She shouldn't be here," he thought. "She might get hurt."

Tony turned.

"Stop this. Stop it," she said, with Chris trying vainly to keep her from leaping from the carriage.

Dr. Gayerré said, "Stay out of this, Isabella. Someone stop her before she gets hurt."

Tony was aiming his pistol at Stephen's head. "Drop the hanky. What are you waiting for?" he said.

278

Jean-Pierre said, "Stay out of it, Isabella."

"No!" Isabella tore away from Chris and Nathan and ran to the field. She stood between both men. "Stop this insanity! I'm the one wounded here. It's my honor, not yours, this man has besmirched. Why should anyone die because of me?"

"Get back, Issy. You and I would be together now save for your family's pigheaded opposition. Let us finish it once and for all this day by allowing God to choose your husband for you."

"He has. Emile Durel is my husband, not you. I owe you nothing. Leave us."

"Isabella, this is all very well for you to say, but it won't solve the problem. The man is a coward and a snake and deserves the strongest punishment I can offer him," said Emile.

Jean-Pierre said, "This is a matter for men to finish. Will someone get her out of here?"

"Drop the hanky. She'll move fast enough," said Tony, dismissing her with his hand as if she were an irritation.

Jonathan Connally said, "Not until the lady is out of harm's way, Tony. The duel has been interrupted. We must start again."

Just then Nathan and Chris grabbed the woman and dragged her back by the trees to keep her away from the pistol fire. The men walked back to their original spots, paced, and turned. The hanky dropped. Isabella screamed. Stephen's eyes involuntarily shifted, so that he could look at her. Emile's steady hand and keen eye helped him aim and fire his gun. It popped on cue. Tony aimed and fired a fraction of a second afterwards. Stephen felt the rush of air as the bullet whizzed by his head. Tony fell. The physician examined him and pronounced Anthony Chesterfield wounded but not in mortal danger. It was up to Tony's second to follow through with his task. Jonathan held the pistol in his hands and looked at Tony.

"Kill the bastard for me," said Tony, crying out in pain as Dr. Gayerré attended to his bleeding shoulder.

Isabella screamed, "*No!* Please. It's over. You know it is."

"I'm surprised by your behavior, Tony. She has condemned you with her pleas. You have shown what manner of man you are this day. The woman loves her husband, and you've done nothing but cause these two families harm. It's over for you in Orleans." The man looked at Stephen. "Monsieur Durel, are you vindicated?"

Stephen answered swiftly so that Emile wouldn't say anything. "I am."

"Then it is God's will that no man should die this day."

Isabella rushed into Stephen's arms. "Thank God, it's all over. Take me home."

Jean-Pierre hugged his sister, and Sam shook Stephen's hand.

Stephen walked over to Tony to examine the severity of the man's wound. The bullet hadn't been driven far into his flesh. He would live with Dr. Gayerré's help. It was over. The scandal, the blackmail, the money, his reputation, hers, the control he might have had on her, the family secret. There was even a stronger bond between Jean-Pierre, Isabella, and Emile now.

Sam smiled at Stephen. "Not bad for a day's work. I know they were expensive, and I'll pay you if you want me to, but can I have the pistols for my brother?"

"Of course. You don't owe me anything. It's the other way around. Give them to Jim."

"He'll be so pleased to know that they were used in an *actual* duel that he might not even sell them."

"She's free, and that's the essential issue. Look at her."

They watched as Isabella hugged Chris and Nathan and laughed away her fears while climbing into the rig—releasing the tension of the last few days by teasing Chris. Happy to be heading home. Free at last.

Dr. Gayerré was administering to Tony's wounds, and Sam and Stephen had a few moments to talk with each other.

"Happy ending?" said Sam.

"For Emile," said Stephen smiling.

"There's still a murderer out there," said Sam.

"Tony?"

"It's highly probable. He had a motive. She'd told him that she wasn't going to pay him any more blackmail money and that she wasn't interested in his false promises of love anymore. Jealousy and ambition are strong motives."

"To kill Emile, but not her, I should think. All right. I'll grant you that he had a motive. Cast-off lover gets even. But what about the weapon?"

"A gift?" said Sam.

"What sort of gift holds death?" said Stephen.

"A love potion?" said Sam.

"Perfume?"

"Hand cream? Melinda!" They looked at each other and smiled.

"She said that she'd given Isabella a special body lotion and would give her more because Isabella liked the exclusivity of the fragrance. Putting it on her body would be the same as swallowing it. Gets into the skin. Some poisons work that way," said Stephen.

"Motive?" said Sam.

"She wanted Tony, Tony didn't want her because he still had this thing for Isabella, and she was in the way. Plus, Melinda had access to voodoo potions, and...well...she's...weird."

"If we could prove she's killing her husband?"

Stephen said, "We can if we can find those honey cakes."

"Honey cakes?"

"I've been tossing these ideas around in my head for a few days but never had the chance to mention them to you what with all the excitement that's transpired after the dinner at Jean-Pierre's. Some things that were said that night just kept resurfacing. Remember the other night at Jean-Pierre's, Chabonnais mentioned how Melinda makes honey cakes for *his* sweet tooth alone. No one else tastes them. That's odd."

"You can kill a man with a honey cake?" said Sam. "I hope chocolate cake isn't a problem, or I'm in big trouble."

"What's the main ingredient in honey cake, Sam?"

"Duh, honey?"

"And honey comes from..."

"Bees."

"Who suck the nectar from..."

"Plants."

"Some poisonous—like mountain laurel or *ivy*. The nectar will not kill the bee, but can kill a human being. If the bees on his plantation create a nasty-tasting honey, we've got her."

Sam queried, "Wouldn't he notice, though, if it tasted bitter?"

"It wouldn't taste bitter if it were baked inside the honey cake. Symptoms are gastrointestinal distress; watering of the eyes, nose, and mouth; breathing becomes difficult; and the heartbeat slows. There is depression, convulsions, paralysis."

"The same symptoms Dr. Gayerré mentioned Chabonnais had—only not as dramatic. But why hasn't he died?"

"She may be administering it to him in small, subtle doses so that it looks as if he's simply falling ill from old age rather than being murdered."

Sam said, "You like the guy, don't you?"

"I think he has a right to live a full life, and his wife—if she *is* murdering him for Tony—has just lost on two counts. Tony will never show his face in New Orleans again, so she's lost him once and for all unless she wants to leave all her money behind and follow him. And if we can sample the honey in her pantry, we may put her behind bars. Dr. Gayerré could attest to Chabonnais falling ill at *infrequent* intervals, but we need to move quickly. If Tony decides to leave town, and she wants to go with him, she may speed up her plans."

"Do you think she's the one trying to kill Isabella then?" said Sam.

"I wouldn't put anything passed Melinda. Tell Isabella you want to have tea at the Chabonnais's. We need to inspect the pantry Melinda is so fond of."

Isabella hugged her husband when he returned to the carriage and refused to leave his side for the rest of the day—and into the night.

She was surprised by the sudden interest in Melinda's home, but assumed Evan was smitten by her lovely friend and agreed to ask Melinda if they could visit the following day.

Chapter Twenty-Eight

Melinda was cordial when she told them that her husband would not be downstairs because he wasn't feeling well. They were ushered into her opulent parlor where tea was waiting for them. The finest china cups, with a rose pattern, sat next to a sterling silver tea service. On a tall server sat a variety of sweet cakes and candy—but no honey cakes. Resting on one side of the server was a gallon jar that contained peaches swirling in rum.

"Your husband mentioned that you were a very talented cook," remarked Stephen.

"I'm not sure what you mean."

"I just noticed that you didn't offer us your famous honey cakes. The ones your husband spoke of with such affection the other night at Jean-Pierre's. He said they were a real treat because *you* made them especially for him."

She smiled and looked at her tea cup. "He fancies them, so I make them just for him."

"I see." Stephen made a move that caused his tea cup to waver and spill its contents onto his leg. Sam hurried to his side with his napkin.

"I'm afraid cold water is necessary to remove the stain. Your cookhouse is..."

"Allow me," said Isabella.

"No, I think Evan and I can handle this."

Without too much formality, they hurried to the back of the mansion. The slaves saw the problem and went to fetch cold water.

"We've got to find the pantry, and then I'll pick the lock."

Stephen was impressed. "Do you know how to do that?"

"I stole one of Issy's hairpins before we left the house. I'm experienced."

He worked the lock on the pantry, but the slave girl came back just as it snapped open. They covered the lock with their backsides. Stephen distracted her by saying that he needed a place to take off his trousers because the tea had burned his leg. She went to find the master's robe so that Stephen would not have to stand there half-naked while the servants tried to remove the stain from his pants.

"Okay. We're in," said Sam.

They searched every shelf. Glass bottles, jars, vegetables, fruit, and meat. Then Stephen noticed a small honey pot hidden behind some jam jars, lifted the lid of it, took his finger and sampled it, and acknowledged victory.

"It's got to be poison. The taste is astringent. She's good. I'll hand her that. No one would have been allowed in her pantry. The lady of the house holds the only key. Heaven forbid she makes a mistake and lets one of the slaves take some of the jellies out of the pantry for toast one morning."

Sam hid the tiny jug in his coat pocket, and they emerged just in time to have the slave return with the robe. She left with his trousers folded over her arm. Sam locked the pantry door, and Stephen searched for a honey cake to prove his point to Dr. Gayerré.

One of the servants walked into the room with the master's breakfast tray. The meal was virtually untouched. On the tray, was a small plate with two honey cakes resting on it.

"The bitch," said Sam.

"What you say, massa?" said the woman.

"I simply said that he should hitch up his trousers so that we can get back to the ladies."

"How soon can I have my pants back?" said Stephen.

"I'll go check on that right now." She left.

Stephen took the honey cakes, placed them in a linen cloth, and handed them to Sam who placed them in his trouser's pocket.

"I wish I had some lab equipment with me right now. I'd like to have one of the lab technicians at Cook County check the contents of those cakes."

"Should we tell Mr. Chabonnais?" said Sam.

"That's a question. I think we should take our findings to Dr. Gayerré since he suspected this all along. Let him handle it," said Stephen.

"But what if she forces him to eat more of the honey cakes and does him in *tonight*?"

"We'll have to end tea directly and do it right now. She'll probably think he ate his breakfast since we took the cakes."

"Unless the slave girl tells her differently," said Sam.

"She probably won't ask. A little too obvious, don't you think? We have no time to waste. Hand me my clothes and let's get out of here."

Isabella was shocked when Stephen and Sam told her that they'd had enough tea, and that the trousers had to be dealt with at home if they were to be salvaged. They bid Melinda a curt farewell.

"Whatever has gotten into the two of you?" Isabella said.

"We have to see Dr. Gayerré today about Monsieur Chabonnais's condition. He seems worse, and we want to know the truth."

"You mean about what's making him sick?"

"Yes, we're very worried about him. He seems like such a nice man."

"May I come with you? I've been concerned on that matter as well."

Sam and Stephen looked at each other. A silent decision was made between them.

"I thought you wouldn't want to travel to the hospital."

"Something isn't right with all this," she said in her oddly intuitive manner. "He seems so healthy for an aging gentleman. Then all of a sudden he's on death's doorstep, and Melinda doesn't tell me much about his condition."

Stephen shrugged his shoulders. "Very well, cher, if you wish to come with us, you may."

Sam said, "Are you sure, Emile?"

"I think we've had enough of lies for a week, don't you?"

"It won't be nice, cousin. The truth may hurt your feelings and a long-standing friendship between you and Melinda."

"Why?"

"We think your friend is slowly poisoning her husband."

"Melinda? Why would she do that? You're wrong. She may not be the happiest wife, but she wouldn't do that to him."

She stared at both of them. "Would she?"

They told her about the honey and the special-order honey cakes and then told Cicero to go directly to the Charity Hospital.

Dr. Gayerré was available to discuss the problem, having just made his final rounds. He tasted the honey and looked quizzically at the honey cake. "How do you know so much about poisoned honey?"

Sam said, "He doesn't. I do. You see, I've traveled extensively throughout France and Spain, and I've been told of such things. One of my dearest friends, a physician in Paris, knew of a wife who married for money and whose husband became ill quite suddenly. She nursed him with a white powder mixed into his drink. It was later determined to be...arsenic."

"Dear me," said Gayerré.

"She was tried and convicted for attempting to kill her husband. There's still time to help Monsieur Chabonnais."

"I will inform the police immediately. We have the honey, and its sour taste is clear proof that it's poisonous. We have the husband's public declaration that she makes honey cakes for him alone, not allowing the servants or guests for tea, to touch the cakes. He has the symptoms you described as being those typical of such a poisoning. I think you might have saved my friend's life. I'm so sorry, Isabella. Your best friend. How this must hurt you?"

"I can't believe she'd even think of such a horrible plan! But now that you mention it, I do remember her having a private conversation with Marie Laveau, though I've always been told that the voodoo queen refuses to help anyone murder another person. I thought it odd that I wasn't privy to her comments because Melinda has allowed me to listen in on all of her other prophecies." She shook her head sadly. "It seems I can't choose anything correctly. Tony. Melinda."

Stephen kissed her on the forehead. "You chose me."

"A decision made by you and my father, and, yet, one that may prove my greatest salvation."

"You can't mention this to her, of course, and you must not go anywhere with her. She loves Tony and may still be upset that he's been ruined by our family. If she's capable of attempting to murder one person, she may try to hurt you too."

"She wouldn't. I can understand why she would want her husband's money as well as her freedom so that she could marry Tony, but why would she want to harm me? I'm married and pose no threat to her."

Sam said, "Tony, for all of his duplicity, may still harbor feelings for you. Stay away from her, cousin."

She agreed to keep close to Evan and Emile during the days that followed.

Dr. Gayerré explained the situation to the police and eventually to Monsieur Chabonnais. For some reason, he wasn't surprised, but the depression that followed was poignant to say the least. She was accused and sent to prison to await her trial. His health improved. The healthier the man became, the more obvious it was to the entire city that she'd been undermining his physical condition.

The wheels of justice spun rapidly, and her trial came two weeks later. Isabella needed support from Chris throughout the trial. They comforted each other on the day Melinda Chabonnais was found guilty of attempted murder and sent to prison for several years. It wasn't easy for her friends to watch her public humiliation.

Monsieur Chabonnais invited all the Durel family to his home for dinner the day after the sentencing. He had much on his mind and wanted to finish his business with them. He proved how grateful he was to Emile and his cousin, Evan, for saving his life by bequeathing his estate to Emile in his will. His reasoning was that he had no children, he was fond of Isabella, and he was grateful that they had earned him the right to live out the rest of his days.

"I'm not going to sell either estate now. You will have many children, Emile, and you know how to run my plantation as well as my home here in New Orleans. As her husband, I have the right to sell her plantation if I wish, but I think Evan might have use for it, so I'm signing a paper that gives your cousin her property. Then you can give your new townhouse to him if you wish and live in mine during the season. I have many years on this earth ahead of me, Emile, but if you will work the farm for me, you may have all of my slaves to help you. If Evan can take over her plantation, he might as well move in now. No one has spent much time at either of the plantations in the last few years."

He turned and smiled at Sam. "Perhaps you will find a nice girl and settle down, Evan. Brother-in-laws should have their own houses, n'est ce pas, Isabella?"

She blushed. "I'm so sorry about Melinda, monsieur. I swear I never guessed."

"Why would you have reason to doubt your friend? Here, this is for you," he said, "I want you to have it." He handed her a tiny ring box. Inside was a four-carat diamond ring that had belonged to her friend.

"I don't think I should take it," she said.

"Sell it then, if you don't want to wear it. I don't care. It only brings back distasteful memories to me now. She hurt you too. Enjoy it. No other diamond in New Orleans can match it. She didn't deserve it, but you do. You have a good heart and a sweet disposition."

She smiled and Sam laughed. "Isabella? Sweet?"

"She took the time to sit with me when I was ill having no idea what Melinda was up to. She was used too; her innocence taken advantage of by one more person she cared about. I heard all about Tony Chesterfield, Issy."

She blushed again and looked at her folded hands.

"Don't be ashamed of following your heart, cher. I know how it feels to love someone who betrayed you. But enough of that. Our lives have been changed by a certain carnival magic. And the magician is here before us."

He took up a glass of wine and saluted Emile. "To an honest, loyal, intelligent, and brave man—Emile Durel. May you and your cousin, Evan, prosper for the good work you have done in the last few weeks. Enjoy Mardi Gras."

After Stephen and Sam quieted the house for the night, they stole away to the parlor, shut the door, and talked.

"I'll write up a contract that proclaims Melinda's plantation to be Emile's because Evan won't be around in another month. Emile stands to gain a lot by this little traveling venture of ours. Talk about giving the guy more than he expected. We just placed him on the top ten planters of New Orleans list.

Three plantations. Two townhouses."

"He's content, at least for now, to stay in the background," said Stephen.

"Do you think Melinda was trying to kill Isabella?"

"My mind says yes. My heart isn't so sure. My gut says no. If she had poisoned the night cream, then why didn't I fall prey to its toxic effects? My lips were all over her skin that night."

"Nice," said Sam, grinning. "So, we don't have a killer or a weapon. We're back to square one?"

"I'm afraid so. I feel as if we have all the pieces save one, and that one clue is the clincher. Unfortunately, I have no idea where to look for it. We've got Tony, Melinda, the Gatous—if we stretch it—and Jean-Pierre which would be really pushing the I-hate-my-little-sister sibling rivalry thing. Oh, yeah, Ernestine if we want to include the fact that Isabella almost got her baby. We have to look at the time frame. The attempted murder happened the night of December 24 continuing into the morning of the 25, and no one has tried to harm her since then. We might have taken their motive away from them. They're pacified, for the moment."

"At least Melinda is in jail and that gets her out of the picture. Tony must have hoisted his bruising loins out of town by now. If Chris were going to kill anyone, it would be you not her. And Ernestine had a boy so that eliminates her motive. Isabella, her brother, and Emile have all made amends. Maybe we don't need to worry. Maybe it's over."

"You mean we can actually enjoy Mardi Gras?"

"If you can't tango better than what you did last night at practice, I'd say even Mardi Gras could be a problem for you," said Sam grinning.

"You said you'd handle the tango, remember. I was to waltz with her."

"Either way, we only have a few weeks left to turn you into Fred Astaire."

"He never tangoed, did he?"

"Rudolph Valentino?"

"Better."

They said good night and headed to bed. When Stephen managed to slip between the sheets of their bed, he noticed how peaceful his wife looked—happy, safe, and alive on the pillow next to his.

"I adore you, sweet, precious ghost." He kissed her cheek and then settled in for the best sleep he'd had in three years.

Chapter Twenty-Nine

Stephen could feel Emile's excitement as the Mardi Gras parade meandered through the city. The festival would be highlighted by the Masquerade Ball tonight, and he could hardly wait to dance with his wife.

They arrived by carriage at nine o'clock sharp. Their disguises were a cut above the rest though no one had the audacity to mention it. Sam wore a gray mask with sequins, Isabella a red one covered with black feathers, and Stephen wore an unadorned, black leather mask.

They had created new reputations for Emile, Evan, and Isabella in high society. People whispered, grinned, and pointed. They talked about the handsome pair and their attractive, bachelor cousin who had saved the wealthiest man in town's life as well as driven a notorious rogue from the city.

The music began, and Emile took Isabella's hand for a waltz. They glided arm in arm, and he felt the most exhilarating chill cover his entire body. He pulled her closer to his chest. She looked at him and smiled. This is where he belonged. Waltzing with Isabella. Holding her in his arms and twirling to the music.

"It has been some time since we've danced together, mon cher," said Stephen.

"We have a lifetime to dance and many waltzes before us."

Stephen noticed that Sam was in an intense conversation with a pretty, young lady. When the dance was finished, Isabella went to find Chris. He asked Sam about her while they sipped champagne.

"This is incredible. The young lady is Mary Jane Michaels. Named after her great-grandmother, Lady Jane Engle Michaels, and her mother, Mary Michaels. She looked so much like this schoolmarm/English lady I used to know from a 1722.

She was on a spontaneous reincarnation transfer. I was on a scheduled genealogical transfer. We experienced one hell of a pirate adventure together. So, I just discreetly asked whether she was related to Lady Jane and Captain Garrett Michaels and their son Trace. It so happens that Trace was her grandfather and Jane and Garrett her great-grandparents. Small time-traveling world, isn't it?"

"The lady is to your liking?" said Stephen with a grin.

"Most definitely. You see, I had this huge crush on Jane, but she was in love with this pirate named Garrett. Karma stuff, so I had no chance with her. Now *this* girl should be in Boston. That's where the story ended. So, I asked her how she happened to be all the way down here, and she tells me that she's digging up her family tree by researching pirates. She likes *your* costume because she's heard stories that her great-grandfather was a *pirate*, and she was wondering if that was the sort of thing he might have worn."

"You're set for the evening."

"Yep. I may travel back here again."

"You can do that?"

"Sure, you can transfer any solstice you wish, as long as you're thinking about the time period and where you want to go."

"So, I could come back here and see Isabella whenever I wished?"

"Sure, and the trip would be free because you really don't need us anymore, do you? As long as Emile allows it. He probably will."

"That gives me hope. I was worried about her—and concerned about myself, as well. I know you said that losing her forever would be the risk I would have to take if I time traveled. I started thinking about how difficult it will be to return to 1999."

"This is incredible. I never had this happen before. I think I may have to leave you for the evening, if you don't mind. This is too good to be true. You have no idea how I lusted for that woman."

Just then the flirtatious, auburn-haired beauty with astonishing blue eyes came over to speak with them and sip champagne. She tilted her head and smiled sweetly.

After she was introduced to Stephen, she said, "You're

such a wonderful dancer, Monsieur Durel. How I envy your flair."

"Why, thank you. I know a few simple steps."

"You're too modest. You must know that your tango is divine."

"What tango?" He stared at her.

"Why the one you just did with your wife."

Sam and Stephen looked at each other. They scanned the ballroom for Isabella. She was nowhere.

"How long ago was I dancing with her?" he said to the girl.

Mary Jane giggled. "Why you just did, and everyone applauded. Don't you remember? Too much champagne? I wish I could dance like that. She was so graceful. There was so much..." she blushed, "passion. You can tell how much in love you both are."

"We've got to find her," said Stephen.

"Why is it that the one chance I get to have some fun, a crisis hits?" said Sam. "Are you having an out-of-body experience? You can't dance the tango well enough to gain applause, and Emile can't leave your body to dance with her. So, who did?"

"The only person who would know before tonight, what costume I would be wearing. The one person who would have an exact copy of our costumes already made, and who could fool Isabella into thinking he was me."

"Tony Chesterfield *Gatou* ?"

"I'm sure his parents could have whipped up a similar costume for him easily and shown him what her costume would look like."

"For what reason?"

"Only one that I can think of."

"Kill her?"

"If he can't have her..." said Stephen.

"I'm right behind you."

They stopped when they got to the street. Looking helplessly up and down the lane for the sign of the pirate and the Spanish lady was pointless.

"The crowd! How in the hell are we going to find them with all these people? We could be searching all night, and she could be dead by then."

"Maybe he's just kidnapping her. We don't know for certain that he wants to kill her," said Sam.

"I'm not taking that chance. You saw the way he acted at the duel."

Chris sauntered by with colorful beads covering his entire chest. "Having a wonderful time? I saw your tango. Very nice."

"I never danced the tango with her, Chris. We think it was Tony, and that he's taken her with him. Any idea where they went?"

"Why, I thought Isabella said that the two of you were going for a romantic walk by the river?

"You just saw them?"

"Yes. Naturally, I thought it was you."

"How could she not know it wasn't me? We don't even have the same eye or hair color."

"How often do you look in your partner's eyes in the tango? Your hair is covered with the hat. The mask? And you and Tony have the exact same build," said Chris.

"Okay. Let's get Cicero and the rig. Are you coming with us, Chris?"

"Sounds like more fun than dancing. Lead the way."

It took a while to find Cicero who was chatting in animation with other black men.

"Howdy, Monsieur Durel," said one rather bold driver who was at least seven-feet tall and built like a linebacker. Stephen recognized him as Jean-Pierre's carriage man. The man's manner showed a confident and independent nature stemming from years of service as a trusted member of the Devieux 'family.' He would not have dared to speak to Stephen otherwise. "Didn't you just walk by here a minute ago with Missy?"

"That was an imitation Emile Durel." He turned to look at Cicero whose face registered total concern for his mistress. "Madame Durel is in great danger, Cicero, we need to find her. She's been kidnapped. A man dressed in the same costume as this one has lured her away from the ball. To the river—fast."

They raced along the streets, looking frantically for a Spanish lady and a masked man in a pirate's costume. Finally,

Stephen stopped the carriage and walked up the hill to have a look at the landscape.

"This is no good. We have to walk. I can't see the river that well from the carriage. She could be in some cove or one of those shacks," said Stephen, pointing to a group of huts near the water's edge. "Or here on the path walking with him."

"You ain't goin' over there alone, is you?" said Cicero.

Stephen looked at the area and knew it was foolish to go asking for trouble by heading near the river, but it seemed like such a good place to hide someone. "You're right, of course. We've got to split up. Cicero, you go that way and look for her. The three of us will follow the other path and get close to the shacks. Safety in numbers, Cicero. Use the carriage if you need to. I trust your instincts. Thank God, the moon is bright tonight."

Two figures, ahead of them and close to the river, darted into a small hut. There was light coming from the building and the sequins on a woman's costume caught it and the moonlight for just a second.

Stephen pointed to the structure, but his two companions said that they'd seen nothing. "It's Isabella," said Stephen, who was now beyond panic. How could he have guessed this would happen, and yet the possibility had been there all along.

"Should we confront him directly? What if he hurts her?" said Chris.

"There are three of us and one of him," said Sam.

"Do you think she's caught on that it isn't you?" said Chris.

"I hope, for her sake, she hasn't. It might be the only thing that's keeping her alive right now."

They cautiously stumbled over the rocks and mud and within seconds stood close enough to hear the two talking.

"What an odd place you've chosen, Emile," she said. "Wouldn't you rather go back home? I should think there'd be some rough men down by the river tonight. My gown?"

"Come to me, mon cher," said Tony.

There was the sound of an embrace and then that of a hand hitting flesh.

Silence.

Stephen motioned for the three men to follow him into the

hut. Tony didn't seem surprised when they entered. Isabella was lying in a red satin bundle on the floor.

"What did you do to her?" said Stephen.

"I knew you would come," Tony said smiling. "Don't worry. Just a little smack to the jaw to keep her quiet. Like the one your cousin gave me only not as hard. I don't think it would be good for her to see what's going to happen next—might destroy her future happiness—with me. Besides, long rides are more fun when you're sleeping, n'est ce pas?"

"She's not going anywhere with you," said Sam.

"Don't be too sure."

Just then three men appeared from nowhere and crowded behind them.

"Right into my trap. Meet my Yankee friends, Durel. They practically work for nothing."

Sam kicked the man behind him in the groin which started the fight. Stephen did the best he could to get away from the man behind him, but with Tony's help, and Chris's complete helplessness, they were soon overpowered by the tougher and stronger dock workers.

Tony bent over Stephen, who was nursing bruised ribs, and stared at him. "I just *knew* you'd fall for my plan. The costume was a great idea, wasn't it? Thanks to Father's and Mother's handiwork. They've always wanted to see Issy and me together."

He walked over to Chris and laughed. "I've written a perfect little play for you, Chris. One I'm sure you'll want to star in. I'll tell you how the plot moves through the three acts, and how it ends. Unfortunately, it's a tragedy as far as *your* role is concerned."

Then he walked back to Stephen, "Shouldn't come to the river at night, Durel. You should know better than that. It's mighty dangerous. But then that headstrong wife of yours wanted to take a walk in the moonlight and you agreed. For protection, you took two other men, but they were of no assistance when you were attacked by these thugs. You see, Durel, Isabella is mine, with or without her money, makes no difference to me. I'd prefer her *with* the money, and if I work things right, by act three, I'll have both. There has always been one major problem; one thorn in my side as far as Isabella is concerned—*you*. A problem easily taken care of with a little cash and some friends in low places."

He kicked Sam in the stomach when he tried to stand.

"Here's how the action progresses in the second act. You are attacked and murdered on your stroll. Isabella disappears. Her brother is frantic when his brother-in-law, a cousin, and her best friend's bodies are eventually found floating down the Mississippi. What terrible thing could have happened to her?"

Tony backhanded Stephen across his face.

"Now in scene two, she awakens in my rig. We're away from town by now. I tell her that she was kidnapped, taken from the city, and held for ransom. I also tell her that her husband, cousin, and best friend are dead. She's sore, weak, and a little groggy. What does she remember? Nothing. Maybe being hit. Could it have been her husband who hit her?"

He grinned and then continued, "She believes me when she sees your grave and talks with her brother. Of course, he's thrilled to see she's alive. I bring her home to New Orleans, to the bosom of her plantation life, looking every bit like the hero who has saved her from a fate worse than death. She is *so* grateful. Maybe she was wrong about me, after all. At the end of act three, she realizes that her life is lonely without a man. I woo her—make her remember our thwarted love from the past—and win her heart, as well as your money."

He looked at the thugs and motioned that they should do what they were hired to do.

Stephen felt the man's fist in his stomach and the hard bite of the same hand across his face. He tried to swing a punch, but another man hit him so hard that he fell. It seems as if the other men were getting the same beating from the sounds of it. Although, he did notice Sam getting the better of his opponent at one point.

When the beating was over, Tony walked over to Chris. "I didn't want to hurt you, Chris. You're my friend, and Issy's too, but what can I do? You chose to follow him here."

"You bastard," said Chris, and then he was smacked into silence.

Stephen found the words to say, "Don't hurt her."

Tony looked at him. "Why would I hurt Issy? I love her. Always have. That was something her family didn't realize.

Sure, I wanted money and a home, but Melinda was always there if I only wanted that. I wanted Isabella, and by rights, she's always been mine. I married her, didn't I? Her father was a fool."

"Then you didn't try to poison her Christmas Eve?"

Tony raised his right eyebrow and seemed stunned by the comment. "What a ridiculous question, Emile! You can't make love to a corpse. That was the one thing withheld from me—her sweetness. The promise I could feel in those delicious lips of hers was forever denied me when she married you. I should have been the one to love her for the first time, not you. She was *my* wife. But that will change after tonight."

Tony turned to the three men and said, "Take all three of them to the middle of the river, slit their throats, and dump their bodies. Make sure it's quiet. How anyone could hear anything with all this reverie is beyond me. Here, I'll give you the money now. I've got a rig waiting, and we're heading out of town, so I'll be far out of the city when they find them. Is this enough?"

"For murdering three men?" said the one man.

"I have to keep something to live on."

"These men are well known in the city. They'll be looking for the murderers. How do we know he doesn't have his slave looking for him right now? More money or do your own killing, Chesterfield."

There was silence, and then he saw Tony's shadow fall across Isabella's body. He took her hand in his. "Here. Madame Chabonnais's ring. That should be worth a lot of money. It'll help the story too."

"We'd have to fence it."

"Take it or leave it."

"Well, it's Mardi Gras night, and no one would have seen them come down this way."

Stephen saw the rough man turn to his friends. They nodded their heads that it was enough.

"It'll be easier to carry them to the boat if you tie them. Here's rope. And gag them too just in case they start to holler."

Isabella moaned.

Tony looked her way nervously. "Get them out of here before she wakes up. I don't want her to see this—any of it.

Hurry."

He covered her face with his body so that if she came to, she wouldn't see Stephen or his three henchmen.

"Isabella," shouted Stephen, and the man beside him tied a dirty cloth over his mouth and glared at him. He felt his hands being pulled roughly behind his back and tied with coarse rope. The filthy rag on his tongue smelled like oil, and its taste made him wretch. The man kicked him in his ribs again for no apparent reason, but Stephen tried to stay alert. He saw them doing the same thing to Sam who was awake. Chris went unconscious after one fist flew across his head. He wondered how the time traveler would get them out of this one.

Tony cradled Isabella against his body, and then kissed her lips. With his fingers, he tenderly brushed back a stray curl from her forehead. He stroked her bruised cheek with the back of his hand. He looked at Stephen and grinned before letting the palm of his hand slide down the side of her body. The gesture was slow and sexual, making sure his hand touched her breast and stopped near the slit in the gown that exposed her thigh. His fingers lightly danced across her leg. Then he moved his hands away and let her body rest in his lap.

This scene was played for one reason only—to show the Creole planter that he had Isabella in the palm of his hand now—and forever, and that Emile Durel's life was over. Final revenge.

He placed her on the floor and then stood up and commanded his thugs. "Get them out of here fast. I can't stay any longer. Do you have a knife?"

The man looked at Tony as if he'd just asked the stupidest question. Then all three men were tugged, pulled, and dragged to the side of the river where a boat was waiting. A light dangled from a hook on the side of it. Stephen looked towards the hut to see what Tony was doing with Isabella. She was his only concern.

Tony was carrying her in his arms and walking down the hill towards the street where a rig was waiting. He had replaced the mask, and to anyone watching the couple, it would seem as if Isabella Durel had had too much Mardi Gras and her husband, Emile, was taking her home. They'd already seen Emile in the pirate's costume dance the tango with his wife at the ball. He had to hand it to Tony; his plan was fool proof.

The three men said nothing to their victims. They placed them in the flatboat and prodded it onto the river.

The water was filled with the odor of fish, and the boat smelled of whiskey and tobacco. One of the men had a cigar which he puffed on lustily. The second man had a bottle of strong liquor, probably bourbon, and drank from it, often wiping his wet lips on his grimy shirt. Another pulled out his knife and examined it in the moonlight.

"How far out should we take them?" said the man, who was infatuated with the glint on his knife's blade.

"We've got to make sure their bodies don't float near the dock—yet. Give Tony enough time to get the woman out of town. The plan is to make it look as if she were killed too, but they'll never find her body—just theirs. Wasn't supposed to be three. Just the man and his cousin. This actor has certainly ruined it all. Everyone will wonder why he was so near the river. Why he would have been asked to walk with the Durels. He's mighty famous."

"So's this Durel fellow. What a man will do for a beautiful woman." He laughed.

The man with the knife whistled low and cackled before saying, "Yeah. She did look sweet in that tight, fancy dress. Maybe we should have killed Chesterfield too. Had ourselves some fun. The money and the lady. It ain't too late to catch up with him. We know where he's headed. Get the rest of our money after we kill him. Won't they think he had something to do with murdering these men? There was talk in town of a duel and how Chesterfield lost to Emile Durel. Pin it on him like it should be."

"Quit talking, Max, you heard him. This is tough enough without your chatter. Chesterfield will be long gone by the time we're done with this," said the third man, who had been quiet until then. "We're out far enough, Ty. Let's get it over with. I got a bad feeling about this."

Stephen felt the man with the hunter's knife lift his body from the floor of the boat so that he was now sitting on his calves and knees.

"I'll take the Creole. Ha, you ain't nothing now, Durel. God, how I hate you French bastards. Always thinkin' you're something. Better than everyone else. Well, that French blood of yours will run just as red when I stick you, n'est ce pas? Dying's the same in any language, monsieur. You scared of dying, Frenchy?"

He was close enough to the man to smell the liquor on his breath. "I've been looking forward to this all night. Come here. I got something for you."

He supported Stephen's back against his abdomen by placing his left hand on Stephen's chest. Then he shifted his weight so that Stephen's body was braced against his hips. He moved his left hand from Stephen's chest to just beneath his chin so that he could keep his victim's neck in the perfect position. His right hand held the blade that would slice Stephen's throat in two. Quick and thorough. The man pinned his victim's head against his chest, making it ready for the unceremonious execution. But then the man hesitated.

Stephen could feel his heart pounding against his chest. The bitter taste of fear was in his mouth. The intimacy of his body being held so closely to this disgusting man who held his life in his hands sickened him. Feeling the coldness of the knife against his skin—the metal that meant eminent death for him with one forceful thrust—sent chills through his body. Oddly enough, his last thoughts were about his companions' safety.

The other man said, "I'll take the actor; he's out anyway. Won't feel a thing."

Stephen saw the man take a knife from the sheath on his belt. There was the sound of weight being lifted, and the grunt of someone moving into an awkward position. "He's heavier than I thought. How we gonna weigh them down?"

The man holding Stephen never moved a muscle when he said, "I got some stones under that tarp. We'll tie them to the ropes around their legs. They should sink fast enough. Eventually they'll float up, but that'll give us time to get the hell out of here. *Fishies* will have done their work on the ropes by then." He laughed at his own words.

"I can't manage the boat and take out the other man. One of you will have to do it for me."

The man holding Stephen said, "We were supposed to do this together. That was the plan. Each one of us has to have blood on his hands. That way we can trust one another to be quiet. Although, I'd welcome the chance to do that one." He motioned towards Sam. "He kicked me in the crotch back at the hut. Bastard. Maybe I'll just let him drown, so's he can wake up just in time to feel the cold water fill his lungs."

They all laughed at the joke. "Oh...well...if that's all we're going to do to him, I can kick him over the side and into the river and still move the boat. His hands are tied; he ain't going to be doing no swimming."

The man with the cigar looked up quickly and said, "Watch it! A boat. Where'd it come from? Do it now before we're spotted."

Stephen felt the cold steel of the knife move to the left side of his throat.

"Wait." The man with the cigar held up his hand. "Damn. Why didn't I see them before?"

The man, who had relaxed his grip on his victim, braced his head tightly again, and Stephen felt the knife's sharp edge cut into his skin and his own blood trickle down his chest. "Bonsoir, monsieur."

The man steering the boat said, "Hold it! They can't make us out yet, but if there's commotion, they might be curious and pull up alongside us. Maybe say they saw something when asked later on. What'll we do?"

"Cover their bodies with that tarp. Hurry. Look like you're night fishing"

"On Mardi Gras night?"

"Better than the truth."

Stephen was dropped to the floor of the boat and felt the heavy cloth being thrown over his body. Sam and Chris were next to him. The man with the bottle of whiskey grabbed a hold of the tarp and uncovered the three bodies, seizing Stephen in the same movement.

"Let's get the hell outta here. Don't you think they'll wonder what we got hiding under the tarp? Ain't no fish that big swimming in the mighty Mississippi."

"Shut up. Look natural. They'll just float by and wave at us. Where'd they come from? I guess we were too busy to notice the boat. Misty night."

"He's right, Carl. If they get too close and notice anything..."

"Oh, they ain't gonna notice three bodies fall into the

water?" he said sarcastically, a touch of panic in his voice. "We do as I say. They look like black men. They won't bother a boat with three white men on it."

"Then If there's trouble, they go down too." He threw the tarp back over the three victims.

"Right."

The boat came very close to the killers'. Stephen couldn't see anything, but he could hear the conversation and judge by the linguistics that the men in the boat were slaves, or at least, doing a fine imitation.

"Well, howdy there, friends. Fixin' to fish the river tonight? We gots some liquor here if you care to take a swig."

They were playing the role of free men of color, but something told Stephen that they were Cicero's friends—the ones he'd been chatting with when they were searching for Isabella. He guessed that it was the tall black man who had said *howdy* to him only fifteen minutes earlier.

"Well, thank you kindly, friend, but we got ourselves a mess of fish here, and are heading back to shore."

"Really? Well, bless my soul. You must have found yo'self one sweet fishing spot. Mind telling us where it might be? My mouth is watering fo' some jambalaya tonight. My old lady fixes one fine meal, but she do need da meat. So she says to me..."

Stephen could hear the voice getting closer.

The man continued, "She says to me, 'Julius, effen yo' want that jambalaya fo' Mardi Gras yo' better git yo' ass down to the river and fetch some *fishies*.' My old lady's crazy. Think I can find da fish in da dark. Women!"

The boat swayed.

"Hey, now, we got no fish to share," said the man, who had placed the knife at Stephen's throat.

"Now that just ain't neighborly," said the black man. "I'd share some of my wife's jambalaya with you. Wouldn't I, boys?"

"Shore 'nuff," echoed a variety of voices.

" 'Sides, yo' got some mighty big-looking *fishies* here."

Stephen heard the sound of many feet boarding the boat. It was obvious by the sound of the man's voice that he doubted the tarp covered fish. There was a skirmish, and Stephen hoped that

Cicero's friends had won the battle, or they were all dead.

The tarp was removed and the carriage man he'd seen with Cicero stared at him. "My, my, Monsieur Durel. Looks like yo' been saved from being fish bait."

The man untied him and took the gag from his mouth. Stephen wretched and spit the taste of it into the river. He noticed the other men helping Sam and Chris. The thugs were nowhere to be seen.

"Look what fell outta dat man's pocket when I hit him." It was Melinda's ring. He let it roll over the palm of his big hand. "Here, you keep it. Effen I takes it, they'll think I stole it offa Missy."

Stephen placed Monsieur Chabonnais's gift under his pirate's belt for safekeeping. "What did you do with the killers?"

The man seemed puzzled by the question. He scratched his head in imitation of deep thought. "Yo' know, I plumb fo'got." Then he grinned expansively. "Timothy, what did we do with dem white-trash dock workers?"

Timothy shrugged and answered, "You know what, Julius, I think I saw dem swimmin' fo' shore."

Julius laughed and clapped his hands with the joy of their joke. "Oh, yeah, das right. They took one look at us and decided to take a nice swim back to town."

Stephen smiled and held out his hand to Julius. "I can't thank you enough...Julius, is it?"

"Dat's my name. Cicero watched the three of you long enough to see the men go into the hut after you went in." His speech pattern changed. "He came back to the hotel to get us. Shore hope our families ain't interested in leaving the party real soon. We watched them take you in the boats. Stole this one from the dock. I guess I can paddle a damn sight faster than that crazy white man. Cicero was gonna take care of Chesterfield for you and get Missy back. Probably waiting for us right now. Hope she's alright. I been with her family for thirteen years now. Ain't no one gonna hurt her without me doing something about it. She used to get me to drive her to see that snake. 'Course she never asked me what I thought of that half breed. I wonder if Chesterfield will ever be able to walk after Cicero's done with him."

"Can you work your magic with the boat and get us back to land?"

"Certainly, Monsieur Durel."

"Again, I can't thank you enough, Julius. I'll reward you, I swear."

"Why you do whatever you wants with that. I enjoyed myself tonight."

"I thought we'd had it for sure," said Chris. "That bastard. And I thought he was my friend."

"I was praying as hard as I could," said Sam.

"It's all right, Sam. I think God's been watching out for her, us, all along."

Sam whispered to Stephen, "Does this mean we've eliminated another suspect?"

"It sure looks like it to me. The only one Tony Chesterfield wanted to kill was *Emile*."

"And with all our testimonies, and these men's story of what they saw, plus Isabella's vague memory of what happened, I think Tony will be spending a great deal of time in prison—with Melinda."

"She'll be so happy."

They managed their way through the darkness and onto the shore where Isabella was holding onto Cicero's strong arm. By the look on her face, it was obvious she wasn't going home until she knew how her husband had fared at the hands of the thugs.

"Cicero told me what happened. I thought Tony was you." She threw her arms around his neck and kissed his cheek. "The costume. The tango. I wonder how he learned to dance as well as you."

Stephen didn't have the heart to tell her that the difference would have been obvious if she'd actually tangoed with him.

Chapter Thirty

Sam returned to the Masquerade Ball and his new-found lady friend, Mary Jane, but Stephen and Isabella went home. The night had worn them both to the brink of emotional exhaustion, and Isabella's jaw ached. Stephen examined the bruise. There was no sign of swelling or discoloration. Tony hadn't hit her very hard. He kissed the spot and she smiled.

"I still can't believe Tony would try to murder someone. He never appeared to me in any form but that of a charming, needy, loving gentleman," she said.

"The police have him now. I'll wager I could obtain a job with them after this last escapade. Cicero and Julius were a godsend." He moved towards a decanter of wine he had Nora place in their room. "Would you like something to drink?"

"Not now." She began undoing the hook-and-eye clasps on the side of her costume. "I have my own plans for celebrating Mardi Gras," said Isabella.

"You have?" Stephen took a sip of wine from the crystal goblet and gazed at her.

"We never tangoed tonight. And you promised me."

"You want to tango—now? With no music?" he said.

"We need no music. Just rhythm." She let the dress drop to the floor. She stood before him in a corset and pantaloons. "Take off your clothes."

He placed the glass of wine on a small table, removed the fancy shirt and the big belt, then sat on a nearby chair to kick off his black boots.

She took off her underclothes—slowly—pulling at each little ribbon of her camisole and then undoing the corset's hooks with careful attention. She sat down on the side of the bed, slipped her pantaloons from her hips, and skillfully rolled each stocking from her long legs, being careful not to slash them with her nails. When she was done, she stood and undid her long hair from its chignon so that the dark mass of curls fell over her shoulders. The look in her eyes would have defrocked a priest.

He stood naked before her, his long legs, and muscular thighs flexing in anticipation of the dance movements they would soon perform.

"Care to tango?" He reached his hand to hers and gave a secret 'thank you' to Emile.

She took his hand, never dropping her stare from his, and smiled. "Mais oui, monsieur. Avec plaisir."

He held her body close to his, and took her right hand so that he could lead her. The touch of her body against his skin aroused him instantly. The smell or roses encircled them.

She placed her left hand behind his right shoulder and put her thumb in his armpit. Stephen automatically lifted his elbow to support her arm. His naked thigh walked her body two steps backwards. On the third move, their outside leg opened to the side while the other leg made a half-step backwards. They paused for a beat, and then her right foot pointed to the side just as his left foot pressed it back to the heel of her left foot. She looked at him for a moment and smiled demurely. Their bodies were very close. He bent her slowly around and over his right hip so that her back rested on his leg.

Stephen hadn't learned this move, and he wondered if Emile was making it up; but, considering where her breasts were right now, he decided not to worry about perfect technique.

He bent his torso over her chest, stretching his back muscles so that he could kiss her breasts. Then his tongue flicked across the flat, taut skin of her stomach. His right hand supported her back. She balanced her weight on one leg while allowing her left arm to hold onto his shoulder to keep her balance. Her right hand gripped his left. She closed her eyes and moaned softly. The danger of the last few hours had stimulated her.

"Only Isabella would find near-death adventures sexually stimulating," thought Stephen.

She allowed her body to drift further down, balancing her weight on one leg, while wrapping her left foot around the calf of his right leg. He pulled her body to his chest in one long, slow, seductive movement. Her graceful arms encircled his neck, and she kissed his lips. Then Isabella turned her head away from his—as if resisting his attempts to seduce her—and returned her hands to their proper positions. Her breasts were pressed against his chest. Their soft, cool touch against his hot skin was so stimulating that he wanted to stop dancing and make love to her.

He moved her across their bedroom floor in the one step, two step, three step, hold position. Then he twisted her body sharply to the side so that they could promenade to his left. She grabbed his buttocks with her fingers and squeezed the flesh when they paused for a quick second before walking to the left. He noticed that she gave a downward glance at his body before they proceeded. She needn't have worried about her effect on him. He felt her body relax, and she seemed agreeable to following his lead. Submission from a woman like Isabella was quite an accomplishment.

When they repeated the basic steps, he paused to guide her body into a corté thereby pulling her towards his body and between his legs. He stepped backwards and when he did this, his manhood brushed against the inner part of her thigh. She arched her back like a cat stretching after a nap, and let her left leg strike out behind her, pointing backwards, then lean into the move so that she could massage him into a stronger erection simply by shifting her weight and lifting her knee. She looked away but continued to tease him. He could move if he wanted to, but he didn't. It was too delicious. The sheer elegance and softness of her skin, her muscles, her femininity, excited Stephen.

In a moment of sweet revenge, he let the top of his right thigh part her hips and push upwards. It caressed the soft skin between her legs. Then he let her body lean against his while he squeezed her buttocks with his right hand. When he finally returned her to the first dance position, she grazed him again and looked up. Her eyes were ablaze with heat and sensuality. He bent to kiss her, but she turned away.

Some emotion, lurking deep inside him, burned to take that fiery arrogance from her. She teased him, and then played coy, taking unfair advantage of his obvious passion for her. It excited him as well as angered him. Her hand dropped from his shoulder and gripped the upper part of his arm. She let her face rest on his chest, caressed and licked the skin of his biceps, kissed his neck, and then bit him. It surprised Stephen, but only fueled his appetite. Another slow corté, and then he led her to the side again. She did a fan flick, her left foot making a small figure eight on the floor. Her breasts bobbed when she moved and brushed his arm.

When they danced the basic steps again, he let his long legs separate hers. He dropped her almost to the ground this time, yet still supported her with his arms. He twisted her body. Her hands fell uselessly to her side; her back arched. He let her torso rest on his hip and thigh. Her lips parted, and she closed her eyes. Compliance? He doubted that it would last very long. He pressed his lips to hers with complete passion, letting his tongue open her mouth. She took her hands and massaged them over his chest, then let them fall gracefully over his back, and lifted her head so that she could taste the skin on his chest.

He pulled her back to the first position, then tossed her to his side so that they could do an open fan. Together briefly. Then a second one. She glared at him. He brought her back to the first position, led her into another corté, pushed her away from him, and forced her into another smaller, side fan. She never left his arms. He had a firm grip on their every move. Their bodies met and parted often, and it was very provocative.

When he maneuvered her into another tango walk, she touched him when they paused, cupping his manhood into the palm of her hand. He let her massage his body for some time before forcing her into a double promenade—slow, slow, quick, quick, hold, repeat to the other side. Then a sharp triple fan.

"Dancing's mighty hot work," thought Stephen, glad that Emile was enjoying himself.

He moved her to his side for a rondé. They held onto each other, side by side, and their outside legs made a large half circle on the floor. Then he lifted her, and she closed with a small fan to his left side before they continued. He pulled her to his body. She lifted her left thigh onto his hip, while he titled backwards so that she was forced to rest her whole weight on his torso. They kissed.

When they opened the space between their bodies and walked sideways together, he could detect the glimmer of perspiration on her breasts and arms.

"I want you," he said, stopping the dance and looking at

her.

"No." She turned her head away and kept her right hand in his left.

He pulled her into his arms again and smiled. *"Chatte,"* Emile called her.

"Oui." She gazed up at him and smiled.

"Non," he said, biting her neck fiercely. *"Suris,"* Emile whispered into her ear.

He dipped her slowly to the floor and dropped over her body, thereby trapping her from scurrying away from him. She tried to push him away, but he was stronger than she was.

"Je suis la chat, mon amour. Vous êtes dîner." Apparently, Emile was finished with the cat and mouse game. Stephen silently thanked him.

"Ah...non." Her back arched helplessly and then rested on the embroidered rug.

He let his manhood slide between her legs, allowing his abdomen to move up and down against her body so that it teased her satiny skin.

"It takes two to tango," Stephen thought. "And if you can tease, so can I."

His arms were taut and held his weight so that he could move above her. When he paused, she sat up suddenly, linking her legs around his hips, placing her arms around his shoulders, and letting her hands fall behind his neck. She moved closer, embracing him, holding his body tightly against her breasts.

"Je t'adore, Emile."

She was so perfectly balanced there, that he could fondle her breasts with both hands and kiss her simultaneously. He then played with her hair, combing it away from her face, and placing it so that it fell behind her. He let her body slip again, so that he could see the love in her eyes and the smile on her face. She let her legs drift apart. He moved his kisses further down, tasting the sweetness of her body's response to their 'dance.' He massaged her gently with his tongue. He heard the small catch in her throat when she crescendoed.

"I adore you, too," Stephen said and then kissed her.

He pulled her back to his body with one hand—letting her rest on his hips again. She held onto him for support, cuddling her face into his neck, and making small cooing sounds.

Obviously, the pleasure she had just experienced had made her obedient to any of his future demands.

He grinned at the expression he saw on her face. Sweet, soft, subtle surrender. He kissed her shoulder. She kissed his lips. He licked the skin on her throat, bit the spot, and kissed her roughly by bracing her head with his hands. She didn't fight him. It was time.

He placed her so that she sat directly on his erection, and then rocked her so that he could examine her face. He wanted to watch her find paradise this time. Together. See her eyes open wide and close, her lips part and shut, her head tilt backwards and then droop downwards, as she collapsed helplessly onto his shoulder. If her eyebrows knit together in a quasi-frown, Stephen relaxed his pressure. His hands held onto her buttocks, so that she couldn't move anywhere he didn't want her to. When she smiled, he increased his rhythm.

He let her fall backwards which naturally allowed him to leave her body. His fingers pinched her erect nipples. She moaned. No resistance.

He let her collapse onto the rug. She was trapped beneath him. His lips covered her entire body. Her skin tasted sweet and salty. Like a cat who has just caught a mouse, he took great joy in playing with his dinner before he devoured it. He growled deep in his throat as he tasted every inch of her. She made those hurt animal noises that he loved her to make. Whimpering, cooing, breathing, deep and fast.

Then he placed her legs over his shoulders and took his own satisfaction with a vengeance. She tried to fondle his hair, but he pushed her hands away. He didn't pin her arms this time, though. He rocked faster and faster until his mind exploded with hers. His body rested on hers. His mind and muscles relaxed. She kissed the top of his head and smiled at him.

"I can't imagine life without you," she said.

"Now the healing begins," thought Stephen, "for both of us."

"Emile?"

"Oui, mon cher."

"Take me home."

He stared at her in disbelief. "But, I thought you liked it here in New Orleans. We still have a few more weeks before we have to leave anyway, and I thought you needed a rest from your chores."

"I'm homesick all of a sudden."

Her depression had been erased by love. Her life sutured with salvation. She had lost Melinda and a con-man who had once been her heart's delight. Stephen had given her back her life—a reason to live. Now, life on the plantation didn't seem so dismal a prospect. It looked like home. After all, she had two townhouses to visit when she grew weary of her farm. She must have been thinking about the peace and quiet of her country life. Considering all that she had gained and lost in two months, it seemed a natural request.

"If you really want to go home, we'll leave as soon as we can. I'll give orders to the servants to start packing. We need to finish some business here first with Jean-Pierre and Monsieur Chabonnais. We have to give our testimony to the court. Three weeks maybe? Is that soon enough?"

"No...but it will do. Will you do something else for me?"

"Anything."

"Free Cicero." She looked at him. Her eyes filled with tears. "I shall miss him so. He's been with me for most of my life, but he saved us last night. You and I would not be together this morning if it weren't for him. Give him some money and legal papers so that he won't have to argue his freedom with any man. Will you do that for me? Tell him that he's welcome to stay on with wages, but that I'll understand if he leaves. Who wouldn't want to be free? No one can live happily when they are caged."

Stephen understood. He kissed her cheek and hugged her tenderly. "Whatever you wish."

Chapter Thirty-One

Isabella gossiped with Nora and Anna as they floated home on the flatboat. Nathan was the only male servant to help load and unload their baggage. Cicero had taken the money, his freedom, and was gone by mid-afternoon. The former slave hugged Isabella, shook hands with Sam and Stephen, and said good bye to his lifetime friends, Nathan, Nora, and Anna.

The long trip up the Mississippi River gave Sam and Stephen time to talk. They spoke in whispers at the far side of the boat.

"Why do we have to leave right when things were looking good for my sex life? I only had a few days with that woman."

"Isabella wants to go home. But listen, you can still go back and use the townhouse if you wish."

"We haven't had much chance to talk lately, and I wanted to tell you all about it." He grinned. "I never told you about the Mardi Gras Ball."

Stephen nodded his head that he would listen to all Sam wanted to tell him, but his stare never left Isabella and the girls.

"I could dance every step I knew with her. I've no idea how a girl from Boston could have learned such moves."

"Maybe she's the reincarnation of the Spanish dancer you once knew."

Sam looked puzzled. "I never thought of that. Well, anyway, we danced and drank champagne and ate wonderful Creole food. It was the best time I've ever had in my life. Well, except for that one night in Egypt...floating down the Nile...on that big barge..."

"I get the picture. Go back to town, Sam. Just hop onto the boat and spend the weekend there. I can manage."

Sam sighed. "She's leaving for Boston next week. Maybe I could sneak back for one last night on the town with her. She's staying at the St. Louis Hotel, and I have her room number. Just being with her is wonderful. The way she talks, laughs, smiles. We moved from strolling in the Vieux Carré and staring at the shops to sharing lunch, but I never made it to dinner. Next date. After that, I make my move. She is *so* hot. I'm getting mental images of that room at the restaurant where Melinda and I had dinner that one night—only this time dessert is one sweet Boston cream pie."

Stephen grinned. "You *are* a scoundrel."

"I'll let you read some of my journals when we get home—especially the one on the pirate ship. All time travelers should write down their adventures. Now, with the invention of computers, we can build our own web sites and read journals from all over the world. You might want to write yours down too."

Stephen's smile faded, and he looked at Sam. "Maybe. I don't know. My heart's about to burst right now. It's almost over, and we haven't found the person who poisoned Isabella. I thought that we would've found the culprit by now. God, if anything should happen to her while I'm in 1999. The idea of finding her grave changed from December 1838 to April 1839 frightens me. Do you have any idea how much I adore that woman? She's more than I expected. Freeing Cicero like that. She's ahead of her time. She's passionate, loving, generous, loyal. I never guessed it would be so wonderful—too wonderful to leave."

Sam said, "Boy, do I know what you mean."

"So, where's this villain who wants my lovely wife dead?"

"We still have time. I figured the answer was in New Orleans. Maybe it still is, and coming home will give us the distance we need to solve the case. We're not doing such a bad job. We busted Melinda and Tony—one would-be murderer and one blackmailer turned kidnapper and attempted murderer. Sherlock Holmes couldn't have done better."

"True." He looked towards his wife. She was showing Anna and Nora the new sewing patterns Ernestine had given her as a farewell gift.

"I still feel that we're overlooking something. That the answer is right before our eyes, and we haven't noticed it."

"Well, getting back to Durel Plantation will help.

Ah—the quiet restful plantation life. How are things going between the three of you?"

"We tangoed naked."

Sam gave a low whistle.

"Emile took her hand to start the tango, and I let him dance with her. We made love while we danced. Nothing can compare to this. Any other life pales in comparison."

"Want to come back?" said Sam.

"What do you mean?"

"As long as Emile doesn't resist you—and I don't see why he would do that considering what you've done for him—you can come back to her every summer and winter solstice. Can you get away from your practice for three months?"

" 'So sorry Mrs. Smith, but Dr. Templeton cannot see his patients until September. No, he's not golfing; he's back in 1839 with his wife.' A new twist to all those doctor jokes."

"You can do it."

"I wonder what Emile would say?"

Sam folded his arms across his chest. "Ask him."

"He'll be okay with it. Right now, I want to enjoy every minute I have with her."

The sunlight bathed her dark hair with a shimmering halo. "I thought I was in love before, when her spirit came to me. I want to spend my whole life with her. Have kids. A puppy. A mockingbird. Thank God, I own her house. At least when I return, I can continue redecorating our home, only this time to its original glory. Maybe even put in a few sugar cane plants to remember how it felt to be a Southern planter."

He paused for a moment and then said, "I wonder if the hospitals in New Orleans could use a surgeon, because I can't picture myself going back to Chicago when my heart is here."

"I'm sure you can relocate if you're willing to give up your former patients."

"The guy who'll take them was Tony Chesterfield in this time period. Seems he followed me into my 1999 life. He's been a thorn in my side for a year. Probably caused me to have this breakdown. He can have my spot in the clinic. Karma. The man's been looking for acceptance and financial security all these years. Maybe he'll get it this time around. I really hate that arrogant son-of-a-bitch. It'd be a shame to give my trusting, loyal patients to that jerk, but staying in New Orleans has become a priority."

"Got to get those priorities lined up correctly," Sam said.

"I can still see my folks for the holidays, but the number one person in my life is sitting there chatting with her servants as if they were her best friends and hoping, deep in her heart, that her husband will be in the mood for making love tonight."

"I'm jealous."

Stephen turned and faced his friend. "Go back and find Mary Jane. Something tells me that she's your destiny. We can both come back together, can't we? Like we did the first time?"

"Absolutely. We know the people, the time period, and the portal location."

"I think answering that e-mail ad was the best thing that ever happened to me."

Sam bowed like a Creole gentleman. "On behalf of the staff at Time Travelers, Incorporated, I thank you."

Loading everything into the house was a colossal problem. Isabella had first thought that she would throw away her new clothes because of the Gatou situation, but then felt that she'd earned the right to wear them. After all, they'd cost her husband a fortune.

The Gatous had been hauled into jail because they'd helped Tony try to kill three people and kidnap a fourth. The three hired thugs never showed their faces in New Orleans again. Julius was rewarded by Jean-Pierre in the same manner Isabella had rewarded Cicero. Jean-Pierre was beginning to show a more sensitive nature. Ernestine was becoming more demonstrative about her needs now that she was the mother of his three legitimate children—two of which were males. Isabella's troubles were all behind her now. Or so it seemed.

Once they were settled into housekeeping, Isabella told Stephen that she was going to begin one of the cross-stitch patterns Ernestine had given her. Apparently, Madame Devieux made her slaves sew their clothing while she spent all of her time creating embroidery. Her sister-in-law had been generous and given her not only intricate, new sewing patterns; but purchased a new hoop, fine needles, and strong, thin thread to make sure her 'sister' made no errors on the complicated pattern. They'd become shopping pals in the last few weeks and even managed to share lunch a few times in their short two-month stay in New Orleans.

The Devieuxs would be returning to their plantation in about a week, and the two women promised to meet and gossip every Saturday afternoon. There was no more animosity between sister and brother either. All had been seamlessly stitched together. Brother and sister, husband and wife, sister-in-laws, *true* friends. Ones she could trust for a lifetime.

Stephen called to her that he and Evan would be outside talking with the overseer while she was working on her hobby. He couldn't wait to see the man, for he had already noticed that his orders had been implemented. The screens were in place, the slave quarters redone, and the yard clean and neat. The slaves grinned and called to him that they were glad he was home. Even the sugar cane was already being planted without a word from him.

The overseer was smiling when he said, "Welcome, Monsieur Durel. Glad you've returned. Things are good here. Hope you like what we've done."

"You deserve a bonus. The work you've done in two short months is incredible."

"Well, I hate to say it, but it was your idea to pay them that really did the trick. Each skilled laborer set goals for himself, and I hate to tell you this, but most of them have enough money to buy their freedom."

Stephen grinned. "Pay them. Good fortune follows me here, and some day we'll have more than enough plantations to run. How's the troublemaker doing?"

"Terence? He's the one who put the screens in. Practically built most of the slaves' houses. He was an inspiration to the others who decided that if their master was really going to let them buy their freedom, they'd have it before the next planting season. And they have. Especially Terence. It appears that he's found a woman who's worth starting a life with. Wants to get married and have his own house and farm. What man doesn't want that? And, by my calculations, he has earned enough to do it."

"Which reminds me," interrupted Sam, "I have that deed for Chabonnais's land and all the papers about the New Orleans's estates to put in the safe. I suppose we should take care of that before I forget."

"You go ahead. I'll be in in a minute."

Sam left as Stephen said, "He has enough credits to buy his freedom, a house, and land?"

"That and then some. He worked around the clock to make it. Says he wants to buy the girl's freedom too, because she isn't a skilled laborer and would never be placed under your plan. Can he buy her freedom? I didn't know whether that would be part of your deal. I told him that I'd ask you when you came home. "

Stephen was thrilled that his plan had worked so well. "Of course. He's earned it. I better get inside. Evan doesn't know how to open that safe. Nice work. I'll see that you get your new house and bonus."

"Merci beaucoup, Monsieur Durel" he said with a smile.

Before going to the library, he decided to go upstairs to retrieve a clean shirt, one that didn't smell of sweat, fish, and the Mississippi River.

While he was changing, he noticed his bureau drawer was open a fraction of an inch. He remembered closing it after he was finished with his unpacking and just before he walked out of the room. Out of curiosity, he decided to check the contents of the small drawer to see whether anything had been stolen.

Isabella called to him. She was stretching material across her new hoop. "Is there anything I can help you with, cher?" she sang out.

"No, my love." He walked into her sewing room and kissed her on the forehead.

"Isn't this the prettiest floral pattern?"

He laughed. "Oh, absolutely. Beyond words."

She turned to regard his expression. "You're mocking me."

"No, I'm not."

"I thought it might look nice on a pillow for the baby's room."

"Oh, of course, the baby's—what?"

She smiled innocently. "I woke up the other morning with stomach pains. That was what I was talking to Nora about. She used to be a mid-wife. She knows everything about womanly matters. I trust her instincts. I was supposed to have my monthly visitor the other day, it's always very punctual, but it never came. She thinks I'm pregnant. I think so too." Her eyes twinkled with the joy of motherhood. It was a look that Dr. Stephen Templeton had seen on many patients at the hospital.

He and Emile were speechless.

She whispered. "The tango, cher."

He pulled her from her chair and took her into his arms. "You're pregnant. I can tell. It's in your eyes. Everything will be wonderful, I promise. I'll tell Dr. Gayerré when we go back into town for Easter Mass."

"Nora's here. I'm frightened, Emile, but excited too."

He cuddled her close to his chest and kissed her forehead.

"Mon coeur. Finally, we have a future. Words cannot express my joy," said Emile.

"You're happy?"

Stephen said, "I'm thrilled." He kissed her.

His little mockingbird had waited for his return. He sat outside the bedroom window on his favorite branch. Stephen noticed he sang a new tune. He secretly said hello to the tiny bird. It was good to be home.

"Then it's a good thing I have all these sewing patterns," she said, "because I think I will be sitting and doing nothing for nine months. I better start making baby clothes too."

"Ernestine might have some you can share."

"I haven't told Jean-Pierre or Ernestine yet. I wasn't sure myself until I vomited breakfast the other day. You were with Evan, so I kept it a secret until I missed my time."

"You'll be treated like a princess. By the way, I have something for you. I meant to give it to you before. Wait here."

He ran to his room, opened his satchel, and took the box which contained the ring and the bow necklace.

"I thought you might like these."

"More gifts?" She opened the box and gasped. "Where did you find them? I sold them. You are so wonderful to have bought them back to me."

She started to cry. "I always wondered why you never noticed that I no longer wore the cameo ring you gave me before you left for France. I thought it meant that we were engaged, but you said that it was just a gift for my eighteenth birthday. I was so angry with you. But then you sent me the fan from France, and I only wore this ring on special occasions after that. And my mother's necklace?" The tears ran down her cheeks. "It broke my heart to give it up. All for that horrible man."

"The past doesn't matter. Only that you have these fond memories returned to you for your future. That's all that matters."

She held his arm and placed her head on his shoulder. "You have made me so happy. At the start of December, I had no will to live, but you gave me back my life, and now we can add this tiny baby to our family of four."

"Four?"

"Evan."

"Oh, yes. That reminds me, he's waiting for me in the library. I forgot all about him. I'll leave you to your work. I'll be up soon to see how you are." He kissed her and raced down the steps.

"About time," growled Sam.

"She's pregnant," sang Stephen, dancing around the room. "That old dog, Emile."

"What?"

"The Mardi Gras night when we made love. The tango. She's pregnant."

Sam gave him a broad grin. "Well, that's a new one for the time traveling journals. Emile must be overjoyed."

Stephen started dancing the tango with himself. "I've changed his life."

"That was our goal. Now, how about opening the safe."

"Oh, yeah, I forgot. Hey, you know I never did get to check this thing out. Look at all these deeds and papers and stuff. Wills. Gruesome thought on a sunny day."

"Well, they'll change anyway now that you three are going to have a little one. Here, let me see that."

Stephen opened what appeared to be Emile's will. Everything was left to Isabella. "Standard stuff here."

"My God," said Sam, and the tone in his voice alerted Stephen to danger.

"What's wrong? Something's wrong with Isabella's will? Didn't she leave it all to her husband?"

Sam showed Emile the line on the document he was concerned about.

"And to my dear sister, whose love I have cherished all these many years, I give her her freedom with my death. Let it be recorded on this day at the reading of my will. This I do in honor of her mother, Tillie, who raised me as her own, and who shouldn't have died that morning. Forgive my mother her cruelty. God has dealt her His own justice, after all. But at least, Father's little girl was able to be my good and true friend all these years."

"But who?" Stephen's whole body went cold.

"A powerful motive, freedom." Sam grabbed Stephen's arm.

"And a revenge factor to boot. Isabella's mother killed Tillie. Let her bleed to death after she'd given birth. But no one ever mentioned what happened to the infant, as I recall. Jean-Pierre said that Tillie could have been saved if the doctor had been called. The woman not only killed her husband's mistress after the woman travailed in her labor, she let Isabella watch , which instilled fear of childbirth in my wife for years."

"But who? She gives no name. It's all assumed."

"Because Jean-Pierre would have known and been sympathetic because even he admitted it was criminal," said Stephen.

"So? Who's the sister? Could be anyone on the plantation."

"Follow this thought with me. Terence suddenly changes his behavior after I give them my plan which was—oh hell—when did I do that?"

"Before Christmas Eve." Sam stared at Stephen.

"All for the love of a slave girl whose freedom might not be part of my plan. Who would never be able to marry him...unless..." said Stephen.

They ran to the backyard and were told that the overseer had ridden a mile or so down the rows of sugar cane to check on the planting. Without saddles, and only reins to guide the horses, the two time travelers raced across the fields until they found him.

Stephen gasped for air so that he could formulate the questions. His heart was pounding. He was frightened and felt dizzy from the emotion. "Terence's girl? Who is she?"

"Why, Missy's girl, Anna, Monsieur Durel. Why'd you

ask?"

He looked at Sam. "And the reason I never was able to finish reading the legal documents in the safe that morning was because Anna knocked on the door and asked me if I wanted breakfast."

They kicked their horses into a canter.

"Do you think she knew about the contents of the will?" questioned Sam as they rode side by side.

"It's possible. Remember Isabella's mental state at that time was suicidal. If she were thinking of killing herself, she might have told Anna, if only as a melancholy pre-suicidal thought."

"But how did Anna do it? We have no weapon."

"But we have a motive now *and* opportunity. Who else is beside Isabella twenty-four hours a day?"

"Okay, okay," said Sam, trying to think the whole thing through. "Let's go back to the night of the murder attempt. What did Isabella say she was doing before she took sick?"

"Ah...,oh, shit...I can't remember."

"Think, man."

"She had been to dinner, played songs for us, and went upstairs. Waiting for me to come upstairs to bed, she said. I think she read or something. Oh, yes, she looked for her Christmas gift."

He smiled at the memory of the mischievous woman who had behaved like a little girl. "Oh, yeah, there was something wrong with her gold gown, and she wanted to make it look nice for Christmas Day. The hem, I think. She said she sewed the hem."

Sam said, "She wore that dress all the time. How could she not have noticed that the hem was torn?"

Stephen's eyes went wide. "Unless someone who could come and go from her room tore it on purpose so that she would have to sew it with a needle laced with poison. Poison that sat in a glove-box drawer and would have been spotted by a faithful servant who dresses and shaves Emile every morning."

"She would have to assume that Isabella would prick herself with the needle."

"Considering the lateness of the evening, the wine she drank, and the lack of direct lighting—such a thing would happen sooner or later and when Anna was nowhere around. But she didn't try it in New Orleans. Change of heart?"

Sam said, "Maybe the location is the key to the modus operandi. Anna was there when Nora told Isabella that she thought she was pregnant. Talk about déjà vue. My mother died in labor—your mother killed her—now it's your turn to die. Why should I wait until I'm too old to get my man, my freedom, and a family? All the things I've been dreaming of for so long. The things denied me by my slavery, but that you have because you're white. I'm Devieux's daughter too, only I don't get what you get—nice clothes, pretty hats, marriage, a big house, a future. Why shouldn't I get what's coming to me?"

"And it all comes my way when you die," Stephen said, finishing Sam's thought.

"Waiting for Isabella to turn senile and ninety is a long time coming. I can't believe it. She was right beside us all along," said Sam.

"And all this time, Isabella thought she had a friend and sister in Anna." Stephen panicked. "Oh, shit."

"What?"

"The bureau drawer was opened when I went to change my shirt. I was looking in it when Isabella called to me. I'll bet the poison is still in there waiting for the new, finer needles to make a better second attempt."

"And Isabella has been chatting like a mockingbird about her new cross-stitch pattern and how she couldn't wait to start it. Perfect timing. You saved her the last time, but if she got sick again, we'd all think it was morning sickness, and not do anything to save her until it was too late. Double homicide."

"Isabella was just arranging the material and the pattern on the hoop. She hadn't touched the needles and thread yet. I've got to get to the house. You grab Anna. I'll stop Isabella."

"Let's hope for a sure hand and a keen eye this morning," said Sam to Stephen's back.

He left the horse in the courtyard and raced up the stairs two at a time. Isabella smiled at him and put down her needle, thread, and hoop.

"Don't touch any needles."

"What?" Her smile faded.

"Don't sew. Where's the needle you were using?"

"Why right here? Why?"

He took it into his room. He looked into the drawer, and sure enough, the poison was there but not in the exact spot he'd last seen it. He talked to himself. "Blow darts. You can lace a sharp object with poison, and it will kill instantly. Apparently, she didn't put enough on it to stop me from saving her life." He analyzed the needle's tip.

"What's wrong with you?" she queried, standing in the doorway and watching him.

"Give me all your needles."

"Are you mad?"

He thought hard for a good reason. "Call me an overprotective father-to-be, but I want them all...boiled for hygiene." He wasn't going to tell her the truth if he could help it. He took the bottle of poison with him as he ran down the stairs with the needles.

"Sit pretty, cher," he called back to her. "Are these all the needles you own?"

Needles were hard to come by in 1839, and Isabella would wonder at his extravagance if he threw them away, but it was the only solution. "What the hell, I'll buy her new ones. I can afford it. Sam can buy them on his next date. So, she waits on the cross-stitch pattern. She'll be alive and that's more important."

He ran from the front door to the dock. "Sorry, *fishies*." He threw the needles and the bottle of poison as far away from the shore as he could. "At last, she's free. Speaking of freedom..." He raced to the back of the house.

He found Sam who motioned for him to come to the barn. Anna was there sobbing and acting repentant.

Their theory had been correct, by the look on her face.

"You tried to kill my wife! How could you even think of such a thing?"

"My man. He told me about how you were fixing to let the men work out their freedom, but I didn't think I'd get to go because I wasn't a skilled laborer."

"I can't believe we never noticed how well she speaks compared to Nora and the others. They all speak with that accent but not Anna. Well, of course, Issy *tutored* her little sister," said Sam.

Stephen exclaimed, "She loved and trusted you. How could you? She gave you all she could. None of this was her fault. Blame her mother. Blame her family. Blame society. But why take it out on her?"

"I couldn't wait until I was an old woman to be with Terence. I was her father's daughter too. I should have some of my own," she wailed.

"Taking a human life, Anna? She's going to be all right. I saw to it. Your man earned enough to buy his freedom—and yours. I gave my permission this morning for him to purchase your freedom. Did he tell you that?"

"I wasn't going to see him until tonight."

"Why did you try to kill her on Christmas Eve? After I gave the men a chance at freedom? Or was that the reason to do it as fast as possible? I don't get it. Why not wait until he had his freedom?"

"Then when they'd read her will, they'd suspect me if she suddenly took sick right at the time Terence was fixing to take off. Besides, I overheard what you said to Dr. Gayerré. I was listening at the parlor door when I heard you shouting and carrying on about her being bad."

Now Stephen and Sam were at a complete loss.

"Refresh my memory," said Stephen, because Emile wasn't talking.

"You were unhappy 'cause she was ruining our family name—Devieux—and Durel. Least you thought so then. Guess you were wrong. You were yelling so much about how you couldn't wait to bury her in that gold gown she loved so much. I heard you tell the doctor that you had reserved a coffin and bought poison. You were going to have a quiet dinner, make love to her, and watch her die real slow. You were going to put it in her wine on Christmas Eve. You wanted the doctor to say she took ill and died from a sickness. Well, then just a few days before Christmas, you bring this cousin home and say as how he's going to save your plantation. How everything was going to be just fine now. You changed your mind about killing her. But how was I to leave with Terence? I'd be brought back and beaten if I tried to run. She told me about the will one night after writing in her diary. She looked so bad that I thought she would kill herself then and there. Seemed like everyone—even she—wanted her out of the way. Seen's how she ruined your family's name, and how I would be free to be with Terence, I decided to act for you. Carry out your death sentence on her. Then her heartbreak and sadness would be over at last. She'd be free too."

"And Gayerré would think that I was the one who poisoned her because I said I would do it on Christmas Eve?"

"That's right."

"Unbelievable, Emile." He spoke the words aloud.

"What?" she said.

"Just talking to myself," said Stephen. "So, when you saw how much I loved her and saved her from death—how happy she'd become—how could you try it again?"

"I couldn't be too sure about my own freedom and my new life with my man. You saved her the last time when she started to vomit, so I figured that when she got ill this time, you wouldn't do a thing to help her. You would think it was because of her pregnancy, and she'd die for sure."

Sam reached out to grab her, but Stephen held him back before he did her harm.

"Don't see how she has the right to have a baby when I can't have one. She had a mother to raise her and teach her things, but her mother let mine die because her husband loved his slave girl better than he loved his wife. Issy's daddy and my mammy." She paused and then said in perfect imitation of Jean-Pierre, "We Devieuxs are handsome people, n'est ce pas?"

She tilted her head upwards and gazed into his face. Stephen noticed her eyes. He remembered that when he first came to 1838 it bothered him that she never looked up at him—never made direct eye contact. He had rationalized that she lowered her eyes out of respect for her master. But now the resemblance was unmistakable. Shining beautifully in her perfect, oval face was the characteristic soulful-brown Devieux eyes looking right back at him. Another little family secret Isabella must have been too ashamed of to tell her husband.

Emile took over. *"I should turn you over to the courts and watch you hang for what you tried to do."*

"I won't ever do it again."

"You certainly will not. Don't go back into the house. Go find Terence and have him come to me in fifteen minutes. Fifteen minutes—no longer, so you better run. Take nothing with you.

You will be off this plantation in an hour. If you go near Isabella ever again, I will see that the law hears about this."

"Yes, master."

"Don't call me that. I've prevented you from killing the woman I love. She was mighty sick that day. Take that as your revenge and get out of here. Because I spoke in anger against my wife, and seem to be part of this demonic plot, I will not charge you with attempted murder. I changed my mind, Anna, because I loved my wife more than my honor. I couldn't do what you so callously could. You have your freedom and a start at a new life with Terence. Ask nothing more from my family and be glad I don't turn you in for what you almost did to my lady. Let God be your judge. Never show your face in New Orleans again."

She ran out of the barn. Stephen was dizzy from the intense emotional outburst. Sam gripped him by the shoulders.

"Are you all right?" Sam asked.

"We did it. We found the killer," exclaimed Stephen.

"But Emile? How could he think such a thing?"

"He thought it, but didn't force me to follow through with his plan. If he'd wanted to do it, I would have known. He must have been devastated when those men told him about her behavior at Jean-Pierre's party in early December. They mentioned how angry he was when he left that night. And remember the conversation with Dr. Gayerré that first day we were in town, how clueless we were."

"Emile is a passionate man when he's aroused and must have been too loud. He knew Isabella wasn't in the house and would never overhear him," said Sam.

"But Anna was always by the parlor, always ready to serve Emile. The only way she would ever be informed of what was going on around the house was to eavesdrop on every word that was whispered behind closed doors."

"And who worries about the servants and what they might or might not overhear? We have to make out a document for her and Terence that both of us must sign. I want these two off my plantation in an hour."

Terence came to the back door and was brought to the parlor by a domestic slave hastily assigned her new position as lady's maid.

"I have yours, and Anna's, papers attesting to your

freedom. Here's the money that you've earned. I want you off my property in half an hour."

"Master?"

"Call no man master from now on. You are a free man of color. And on your own. Ask nothing more from me."

"Anna told me what she done. I just want you to know that I didn't know nothing about it. I swear."

Emile's emotional tirade lessened.

"I mean it," he continued. "I wanted my freedom, tha's no lie. And I wanted my girl. You gave me a way to do it, and I won my freedom and hers. I'm real sorry." The man was terrified.

"Let me give you a word of advise my good man."

"Yessir."

"I'd never make her angry or jealous if I were you. She's your woman now. Get off my land."

The man left without speaking another word.

The new lady's maid came down the stairway. "Missy wants you, massa."

Stephen turned to Sam and said, "I swear if I hear one more 'massa' I'm going to strangle someone. Emile," he said outloud so that Sam could hear, "you'd better do something about this slavery issue, or I'll come back on the next solstice, free them all, and take her to France to live happily off your money—and mine—for the rest of our lives. Think about it. You've got the real estate. Sell it all and you both won't have to work a day for the rest of your lives. Her dream life can be yours too."

Sam and Stephen walked slowly up the steps to her room.

Isabella appeared puzzled. "What's going on? Where's Anna?"

Stephen swallowed hard before he said, "Her man, Terence, earned his freedom today. He had enough money to buy hers too."

Isabella's lips trembled with emotion, and she started to cry. "Anna's gone? After all these years, she didn't even come to say good bye?" Her hands went to her face to hide her emotion. "She didn't even come to say good bye to me?"

It broke his heart to see her upset by the departure of another lifetime friend who had proven just as false as the rest.

328

He held her in his arms to comfort her. "Better this than the truth," he said to himself.

   "Much better," said Emile.

Chapter Thirty-Two

It was March 20, 1839/March 20, 1999. Time for the equinox that would return all things to their rightful place.

Sam had had a good time with Mary Jane and had won her heart. She'd given him her address in Boston, and he'd told her that he'd be in touch.

Stephen prescribed certain foods and a physical regime for his patient and pregnant wife. Nora was acting as if she were having the baby instead of Isabella. The household was running smoothly; the plantation ready for the sugar cane plants to grow. But, Stephen was *not* ready to leave Isabella.

"Meet me by the dock tonight at midnight. Tell her you can't sleep and want to take a walk. Emile will come back to her."

"The man who thought of killing his wife?"

"But couldn't. You've given him something to live for—a loyal and loving wife and a child. Dr. Gayerré will do just fine with the techniques we told him we learned in France. Isabella got her second chance. So did Emile. And so did you."

Stephen laughed. "Dr. Gayerré must be so confused." His mood shifted. "I'm going to miss it all."

"We'll come back."

"We sure will. Tonight at twelve?"

"Bring anything you want to take home as a souvenir in your satchel. Remember, everything will transfer with you. Can't wait to tell my brother about Mary Jane Michaels. I'm going to miss that little cutey, but I have her address in Boston. Maybe I should transfer to Boston 1839 this summer. Big surprise—this Durel Frenchman at her gate."

Stephen said, "I can come back as soon as this summer?"

"Yep."

"She'll be having the baby in November. If I traveled in June, could I watch over her while she's pregnant?"

"Sure."

"I could use the interim to find a part-time position on the staff of some hospital in New Orleans."

"Take something back that you can sell to that antique store guy. Helps pay for your trip."

"I'd like to see my parents. I'll have to take at least one trip back to Chicago to say good bye to my friends. And it might be nice to inform my psychiatrist that I'm healed."

"Good trip, man. Good trip."

"In so many ways." He turned and looked at Sam and smiled sadly. "I'll see you at midnight."

A hint of melancholy surrounded him the rest of the day. He inspected each slave's face and made them laugh so that he could affix their smiles into the journal he kept in his heart. He ordered his favorite food prepared—jambalaya-Nora style. He'd taken over the pantry and was doing Isabella's chores as well as his own, so it was easy to prepare the menu the way he wanted it. He and Sam rode their horses around the plantation one last time. And then it was time to say farewell to his wife and make love to her one last time.

When they were resting in each other's arms, he said, "You freed me." He felt his eyes fill with tears.

"Oh, I think it's the other way around, don't you? What you've done for my friendship with Chris, how you healed my relationship with Jean-Pierre and Ernestine, and uncovered the truth about my not-so-nice friends Tony and Melinda. I would have been devastated to learn that she'd poisoned her husband, and that I'd done nothing to prevent it. You've created this wonderful new life for us. And then there's Evan. I love him so. You've been my salvation, mon cher, and I shall spend the whole of my life thanking you. You freed me from the cage I'd created for myself."

"Ah...well...about Evan. Evan will be leaving us...tonight."

She sat up. "Tonight? Why?" Her expression registered pain.

"Remember how I told you that he'd fallen in love with this girl from Boston?"

She nodded her head that she remembered.

"Well, he's going to make a surprise visit to her. Can't live without her, I guess."

She smiled finally. "So. Very soon we shall have a wedding?"

"Maybe. Would that please you?"

"The more family I can have around me, the happier I will be. I shall have to go to town this weekend to tell my brother and his wife the wonderful news about our baby."

"Be careful traveling, cher. The first three months are critical."

"There you go again, sounding like a doctor." She fell back onto the mattress and smiled at him.

The tears were hard to cover now. He felt a sudden stab of pain in his heart. "Funny little habit I have, huh?" he said softly.

"What?" She rolled over on her side so that she could look at him. "Why are you crying?"

"Because," he said, pulling her naked body close to his and touching her abdomen. "I love you both so much. And I don't want anything bad to happen to either one of you—ever. All right, cher?" He brushed the thick dark hair from her cheek with the back of his hand.

The mockingbird sang his love song.

Her voice was as gentle as the warm breeze that tossed their curtains into the air. "And I love you, mon mari, more than words can say."

"Remember that song you sang to me that morning...after the first time we made love?"

"Oui."

"Will you sing it for me again?"

"Now?"

"Oui."

She sang her song with the same sweetness as did the mockingbird. "When we do meet again, when we do meet again, when we do meet again, t'will be no more to part."

She giggled at the chorus part of the song while she sang it. "Brother Billy fare you well, Brother Billy fare you well, Brother Billy fare you well. We'll sing hallelujah when we do meet again."

"Who did you say taught you that song?"

"Tillie."

He stopped the flow of his tears by closing his eyes. "I see. I like it." He opened his eyes and looked at her. "'When we do meet again.'" The tears fell rapidly, and he held her tightly to his chest and kissed her, refusing to let go of her until she broke away from him to catch her breath.

"What's gotten into you tonight?" said Isabella. She examined his face—his eyes.

"Ask me that tomorrow morning."

They made love one last time, and then it was time to go.

At eleven-thirty, Stephen took out his satchel from under Emile's bed, returned Emile's pocket watch to the velvet box on the bureau, and looked around for a souvenir. What could he take home that would remind him of her?

He stared at her sleeping face and then kissed her cheek. There wasn't anything that could remain a symbol of the woman he loved save for the portrait Chris had given them when they returned to the plantation—and home on his dining room wall it sat. Like Chris, he would have to be content with coming down each morning for breakfast and looking at her portrait instead of her face. Until June 22, 1999.

The mockingbird sang farewell from his tree branch. He was actually able to make out the tiny bird silhouetted in the sliver of moonlight that peeked through the clouds. It lifted its left wing and used its beak to scratch under its feathers. It tilted his head and looked at Stephen.

Stephen closed his eyes, dropped his chin, and thought to himself while speaking aloud, "Bon chance, Emile."

The man's voice was clear. *"Words cannot express my gratitude, Dr. Stephen Templeton,"* he heard him say in his mind. *"May God grant you your dreams as He has granted me mine. Merci beaucoup, mon ami. Bon chance."*

Sam was waiting for him at the dock, and the transfer happened on schedule.

Chapter Thirty-Three

Bruce Wainwright was waiting for them as per the contract's clause.

"Welcome," he said, like some tour guide.

"How's my brother?" said Sam.

"Much better after I tell him *you're* home. He's had those psychic vibes of trouble he sometimes gets. So, how was the trip?" he said, taking their luggage for them and walking them towards Durel Plantation as if it were his own bed and breakfast.

Stephen took one look at the house and collapsed. He refused to stand and covered his face with his hands while he rocked back and forth. "No! God, no!"

Sam said, "I was afraid this would happen. The ghost been around? That might help."

Wainwright shook his head that it hadn't. "She left two weeks ago. Haven't seen her since. Kinda glad of that. Not my cup of tea, y'know. But then I'll catch you up on everything that's been going on at the old homestead. You can tell me everything that happened on your trip while I make you a nice pot of coffee and something to eat." He watched as Stephen writhed in agony on the ground. "I think we'll need to give him something to help him sleep tonight."

Sam said, "Good idea. Hey, you'll never guess what happened—I met Lady Jane Engle/ Michaels' great-granddaughter."

"Not the schoolmarm's offspring, right?"

Sam shook his head. "*No,* the original Lady Jane who married the pirate Captain Garrett Michaels' heir? Their great-granddaughter? From Boston?"

"No kidding. Well that may be a first for the modern time traveler."

Stephen cried out. He wrapped his arms around his legs and rocked in anguish on the ground near the dock. "Isabella! God, no!" His voice quivered with emotion. "Cher!" It seemed as if he were calling across time to her. His hands shook and his body trembled. "I can't live without you."

"We warned him, right?" said Wainwright, glancing at Sam.

"Correct."

They helped Stephen into the house, but that only made his emotional trauma worse when he saw her portrait on the wall. Emile stared at him from the other side of the room.

"Chris paint that one too?" he said to his alter ego who could hear him no more. "Oh, God, Emile, *you're gone too*."

He pulled away from the two men and fell in front of Emile Durel's portrait. "I'll miss you. Oh, God." The tears fell swiftly. "Tell me they're not dead, Sam." He looked at Sam for comfort, but the seasoned time traveler could offer him none.

"Please, no. They can't be dead. Nora?" he screamed for a woman who could not come to him. "She's in the cookhouse, right? Tell me they're not all gone. Isabella. Cher. My wife. Our baby." He stood up and walked over to Sam. "Sam, I had no idea it would be like this."

Sam touched Stephen's shoulder. Then he gave him a brotherly hug and said, "They aren't dead. Only on a time loop that never ends. You can go back and see them whenever you wish. This is what they mean by eternity, Stephen." The words seemed to pacify the hysterical physician.

"Trapped in a never-ending time loop?" Stephen asked.

Sam said, "That's right." He stared at him for a long time before saying, "Sooner or later, we all become part of past time. Over and over again. You were Emile once. Don't forget that. But eternity is ongoing. It never ends. We only say goodbye temporarily. Sooner or later we all meet again."

"'When we do meet again,'" mumbled Stephen.

"What did you say?" asked Wainwright.

"Just a song." He turned to look at Wainwright. "A slave song Isabella used to sing to me. When the mockingbird sang its song of love. It goes, 'When we do meet again.'"

"I see," said Wainwright, unable to comprehend. "He's in shock."

They managed to get Stephen to his room but that didn't make the situation any better. Their room was there, but she wasn't.

"These curtains are all wrong, you know," Stephen said,

as they helped him into bed.

They gave him a sleeping pill which he refused to take at first. He told them that he wanted laudanum. His body quivered, then mercifully relaxed as he drifted into sleep.

The next few days were tough for Stephen who grieved as if he were in a state of mourning. He e-mailed all of his friends about his 'vacation' and his decision to find work in New Orleans because he liked the locale so much. His family was well, and the surgeon who looked like Tony was being sued for malpractice. "Serves him right," thought Stephen to himself.

Wainwright left River Road two days after their arrival to return to Jim Cooper in New York. He took Sam's new journal entry with him. Sam, however, decided to stay a few more days to make sure all was well with their client.

"The ghost is gone too," said Stephen, with a weak smile and a shrug of his shoulders.

"Well, of course. She isn't in limbo anymore. She's in paradise. Thanks to you, she's with Emile and her family. You should be very happy. You were her savior, after all."

Stephen looked down at his feet. "I miss her. I miss Emile too. I miss our townhouse and Chris's simple jokes. I even miss Jean-Pierre's arrogance. He had so much courage and pride that man."

"I understand."

He looked at Sam. "You have to go, don't you? You have other jobs, other clients."

"And some dueling pistols for my brother, thanks to your kind generosity. Plus a lot of wonderful memories." He hesitated and gazed directly into Stephen's eyes when he said, "Do you want to go to the tomb to see whether you've changed the dates?"

"No. They've changed. I know that. She's not dead. Not in my heart." He touched his chest with his index finger and shifted his gaze to the wall so that Sam couldn't see his tears.

"Are you going to travel back to her in June?" Sam asked.

Stephen smiled. "I'm living for it."

Sam departed the following day, leaving Stephen alone in an empty plantation house that could not compare with the one he'd left. Ruined, destroyed, and with all the wrong colors. No slave girl to run up the stairs with a cup of coffee for him each morning, no Nora to joke with him, no Sam/Evan to tease him, and no Isabella to make love to him.

He went to the city and walked to every single location he could remember. He smiled ruefully when he saw a building still standing proudly after all these years, and mourned when he saw that another one no longer existed. He had to stare for a long moment at a site that had been converted into a restaurant, and clapped his hands excitedly when he recognized the old window frames that proclaimed what it used to be. He lit some candles in "their" church and prayed for Isabella's soul.

Then he walked past his townhouse, and the one that had belonged to Monsieur Chabonnais. A tour guide was speaking outside the door of Jean-Pierre's seasonal retreat. She was telling a story about the family who had built the home. Isabella's great-grandparents. He listened to all she had to say. Then she walked the small group through the beautifully decorated rooms. He thought about spending the six dollars to go on the tour but then felt awkward about it. Why should he pay to visit his own brother-in-law?

He looked into every window and every doorway in the hopes of seeing Isabella's face—but she wasn't there.

He drank hot, chicory coffee and ate his favorite beignets at Cafe du Monde. It wasn't 1839 anymore, but if he closed his eyes, he could swear he heard her proclaim some exciting find in one of the shops at the Vieux Carré. A new hat, perhaps?

He whispered aloud and in French, "If you want it, cher, buy it. I'll deny you nothing. Whatever makes you smile, mon amour."

He went to the address of his father's old friend who might be able to give him a spot in his new clinic. The interview went well, and Stephen knew that he would be asked to stay on. His credentials were perfect. He left out the nervous breakdown part by saying that stress had caused him to take a sabbatical, and, after all that was partially true.

That night he opened a bottle of champagne, poured himself a glass of the wine, and looked through her diary. Touching it, rereading every entry, remembering that these were her words
speaking to him from the past. He ate caviar on crackers much

337

as he had the night he'd tried to seduce her ghost. Her spirit never came to him.

At twelve o'clock on the dot, a breeze tossed the front window curtain aside, and he ran to it, hoping that it was her ghost, but of course, it wasn't.

He sat at her harpsichord and fingered the keys. "Play something for me, cher." He closed his eyes and listened, believing that he could will her spirit to play her melancholy songs. In his mind, he heard her playing the song she'd played at Jean-Pierre's dinner party, but he couldn't hear the soprano sing—he heard only Isabella's sweet voice singing the slave song over and over again. *"When we do meet again."*

Eventually, he blew out the candles and walked up the stairs, stripped off his clothes, and snuggled into his empty bed. "Care to tango?" he asked his pillow. Then he cried himself to sleep.

He slept late the next morning. At ten o'clock, he threw on his jean shorts and a T-shirt, and walked downstairs, saying good morning to their portraits as he passed. He made himself breakfast and sat outside on his patio to drink his coffee. It was a beautiful, hot spring day, and the flowers were starting to blossom around the foundation of the house. Still, blooming after all these years? Was that a French lily? He'd have to find a book on the flowers of New Orleans. Funny how he'd never really noticed them before the trip.

He then went back into the house to take his shower before starting to paint Evan's, Sam's, the guest room's walls. He turned on the shower and sang sadly, "Dance with me, Isabella—love's sweet memory." The pain returned, and he let the water trickle over his face so that his tears would be washed away.

That's when he heard the knock on the door. It wasn't a tentative, little knock, either, it was as if the person wanted to break down his door.

"Ah, shit," he growled, turning off the water. Stepping carefully out of the shower stall so that he wouldn't slip, he wrapped a towel around his waist, and headed for the front door. "Now what?"

He answered the door in his half-naked and highly agitated condition.

"What the *hell* do you want?" he said to the woman. His body was still quite wet, and his hair streamed its wetness down his neck and back.

She blushed. "Ah, well, oops, sorry," said the woman nervously. "I just thought this house was one of those River Road tour plantations." She waved the brochure at him as if it were some sort of passport to bother anyone she pleased. "I guess I was wrong. Sorry for disturbing your shower."

"Do you see a sign anywhere out there that says TOUR?" he yelled.

"I *said* I was sorry. Okay," she replied in an equally angry tone.

She inspected his body, draped in a French blue, Egyptian pile, 100 percent cotton towel, and tried to avert her gaze, but gave him a second look anyway.

He examined her perfect oval face, angry brown eyes, waist-length, dark-brown hair, curvaceous body, the way her eyebrows knit together when she was irritated, and that mischievous expression she wore.

He changed his tactic immediately. "Ah, look, I'm sorry. Got up on the wrong side of the bed today." He swatted at his hair, patting it into its rightful spot, and hopped up and down in place as if he could dry off that way.

"Listen, let me put some clothes on," he said.

She must have thought he was crazy because she turned to walk away.

"Hey, don't go away. I said I was sorry. Thought you were some door-to-door solicitor." He opened the door for her to enter. "Don't go. Please? Come on in."

She stopped, turned around to look at him, and placed her hands defiantly on her hips. "Why should I do that? Are you some kind of pervert? I'm not coming in there." But she didn't try to leave.

He leveled his stare directly into her eyes and did his best Emile imitation. "Oh, yes, you are, *cher.*"

She tilted her head to one side. Something had caught her attention. "Why the hell would I do something stupid like that with your attitude and your..." she waved her hand at his waist. She crossed her arms in front of her in an attempt to demonstrate to him that she had complete authority over any man

339

wearing a towel.

Stephen smiled. "Because I have a portrait in here that you've just got to see." He tied the towel tighter so that it wouldn't slip off his hips.

"Let me show you my etchings? That's an old one. And you're standing there in a towel? Yeah, right." But she didn't stop staring at his face. He used that. Direct eye contact right into her soul.

He wanted to say, "Come on, baby. Think. Because it's in there, and you can feel it, can't you? Eternity. Across time. Don't I look like a man you tangoed with back in 1839?"

He opened the door wider and beckoned to her with his free hand that she should come into the foyer. She hesitated and then took one step forward.

"Look on the wall in the dining room, cher." He whispered the familiar term of endearment to her, hoping that it might trigger a memory. "You don't have to stay if you don't want to."

He could tell she wasn't sure of him, but, he hoped the same emotion was compelling her to trust him. She walked into the hallway, stopped, and looked around. He left the door wide open so that she wouldn't feel trapped, caged.

She saw the portrait. Walked over to it. Stared.

"Why, that's me." She pointed to it and then looked at him. "How do you happen to have a painting of me?"

He folded his arms across his chest and leaned against the door frame. "It's a long story, both yours and mine, but they both start with, 'I was just driving along River Road when suddenly I saw this house and, for some odd reason was mysteriously drawn to it.' Odd, isn't it, how a house can have that effect on you? "

She gazed at him for some time. The expression on her face told him that he'd guessed correctly as to why she'd come to 'tour' a house that had *not* been mentioned in her brochure. He started to shut the door behind the bewildered woman, when he noticed something perched on one branch of the twisted, old oak tree that had grown in front of this plantation for centuries. A mockingbird tilted its head, regarded him closely, and then sang its sweet song of love.

The End

Lightning Source UK Ltd.
Milton Keynes UK
UKOW051537250412

191444UK00001B/153/A